PICK-UP

PICK-UP

A Novel

NORA DAHLIA

G

GALLERY BOOKS

New York London Toronto Sydney New Delhi

G

Gallery Books
An Imprint of Simon & Schuster, LLC
1230 Avenue of the Americas
New York, NY 10020

First Gallery Books trade paperback edition December 2024

GALLERY BOOKS and colophon are registered trademarks of Simon & Schuster, LLC

Simon & Schuster: Celebrating 100 Years of Publishing in 2024

For information about special discounts for bulk purchases, please contact Simon & Schuster Special Sales at 1-866-506-1949 or business@simonandschuster.com.

The Simon & Schuster Speakers Bureau can bring authors to your live event. For more information or to book an event, contact the Simon & Schuster Speakers Bureau at 1-866-248-3049 or visit our website at www.simonspeakers.com.

Interior design by Esther Paradelo

Manufactured in the United States of America

10 9 8 7 6 5 4 3 2 1

Library of Congress Cataloging-in-Publication Data has been applied for.

ISBN 978-1-6680-6116-9
ISBN 978-1-6680-6117-6 (ebook)

For Claudia, who has had my back since birth

1 | Drop-Off

SASHA

On my walk to school, there's a mother with red hair. I see her every morning.

We exchange looks, in silent kinship, over our kids' heads. Triumphant looks. Tortured looks. Looks, though I don't know her name.

She is my barometer for the day. My Weather Channel. My forecast of what's to come.

Only, instead of two, she has too many kids—and a very large dog, who also has red hair.

On good days, she walks him with swagger. On bad days, he walks her.

2 | Drop-Off

ETHAN

On the walk to school, there's a dad I see. He has shaggy surfer hair and wears flip-flops in winter.

Some days, I envy his chill. Some days, I think he's deranged.

But he and his son are always smiling. Hands in their pockets, they saunter.

My kid and I trudge.

Waiting for the light to change, I catch myself frowning. I review my mental to-do list:

- Do not forget to buy the school sweatshirt.
- Do not forget the sweatshirt.
- Do not forget—
- Holy shit. I'm a grown man! I will not forget the fucking sweatshirt.
- *Just don't forget the fucking sweatshirt.*

"Dad!" barks my third grader. "Hello?"

I look up. The light has changed. But I am standing still.

3 | Drop-Off

KAITLIN

There's a nerdy mom with one kid. She's always late.

There's a mustached dad with three. He's always shouting.

There's a skinny mom who always feeds her kids doughnuts as they walk. They run into school, high as kites, faces smeared with frosting and glaze.

I see them all.

I once had drop-off by the balls: I was never late. I never shouted. I made free-range eggs and organic oatmeal for breakfast. And everyone left with their faces clean.

In those days, I lingered outside the gates after the children hustled inside. Chatted with other parents about TV shows we liked and Common Core math homework we hated. Took morning walks in the park with mom friends.

Now, instead, I linger in bed until the last possible second, scrolling through ads for workout gear I am told I'm deficient without. I look at pictures of other streets, in other cities. Of other parks and other families. Of hipster dessert spots and canyon hikes. Of younger people who stay out late and never venture into the light at all.

There's a sparkly mom who I actually knew growing up. But she always looks right through me.

At drop-off and at pick-up too. I see that mom who I once knew.

4 | Silly Socks

SASHA

Sometimes it feels like I'm being *Punk'd*. Then I remember that the show went off the air like two decades ago and Ashton Kutcher is someone's dad and, also, why would anyone want to punk *me*?

I should be so lucky as to garner that much attention. Lately, work is so slow, it feels like my email is broken.

And maybe it is. Because somehow, I have been left off the school email reminder about Silly Sock Day again, though I have tried to correct this issue four times already. And that is how I wind up at drop-off at 8:27 a.m. with a weeping five-year-old in my arms. A five-year-old wearing boring gray socks instead of the baseball-themed ones he'd been saving for this very occasion.

"Is Bart okay?" asks a school administrator standing at the entrance. The same one who is always standing there.

Bart is clearly not okay. All around us, parents play chicken on the crowded sidewalk, hurrying kids in oversize State backpacks toward the schoolyard before the bell. The deed done, they exhale and walk a little taller toward their cups of coffee, the morning's chaos resolved. Helmeted grown-ups unchain bikes, some with enormous trailers attached for lugging kids, and cycle to work. Others matriculate toward the Prospect Park loop for a run, a prerequisite hobby in this green neighborhood. A few—one crew in particular each morning—stand around in clusters and chat, lingering long after kids disappear inside, the last guests at the procrastination party.

The stragglers eye me and Bart with equal parts amusement and pity. Most notably, we are being surveyed impatiently by my eight-year-old daughter, Annette, who stands at a far enough distance to separate herself from the scene.

"Can I go in now?" she says, widening her eyes. This is *so* uncool. "A little help?"

She shrugs behind Bart's back. "How? I don't carry an extra pair of weird socks in my pocket!" She's not wearing silly socks either, but she doesn't care. She's not particularly interested in anything silly lately. She is tweening two years too early.

In her defense, she is usually very helpful. More helpful than an eight-year-old should be. And she has spent the whole walk to school trying to convince her little brother that, in her vast experience, Silly Sock Day is just a blip on the radar. That after the first five minutes of circle time, no one even remembers what day it is. Usually, Bart hangs on her every word, an unwavering disciple of the cult of Nettie. Today, he's not having it. And so neither is she.

Triggered by the word *socks*, Bart begins weeping anew. Surrendering, I wave my daughter inside so she's not late.

"I love you, Nettie!" I call. "Have a good day!"

She sprints away from my embarrassing sentiments and inside the black metal gates.

I am so tired.

"Bart," I try, turning back to face him with practiced patience. "How about I give you my socks?" See? I am the Giving Tree.

He looks down at my feet, socks peeking out the top of my Nike high-tops. "They're just black," he hiccups.

"But they'll be really big on you. That's silly! Right? Giant socks?"

"Mom!" he groans like I know he will at fifteen too.

"What's wrong?" the administrator presses, hovering over us now. Her requisite statement necklace sways as she moves.

Bart looks up at her, despondent. His tiny chin quivers. Then he looks back down at his feet. Can she not *see* his gray socks? Can she not understand the atrocity she's witnessing? He dissolves into tears again.

"There was a mix-up this morning," I say, as much to him as to her. "No silly socks."

"Ah. Did we miss the reminder?" she asks.

By we, she means *me*. She looks at me with the same condemnation as she did on Pajama Day and Sports Day. I resist the urge to hiss at her.

"I didn't *receive* the reminder!" I insist, while my son wipes snot on my shoulder. It's bad enough to be the "divorced mom." I don't want to be the "bad mom" too.

She nods like she doesn't believe me. "Oh, well, that's no problem," she says.

Bart and I look up at her in her sweater set. *Really?* It sure seems like a problem. The mucus on my jacket is confirmation of my colossal transgression.

"We've got some supercool fabric stickers inside for decorating socks to *make* them silly. That's even more fun than wearing the store-bought kind! Do you want to come check out the stickers, Bart? Make your own silly socks?"

He considers this, his grip on my sweatshirt loosening. "Do you have sports ones?"

"Maybe? We definitely have unicorns . . . and dinosaurs."

Bart considers this. He has no use for unicorns, but a *T. rex* might do the trick. Before he can overthink it, she takes his little marshmallowy hand and leads him just inside the door to where his teacher is waiting.

I watch them go, then rise to standing with a creak. I feel more like lying on the sidewalk in fetal position. A minute later, the administrator returns.

"Thank you for your help," I say. "This morning was a doozy."

"That's fine. *This* time. You can sign up for reminders and the weekly newsletter on the school's website."

"I have. I swear. Multiple times."

"Uh-huh. Okay, Mom. Have a good day!"

At school, I don't have a name. I am Bart's Mom. Nettie's Mom. Sometimes, I'm just "Mom" when the teachers and administrators are feeling cute and can't place me among the myriad other women in their shearling jackets and jogger pants.

I have been dismissed.

By now, the street has grown quiet, returned to its almost suburban calm. This is New York City. Two blocks away, the subway rumbles underground, a convenient yet apocalyptic hellhole drizzled with urine. Ten blocks in one direction, the bodegas get dustier, the streets become less Sesame. But here, in this tiny enclave, robust trees, manicured sidewalks and the sweet school building, with its colorful flags and murals, betray its domestication. This is no concrete jungle. It's more like a well-tended zoo, its edges babyproofed and softened.

Normally, I go straight home to work after drop-off or take a run, like all the other parents. But, today, I am on a mission. It's Spirit Day on Monday and I will not fuck it up like Silly Sock Day. I'm already patting myself on the back for all my good mommying.

The school swag table, set up outside only on Friday mornings, waits ahead of me like a winning ticket. No line!

Just as I'm about to approach though, I am intercepted by a creature who will not be put off. Mom Who Never Stops Talking.

"Sasha, hi! It's been *forever*."

She's nice enough. I'm pretty sure her name is Lisa, but sometimes I think it's Lorraine. Or maybe Laur*en*. Either way, it's too late for me to ask. We've chatted on the street and at school events on and off for years since Nettie started kindergarten. She's one of the few moms I know at this school, where circumstance and maybe marital status have rendered me largely antisocial. Still, I'm clued in enough to know she's a patrol cop on the school's information highway. And, for all the reasons, you don't want to get on the bad side of a gossip.

"Hi . . . you!" I say. "It *has* been so long! How's Olivia doing this year?" Of course I know her daughter's name. Because, like me, this mom doesn't have her own name. She is *Olivia's Mom*.

Asking a question. Rookie mistake. Because, my Lord, once you get this woman going, there's no end to her rambling. Don't even think about trying to interrupt.

"Oh, I'm glad you asked, actually, 'cause I'm kind of freaking out!" She leans in and begins stage-whispering about her daughter's struggle with waking up for school. Sometimes Olivia wakes up on time. Sometimes Olivia is cranky. Sometimes Olivia melts down on their way out the door if she can't find her snowflake pom-pom hat.

Oh, Olivia.

Olivia's Mom is wearing an electric-pink helmet—like maybe she borrowed it from one of her offspring? And she's leaning on a bike, but she doesn't seem motivated to leave. There's a fall chill in the air, but somehow she is perfectly at ease in a tie-dye T-shirt and spandex bike shorts that I'm guessing might be maternity (no judgment!), her shoulder-length black hair pulled back in a low ponytail.

"Like somedays, I come upstairs and she's already awake," she says, her pale cheeks flushing pink as she gets worked up. "But then on other days, it's like after seven a.m. and I have to wake her up and, just this morning, she was lying on the ground—I mean, you know how kids are—just kicking and screaming because we didn't have any Frosted Mini-Wheats left, and I mean . . ."

I am eyeing that table of school-branded T-shirts, sweatshirts, and hats with mounting anxiety. The stacks are dwindling, and it looks like the VIMs manning it are beginning to pack up.

(VIMs or "very involved moms" is shorthand my friend Celeste and I created one night while drunk on orange wine to refer to the mothers who are somehow able to juggle constant volunteering and their lives. Moms of whom I am in awe because—when do they watch TV? Celeste's own mother was a VIM, and she still falls short. Every time I feel guilty, I play that single-mother card in my head—and I am magically off the hook.)

"Do you know what I mean?" Olivia's Mom is saying. She's kind of a VIM herself. "Of course, you don't. Nettie is basically perfect. And so are you. Even your yoga pants are cool. Where did you get those? I grabbed some at Target the other day, but have you noticed lately that—"

I open my mouth once, twice, three times to interject. I raise a hand to interrupt Lisa/Lorraine/Lauren's athleisure monologue midstream and excuse myself, but there is no oxygen. I can't make it past a single syllable. *Tha—! Ma—! To—!*

The other VIMs—a white brunette in a PS421 baseball cap and a red down vest and a Black brunette with sunglasses on her head and the same vest in green—are opening the cardboard boxes at their side and beginning to transfer mugs from the display table back inside. I get a jolt of panic, a vision of Bart's tear-streaked face playing in my head like a horror show.

So I behave like any trapped animal would and begin backing slowly toward the school paraphernalia. For every step I take backward, Mom Who Never Stops Talking takes one forward, rolling her bike closer to me. I have stopped listening to her verbal diarrhea. She is not deterred.

As I speed up, she speeds up—step back, step forward, step back, step forward—and then suddenly I am smashing into something hard. I lose my balance and fall on my ass on the sidewalk. The sidewalk is also hard.

"What the hell?!" I hear someone say. And I'm pretty sure it's not me.

Once I get my bearings, I swivel to see what I've slammed into. Only it's not a what. It's a who. He is tall with that combination of tan skin and sandy hair that no one actually has. Perfect bedhead, perfect five-o'clock shadow. Simple, cool, well-cut clothes. Throwback Jordans on his feet. Basically, he's too good-looking not to be an asshole. And he is looking down at me with confusion and, *yes*, disdain.

Oh, this day!

"What the hell?" he repeats.

And they say chivalry is dead.

"It was an accident, Ethan!" says Lisa/Lorraine/Lauren, with a forced chuckle. "She was walking backward and didn't see where she was going."

"Walking backward? Why would you do that?" he says to me.

"Why?" I repeat.

I am incredulous, and it has to register on my face.

We hold each other's gaze for a beat. His eyes would be nice if they weren't glaring at me.

"I am literally on the ground," I say finally.

The VIMs, and even L/L/L, are unsure of what to do next. It is awkward. They watch us, mouths slightly agape.

"Right. Sorry." My douchebag in shining armor—Ethan, apparently—offers a hand to help me up. It's a nice, strong hand. But I don't give a fuck. I look at it with my own disdain, like it might be coated in excrement and I might be the late queen of England. Then, I brush the granite pebbles off my palms and push myself to standing.

Once up, I hold my posture ramrod straight to show him how haughty I can be. It's hard to look superior when you've just fallen on your ass, but one does what one can.

"Um. Well, look at the time!" says L/L/L, who has not looked at the time. "I better get going!"

I guess now I know how to get rid of her. She leaves without anyone saying goodbye.

This Ethan person has retracted his hand and is now using it to sort through forest-green T-shirts on the folding table in front of us.

"You should watch where you're going," he mumbles. "You could get hurt."

"I'm fine," I grunt. "Thanks for asking."

Simultaneously, we both plaster smiles on our faces and look up at the women manning the booth.

"Can I help . . . one of you?" says Red Vest. "I'm not sure who's next?"

"I think it's me—"

"I am—"

We say on top of each other.

"If you don't mind . . . ," I begin.

"I'm running late . . . ," he finishes.

It's amazing how busy men can be.

Red Vest looks at Green Vest in a panic. And it is because I feel for her (a.k.a. don't want other moms to hate me) that I say, "Fine. He can go ahead."

I am obviously the bigger person.

"Okay," says Red Vest. "What can I get you?"

"I'd like a hoodie," he says. "For a third grader. What size would you recommend?"

"Oh, great! A youth medium, for sure." She sorts through the pile for the right size. "Oh, look! You got the very last one!" Green Vest pulls out a tablet to run Ethan's credit card.

"Thanks for your patience," says Red Vest, turning to me. "Now, what would you like?"

"A T-shirt in 5T for a kindergartner," I say, gritting my teeth. "And a hoodie. For a third grader. In a size *youth medium*."

"Oh *no*," peeps Red Vest, her eyes going wide.

Oh no indeed.

This Ethan person sneaks a nervous peek at me as he slides his credit card across the table like a job offer. He doesn't dare meet my eyes.

I'm reminded of the time Nettie bit a kid on the playground who stole her toy—and I'm thinking I get it.

This guy is exactly the kind of handsome Brooklyn man who gets everything he wants. And I suddenly want to murder him. Not only because he has taken the last hoodie in Nettie's size. But because men like him always get the last hoodie.

If I've seen him around before, I haven't noticed. This is a big school. He's probably one of those dads who rarely makes an appearance. And I keep to myself, anyway.

I don't know this man. But, in that instant I realize, the VIMs do.

"Thanks," the hoodie hoarder says, as they hand him back his card along with the folded sweatshirt.

"You're welcome, Ethan!" Red Vest simpers.

I never stood a chance.

He turns to face me, opens his mouth like he's about to speak, then thinks the better of it. "Bye," he says to the sidewalk. I watch him retreat.

5 | Sweatshirt Blues

THIS ETHAN PERSON

Welp. I got the sweatshirt.

For fuck's sake.

I drag a hand down my face as I walk toward the train.

That kind of day. That kind of year.

I shake my head at the failed exchange. Usually, women kind of like me when we first meet. Plus, I know that mom, though she may not realize it. Once, when our kids were only toddlers, we spent hours talking while we trailed them on the playground, blocking for them like linebackers.

Not that she looks like a lineman. More like a pixie with her shaggy honey-colored hair and cat eyes.

That talk stayed with me. Not just because she's hot. Which she is, even if she's cranky as hell. But also because our conversation was so easy. About nothing and everything. Like a throwback from teen years when you'd sit on the phone with someone for hours and just talk shit. For the first time in a long time, I was just me.

It did not stay with her though—our talk. I know because she waved once or twice at drop-off after that and then she stopped saying hello.

Some days I think it's intentional. Most days I think she forgot. On days like today, I don't blame her. I would ignore me too.

TO-DO
- Drop off sweatshirt.
- ~~Apologize about sweatshirt.~~

- Forget about the stupid fucking sweatshirt and get to work.
- Call with corporate.
- Don't forget to log on for after-school registration or suffer the consequences!
- Don't forget!

6 | Back in the Day

KAITLIN

It's ten minutes after pick-up and most everyone has left. My daughter, Ruby, is still inside at after-school toy-making class. But, since I work from home in research marketing and am not currently super busy (read: am mostly hate-scrolling through other people's photos of family vacations in Hawaii), I have volunteered at the last minute to work the bake-sale booth until 5:00 p.m. Some second-grade dad canceled because he got the "stomach flu" (probably code for Nets tickets).

I glance up and around. *Again.* Sasha was nowhere to be found today. Which makes standing outside school alone extra boring.

See, the Sasha I see at school pick-up every day in a sea of other parents doesn't look much like the one I used to know. And I find it fascinating.

When we first met, we were children—about to start eighth grade. She was sitting on a stoop on Eighty-Sixth Street between Riverside Drive and West End Avenue. I remember because I had just moved from the Upper East Side to the Upper West after my parents' divorce and I still felt out of place. Eighty-Sixth was one of the only streets I knew and not in a good way. That past summer in the Hamptons, the daughter of a Park Avenue family friend had proclaimed in no hushed tones that where Eighty-Sixth Street intersected Broadway "might as well be Harlem."

I wasn't sure exactly what that meant, but I sensed it was not supposed to be good. I also sensed that it was vaguely offensive—to my family and to Harlem, for that matter. Nevertheless, I lay awake on more than one night worrying about it.

That girl was an idiot. I saw that in no time. But I also observed, with some discomfort, that this neighborhood didn't mind showing you its stitches and scars. It juxtaposed upscale prewar buildings—historical landmarks with glamorous deco detailing and doormen who loitered under grand awnings—with neighborhood staples like William's Chicken, where they gave you crunchy pickles and fried drumsticks to gnaw on while you waited if you managed to look cute and young enough. The buildings and sidewalks were so often scaffolded and repaved that they existed in a state of constant reinvention, edits enacted gradually to avoid upsetting the ghosts of carved initials past.

You wouldn't have thought that the Upper East Side and Upper West would feel so different, being just across Central Park from each other. They were both populated by prep schools and museums and beloved mom-and-pop businesses of another era. And yet there was an energy that felt diametrically opposed—one straight-backed and proper, while the other slouched in casual defiance, a hunched middle finger to the etiquette that I understood. There was a proud clutter to this new neighborhood, a brisk warmth, an eclecticism, no apologies.

That first evening when we met, Sasha and I were both newbies, dragged along out of obligation by other kids, in my case a cousin. Two square pegs, milling on the outside of a closed circle of teens whose drama didn't yet include us. But, unlike me, she looked like she belonged. Her bleached platinum-blond bob was tucked back behind her elfin ears—with multiple piercings already—to reveal matching fairy features. Short floral baby doll dress, shit-kicker platform sandals. A less-vanilla white girl than I. Pale skin, a smattering of freckles, small nose with the most subtle ski jump, green cat eyes accentuated with liquid black liner I was not yet skilled enough to apply myself.

But, for those first few months, we glommed on to each other, the way you do when you're new to a place. Meeting up on corners we were still memorizing, baking chocolate chip oatmeal cookies during sleepovers at each other's houses, gossiping about kids who didn't know we existed.

Until, one day, they did. Well, not *us*. Her. And, as soon as she came alive for them, she began to fade for me. We'd been tight for only a few months, and we didn't go to the same school, but it felt like getting dumped. Hard.

And, Lord, I envied her sparkle.

These days, Sasha is someone else entirely. For one thing, this is deep Brooklyn, not Manhattan. (What would that Park Avenue girl say about this place with its patchwork of dilapidated and gentrified row houses?) For another, it's been decades, *decades*.

Yesterday, at school pick-up, I noticed Sasha hadn't changed out of her workout clothes for whatever exercise she's using to stave off perimenopausal pounds. But, of course, she still looked annoyingly incredible. Even the dark circles under her eyes gave her a cool edge. (*Did the concealer pen run out, Sasha? Add that to the to-do list!*)

Grown-up Sasha has less swagger as she walks—no, *runs!*—to grab her kids just in time, her pink-tinted sunglasses always threatening to topple from her head. And, when she nodded to me yesterday, I noticed she ran a hand along her hair, and, obviously self-conscious about its untamed state, threw it in a ponytail. But she is still magnetic, despite the waning collagen and waxing stressors of adulthood.

Thinking about it now, I run a hand over my own hair. I need to get my roots done. Add that to *my* to-do list.

Sometimes, I think she avoids me because I knew her when.

Yesterday, I watched her—purely for anthropological reasons, naturally—hurry away from school and toward her apartment. She waved at the few other parents she knows, some of the dads watching her for a beat too long. She ushered her kids across the street. Asked them about their days. Listened distractedly as they reported on art projects, recess kickball and friend dramas. Sighed as they confessed to leaving half their lunches uneaten—the healthy halves. She ran her hand over her hair one more time as she faded into the distance, pulled out the hairband and shook it free, scrunching up her perfect nose as she caught her reflection in a car window. Never pleased.

Does she look as bad as she thinks she does? Is she as boring as she feels? Sasha. *Are you okay?*

It doesn't really matter. She looks worse than she used to. And "used to" has become a part of her lexicon, as it has all of ours as we've aged.

God. How did we get here?

The truth is she looks just fine for her age. Even annoyingly chic, I think, as I frown down at my frumpy sweater. But "for her age" must be added at the end of every sentence when describing a woman over forty. She's successful *for her age*. She looks good *for her age*. She's in good shape *for her age*. She's got good style *for her age*. At least, she *used to*.

But Sasha is MIA this afternoon. Although her daughter, Nettie, stands outside beside her third-grade teacher in front of the gate, looking mortified. Her arms are crossed over her chest, her lips pursed tight, as she is marched back inside to the office where forsaken children wait for their late parents.

If Sasha has not arrived in ten minutes, there will be a call to her cell phone. If she does not pick up that call, there will be a call to her backup emergency contact.

It will not be her ex-husband, Cliff, because he lives in LA.

Cliff didn't leave her suddenly. Or maybe he did. But it didn't appear that way from the outside. I'm not on the inside despite our history. I thought perhaps since our children ended up enrolled at the same school and live in the same neighborhood, we'd finally become real friends again, but Sasha prefers two-person huddles with her buddy Celeste—when Celeste actually shows up.

So I can only speak to what the rest of us observed about her marriage, which was not very much. After all, we barely saw Cliff before the separation either, except as a blurry figure materializing, rushed and disruptive, at the back of the classroom or auditorium at the tail end of some curriculum night. (Of course, that's true of a good percentage of the dads.) He was good-looking in a quirky way with jet-black hair, pale skin and a resting snark face. Like Reggie from *Archie*.

He looked up to no good.

At the one Monster's Ball Halloween festival I believe he attended, he hung at the edges against the schoolyard's green chainlink fence, sullen and glued to his phone. Some of the other parents got wind that he was a screenwriter and thought that seemed cool, so he drew some focus. I saw Lisa corner him that night, going on and on as she does. He barely tolerated her, his eyes darting impatiently over her shoulder again and again until he made some excuse to walk away. She is extra, but there's no reason to be unkind.

Once, when the kids were really young, he got tipsy at our eighties-night auction and fundraiser, laughing too loudly about how *disinterested* he was in the *Tonight Show Starring Jimmy Fallon* tickets we had on offer. (I also think Jimmy Fallon has the personality of a flaccid penis, but I wouldn't shout about it at the top of my lungs.)

So, when he didn't show up for drop-off or pick-up at school, we didn't notice. He never showed up anyway. We just saw him less and less until he never made an appearance at all. It was as if, instead of leaving, he had effervesced his way out of our neighborhood like dust particles floating into nothingness. And who knew where they landed? Who cared?

Except we all did. Because at some point during that time, he sold one of his moronic superhero screenplays to a giant studio. His participles realigned in a state of quantum entanglement on our TV and movie screens. Suddenly, we saw him—or at least his name—on billboards, in scrolling credits and everywhere else.

Unless you were his kids. Then you barely saw him at all.

Then came the scene the world saw: Cliff at an awards show with his hand inside the dress of a seat filler. No one there knew or cared who he was. He was probably just someone's plus-one at that point. But the indiscretion was caught on camera during one of those televised commercial breaks at the Golden Globes. One minute, you were watching drunken celebrities stumble around in their natural element; the next you saw Cliff, hand cupping someone's tit in graphic relief. The clip went viral, of course, and the term *Golden Globes* took on new meaning, inspiring a hashtag and pernicious punch lines. (Okay, *fine*. My mom friends and I may have giggled over the puns some.) Eventually, the fervor died down.

But maybe Sasha died a little inside too.

In fact, if Cliff's disappearance was observable, it was by watching Sasha instead. As he vaporized into something lighter than air, she darkened and solidified. For a while, her highlights got touched up less often and, at drop-off and pick-up, she appeared with less and less makeup, her clothing more wrinkled as she sprinted away at warp speed. It was hard not to sense her back ache as her shoulders hunched during that time. She found her posture again; but she remained at arm's length.

When she shows up at school now, forty-five minutes after pick-up, I am still outside. There are only a few chocolate cupcakes left with pink and purple icing, dusted with broken sprinkles.

I am contemplating the pastel of it all and considering eating one myself, so I almost miss Sasha as she races past and up the stairs to the school's entrance, harried, flyaways framing her face. She doesn't notice me. Or, if she does, she doesn't show it.

Are you feeling frazzled, Sasha? Do you feel at fault? Give yourself a break. We can all only do the best we can.

7 | After-School, Before School

Nettie is not pleased.

It is School Spirit Day and, although she has had the weekend to process, she is still upset that I was only able to procure her a hoodie in size large.

In her defense, she is swimming in it.

I have tried to convince her multiple times that she looks like Billie Eilish—that it's an oversize *lewk*—but, unfortunately, she is not dumb.

Maybe she's also still not over the fact that she had to wait in the office for over an hour on Friday because her after-school registration got screwed up.

When I got the call that Nettie needed to be picked up that afternoon, I was producing a quickie shoot for a cat clothing line at a loft in lower Manhattan. Creating video content for Do It Furr Fashion's website, which meant coordinating all the feline talent and then overseeing the shoot itself, wasn't the greatest thrill of my career, but I'd jumped at the last-minute job since freelance work has been so slow. Luckily, we were already wrapping when my phone rang. As I rushed out the door, DIFF's owner gifted me a camouflage jacket for our giant cat, Larry, who would kill me in my sleep if I ever tried to make him wear it.

By the time I arrived to grab Nettie, the parent-teacher liaison, Ms. Choi, had left for the day, so I wasn't able to resolve the mix-up. But the office staff promised me I could find her this Monday morning—the last day to make after-school enrollment changes—and rectify the problem.

Nettie swore she was fine when I arrived to pick her up. "These things happen," she said mournfully, with a pat on my shoulder. Like she is the grown-up. "Don't worry about it."

Someone gave her a chocolate cupcake with sprinkles while she waited, which I imagine went a long way. Her mature response was a relief for me. But she has to be sick of these snafus. Of having a stiff upper lip. I know I am.

I am really missing a step lately.

When I finally collected Nettie from the office and we exited the building, knowing I'd have to return for Bart an hour later, I felt eyes on us. Kaitlin, that mom I knew a little growing up, was scrutinizing us from behind lopsided baked goods. *Of course.* Of course she would see us now. She always seems to catch my worst moments. I pretended not to see her.

Bart is at least happy this Monday morning, though he has insisted on wearing his new PS421 tee and no jacket despite the windy fall weather, and his lips are turning Smurftastic blue. He is walking tall, chest puffed out, to display his shirt like he's done something to deserve it. He's got the spirit in him! *Hallelujah!*

He's not the only one. If the families flowing toward school today are a stream, the children, in their green gear, are the algae. The occasional overzealous parent is dressed like the Jolly Green Giant in solidarity. I pass Green Vest VIM in her school earmuffs. Were the parents meant to participate?

One by one, the kids march proudly into the schoolyard to find their teachers. Bart gives the school administrator at the entrance a high-five and doesn't look back. Even my grumpy third grader allows me to kiss her goodbye atop the head, hurrying toward the entrance with the rest of the kelp. I picture them emerging at the end of the day as salted-seaweed snacks.

She needs to wash her hair. That's my first thought as I watch Nettie drop her backpack and join her friends. For a moment, I'm transported to when she used to smell like baby. Time moves so fast. Then, as an oversize fifth grader jostles me trying to beat the bell, I remember to haul ass to the school office.

I dodge dogs and parents, rushing toward the school's main entrance. As I'm smiling at the faces I think I recognize, my eyes land on one I know well: Celeste! She is a vision in not-green. I stop short in front of her.

"Where's your spirit?" I ask her.

"Floating somewhere above the Maldives." She grins.

I already wanted to hug her. Now, I want to even more. So I do. I need the squeeze more than I expect.

"So what's a girl like you doing in a place like this?" I ask as we separate.

"Just thought I'd drop in. Check out the *greenery*."

"Oh no," I say. "That was terrible."

"It was," she says, nodding.

Celeste is a rare sight at drop-off and pick-up. She's the CEO of a very successful interior design firm. And she looks it. Always. Even in jeans and a puffer vest. She has olive skin and wide lips, shiny dark hair piled perfectly atop her head—her Middle Eastern birthright. Her adoring and adorable husband, Jamie, is a stay-at-home dad who shepherds their son, Henry, from place to place.

Her own mother stayed at home, and Celeste felt her mom never got enough credit. She vowed never to repeat that pattern. In fact, she turned it on its head.

"Where's your sainted other half?" I look from side to side and behind her as if Jamie definitely could be hidden there. He could not. He's got the build of a linebacker. He is a rare bird—and not just because, as he likes to say, he's a Black man from Wyoming. He's also got the patience of a preschool teacher, the tech skills of a creepy IT guy (sans heebie-jeebies) and the baking skills of Paul Hollywood. There is no better human on earth.

"Apparently, even deities need to visit the dentist now and then."

"Very inconvenient."

"Indeed," she sighs. "I had to take the whole morning off! Got time for an impromptu walk?"

"I do," I say. "Sadly, and happily, I have no pressing work to do."

We take the first few steps on our stroll before I remember my mission. "Oh, wait! Shoot. I have to run in and handle something at the office. Can you wait? I'll be super fast."

"No problem." She nods, leaning against a parked SUV and pulling out her phone. "I haven't listened to *The Daily* today. There is work to be done!"

Inside school, the mood is chill. First-period classes are in session. Officer White, the security guard at the desk, flashes me his always winning smile as he checks my ID and directs me to the main office. Once there, I wait for the administrators to look up, through mostly cat-eye glasses, from their desks.

"Can I help you?"

"Yes, thank you. I was hoping to talk to Ms. Choi. My daughter was supposed to be signed up for drama after school on Fridays and somehow she got unenrolled."

"Oh, right." The woman nods, gesturing toward a closed door across the hall. "I remember. Ms. Choi is in with another parent currently, but if you have a seat, she should be out soon."

I sit down. A box of doughnuts for the staff is open on the counter in front of me with a sign that reads, "Take one!" I know they're not intended for me, but the Boston cream at the top is really calling my name. I'm debating whether I can get away with snagging it when Ms. Choi emerges, which is why, at first, I don't notice her companion.

"Mom," the office administrator says to me. "It looks like she's out of her meeting."

I pop to standing and turn the corner, just in time to hear that Ethan person saying, "Thank you so much, Ms. Choi."

Twice in one week? Who *is* this man?

He is still tall and irritating and now freshly showered standing beside Ms. Choi, who smiles up at him from below heavy bangs.

"No problem," she is saying. "Happy I could help."

"Oh, I had one other question—"

"I'm so sorry," I interrupt. "Hi. I'm just in a bit of a rush. If you don't mind." I look at him meaningfully. *Remember Friday?* I say with my eyes. *When I let you go first and you took my hoodie?*

"Do you mind, Ethan?" asks Ms. Choi.

Ethan. Why does he get a name?

To be fair, I've had limited interaction with her. But I know she is fair, efficient and from Seattle—because, when we chatted once at a first-grade picnic, we had a long conversation about coffee.

And I know her name.

"Of course not." He shakes his head. "Go right ahead."

Charmed.

"What's up, Mom?" Ms. Choi says to me.

I explain the situation with Nettie and after-school. "I'm not sure how she got unenrolled. I have an email confirming her place in drama," I say, referencing my phone. "I can show you if it will help."

Ms. Choi bites her lip in a way that spells nothing good, fingering a stack of papers in her hands. She looks from me to Ethan, who is shifting in his perfect beat-up brown leather boots in obvious discomfort.

"Unfortunately," she begins, as my heart sinks, "when Nettie got unenrolled, the system repopulated as if there was one space left in the class. There's a record of Nettie's enrollment, but also of her dis-enrollment. And Ethan, here, has just secured that open spot for his daughter."

This fucking man.

"Okay," I say, propping up my wobbly voice with an emotional matchbook. "But can't you make space for one more kid? She's small for her age," I joke. But nothing is funny here. "I really need to have her in after-school on Fridays. For work."

"I'm afraid we can't." Ms. Choi shakes her head. "There are DOE and building regulations about how many children are allowed at once in certain spaces for certain activities. There was only space left for one more child."

I look up at Ethan, who is studiously avoiding my gaze, examining some wall-mounted kindergarten scribbles like they are Van Goghs. He clears his throat. Scratches his stubble.

He is not wearing a ring. *Shocking* that someone divorced him.

I watch his Adam's apple bop up and down like buoy.

"Is there any chance—?" I begin.

"I can't!" he barks before I can finish. He turns to Ms. Choi and shakes his head. "I can't help her."

"Sasha," I bark back.

"What?"

"My name is not *her*. It's Sasha. I'm standing right here."

We stare at each other while an uncomfortable number of seconds pass.

"I've got to . . . go somewhere else," says Ms. Choi, backing away down the hall, papers in the crook of her arm. "But email me, Mom, if you want to get Nettie signed up for a different Friday after-school activity. I believe there's space left in Mindful Soccer and Intermediate Ukulele."

I can feel more than imagine my daughter's cataclysmic disappointment. I am nauseous in anticipation of telling her. She's been talking about drama class all summer. I wanted so badly to deliver her this. After-school sign-up is basically the Hunger Games. I prepared a ranked cheat sheet; set multiple alerts and alarms at sign-up time; sat at my computer and refreshed until the after-school offerings appeared and, with shaking hands, snagged a spot before everyone else. And yet, I have failed. I feel horrible.

Ms. Choi hurries away until all that remains is the echo of her ballet flats slapping against the floor. Whatever Ethan's follow-up question was for her, he will have to ask it at another time. Once again, this infuriating man and I have sent onlookers fleeing.

"Of course!" I humph at him, as I turn and storm toward the exit. I shouldn't feel horrible! *He should.*

"How is this my fault?" this Ethan person says, following behind me.

Even Officer White, sitting at the security desk, averts his eyes as we pass.

"How is it *not* your fault?" I spit. "Apparently, everyone is about pleasing you and you're more than happy to take, take, take." Ethan. With a *name.*

We make it outside the enormous red school doors at the top of the steps and into the crisp air as he says, "Nobody is about 'pleasing' me!"

"Oh yeah?" I whip around to face him. He is annoyingly good-looking. I want to smack that cuteness off his head. "Then why do *you* keep getting what *I* want?"

He shrugs. "Look, *Sasha.* Maybe if you were more on top of things?"

The words hit me hard, unleashing a rage flash flood through my body. Now, I am literally vibrating. "*Excuse me?* What should I be more on top of?"

"What I mean is—" Ethan begins, my red-hot anger reflected as fear in his deep brown eyes. "I didn't mean that how it sounded. What I'm trying to say is, if you sign up early for things, and, like, prepare, then maybe you won't wind up getting screwed."

"Screwed?! Screwed?! The only person screwing me is *you!*"

If I committed homicide in this moment, would anyone blame me? An all-female jury would surely acquit. But no. Even then, they'd probably take one look at his chiseled jaw and leave me to rot in the clink.

It is too early in the morning to be this pissed. It's too early to feel this defeated. From the bottom of the stairs, Celeste is staring up at me, eyes wide. I take a moment, weave my fingers together behind my head, look up at the murky sky and exhale. I want to take his stupid messenger bag and shove it up his ass. Instead, I take the high road.

I growl at him, loud enough that he jumps back. Then, I stomp down to the sidewalk, leaving him standing at the top alone.

"Who's your friend?" Celeste asks when I reach her.

"Satan," I say.

"He's kind of cute." She toggles her head.

"That's how they get you."

"He looks familiar." She narrows her eyes.

"Let's go."

I grab her manicured hand with its stackable rings and drag her away toward the coffee shop to get sustenance for our park walk. If he watches us go, I don't know. I'm sure if I look back, I'll turn him to stone.

8 | The Name Game

SATAN

I watch her go. Because of course I do, even though she doesn't look back. And I do the hard work of not noticing her ass.

Mostly.

I get why she's pissed. But why is she *so* pissed? Why is she *always* so pissed? She actually growled at me. Like a rabid raccoon.

It would have been a cute kind of growl, in another context. A context where my reptilian brain automatically goes now. But, in my defense, women don't usually make that sound in my presence—unless that's my mission. And then less clothes are involved.

Shit. Why am I thinking about her in bed? Her thick hair tangled around her flushed face? *What the hell is wrong with me?*

It's bad enough that I just stole her daughter's theater slot and wouldn't give it back. How has this become my life?

I sigh. Shake my head. Adjust the strap of my messenger bag and reset before starting down the steps.

Once on the sidewalk, I stop and text my ex:

> Hey. Was able to get a drama spot as you predicted. Didn't even have to beg. There was actually one slot open.

A mom I know vaguely walks past, shoots me a lascivious look, like I'm edible. I nod in greeting, but can't bring myself to smile.

I did my job. So why do I feel like such crap?

It's only when I'm headed down into the subway, running to

catch a train rumbling into the station, that it occurs to me: I knew her name. I should have told her: *Sasha. I know your name.*

TO-DO

- Stop making her hate you more.
- Sasha. Stop making *Sasha* hate you more.
- Stop noticing the way she bites her lip when she's mad.
- Stop admiring how she advocates for her kids—in your face.
- Lunch with new CEO.
- ~~Apologize about the after-school drama.~~
- Stop thinking about the after-school drama and get the fuck to work.

9 | Kiss Kiss

KAITLIN

Sasha is on time for pick-up today. Bart high-fives his teacher to be dismissed, then grabs his mother's hand, as they hurry around the corner to where Nettie waits with her teacher too.

Once they grab her and all reach the corner, having maneuvered their way through the eye of the pick-up storm, they pause to regroup. Sasha slings Bart's dinosaur backpack over her shoulder, so he is freewheeling.

Nettie is upset again.

I am standing a few feet away, waiting for my daughter's class to be dismissed, under a dogwood with leaves that have yet to change. Like my kid's teacher, this tree is always running behind.

I pretend to keep scrolling on my phone, through pictures of a former coworker-cum-real-estate influencer—but I'm watching.

Early on, Sasha and I used to chat at pick-up and at school events in the yard occasionally, as old acquaintances. In addition to the usual mom small talk—about dance classes, school lunches, sleep deprivation—we'd swap updates on high school friends with whom we'd kept in touch. We'd make eye contact or smile knowingly when some nineties song blared from the subpar speakers. Any tension about the abrupt ending to our childhood friendship was long buried below pleasantries.

Once, we—well, *I* really—organized a playdate after school at the playground for our two girls. But our kids never really gelled.

Her Nettie almost seemed to have been born a thirty-five-year-old adult or at least a teenager, disinterested in the imaginary play and jungle gym climbing Ruby and the other kids preferred.

When we were still teens ourselves, for years after we stopped hanging out, I would see Sasha around. Even then, I got used to acting like we were fine—like *I* was fine. But, the truth is, I never got good at connecting with the aggressively chill Upper West Side kids like she did. And I still blamed her for abandoning me. I stuttered as I searched for replies to boys who told me my "kicks" were "dope" and girls who asked what music I liked. *I don't know. Everything?*

One night, near the end of tenth grade, I ran into Sasha. In a cropped top and baggy jeans, she was lounging on her elbows against the steps of someone else's swanky building, surrounded by a crew of friends—some of whom I knew too. They were always so dedicated to her. In my life, I never inspire that kind of loyalty—unless I demand it.

She smiled warm and big when she spotted me, chatted for a bit while most of the others ignored me. Then, she went back to laughing carelessly, shooting the boys who liked her playful dirty looks as they paced the sidewalk, battered skateboards and blunts in their hands. Soon enough, she slung her mini backpack across her shoulders and kissed each and every person on the cheek goodbye—even me—as they booed her for leaving.

In those years, when we happened to find ourselves in the same place, it seemed to me she was always going. Always the first to say goodbye. Always leaving them wanting more.

The hangout continued without Sasha that night, until everyone was gone, including me. But something had gone missing after she left. A little luster worn away.

Even as an adult, she seems to effervesce in and out of school events. One minute she's there; the next she's gone. At the winter carnival one year, maybe when the girls were in first grade, we were chatting by the painted rock garden while the kids played makeshift carnival games. Sasha had never been much into volunteering, but she and Celeste had taken the lead on decorating. I had to admit the schoolyard looked magical—twinkle lights, shimmering white streamers, metallic glitter and run-of-the-mill holiday tinsel somehow metamorphosed into an enchanting wonderland. Of course, Celeste is a professional, so she had a leg up. Sasha herself was not dressed up in any festive way, just bundled in neutral woolens, and I felt dumb in my reindeer headband and glitter eyeshadow, which I'd applied based on a TikTok trend and thought looked cute in the mirror at home.

"Have you ever run into Hugo?" I dropped, in context. I'd been dying to ask for months, playing the long game, but it was impossible for me to hold her attention for any extended period.

"Hugo?" she said, scrunching her nose. "Which Hugo?"

"You know," I said, forcing a smile. "Hugo Reyes! How many Hugos do you know? And, by know, I mean . . ." I raised my eyebrows suggestively.

She looked genuinely confused. I felt my frustration ratchet up. I was already in a bad mood. My husband had just called about extending his business trip and I had hit a solo-parenting wall.

"I think I remember a Hugo," she said. "Was he the tall one with dreads who always wore the Saints Starter jacket?"

"No, no. Medium height. Skateboarder. Shaved head."

Had she really forgotten? 'Cause I hadn't.

"Ohhh." She nods. "Okay. I think I know who you mean."

I could tell she was only humoring me. Maybe, it occurred to me, she was always humoring me.

"You guys dated," I said, impatience creeping into my voice.

"My God. We probably did. My memory is the worst for that time!" Sasha smiled. "Maybe it was all the weed and malt liquor. Or maybe it was Rebecca who went out with him, not me?"

Rebecca. One of her mean-girl best friends.

"No!" I insisted. "You must remember! It was spring of junior year. Right after you broke up with Josh."

"Wow. I'm surprised you remember that."

Of course I remembered. She and Josh had sparkled. We all knew he cheated on her, but everyone envied her anyway. He was *that* adorable. We were equal parts gleeful and disappointed when they ended. That put her on the market. That led her to Hugo.

"I saw you guys together—you and Hugo—at a party at Crane Club," I said.

I saw them together all right. His tongue deep down her throat; their bodies pressed together against the quilted wall, illuminated intermittently by strobes. Her skimpy cropped top, miniskirt and clunky Doc Martens. His Champion sweatshirt pushed up above low-slung jeans, revealing the waistband of his boxers and her hand resting against the shadowy divots below his six pack.

The image was burned on my brain.

"Oh, right," she said. "Crane Club. That's a blast from the past."

I could tell I was making her uncomfortable, but I couldn't stop myself.

"You really don't remember? Like, at all?"

"No, I think I do, kind of," she said, pulling her hat down on her head to protect against the cold. The sun was going down, a final curtain call on warmth for the day. "I was pretty sad after Josh. There were some rebounds. Probably at Crane Club." Sasha shivered. "I should go make sure Nettie is doing okay."

"Right," I said. I couldn't bring myself to smile.

With a wave, she walked away in search of anyone and anywhere else. She did it again. Receded. Left us—*me*—wanting more.

That might have been our last substantial conversation.

And, standing there, alone, for a moment I returned to the body of a fourteen-year-old me, loitering at the edge of a circle surrounding her.

I returned to the body of a fifteen-year-old me, saying hi to Sasha under the nasty gaze of that Rebecca girl.

I returned to the body of a sixteen-year-old me. Mary J. Blige belting "Real Love" through the speakers with too much bass. Standing alone in a frenetic club, jostled by my drunk and drugged under-age peers. Reeling from the gut punch of seeing the boy who just dumped me, the boy I believed I loved, making out with the girl who had also dumped me and who rarely gave me the time of day.

"Disaster!" I heard someone exclaim.

I looked up. Lisa was standing next to me in a Santa hat. Like me, she had dressed up on theme for the fair. "We've run out of chocolate elves!"

I was shot back into reality. I am an adult woman. In a school-yard. At my daughter's school. And we needed more chocolate elves.

I focused my attention back where it thrives: on my daughter.

"I know what to do," I said. Lisa followed at my heels.

"There's nothing I can do," I hear Sasha saying now, as Nettie hangs her head, her shoulders slumping. "Drama is full. I'm sorry. I tried. But I'm looking into alternatives."

This is getting good. I put my phone in my pocket.

I see Sasha see me, then pretend she doesn't.

"Whatever." Nettie turns and begins trudging in the direction of their apartment.

Bart looks up at his mother. "Nettie is walking without us."

Sasha nods. "I see that."

"Why is she doing that?"

"I think she's angry."

He pauses to watch. "I think she's sad."

Sasha closes her eyes tight for an almost imperceptible moment. I know that look. She is holding back tears.

Don't cry, Sasha.

"Let's catch up!" shouts Bart, running ahead. And the spell is broken.

10 | The Runaways

SASHA

It's a beautiful day in the neighborhood. The morning sun is shining, the leaves are changing to a yellow and coral ombré that makes me feel all is right in the world. On the way to school, I nod cheerfully to Redhead Mom like, *We got this.*

After I kiss the kids goodbye, I spot Jamie, Celeste's husband, dropping Henry off. I wave and cross to him, as he waves back at me. It feels good to see a friendly face.

"Did your wife tell you about my freakout yesterday?"

"She may have mentioned a minor meltdown."

"As long as she called it 'minor.'"

"Sure. Let's say she did."

"No, but really." I laugh. "She saved me."

"Yeah," he says, running a hand over his bearded face. "She has a way of doing that."

It's then that I notice bags under his eyes, an existential malaise in his expression that I'm used to peeping in my own mirror but not in Jamie's inexhaustible face.

"You okay?"

He shrugs. "Just tired."

"Minor meltdown?"

"Minor meltdown."

"Life!" I say.

"Life," he agrees.

We part ways.

The truth is Celeste really had helped me the day before—and not just with decompressing from my run-in with Demon Dad (my new nickname for that Ethan person). She also talked me down from the drama over after-school drama, reminding me gently that no lives hung in the balance.

"After-school theater is kind of terrible anyway," she said. "I know. I sat through Henry's Pokémon adaptation last spring." She turned to face me. "I'll never get those minutes back."

"I know." I nod, rubbing my eyes and smiling despite myself. "But poor Nettie. She really wanted to take theater." I wonder if this was some abstract way of connecting with her director dad.

"Well, I've been hearing awesome things about Brooklyn Theater Center on Eighth Avenue. And they do pick-up!"

I don't know how Celeste knows about these things despite rarely making an appearance at the actual school. But she always does. As soon as I got home, I threw my keys on the sideboard by the door (where I would inevitably forget I left them), kicked off my high-tops, raised the shades to let light in and then padded across the muted mauve Moroccan rug to the open-floor-plan kitchen. What the apartment lacks in size, it does make up for in nice appointments—almost. I confronted and cleaned up the Pompei of my kids' lunch assembly—half avocado, bag of baby carrots, cream cheese container with the top flung aside. Finally, I wiped down the granite counter, then sat in front of my laptop at my kitchen table, a beautiful wooden farm relic, and googled that theater program.

Celeste was right, as always. Not only did they offer after-school drama for third and fourth graders right near our house, but the theme for the coming session was Enola Holmes. Score. Only downside? It was pricey. Now, I just needed to figure out if I had the budget.

As if all-powerful Celeste had magically manifested it, I scrolled and discovered an unexpected email waiting: a potential freelance gig that might enable me to pay for the class without having to harvest an organ or interact with Cliff! Equally painful experiences—

not because I harbor regret or hurt feelings anymore, but because my ex-husband is insufferable. Cliff, who is busy being a *serious director* on his movie set in Canada or New Mexico or somewhere else with "great tax credits" and likes to let me know it. Cliff, who, when we met in film school, had once had a sense of humor. Or had I imagined that?

> Hi Sasha,
>
> Nice to meet you! I hope you don't mind my reaching out cold. I've heard wonderful things about you and have seen a bit of your work for myself (a.k.a. went down a rabbit hole on your website and social). Very cool!
>
> We have an upcoming project for which I think you'd be a great fit, which involves producing video content to accompany a sprawling feature we have planned for the cover story of our March issue. The only caveat is the deadline is quite tight!
>
> If you're interested and available, I'd love to have you come meet the team this Thursday afternoon. Would 4:00 p.m. EST work?
>
> Please revert at your earliest convenience.
>
> Best,
>
> Derek Perez
>
> Managing Editor
>
> *Escapade Magazine*

I waited forty minutes to respond so as not to seem desperate. Which I am.

> Derek, hi!
>
> Thank you for getting in touch. It's lovely to meet you. Fortunately, you've caught me at the perfect moment, in a short gap between projects. I'd love to learn more about this opportunity.

And, yes, I'm available on Thursday afternoon. Looking forward!
Best,
Sasha

Derek confirmed the next morning.

Though I claimed to be free to meet at 4:00 p.m., of course I am not. Because that's after pick-up, when I'm with my kids. Which is why, later that morning, as I walk from drop-off toward the park for my run, I text my mother to request backup. If my parents can help out, I won't have to harvest another organ to pay a sitter.

> Mom. Hi! Possible for you to babysit the kids on Thursday afternoon, starting at around 3pm? I have an important meeting!

Seconds after I press Send, my phone rings with a FaceTime call. This is my mother's move lately. FaceTime all day, every day. It's my nightmare. Especially inconvenient when you're texting from the toilet.

Out of options, I accept the call, ducking into a corner by the eco dry cleaner (which I suspect is just a normal dry cleaner) so I can talk without blocking street traffic.

Of course, as soon as her image pops onto the screen, a fire truck zooms past with sirens blaring.

"I can't hear you!" she shouts.

"One second," I say, holding up a finger.

"What?!" she says.

"Hold on!" I say, holding my hand up.

"What?!" she says.

I consider throwing my phone, or myself, into oncoming traffic.

"HOLD ON!" I yell into full quiet. The siren has passed.

A woman walking her collie brings a hand to her chest, startled, and shoots me a dirty look. The collie shrugs. They resume walking.

"What was that?" my mom is saying. "I think it was on your end."

"It was definitely on my end," I say. "It was a fire truck. I'm on the street. You're on your couch."

She is indeed sitting on the modernist couch my parents have had for at least ten years, squinting at me through her wire-rimmed glasses, a *New Yorker* issue castoff beside her. This is my mother in a nutshell.

"True, true," she says, slipping her glasses off. "So, I got your text."

"I figured."

"What?!"

"Mom, should I just call you? It might be easier to hear."

"No, this is great. You're just in a loud place. Where are you? Can you go somewhere quieter?"

"Not really, Mom. I'm outdoors. In New York City. Where we both live."

"Right, right."

"Anyway, how are you?"

"Fine. The doctor recommended a new pain medication that I'm taking for my neck, and I think it's helping!"

"Oh, great!"

"Yes. Don't get old. It's not for the faint of heart."

"I'll do my best. I hear there's a cool new fountain of youth in Bushwick."

She does not laugh. "Anyway. I'm available on Thursday, but we can't come any earlier than three p.m."

"That should be totally fine." I nod vigorously.

"I have a doctor's appointment and then a meeting with that anti-censorship advisory council at the public library," my mom continues. "You know, they're trying to ban *To Kill a Mockingbird* in Florida. It's an outrage!"

"I also have a meeting!" my father interjects from somewhere beyond my view. "But it's a breakfast meeting!"

"What does that have to do with anything?" my mom asks my father, swiveling so that her back is fully to the camera. So that I am looking at her sweater seam.

"Just contributing to the conversation."

"Who's your breakfast meeting with?" my mother asks him.

"It's Bill. I haven't seen him since he left Columbia."

"That's right. I wonder how he's doing. His wife must be losing her mind with him home all the time."

"Well, he won't be home on Thursday morning. He'll be at breakfast. With me."

"Hey, guys," I try, but they have forgotten I exist.

"Where is brunch?"

"Guys?"

"Fairway."

"Oh, that sounds good. I haven't had their cranberry muffins in ages. Maybe you could bring me one?"

"GUYS!" I yelp, just as the woman with the collie circles back around. She balks at me. She is not a fan. "I'm still on the phone!"

"Oh, sorry." My mom shrugs, turning back to face me. "Where were we?"

"Thursday. Three p.m. Sounds good!"

"What's the meeting, by the way?"

No way I'm getting led down this path again. "I'll tell you all about it when I see you in person!"

"One last thing," my mother says as she puts her reading glasses back on and picks up the *New Yorker*. "I was wondering what you're planning for Chanukah?"

"For Chanukah?"

"Yes."

"Is it early this year?"

"Not especially."

"Why are we talking about it two months in advance? I'm still recovering from Yom Kippur."

"Just planning ahead."

"Let's talk about this later too."

I both appreciate my parents' help so much and feel a bit nauseous with self-loathing for having to request it so often. Of course

I will work around their schedule and the insanity—but why does everything feel like an uphill battle?

"Suit yourself." My mother shrugs. "See you Thursday!"

I hang up, sigh and take a single step toward the park for my run when my phone rings out again. It reads "MOM." For the love of all things holy.

"Hi?"

"Me again!" my mom says.

"I see that. Want to plan Passover? It's only six months away." She ignores me.

"I just wanted to tell you that we can't come on Thursday until three p.m."

"Right," I say. "You mentioned that before." My stomach sinks. Does she not remember?

"I did?" She frowns. "Huh. Well, now I've said it twice."

I nod. "Consider it computed."

"Okay, sweetie."

"Oh, and Mom?"

"Yes?"

"Thank you."

"You're welcome."

I wait for a beat after she hangs up. I will not frighten that collie again.

But the phone doesn't ring. For the moment, it seems, we are good. Though, if I'm honest, the conversation left me feeling anything but, unease prickling below the surface. *Is something up with my mom?* It's not like her to be so forgetful.

Sighing, I head to the park to blow off steam.

I run. But I am not a runner. That's an important distinction in a neighborhood that attracts this earnest and committed a running crowd. I have never attempted a 5K, a half marathon or a marathon. I do not carry energy chews or own a holster for my iPhone. I have never consulted an expert about my gait. And, while I do use an app to track my mileage, it's only so I know when I can be done. At exactly three miles. No matter what.

The truth is, I don't like running. But I *love* stopping. The feeling of finishing and basking in the rest of a podcast or power ballad while I stroll out of the park like a champ is transcendent. Like everyone else, I have endured boring-ass lectures on the importance of exercise my whole life—by school health teachers, doctors at annual checkups, fitness articles in waiting-room magazines. But I never actually absorbed any of that endorphin mumbo jumbo until after my divorce, confronted with the vision of a future spent as a blob on my couch.

Each morning, I would blink my eyes open to another day of solo parenting without reprieve, no matter how great my kids, of feeling sad and like a failure. Of worrying about a dearth of money and time. Of feeling lonely—though never as lonely as when Cliff was still pretending to participate. Nothing like someone ignoring you in the same room to make you feel like an island. I've realized I prefer to be ignored from three thousand miles away.

Jogging helped.

So, now, I run my way through bits of native forest onto the main path, finding my rhythm as I get warm. I often switch up my route, but, on tired days or when I don't feel like pushing that hard, I go against the current, jogging the opposite direction of most other runners to avoid the giant uphill swing on the opposite side of the loop. This is one of those days.

Today, the park is alive with people—runners, bikers, preschool teachers guiding groups of tiny humans in matching T-shirts, gripping a shared rope or a partner's hand. Set free, kids toss leaves in the air. No surprise. The weather is spectacular. There's a hint of crispness, like biting into an apple, but it's on the tail of warm, enveloping sunlight. I love this gift of early fall, when the foliage is only beginning to make an appearance, transmuting into pinks, oranges and yellows.

Almost every morning as he eats breakfast, Bart asks me my favorite color of the day. I appreciate that he doesn't expect me to pick one and stick with it, always. He understands, every day is different. Some days are green tea tinted, while others burst out in crimson. As I run, I lift my phone, awkwardly, to snap a photo of a particularly flamboyant maple. I'll show it to the kids later. *This* is my favorite color today.

But, between my deep thoughts, photographic endeavors and the running app that periodically interrupts my podcast of celebrities interviewing celebrities, my brain and body get jumbled up and I stumble. Luckily, I catch myself before I hit the concrete and dirt path, but I look up just in time to see *him* see me. Demon Dad. Coming from the opposite direction. Looking like a catalog model for *Runner's Monthly*, with just a dash of curated scruff.

He looks shocked. Which is how I feel too. Who knows why, since we live in the same tiny neighborhood and literally *everyone* runs here. Caught off guard, he waves in greeting, aborts halfway, then seems unsure of what to do with his hand. He scrunches up his nose like he's caught a whiff of the sulfurous ginkgo tree to our left. Then, as we pass each other, at the last second, he opens his mouth to speak. Mucked up by ambivalence and the speed of sound, all I wind up hearing is a garbled rumble as if from a trapped animal surrendering. Kind of like *mleghhh*.

That's when I realize that, in the midst of this profound millisecond exchange, I have been staring dumbly, my mouth hanging open like a bulldog. *Dammit*. A missed opportunity to glare at him or snub him or at least look "on top of things."

I am left with a buzzing feeling, like something significant has happened when it hasn't. Like suddenly I am awake. I try to recenter and think about something else. Not the hoodie. Not the lost drama class. Not the ways in which I have disappointed my children and this man has made it worse. Not how the divorce still feels like a failure akin to original sin. All of that sits solid in my chest, a burden to carry and keep moving.

To my chagrin, instead of waning, the shot of adrenaline from seeing that Ethan person shifts into a nervous drip. Anxiety trickles through me.

What if I don't get this job? Is my mother losing a step? Did I leave the oven on?

I try to think hopefully about my meeting on Thursday. Plan an outfit for it. Envision it going well. Them hiring me and inexplicably paying me $2.5 million for a four-day shoot. But even that fantasy can't settle me.

What is with this guy? Is he destined to destroy any semblance of serenity for me? Has he come into my life as a hurdle I must somehow leap in order to ascend to the next level?

The more I think about him, the more I spiral into anger. My run is sacred time! And I've never noticed him here before—not like the Orthodox Jewish girl who still manages to run with a wig or the inexplicably pale eighty-year-old man in full race regalia who I pass on every jog. How dare Demon Dad disturb my run by . . . existing! That's right: how dare he exist!

Also, is this run almost over? Because this is not one of those easy, breezy jogs. I am huffing. I am puffing. There's a crick in my neck.

I look down to check the remaining distance. How am I not done? Of course, when I glance back up, I make eye contact with Demon Dad. *Again!* What is this karma?!

This time, he looks more prepared, maintaining an even expression with only a slight raise of his eyebrows. But I am exponentially annoyed. Really? He lapped me? In the time it has taken me to move ten feet, he has run three-quarters of the loop again?

I'm contemplating to what far-flung land I can relocate my bi-weekly run—is it disrespectful to jog in Green-Wood Cemetery?—when I sense more than see someone jog up beside me. Like the Angel of Death, his shadow overtakes mine.

"You're running the wrong way," Ethan says. He has clearly hung a U-turn and is now jogging in my same direction.

I do not look his way. "There is no wrong way," I say, between pants. "There are only wrong people."

"Well, most people are running the way I was running. The *right* way."

"Please feel free to resume running in the other direction. Away from me."

I speed up. He keeps pace with me, easily.

"You don't like me."

"That's surprising to you?"

"Maybe just the depth of your contempt."

"I have great depth."

"I have no doubt."

He continues running beside me, quietly for a few paces. And, to my chagrin, I can sense him there almost physically. At my side. Like an itch. "You know, you should really run with your hands held higher up in front of you." He demonstrates as if he's about to start a boxing match. Punching him *does* seem like a good idea.

"Weirdly," I say, instead, "I don't remember asking for your advice." I am reminded of Cliff's unsolicited note on my *finished* final film project in college. "You might want to do it more like . . . me."

"I'm just saying"—Ethan shrugs, with irritating ease—"holding your hands up allows you to protect your face and body if you fall."

I say nothing. I am honestly just trying to keep breathing. This is faster than my usual pace. But there is no way I'm slowing down.

"'Cause I saw that. Before," he says, pointing his thumb behind us, "when you almost ate it back there."

Of course he did.

"Oh, good," I say. "I'm so glad to hear there were witnesses."

"I'm only trying to be helpful."

"Let me confirm that you're not."

I sprint farther ahead. I don't think I've ever run this hard. The trees are blurs in my peripheral vision, and yet this annoying man remains in focus. And then, like a miracle, my running app chirps through my earbuds: "Distance: three miles. Split time: eight minutes, fifty-four seconds. Average pace: nine minutes, forty-three seconds per mile."

I stop short, gasping, and squat to catch my breath.

Ethan overshoots, realizes I'm gone, then turns around and circles back, still jogging in place.

"What happened?" he says from above. "Are you okay?"

"Yeah," I manage. "I'm fine."

"So, why did you stop?"

"I was done."

"Done? You finished the loop?"

"Nope. I run three miles. The loop is three and a quarter."

"Really? But why not just finish? You're so close."

I gape at him incredulously. "Because I don't want to! Oh my God! Why am I having this conversation? Who *are* you?"

I start speed-walking away, my arms swinging. I'm still breathing hard, but it's an improvement. He stops running and falls in line, walking beside me.

"Okay, sorry," he says, running a hand through his mussed hair. "I'm making things worse. Sometimes I do that when I'm . . . awkward."

"Are you sometimes not awkward?"

"Occasionally."

"Okay. Well, good luck with that. I'm gonna go." I turn my back on him.

"Wait." He reaches out and rests a hand on my shoulder. His touch is totally gentle, but it sends such a strong shock wave through my body that I startle and step away.

"What?!" I yelp, my body reverberating.

An enormous man in a Yankees cap and tracksuit sitting on a bench nearby shoots me a questioning look: *All okay?* Like if I needed, he'd take Ethan by the scruff of the neck and toss him over the fence and into the zoo.

I nod. It's cool. No need for intervention. But good to know that's an option.

"Sorry!" Ethan says to me again, holding up his palms. "Look"— he sighs, dropping his hands, flexing the one that grazed my shoulder like he got shocked too—"I haven't been able to stop thinking about yesterday. About what happened. And your daughter. So, when I saw you, I figured I'd take the opportunity to—"

"Mansplain about how to fix my running stance?"

"Um, no. Apologize. And explain. If you're open to it."

I cross my arms over my chest. I'm trying to maintain my level-orange hatred, but he's making it difficult. His charming half smile. The crinkle of his eyes. The way he gazes at the ground like a contrite little kid.

Plus, now that we've stopped, it's impossible not to notice his muscular arms and legs, the way his damp T-shirt clings to his lean chest. He's stupidly handsome and the crookedness of his smile only exacerbates the issue. I smooth my ponytail, catch myself primping and almost groan out loud. *Ugh.* This guy is every woman's worst nightmare.

"Okay," I say, recovering. I will not groom for this man. "Go ahead."

Ethan gestures over to the side of the path, and I nod. We step a few feet into the grass, so we're not blocking other runners. We are awash in kinetic light under the flickering leaves of a now-orange oak.

"I know I should've given you your daughter's spot in drama back."

"But you didn't."

"But I didn't. Because, well, I was caught off guard and also . . . it's complicated with my . . . ex-wife."

I like to think only a seasoned veteran like myself could detect the subtle clunkiness of the way he delivers the moniker. The way he is still trying *ex* on for size. The divorce is fresh.

Of course, I, of all people, understand this. The complication of factoring in the impulses of a person with whom you're no longer romantically entangled but to whom you will forever be logistically chained. The desire to avoid engaging. It's the only reason I'm sometimes grateful that Cliff is so checked out.

"I'm trying to take on more, but it's all kind of new for me. She was already angry that I hadn't secured the spot in drama in the first place—I didn't realize how cutthroat after-school sign-up is—and then, when Ms. Choi said that a waitlist spot had opened up, I was so relieved to diffuse things. Giving it up to you would have meant contending with my ex. Which is not your problem. Sorry. Is this too much information?"

I sigh. "No. It's okay. Unfortunately, I can relate."

I watch him process this information. "Right. The point is, I took the easy way out . . . at your daughter's expense. And if you want the spot back, it's yours."

I study him for a moment. The clear look in his brown eyes. I even feel a little bad for him. Does he have an angle?

Well, he has many angles. But I'm trying to avoid noticing those—because of the warm feeling they're giving me in my stomach.

I really need to get out more.

If he has some nefarious plan, I can't see it. He's just some semi-absent dad who's on a mission to be present now, fueled by divorce guilt. It explains why I haven't noticed him before. He was probably never around until now.

"No, it's okay." I shake my head, opting to take him at face value. "I appreciate that, but, at this point, I think I'll spare my daughter the whiplash, never mind disappointing your kid too. I imagine she doesn't need more upheaval in her life."

He nods, sighing, like the thought of his daughter's forlorn face stresses him out as much as Nettie's does me. He tugs absently on a leaf dangling from a drooping tree branch, which rebounds mildly. We both watch it bounce.

"Anyway," he says, remembering himself. "I'm sorry for saying you should be more on top of things. And I'm sorry I screwed you." He pauses, then smirks. "Especially because that's really starting to sound wrong."

I grin despite myself. "It really is."

We both snicker. Maybe we're parents, but we're all still seventh graders at heart.

He runs a hand through his hair, clearly a habit. "Let's start over," he says.

"Fine," I say. "I'm Sasha. Officially."

He narrows his eyes. "I know who you are."

I am startled by the way he says this. As if he really does. As if maybe I should know who he is too. As if he *sees* me.

For a disorienting moment, I can't tell if he's being literal or not. I am struck dumb. There's an awkward pause.

"Sorry. I don't . . ."

"We've met before," he explains. "At the playground."

"Okay," I say. "I'm sorry. I'm bad with faces. And names."

He nods. Maybe I'm imagining it, but I think I see a look of disappointment flit across his face, then disappear.

And I'm confused. This man hates me—right?

"Well," I say, suddenly unmoored. "I better go."

As I begin walking away, cutting across the lawn to the nearest exit, he starts up the path ahead, revving back up to a run. But then he turns to face me, jogging backward.

"You really should keep your hands up when you run though," he calls, modeling the position.

"You really should stop dispensing unsolicited advice."

He cocks his head, unbothered. Shrugs. "Fair enough."

And, with that, Demon Dad turns and sprints away. I press Play on my podcast and bask in the afterglow of my run.

11 | Pony Up

DEMON DAD

She really doesn't remember meeting when the kids were small. I can't decide if that's bad or good. Either way, I am clearly delusional.

Why do I care? What is happening to me? I'm never like this.

I guess, if I'm honest, all those years ago, even though we were both still married, I thought we'd connected. One parent, one *person*, to another. Like we could have been real friends.

Maybe.

Could I just be friends with Sasha? Sure. I'm evolved. Why the fuck not?

Because. That's why not. Even when I talked to her now, when her brow furrowed in that adorable way, when her green eyes filled with irritation and something harder to name, I just wanted to reach out and tug her ponytail.

I shake my head, like I'm clearing an Etch A Sketch. I can't let my brain wander beyond that. I won't. I'm cut off.

And I have the rest of my run to try not to think about it. About *her.* I close my eyes against the breeze. Against the image of her scowling. Of her on top of things. Turn my podcast louder. Focus on work. Blast out the noise.

I ruined my pace. But at least I apologized.

TO-DO
- Finish the run, extra fast.
- Get over yourself.

- Stop thinking about Sasha.
- When that fails, try harder.
- Try harder.
- Try.
- Harder.

12 | No Time to Say Hello, Goodbye

KAITLIN

On Thursday at pick-up, I almost don't recognize her. There's a bit of the old Sasha in the way she struts up, posture at once straight and relaxed, smooths her hair and waits in oversize sunglasses for the children's classes to emerge outside. She knows she looks good. She is "feeling herself," as the kids say.

In place of her standard hoodie and Nike high-tops, she's wearing an actual blazer in leopard print, high-waisted wide-legged black jeans and suede booties. She's dressed for *something*.

I gaze down at my own skinny jeans, cross one leg in front of the other. I know they're not on trend anymore. And they need a wash. But they're comfortable, and it's just pick-up.

Once, I wouldn't have been caught dead looking basic. I would have known what was what. Seemingly, it's still effortless for Sasha. Or maybe she's trying hard. Either way, it's exhausting to me.

It's amazing how quickly something that feels essential can become obsolete. That could be the title of my autobiography.

I think about how much my daughter wanted to spend time with me last year, how distracted I was by my own impulses, how different our lives looked. I'm nauseous. The salmon I bought for dinner has turned in my mind.

I pull out my phone, open my to-do list in my notes app and type: *Buy Ruby new clothes.* I'll troll H&M tonight. I may have come up short, but there's still hope for her.

Sasha pets a passing dog, notices me and shoots me a perfunctory smile, checks the time on her phone multiple times. Begins tapping her toes.

She's late. She's late. For a very important date.

13 | Let Me Take You On an Escapade

SASHA

Derek at *Escapade Magazine* makes spreadsheets about spreadsheets. That's something I learn in the first five minutes of our meeting. It's also something I should have guessed after he sent a calendar event, a backup calendar invite, a confirmation email the day before and another this morning. The man is organized.

I can respect that.

After I hustled my kids back to our apartment post pick-up and my parents arrived to babysit at 3:00 p.m. sharp, I made my own pre-meeting confirmations: I checked my bag for lip gloss, earbuds, anti-anxiety meds.

As I gathered my belongings, my mother began banging around in the white kitchen cabinets. Bart watched from the table, already knee-deep in his packet of rainbow Goldfish. Nettie was in her room reading.

"Mom," I said, holding the front door open as I grabbed my shoes from the charcoal-gray mat in the hall and readied to leave.

"Yes, sweetie?" she asked.

"What are you looking for?"

"You moved your glasses!" she said, rummaging through a selection of ceramic vases.

"No. Nope. I haven't," I said.

"Really?" she said, now rummaging through my tea selection, which had been neatly stacked against the teal backsplash—probably my favorite detail of the whole place. "I could have sworn the cups were right here!"

My glasses—short, squat tumblers with ribbed edges—have been in the same cabinet since Cliff and I first moved to this apartment four years ago. They remained there through our arguments—over his constant travel, over prioritizing his career over mine, over his phone addiction, over the way he opted out of watching our children, over the way he would lie down on the couch and, without guilt or irony, just watch me clean while he critiqued some movie he thought he could have made better. Over the fact that he was not who he had seemed. Or maybe he was.

Cliff moved. The glasses did not.

"Well, then, where are they?" my mother asked, now cross. As if the glasses and I were colluding against her.

They are most certainly not on the counter.

"Over there!" I pointed.

"Here?"

"No, the next one."

"Here?"

"No. Up."

"Up where?" she snapped, exasperated.

"Two cabinets to the left," said Bart, surprising us both. He picked up a Goldfish and swam it through the air, making a fish face.

My mother had forgotten where the glasses are kept. There was a drop in my stomach that I didn't enjoy. An uneasy flutter in my chest. I brought a hand to my heart to still it.

She finally located two glasses and pulled them down. I watched her take them to the sink and rinse them. This habit of my mother's drives me insane. They're already clean! That's why they're in the cabinet! Where they always are!

At least she could find the sink.

"What's this meeting again?" she asks.

"Just a possible gig—a shoot on a tight deadline," I said, as if I wasn't nervous. "I'm not sure of the details yet."

"So, not a hot date?" she asked, swallowing multiple pills.

"Not a date," I answered.

"What's a date?" asked Bart.

"A stone fruit," said my dad from the couch, looking up from the same *New Yorker* issue my mom had been reading the other day.

Larry, our giant gray cat who looks like a cross between Jerry Orbach and my late grandfather, grunted in his sleep as if to confirm this fact. I'd almost forgotten he and my father were sitting there.

"I gotta go," I said.

I really did. For all the reasons.

In addition to keeping my eye out for any homicidal maniacs boarding my subway car, I spent the train ride trying not to panic about my mother's sudden dottiness—the repeated calls about the 3:00 p.m. arrival time, the disorientation over the standard arrangement of my kitchen. The clear confusion.

I also tried to block out her insinuation about my love life. Or, I should say, lack thereof. Lately, she has been trying to convince me to join some dating app called Grattitude, where, instead of swiping a certain direction, you "bless" people. She says it's more positive.

And I am positive I don't want anything to do with it.

I hate first dates. And it turns out you usually have to go on one in order to have a second date. So, I will remain celibate for the rest of my life. Easy solve.

I met Cliff in college, so I didn't have to confront that barrier. We went to class together, lived in the same dorm, had mutual friends, watched pretentious movies, went out and binge drank in groups and eventually—after due persistence on his part—found ourselves making out against the refrigerator in the communal kitchen one night instead of watching a pivotal scene in *Revenge of the Nerds*.

Cliff always insists we were watching Hitchcock's *Rear Window*. Revisionist history.

He hadn't been my type. In high school, I'd dated DJs and basketball players, one hot brooding musician who turned boring quickly. My long-term boyfriend, Josh, had been a social beast, everyone's favorite . . . everything. But he'd broken my heart again and again, and I was still licking my wounds in college. In an ironic twist, Cliff seemed just nerdy enough to be safe. Not. So. Much.

Now, I'm sitting in a stark conference room around a glass table with sharp edges. Out the window, we are blinded by the reflection of sunlight from other windowed skyscrapers. Derek, who is *Escapade*'s managing editor and clearly the engine behind the operation, is sitting across from me.

I have been offered filtered tap water, bottled water, spring water, sparkling water, Hint water, coconut water, collagen water, Vitaminwater and coffee.

"Hmm. I could really go for some Smartwater," I deadpan.

My joke is met with uncomfortable grunts and fake laughs from the members of the staff sitting around the table, in addition to Derek. Stephanie (deputy editor, like a bustier Blake Lively), Peter (a burly, white, lumberjack-looking cameraman in a flannel shirt) and Jackie (a graceful, dark-complected set stylist wearing a black jumpsuit and necklaces layered in a way I can never get right).

Derek shoots me a compulsory smile. I give it a 6.3. The technical skills are there, but there's no passion behind it.

Even though I cyberstalked him, he looks different in person than I expected. He's smaller, lither, with shiny black hair. He's wearing nerd glasses, a denim-on-denim ensemble and oxfords. And he has the tightly wound energy of an ostrich but with kind eyes. I like him right away. I vow silently to win him over.

"So, as I was explaining, we don't usually outsource our content, but the previous HP—"

"That's head producer!" Stephanie chimes in. Her neon pink lipstick is aggressive, and maybe so is she.

"Yes. That's head producer. Anyway, he just left us suddenly to produce interstitials for a streamer. I won't say which one—"

"Netflix!" Stephanie winks meaningfully.

Derek clears his throat. "So we're in kind of a spot. There have been a lot of changes here lately and things are a bit in flux. The bad news is that we only have a few weeks to pull this all together. The good news is that—"

"We're going to have the best time!"

Derek turns to Stephanie and looks at her long and hard. She shrugs at him. *Deal with it.*

"I was going to say, the good news is, if you're interested, we are looking to fill that full-time position too. Should this go well and should our new editor in chief and you both feel this is a fit, there's a potential permanent producer role on the team for you."

"I see," I say mildly. "So great to know."

But I am only playing it cool. Suddenly, this meeting has taken on extra significance. My heart is pounding.

As it turns out, freelance video production work isn't the best job for a single parent. It demands long hours, networking drinks, days spent pitching just to get a job in the first place. But then a lot of things that seemed like good ideas in film school in the late nineties and early aughts really don't now. Cliff. The arts. Low-rise jeans. In those days, Cliff and I both figured we'd skyrocket to fame as multi-hyphenate writer-director-producers. Make our own hours; be rolling in cash. We certainly weren't thinking about insurance benefits. We knew most people had to claw their way to the top, but we were already at the top of our class. Obviously, those challenges wouldn't apply to us.

We would stay in New York, not sell out in Hollywood, and be acclaimed for our commercial and artistic success!

In retrospect, if I had only looked for equivalent examples— filmmakers in a romantic couple who rose to great heights together— I would have realized that both members of the duo rarely build equal careers. The reason why seems pretty clear: someone becomes the ritual sacrifice at the altar of finances, children, and real life. Someone has to pay for health insurance.

Nine times out of ten, who do you think that person is?

Cliff wasn't the most talented filmmaker in our class. He wasn't top five. I knew that even then. But he was the best operator. He overflowed with entitlement, which turned out to matter more. As time went on, and we had babies who someone needed to actually raise, I realized he'd happily throw me under the bus for the chance to direct a lowly Chevrolet ad, let alone write a studio movie. That realization didn't endear him to me.

I thought he was enamored of me, had my back, but really he was enamored of winning—which, when we were young enough, he thought he could do with me standing slightly behind him. My work became producing corporate videos for fast cash—and he went off to LA more and more often to try to drum up screenwriting work. The rest wrote itself.

Well, actually, the Golden Globes incident was his to own. A truly astounding show of indiscretion, disrespect and grossness that I cannot attribute to fate. By that time, I couldn't have cared less who he felt up. But I could have done without the public humiliation.

Maybe some people in our film program at college were surprised that Cliff was the highest achiever of us all—with success that came, by the way, largely *after* our divorce two and half years ago. I got to be his shoulder to cry on for decades of struggle and insecurity, during which he often turned red-faced and ugly, blaming me for holding him back. Then, just as we broke up, he was subsumed into some sugary-sweet movie-industry dreamscape. Only then did the money roll in. And it didn't roll my way since we were already broken up. The terms of the divorce were settled before his financial success was full-fledged, and maybe I should have revisited the arrangement once he was so flush—but I preferred not to need him. Either way, it should have been obvious to everyone that he'd get ahead. For one thing, he wanted it most. For another, he had no pesky ethics to get in the way.

So, a full-time job? With benefits and regular hours and a dependable salary? At an established publishing company with a legit HR department, bonus structures and obligatory holiday parties at the end of each year? The thought of it now gets me hot and bothered. These days, *this* is what turns me on. For the briefest instant, my mind flits to Demon Dad in the park the other day. His crooked smile, lean abs. I shake my head clear. Who needs first dates when there's a 401(k) and a weekly staff meeting to keep you warm at night?

Derek has synched his computer to a giant flat-screen at the front of the conference room and is walking us through dates and line items, all of which I understand like the back of my hand. This is my safe space; my happy place. A set. Production. Lighting. Coverage. A crew.

"We're imagining the shoot will take about—"

"Three to four days!" interrupts Stephanie.

I think Derek might actually murder her.

Bristling, he moves on to his fourth spreadsheet, this one focusing on next steps, and asks Jackie to lead us through some set decoration details, when I realize I'm missing an essential piece of information:

"I'm so sorry if I missed this, but where did you say we'll be shooting?"

"Citrine Cay!" Stephanie and Derek say in unison. Finally in agreement on something.

"Citrine Cay?" I repeat. "I'm sorry—I'm sure I'm being clueless— but I don't think I've heard of that."

"It's an island!"

"Oh! Like Governors Island?"

They shake their heads.

"Roosevelt Island? Randall's Island? Long Island? Staten Island?" I am out of islands in the New York area.

"No, silly," says Stephanie. "Like a tropical island! In Turks and Caicos!"

My mouth drops open, followed by my stomach. "Oh, wow," I say, trying to keep the deep stress out of my voice. "The Caribbean!" I will need to organize way more than supplemental babysitting and extra after-school hours. But I will make it happen. I need to make it happen. I *need* this gig.

Stephanie leans in. "It's this amazing private island! No one has even been there yet. It's not open to guests until the end of the month. We're going to party so hard!" She throws her hands in the air and waves them like she just don't care.

"She means *work* so hard." Derek's lips are pursed.

"Totally," says Stephanie. When he looks away, she shakes her head at me and mimes taking a shot.

"Anyway, Stephanie is right. It's a big-deal exclusive. We're first to the property. And it's exquisite! We've even agreed to shoot without models, though it's somewhat unorthodox, to let the landscape speak for itself. So, this group here will be our bare-bones crew. Plus, our photographer, Charlie. Our editor in chief may join as well, if schedule permits."

"Of course."

"If you don't have any additional questions for us, we'll discuss internally and circle back ASAP on the position. But you seem like a fantastic fit. Thanks—"

"So much!" yelps Stephanie.

"For your time."

As we shake hands and part ways, I smile big, all happy camper. Inside, my intestines are stomping a line dance. Finding childcare for four days and three nights is no piece of cake. But now that I know this could turn full-time, I am desperate for this job to work out. This would relieve so much financial stress, not to mention save me from having to hustle so hard for freelance stints.

Instead of heading straight home, I meet a high school friend for a drink at a sake bar in the East Village. I'm so nervous about jinxing the gig, I don't even mention it although I can think of nothing else. Instead, I let her go on and on about whether cheating is still unethical if your spouse is super annoying. (It is. She will do it anyway.)

Then, at around 9:00 p.m., I head home and relieve my parents. I walk in to find them both dozing on the couch, pretending to be watching TV. *Classic.* They fill me in on Bart's bowel movements and Nettie's tween attitude, tell me how spectacular my children are in their unbiased opinion, then climb in a cab and head home.

The kids are already asleep. Quiet settles over the apartment.

Here's how you know you've gotten old: you come home tipsy, dismiss the sitters, binge on the kids' leftover roasted brussels sprouts and that's close enough to bliss.

I take this moment alone to check in with myself. And, leaning against my kitchen island, I realize I am excited. Truly. For the first time in a long while. My heart is flipping in my chest. I know I'll find a way to take this job because it's essential. For years now, I have been running on empty, moving gig to gig, struggling to make ends meet despite receiving mandated checks from Cliff. Even when I've had enough work, there haven't been enough hours in the day. And this job seems like it might be more interesting than what I've gotten to cover in the recent past too—maybe it's a chance for some actual creativity. Maybe there won't be cat boas involved!

I definitely haven't gotten a shot like this since the kids were born; and I also haven't taken a proper adult trip in years. With other grown-ups. Even the concept of sitting on the plane, alone, without any bathroom emergencies or spilled juice sounds like heaven.

For reasons I can't explain, I have a sense that maybe things are changing, plates shifting ever so slowly beneath my feet until they lock into place. Is it possible? Dare I dream? Could things be getting easier? I exhale. Maybe I am headed for more stable ground.

14 | Desk Jockey

DEMON DAD

I don't leave my desk from lunch until the end of the day. There are Zooms, emails, plans to be made. Higher-ups to keep happy. I let my staff know not to disturb me. It's legit. I'm busy—and overextended—as hell. By the end, my eyes hurt and I'm bleary.

And, honestly, that's just fine. It keeps my mind from drifting to all the wrong corners. It keeps me from facing how I kind of *like* this veritable stranger, who kind of hates me. And not in the way it was with the few rebounds, late nights or false starts I had with other women when the breakup was brand-new.

In a way that is distracting.

So I'll take the stress.

It keeps me from wondering about her.

TO-DO

• Get your shit together.

15 | Orange You Glad?

KAITLIN

Celeste is too tall to talk to. Not that she wants to talk to me anyway.

That's my first thought when she shows up at pick-up today like it's perfectly natural for her to be here, like it's not the first time *this whole year*. She's wearing some incredible rust-colored jumpsuit that would make the rest of us look like inmates.

Even I know it's the color of the season. All the momfluencers I follow are hawking terra-cotta turtlenecks and amber BabyBjörns. But what's with her and Sasha being all glammed up this week? I roll my eyes. I don't even care. At least I don't want to.

It's Friday, which means I'm hawking PS421 gear at our make-shift kiosk to raise funds for the school's new media system. I sometimes let other parents handle minutiae like this, but it's important for me to stay involved. That's also the only way things get done right—in the only arena I can still control.

It's not like my time is so precious anyway. Yesterday, I spent forty-five minutes trying to take one decent selfie. Even with all the Face-tuning and filters, I can't hide my haggard state.

Celeste is a few minutes early to pick-up, so she wanders over to check out my wares. I suddenly feel like an idiot standing behind a folding table wearing a school-branded scarf. I pull out and apply my new lip balm. Like that's going to make the difference.

I am spiraling.

She sorts through the T-shirts and mugs, her fingers long and graceful like a journeying daddy longlegs. I scan her for flaws. High cheekbones. Perfect understated manicure. Large antique diamond ring. Not a hair out of place. Golden tan coloring that never dulls. She looks up at me.

That's when I notice that her eyeliner is smudged on one side. Almost like she's been crying. Her nose is just slightly pink in an adorable way. Something is up. *Interesting*.

"Hey, sorry—how much is the pencil case?" she asks.

"It's twenty dollars. And it comes with cute PS421 pencils and an eraser inside." I pick one up and unzip it to show her. Like I'm on QVC. Which, lately, I've been staying up watching because I don't sleep.

"Oh, adorable! I don't even think I knew the school mascot was a chipmunk!"

Shocking that Celeste is not in-the-know.

"I'm sure Henry would love it," I say. "Isn't he into animals?"

She looks up at me wide-eyed. She's surprised that I know her son's name. But of course I do. I remember everything. "He is. Yes. Good memory!"

"I remember from his first-grade birthday party . . . at the zoo." It was the only one of Henry's birthday parties that we'd attended. They invited the whole class to watch a woman in a khaki jumpsuit take reptiles out of cages and let the kids pet and hold them.

I also remember that Nettie declined to touch any of the creatures. "I'm more of a mammal person," she said, always precocious. It made Sasha and Celeste laugh and laugh.

Celeste pays, then tucks the pencil case away in her snakeskin embossed tote. No standard off-white canvas for her.

"Have you volunteered for Monster's Ball this weekend?" I ask. "Or is that more of your husband's thing?"

She twitches, as if stung. "Actually, I already volunteered to work the photo booth. With Sasha. You know, Nettie's mom?"

For some reason this drives me insane—her telling me who Sasha is. Like she doesn't remember that Sasha and I knew each other long before she was in the picture.

"Great!" I force a smile.

"Oh, here come the kids!" Celeste says. "Better run."

I nod. "Bye, Celeste."

She looks back at me as she hustles away, and, by the panic in her eyes, I can tell she can't recall my name.

"Thank you . . . ! Um. Good to see you. Bye!"

Just as the first teachers begin to lead the kids out of school to stand against the gate, Sasha jogs across the street, waving to the crossing guard. She looks distracted, worried.

What's bothering you, Sasha?

But when she spots Celeste, her furrowed brow releases into an unfettered grin. The two women embrace.

"Twice in one week!" Sasha exclaims like she's won the lottery, joining the stream of parents flowing down the block to where the third graders stand. "To what do I owe the pleasure? Jamie's terrible teeth again? I don't want to wish root canals on the man, but if I get to see you . . ."

Celeste laughs. It sounds like church bells chiming. It takes everything in my power not to gag.

Lisa scurries up next to me, follows my gaze to Celeste and Sasha. "You know," she says, "I have an orange jumpsuit just like that one! I got it at Target. I wonder if it's the same one."

I look from Lisa—in her floral fleece—to Celeste. They are different species. But Lisa is blessed not to know.

"Maybe," I mutter. Then I turn with a smile to the next parent in line.

16 | On the Ball

SASHA

It's late afternoon. It's unseasonably warm. And I am in a good mood, walking toward the school with my two costumed kids.

Bart is dressed as a volcano with a red hat as lava. The child loves an eruption.

Nettie is channeling Angelina Jolie as Maleficent. I can't help but see the ghost of teenage future in the dark eyeliner, red lipstick, black hair. The moment we arrive inside the schoolyard gates and get wristbands and tickets, which serve as free passes to games and treats, she finds her friends and takes off with Bart in tow. He brings up the rear like a champ, the cutest natural disaster.

Last year, on the night of the school's outdoor Monster's Ball festival (a precursor to Halloween, when, in theory, the kids dress up as book characters or something related to what they're studying), the weather was cutting. We were shivering before we even set foot inside, the wind pummeling us and sending witches' hats flying. Not long after that, it began to rain.

That was a special kind of torture. But today it is sunny. And I am prepared. I'm wearing my favorite jeans and vintage Toxic Avenger T-shirt (so on theme). I've packed layers and a flask full of bourbon to share with Celeste when the sun goes down.

I owe her a drink. Or twenty.

By Friday morning, Derek had sent me an email officially offering me the job in Turks and Caicos and two options for flights. He cc'd the rest of the team too, but, after I wrote back saying I'd be thrilled to come on board, Stephanie emailed me on a separate thread.

"We're gonna get so lit, woman!"

She is starting to scare me. I can't tell if I want to avoid her or be her when I grow up. In all seriousness, I feel sure I'll disappoint her. I'm kind of a lightweight, and I really want to ace this assignment. I'm way too square for her squiggles.

With such a tight turnaround, I set out right away to secure childcare, imagining I could cobble together ample coverage between my family and babysitters.

Not so much.

Finding babysitting is like anything else: sometimes it happens with ease. Other times, it's like apartment hunting in New York City without a broker—depressing, futile and almost reduces you to giving up and moving to New Jersey.

My parents are traveling to an education conference over the same dates. And my mother, true to her new spacey persona, called me back once to say she was mistaken—they actually *could* babysit!—and then again to crush my dreams and say she'd actually been right the first time. Maybe it was okay. As horrible as it felt to admit to myself, I wasn't totally sure I could rely on her.

None of our regular babysitters were free either, even for an exorbitant fee. I sat at my kitchen table staring at the linen runner, both hands on my head, racking my brain for a solution.

Out of ideas, I did the unthinkable. I called *him.*

"Sash?"

"Hi, Cliff."

"Wow. Great to hear your *actual* voice!"

"Oh. Is it?" I said. "Okay. I'm glad."

"Well, usually, you text or email. Like most people. Which is less invasive, it's true. But you miss a kind of real connection that way. You know what I mean?"

Original-thought alert.

"Yes, of course." I do know what he means—and so does every other cogent adult in the modern age.

"I was actually just talking to Ryan about this exact thing," Cliff was saying.

"Ryan?"

"Oh, sorry. My friend Ryan Reynolds. Do you know who he is? We're in development on a movie together."

"Yes. I know who he is."

"You'd like him. He's actually so cool. So down-to-earth. Really kind."

"Yes. Well. He's Canadian."

"Right, right. Hang on one second."

I was treated to some rustling and then the clinking of utensils. "Hey, can I get a matcha latte with oat milk and a wellness booster?" I heard a distant woman's voice, muted like the adults in *Muppet Babies*.

"What are the options?" Cliff said.

Murmur, murmur.

"Um. I think I'll try the vanilla adaptogen powder with chaga mushroom dust? Thanks, love!"

I rolled my eyes in solidarity at our cat, Larry, who never liked Cliff. His expression was resigned. *What did I tell you?*

"Sorry," said Cliff. "I'm at a Café Authentique. Meeting an exec from Sony to talk about this pilot I'm shooting next month. And then I've got to meet Ryan to plan our trip to the Himalayas. That's where he likes to brainstorm his next projects. So, unfortunately, I don't have long to talk."

The only person more annoyed than me by this conversation had to be the person sitting next to Cliff in real life, trying to drink their mushroom latte in peace.

"I'll be quick, then," I said, so very accommodating. I am revving up for the big ask, swallowing a supersize serving of pride. "I just got an important opportunity, maybe the one I've been waiting for, and I'm having a ton of trouble finding childcare. Is there any way you'd be able to fly in to New York next week for a few days to hang with the kids? Spend some time together? You'd be saving us, and I know they'd love to see you."

He lets out a slow stream of air. A whistle through his teeth. "Oh, wow. Sash. I'm so happy for you. That's amazing! You deserve it."

"Thanks, Cliff."

"Really. You're an incredible talent. And it's wasted on those corporate videos."

"I appreciate you saying so. Does that mean you might be able to help?"

I hold my breath.

"Oh, no. Definitely not," he says. "I'm booking months in advance these days."

Like I was trying to schedule a facial with a celebrity aesthetician. He is all booked. And I am all fucked.

"You know how it is," he added.

"Do I?"

There was a time when I would have called Cliff on his shit. On how selfish he was being. On the fact that it wouldn't kill him to miss a couple of days of wellness smoothies to be with his children. On the fact that he had kids only to leave them—and me—to fend for ourselves. But somewhere along the way I realized that my ex-husband was acting like a douchebag because he *is* a douchebag. And no amount of protesting or courtroom shenanigans would change that.

Sometimes it still breaks my heart. For Nettie and Bart, who have yet to fully surrender to this truth.

"Send the kids my love though," he said. "Tell them I can't wait to see them over spring break!"

"In five months?"

"My accountant is sending the child support checks on time, right? You have enough diaper money?"

This just makes me exhausted. I drag a hand down my face. "Cliff, Bart hasn't worn diapers in two years."

"Right. I knew that. Just, you know, diapers, so to speak."

How had I ever wanted to have sex with someone who said "so to speak"?

"Anyway, I better run. The unsolicited phone call has thrown me off my game. It really is an intrusion. I need to get centered before this exec arrives."

"Centered. Right."

"But, hey, Sash. You've got this! You're incredible, baby. Love and light."

How had I ever wanted to have sex with someone who said "love and light"?

With no other recourse, I hung up the call, rested my "incredible" cheek on the kitchen table and stayed in that position until Larry jumped up and sniffed my face for signs of life.

When I ran into Celeste at pick-up in her amazing rust-colored romper, I had no intention of asking her for help. But, as we made our way beyond the throngs of parents and kids and stopped on the corner to chat as our kids played some invented game called "hot dog tag," I was already complaining about my situation.

"And so I have no idea what to do. I basically either have to give up the job or leave the kids with a stranger. Which I don't love and they *definitely* won't love."

"Your ex-husband is kind of the worst."

"Kind of?"

Celeste shrugged. "Just leave them with us."

I stared at her. "Yeah, right."

"Yeah. Right."

"Wait, really?"

"Really."

"I couldn't."

"Why not?"

"Just like that?"

"Just like that."

"But what about . . . ?"

"What?"

"How annoying it will be to have two extra kids around?"

"Henry will be thrilled." She shrugged. "And it's only four days. During which they have school. Cumulatively, it's not even very many waking hours."

"Celeste." I gazed up at her glowing face. I was tempted to ask her what serum she's been using, but this didn't seem like the time. "I can't thank you enough. Are you sure? You can still back out. I won't hold it against you."

"Positive," she said, smiling. "I will not be a party to you missing out on this opportunity. Also, your ex-husband really blows."

"It's true. He does. Speaking of which, do you need to discuss with your husband? Before you sign up for this?"

"Jamie?"

"That's the guy. Big. Burly. Loves to make his own ice cream. Inexplicably sometimes in gross flavors like banana."

She exhaled. "Nah."

I thought I read something complicated in her expression, but I couldn't say what.

"He seemed a little out of sorts when I saw him last," I tried. "Is something up with him?"

"A bit. Maybe a change of pace will help." She gazed into the middle distance for a beat, then seemed to return to her body. "Anyway, I'm happy to help, if and only if, you address some essential questions."

"Of course!"

"First, any more combative arguments with Demon Dad?"

I laughed, taken aback. Why did I feel caught? Like she could see inside my head, where he'd been making uninvited appearances lately?

"I thought you meant questions about my kids."

Celeste shook her head. "Them? Nah. That's not interesting. Plus, I already know all about them."

More parents had begun to arrive for pick-up, lining the curb in staggered formation. They glanced down at their phones, up at the exits, around for other parents they knew. Younger siblings munched snacks in strollers or practiced balancing along the fenced edges of tree pits surrounding microgardens. The truth is, lately, maybe I had found myself looking a *little* more closely than usual at the crowds for signs of Ethan. I don't know why. Probably just basic curiosity. I had caught sight of him a couple of times after drop-off since our park run-in (no pun intended, but no apologies either). We only nodded politely.

I noticed that he never did pick-up, but that wasn't surprising. (More annoying was that I took the time to notice.) Since preschool days, it had become clear to me that—in heterosexual two-parent families—most often the men did drop-off before it could disrupt their workdays and made pick-up the purview of their wives, the primary caregivers. It was the women who stopped work early to make snacks and play games. Why should Ethan be any different? Cliff never even did drop-off.

Why was I even wasting time thinking about this dude?

"I've seen him around little," I said. "But he hasn't stolen any outerwear from me lately. How come?"

"Just looking for some intrigue." She surveyed the crowd, scrunching her nose. "Everyone here is so well-behaved."

"Ah. Sadly, intrigue-free." That was technically true. "What's question number two?"

Celeste looked right, then left, then stepped in closer to me, lowering her voice. "See the woman selling the school paraphernalia over there? The blond one with the coppery lowlights and the peacoat?"

I scratched my head, pretending to glance unseeing over my shoulder. So nonchalant. An expert spy maneuver. Then I realized who she was referencing and grimaced. "Oh, you mean Kaitlin?"

"Ah! *That's* her name! She looks different. Like, less together maybe? How do we know her again?"

"I know her a little from growing up. From my whole high school scene. Not well."

I chanced another glance over at Kaitlin, whose own gaze skittered away. I guess maybe she did look a little less together. She usually had a kind of preppy, tightly wound vibe. Today, she looked like maybe she hadn't brushed her hair. No judgment.

The truth is, I kind of avoided her. There was something about the way she looked at me, talked to me, that made me uneasy. She was definitely a VIM. Maybe she thought I was slacking on the mom front? Maybe she just didn't like me?

Once, early on at some festival, she had introduced me to her circle of school moms as "a close friend from middle school" and "that untouchable high school girl." I thought about that periodically afterward. We'd hung out the summer before eighth grade, but we hadn't remained close, at least not in my memory. It was more like that friendship that sustains you—at any new place—before you find your actual people. Like an unspoken understanding. Also, the idea that I seemed so inviolable as a teenager was hard to fathom, since, like all teenagers, I'd felt exposed. I guess I did a good performance of Teflon. Of course, later—after Cliff—I found better ways to protect myself. By being literally untouchable.

"Right!" said Celeste. "I could not remember!"

"Uh-oh."

"Yeah, she was like, 'Oh, Henry this and Henry that' and I was like, 'Who are you again?' I'm the worst!" Celeste clapped a hand over her eyes.

"She must have liked that."

She grimaced with genuine remorse. "Hopefully, I played it off."

"Probably not."

"Probably not." She sighed.

"But, honestly, there's no reason why you should know her. I barely do."

I glanced back at Kaitlin then and caught her looking at me. I smiled, reflexively, and the corner of her mouth ticked upward too.

But, as her gaze lingered, her smile faltered. And her eyes seemed to tell a different story.

Now, all is right with the world. I get to go on my trip. I can pay for drama classes and, oh, you know, rent. My kids have a safe place to stay while I'm gone. And, on Monday, I can begin planning the Citrine Cay shoot in earnest with the *Escapade* team.

For this evening, all I have to do is hang with Celeste at Monster's Ball, help some cute (and some not so cute) kids use the photo booth and sneak swigs from my flask. Heaven!

Only, that's not in the cards. Because there's been a mix-up. Of course, there has.

When I approach Celeste, who is already working our station, she is wearing a cable-knit sweater, sailor jeans I wish were mine and a look of resignation.

"There was a mix-up with the sign-up sheet," she says to me, eyes filled with unspoken expletives and boring into my own. "Apparently, your name did not appear with mine in the photo booth slot. So, Lisa, here, signed up as my partner."

Lisa! Mom Who Never Stops Talking's name is confirmed. That's one tiny silver lining.

"We're going to have the best time!" She grins.

Celeste bites her lip.

"Oh, okay," I say. I am bummed, but not that bummed. Now, I don't have an assignment. I can just hang around, chat with the two parents I know, visit Celeste. "I guess I'm out of work!"

"Not quite," says Celeste, eyes wide.

And I can feel the universe readying to wallop me from a mile away.

"Oh, there you are!" I turn around to find the school administrator, the one who is always at the drop-off entrance, waiting behind me. "Are you ready to start?"

"Ready to start . . . what?"

She raises her eyebrows.

And now the pity in Celeste's eyes is starting to concretize. It wasn't for herself. It was for me. I have been given the most dreaded job in the entire Monster's Ball festival:

I am the cotton candy lady.

There is no longer line. No more relentless demands. No messier station. No booth more likely to attract sticky kids to "help" (a.k.a. make everything worse). And it's all mine. The position is for two, but is so reviled that, of course, no one signed up.

Last year, the poor dad who got suckered into running the booth got so frustrated with some fourth grade "helpers" that he banished them, making them weep, and had to contend with a mob of angry parents. Rumor had it that, in the end, he too was reduced to tears. He was never quite the same.

There will be no relaxing tonight. No carefree swigs of booze or amusing chats. No stealing Twizzlers and mini Three Musketeers from the kids. There will be no rest for the weary. There will be only spun sugar.

And, forty-five minutes in, it's more in my hair than in anyone's mouth. Strands of pastel pink and blue crisscross my face and body like I'm headed for mummification. I am frenzied; I am sticky; I am no closer to mastering the art of wrapping a fluffy cloud of cavities-in-waiting around a stupid white paper tube.

My cotton candy creations are more abstract than cylindrical. Lopsided and lumpy in a way, I've decided, more closely reflects our true humanity. Sure, it might fall off the stick and onto the ground, causing multiple children to wail in torment. But a little adversity is healthy. Perfection is only a construct. I am taking a stand.

Celeste and a couple of other parent acquaintances have come to visit me. But I have no time for solidarity or chitchat. No time to help Bart put ketchup on his hot dog (an act I don't condone anyway since mustard is clearly superior). A line of restless, hungry beasts extends past the basketball hoops and behind the fortune teller's tent. They will not be satiated.

This year, the fourth graders are not offering help so much as heckling me from the sidelines.

"You call that cotton candy?!" they yell, laughing as it congeals on my hands like superglue.

"That one's upside down!"

"It looks like my grandma's wig!"

I stick my tongue out at them like a deranged maniac.

The people in line are starting to complain too. "This is taking forever," whines one of six mermaids to a first-grade ladybug.

"Patience!" I snap. Like a Disney villain.

I am starting to descend into madness in part because I keep eating the cotton candy I mess up. Which is all of them. I am on a sugar-high bender that can only end poorly.

That's when he comes to the head of the line. Of course. Demon Dad. With a front-row seat to my failure. Dressed in a Yankees cap and his regular immaculate casual wear: perfect gray hoodie, perfect black T-shirt, well-worn Levi's, work boots. Here to pour Maldon salt in my wounds.

I write off my accelerated heart rate to sucrose overload.

"Hi," I say. I hope with hostility.

"Hi?" he says. He cocks his head sideways, examining me in my state.

I refuse to let him rattle me. I swirl the cardboard stick in the machine, then hand him a wispy uneven bulb of pink cloudy poison.

"Two tickets, please."

He examines my masterpiece. "This is terrible," he says.

"I am aware," I seethe from beneath a bat-ear headband that has somehow landed on my head.

"It looks like a tumor."

"You look like a tumor."

He opens his eyes wide at that.

"Okay. No, but seriously. This is supposed to make the kids happy. Not terrify them." He studies the cotton candy like it might bite him.

"Well, I don't see your kid anyway. So, hopefully you can be a big boy about this. You get what you get and you don't get upset."

"It's not for me!" he protests. "I said I'd grab one and bring it back for her. Now, I'm not sure I should."

"I think you're being a little dramatic."

"I think you're going to traumatize countless small children."

"Hey!" shouts a fifth-grade Captain Underpants. "What's the hold up?"

"Hey, kid. Get some manners!" I yell back.

"Okay, okay," Ethan says, a hand up as if to stop me. "Try to remain calm. I'll be right back."

"Yeah, sure. That's what they all say!" I call after him.

He looks at me quizzically, but even I don't know what I mean.

He leaves me feeling even more tweaky.

I am doing my best to serve the next people in line when Ethan returns and, without warning, takes a spot beside me behind the table.

(A) He is close to me. (B) Why is he close to me? (C) Why is he close to me in my current state, as a feral cotton candy beast? (D) Why do I care?

Extra credit question: Why am I suddenly warm?

Startled and suspicious, I narrow my eyes at him. "What are you doing over here?"

"I'm helping you."

"Helping me . . . or taking over?"

"Are you really in a position to make that distinction?"

He has a point, though you couldn't torture me into admitting it. I smooth my hair, pulling tacky fluff through it.

"I don't need help."

A runaway strand of cotton candy stretches like a tightrope across my face. I watch him raise his hand, as if to help, then reconsider and drop it back down. I try to blow the sugar out of the way, but suck it into my mouth and choke instead. The resulting coughing fit does not feel hygienic. The crowd eyes me like I've got typhoid.

"Yeah," Demon Dad says. "It seems like you've really got it under control." He leans in close to my ear, whispering so the people in line can't overhear. "Just let me help."

I am preoccupied by his proximity, can feel his breath on my neck. It ignites a kind of pulsing beneath my skin. Does he smell like sugar, or have I inhaled cotton candy up my nose?

When he stands up straight again, leaving my orbit, I'm alarmed by an impulse to drag him back.

What is happening to me?

I shake it off. I will not be distracted from my suspicion! "Why are you helping?"

"Maybe because I'm a nice person?"

"That's definitely not it." He rolls his eyes, and I cross my arms over my chest. "Why should I trust you?"

"Because I actually can't watch this."

He gestures between me and the angry crowd. Before I can protest more, he edges me to the side.

"You're on order, paper cone and ticket duty."

I look at him dumbly. Does not compute.

"Ask them which color they want. Take their tickets. Hand me a cone and I'll scoop the powder into the machine and make it. Assembly-line style."

I acquiesce, grumbling all the way. So *bossy*.

Sure enough, after a few minutes, I am able to exhale. The pace is still fast, demand remains high, but it's more manageable at least. And, of course, Ethan is annoyingly capable. His creations are the platonic ideal of cotton candy—fluffy, joyful, effortless, smooth. *Jerk*.

There is no time to argue—or chat. After maybe an hour, he announces that it's time to take a break.

"A break?" I eye the still epic line. "We can't."

"Ah, but we *can*."

He grabs a piece of cardboard and a Sharpie out of a craft box under the folding table and scrawls: "BACK IN FIVE!" Then he props it up in front of the machine.

There are groans from the peanut gallery, particularly one dad dressed as a superhero who grunts, "What the hell?" But Ethan holds up his hand. "Hey. Take it easy, Iron Man. There are labor laws in this country. It's called a bathroom break."

The crowd grumbles but has no choice but to accept this setback. Before we officially start unionizing, Ethan and I step back from the table. And it's like freedom! He gestures toward some empty folding chairs in the yard's back corner. I grab my bag, and we stroll over.

I'm so elated to have escaped that I don't even care that it's with him. Alone.

"Holy shit," I curse loudly, as I collapse into a seat. Definitely within range of small children and their innocent ears. But I don't care. Cotton candy duty has made me hard. "It's never felt so good to sit down, ever."

"It's a slog." He nods, leaning back in his chair. "Especially if you're inept at making cotton candy."

I glare at him and his stupid cute face. His eyes glint. He has a single dimple that pops when he smirks.

But that's clearly the cotton candy fugue talking again.

"Why did you volunteer for the suicide mission, anyway?" he asks. "Just for the glory?"

"I didn't!" I protest. "I was supposed to be . . . part of this." Only now do I take a moment to glance around. I've been so laser-focused that I haven't even noticed my surroundings. Darkness has descended. All around us, children with glow sticks squeal and run around in packs, roaming constellations. Taylor Swift plays on the loudspeakers. In one corner, the fifth-grade girls dance as a unit, jumping up and down. Parents—normal ones, with normal shifts at normal Monster's Ball jobs—bunch in groups, chatting, commiserating, laughing, sipping steaming drinks. It's kind of magical.

"Wow," I say. "So this is how the other half lives."

Ethan laughs, like a hiccup. It's dorky and unexpected. In a good way. Is Demon Dad part human?

"Sorry I kept you from your kid," I say.

"Oh. She was with her friends. I was only a humiliating append-age." He sighs. "Are you hungry?"

"Yes. But, wait! I have a better idea!" I dig around in my tote and unearth my flask. "Aha!"

He raises an eyebrow, nods, impressed. "Good move."

I am a bad influence, and I like it.

I take a swig and then, despite my wariness, risk cooties and offer him the hooch. He takes it gratefully.

"What are you supposed to be? A bat?" he says, eyeing my head-band. He drags his gaze all the way down my body, then catches himself and snaps back to attention. *Surprising.* In our interactions, he has thus far been almost chaste.

"I don't know," I manage, still recovering from feeling his gaze on me like radiant heat. "I don't even know whose ears these are."

"That's a pretty half-assed costume."

I roll my eyes. So many opinions. "It's actually not a costume at all. Anyway, look who's talking. What are you dressed up as? A basic Brooklyn dad?"

"Sheesh. *Basic.* Harsh."

I shrug. I call 'em like I see 'em.

He shakes his head like I'm naive, then rotates to the side. I can't help but notice the way the cords of muscles flex in his neck as he turns, his skin still holding a hint of a summer tan. That is until I spot a giant bloody gash in his neck and (unfortunately) gasp. Like a sucker. He chuckles.

"What the hell?! Why does that look so real? Are you a low-key makeup artist?"

"Let's just say it's not my first rodeo."

"What are you though? A chain saw massacre victim? A soon-to-be headless horseman?"

He shakes his head. "I'm 'cutthroat.'"

I drop my head in my hands. "Noooooo. See that? You took some-thing cool and made it a dad joke."

He shrugs, his eyes twinkling. "I'm a dad."

I study his profile—strong jaw, small scar across the bridge of his nose that only makes him better-looking, eyes that crinkle at the corners, full lips. "So, how come you've got the cotton candy skills to pay the bills?"

"Did you just say that?"

"I'm not responsible for anything that comes out of my mouth tonight," I say. "I have been robbed of my humanity and filter."

"Fair enough," he says, stretching his arms above his head. I do not notice his arms flex.

"So? Dish. How come you're a cotton candy maestro?"

"I guess I'm just gifted."

I cant my head. Nope. "Bzzzzzz. Survey says that's not a thing."

He snickers, handing me the flask back. I take another swig. It burns so good in my throat. Now that I'm sitting still, I realize the temperature has dropped. I hand him back the drink and he takes it without a word, grab my fleece from my bag and throw it on, cozy. I realize, now warm in this moment, I am kind of happy.

Strange.

"Truth?" he says.

"Obviously."

"I've manned this station before."

"Manned. That's got to be a canceled expression."

"Well, to be fair. I am a man. And I did run the show."

"When?"

"Last year."

"Last year?"

He nods.

"Wait, what?!" I sit forward in my seat. Point a finger in his face. "You're *that* guy? You're the cotton candy dad? You're legendary! Both for your gifts and your epic meltdown!"

"Whatever." He frowns. "Let's not get carried away. It just took a second to find my groove."

"I heard you almost got into a fist fight with a kindergarten dad when you ran out of blue sugar!"

"Don't believe everything you hear," he mutters. "But that guy was a dick."

I start to laugh. Suddenly, it strikes me as so absurd. That parents could get so worked up over a janky school fair confection! That he and this other dad literally had to be held back from punching each other in the face!

Ethan starts snickering too. Soon, there are tears streaming down both our faces. We can't stop. I don't even know if it's funny or if I'm just in a post-sugar-withdrawal free fall. I might require a formal detox. Whatever it is, it's been ages since I laughed this hard and he's right there with me.

Wiping tears mixed with cotton candy remnants from my face (what manner of hot mess must I look like right now?!), I sigh as our laughter finally begins to dissipate. "You asked why I signed up!" I manage. "Why'd you take the dreaded job last year?"

But even as I ask it, I know the answer.

"The ex-wife," we say in unison. Then we start laughing again.

This guy is a pain in the ass, but he sure is easy to hang out with.

"She signed you up? For this torture? Without asking?"

"She sure did."

"Is that why you got divorced?"

"It didn't help."

"Wow. She *hates* you."

I take one more sip from the flask as he eyes me. Across the court-yard in the shadows is a woman I don't know, working the apple cider stand. I think I notice her glancing at us—birdlike, severe black bob, chic camel trench. I wonder briefly if she's Ethan's ex. Then I realize I don't want to know.

When I look back at him, he's peering at me a little shyly like he wants to ask me something. And the intensity of his gaze makes me shift in my seat. I suddenly feel like maybe no one has really *looked* at me in years. At least not like this.

"So, you're divorced too?" he says finally. "I mean, I know you are, if I'm honest."

I flush. Everyone knows. Even people who don't know me. Did he see the Golden Globes meme like everyone else? "Almost three years in the club," I say.

"When you were married, would you have signed him up for something like this?" Ethan asks. "Did you hate him enough?"

I think for a moment, then I shake my head. How to articulate this? "He wasn't that kind of husband," I say finally. "And he's not that kind of ex-husband either. I could have signed him up, but it doesn't mean he would have come."

He nods. "He's not in Brooklyn, I take it."

"He is not. Which, most of the time, I'm kind of grateful for."

"I guess that explains why you got divorced. If you didn't want him in the same state?"

"Well, he didn't want to be around," I say. Maybe the alcohol is going to my head, but, for once, I don't bother censoring myself. "I feel like people always want a concrete reason why it didn't work, you know? But it's a lot of things. Offhand, I can think of, like, twenty. Not the least of which is the frequency with which he said, 'It is what it is.' There's only so much a person can abide."

"It's always a lot of things," Ethan agrees. "It is what it is."

I kick him lightly in the shin. He reacts as if he's been mortally wounded—then grins. And the way it lights up his face is impossible to ignore in the glow of the schoolyard festivities.

"But yeah," I continue, if only to distract myself. "He traveled to LA a lot for work. And the business trips got closer and closer together until the scales tipped and he was there more than he was here."

"Happens to the best of us," Ethan tries.

"Does it?" I say. "I hope he's not the best of us."

There's a pause while we digest this.

Ethan looks down at the rugged blacktop, with a furrowed brow, and then back up at me. "You asked why I wanted to help you before?"

I nod, unsure of where this is going. I realize I'm holding my breath.

"The truth is, someone needed to step in before you caused an international incident, obviously. But, to be honest, I also wanted to avoid talking to people. This is a small community. The divorce thing . . . it's hard."

Ah. I get this. "It is hard."

I think back to some of the moms, and a couple of dads, who greeted Ethan at the cotton candy booth with extra exuberance. Was it hard for him because he felt like an outcast? Or because, now that they knew he was available, parents kept hitting on him?

Before I can ask, he continues and I snap back to attention, oddly flustered: "I think I mentioned, I didn't used to come to school events like this much. I worked a lot. Things are different now. Maybe that's why my ex wanted to torture me with the cotton candy gig."

"Fair enough, then," I say. "I get it. None of it is easy."

Ethan catches my eyes with his own. Shoots me a small smile. It's pretty disarming—bordering on a panty dropper. "Sorry your ex-husband's not on top of things," he says meaningfully. "Sorry he screwed you."

I laugh, but I am also oddly touched. Because he is joking, but he also seems genuine.

Maybe to avoid eye contact that's too full of stuff, I look up at the sky pockmarked by the occasional star. Or maybe they're airplanes and planets. These are things I do not know.

Warily, I let my eyes settle back on Ethan. The way he's studying me, like I'm the *New York Times* Spelling Bee, is making me shift in my seat. He leans forward, resting his impressive forearms on his thighs. Lets his head drop for a beat. He feels too close for comfort, close enough that I can smell his grassy cologne (not cotton candy!). But I can't will myself to move. Then he drags his gaze up to meet mine, leaving a trail of sparks in its wake. "I think we both know it's time."

I am caught off guard. For reasons I can't fathom, panic courses through me, followed by a shock of heat between my thighs. "Time?! For what?"

He nods his head toward the cotton candy line. The crowd has multiplied like soggy gremlins in our absence.

As I realize what he means, I catch a wave of something complicated, on the continuum between relief and disappointment.

"Damn." I'd lost track of why and how I landed here. "The hungry hordes."

He rises. "Ready?" He stretches out his hand to pull me to standing. I am in no way about to take it. Instead, I shove the flask in his direction one last time.

"To fortify," I say.

He looks surprised, but he accepts it. As I hand it over, his fingertips graze my knuckles. A shudder passes through me like it's Jane Austen era and I've caught a chill. We freeze for a beat, looking at each other. I can't look away.

What is happening?

His lips part, as if he's about to speak.

"Hey, Mom!" Nettie's voice breaks the spell. Or curse. Or whatever the hell this night of cotton candy, bourbon and Halloween magic has done to me. Either way, she offers an out. I whirl around to find my daughter waiting, her Maleficent makeup cheerfully smeared. "Are you going back to the cotton candy booth?"

"Yes. I think maybe for all eternity. Why?" I ask, coming back to myself.

"Bart and I want to know—can we get a cotton candy without waiting on line?"

I smile at Ethan and then at Nettie. "Oh, hell, yes, sweetie. You're a VIP."

What seems like days later but is probably only hours, the very last fairy-unicorn-witch-princess-Violet-Baudelaire procures a blue cotton candy and our job is done. We are awash in a sea of red tickets, the hottest show in town.

As Ethan and I ready to part ways at center schoolyard, he in one direction and I in the other, I swallow enough pride to say, "Hey. Thanks for helping me."

"No problem." He shoots me that charming half smile. "But I didn't help. I took over."

I dig into the supply box I'm carrying back toward the cafeteria, grab a paper cone and throw it at him. I miss by a mile.

"Good throw," he says. He picks the tube up off the ground, returns it to the box I'm holding. Lets his hand linger there, on the box's edge. It is a conduit between us that I can feel.

I blink up at him.

"Have a good night," he says, finally.

But I already have.

17 | I Want Candy

DEMON DAD

If Monster's Ball had awards, I'd win the one for self-control. No joke.

Sure, I let myself step in to help when I spotted Sasha all tangled in spun sugar and that vintage Toxic Avenger T-shirt (which I kind of covet). That was just basic decency. She was drowning.

But there are a lot of things I didn't do: I didn't gently wipe the stray cotton candy from her cheek with my thumb.

When it felt like there was a moment between us during our break, I didn't even think about leaning in and kissing her sticky lips—until long after I went home. (Then I *may* have thought about it a lot.)

And when we said good night, though she's beautiful as hell, even covered in spun candy webs, I only let myself watch her walk away for a hot second before I left too.

See? Self-control.

TO-DO
- ~~Sign up for cotton candy every year.~~
- Become a professional cotton candy maker and take this show on the road.

18 | Night Times

KAITLIN

Sasha turns cotton candy duty into a meet-cute. At least that's how it looks from the vantage point of the arts and crafts table I'm running, where I'm knee-deep in orange glitter and glue. How does she do that? Everyone knows that job is torture.

But of course she does.

Anger rises in my chest.

After the festival dies down, I check the picture I posted of Ruby in her Marie Antoinette costume on Instagram. Only thirteen likes in three hours. WTF? I spent real time on that thing!

I plaster a friendly look on my face for the other parents and finish packing up. On my way out, I pass Sasha in the schoolyard, carrying a box. We're walking toward the opposite exits leading to our respective homes. It would be awkward not to acknowledge each other.

"Good job tonight!" I say.

She shoots me a smile, which I return. It's more genuine than average. "Thanks, Kaitlin! Have a good night!" Sasha seems *happy*.

Is happy even a thing anymore?

It's the end of the evening. She looks tired though it's only 8:00 p.m. We all do. We are parents on a burning planet. This is our idea of a late night. Children are exhausting. Work is exhausting. Staying afloat is exhausting. But there is something in her flushed cheeks that's energized too. Something shiny in her eyes.

Suddenly, I am bombarded by a memory I had forgotten: Sasha wearing that same expression. For a moment, I can put myself in that place, in my own seventeen-year-old body too.

It was late—or early. We were old enough for life without curfews and, those of us who still had restrictions, slept out. In those days, New York City was a more lawless place. For reasons I can't begin to fathom, our teenage friends were able to act as full party promoters, throwing massive alcohol-fueled parties at grown-ass clubs.

Assuming you didn't come up against some terrifying and cruel door girl who barred entry, you'd slide past the gargantuan bouncers in their black leather coats and enter a playground of possibilities. I say playground because everyone there was a child—cute boys, statusy girls. Not a single one of us was of legal drinking age.

Biggie Smalls blasted from the speakers. A Tribe Called Quest. De La Soul. The ground was sticky with cosmopolitans and malt liquor, spilled for fallen homies and by accident. The boys smelled too strongly of Cool Water and Fahrenheit colognes—a crisp and over-compensatory Gillette deodorant scent. These parties were the meat and potatoes of our teenage social life. And this one was a classic.

We danced in a kind of undulating circle with five or six of our mutual girlfriends. The boys—the ones who danced—popped by periodically to freak one of us for a minute, a silent conversation. *Any interest?* Usually, no. Sometimes, yes.

Eventually, the music propelled us—sweaty and serotonin-flooded—out the doors and up industrial side streets, past warehouses whose graffiti-tagged metal gates waited to be lifted. The sun threatened to rise.

While the most assertive of our group hailed taxis, the rest of us hung back and smoked cigarettes. Some flirted with the boys, playing tag and giggling like elementary school kids. *Not it!* Sasha leaned against the building's facade, her eyes hooded from fatigue. She pulled a thin flannel around her shoulders.

We were rarely with the same crowd at this point. And, even then, we barely spoke. But, out of nowhere, she turned to face me. "That was fun. Wasn't that fun?"

I glanced behind me, looking for the person she was addressing. No one was there. Just a trash-strewn sidewalk. Crushed McDonald's cups. Cigarette butts. Gray matter.

Part of me wanted to ignore her, walk away. Show her how little I cared. But I still craved her attention too. "Totally." I nodded. "That was a fun one."

Her cheeks were pink, flushed from dancing. The rest of us were sweaty, haphazard ponytails frizzing at the hairline. But she looked lit from within. "What a beautiful night."

I think she was talking about the weather. It was spring, and winter's spite was finally lifting off the breeze. We were too warm from dancing to care about what was left of the cold, anyway. All endorphins and ego. "Just look at that moon."

I hadn't thought to look up. I was too busy navel-gazing. But, when I did, I realized it was enormous. It must have been full.

Full, like we were. Of possibility. Of hope. Of misapprehensions about what the world would offer.

She yawned dreamily. And I opened my mouth to speak, recognizing that this was finally my moment. With Sasha as a captive audience. Something I'd thought about many times before. To remind her of how tight we'd been that one summer. To ask her why she'd been careless with me. Maybe to tell her off.

About ditching me. About ignoring me. About Hugo, who she'd kissed hours after he dumped me.

"Hey, Sasha," I said.

She turned her gaze on me again. Just then, one of her besties, Rebecca, one of those loyal girls, tugged her by the arm and, of course, loaded her into the *first* waiting cab.

"Who *is* that girl, anyway?" Rebecca said loudly enough for me to hear. Definitely on purpose. We'd met plenty of times. Had plenty of friends in common. "Why is she even here?"

The rest of us would wait twenty more minutes before finding our own taxis home, racing uptown without traffic, the buzz of the night wearing thin.

But, through the window, Sasha waved goodbye to me, her fingers fluttering like hummingbird wings. By the time I waved back, she was gone.

19 | When It Rains, It Pours

SASHA

Though I do not get to hang out at Monster's Ball with Celeste, we do get to walk two blocks toward home together afterward. The moon is giant, and I can't stop talking about it. I have always loved the night sky.

I know, because of a clickbait article I read this morning, "What's in the Stars for You," it is called the hunter's moon. Bart insists that it's following us and, bolstered by the magic of being out after dark, Nettie and Henry are goofy and content enough to play along. The kids skip ahead awash in moonbeams, a xylophone of giggles.

"I can't believe you got cotton candy duty!" Celeste says. Like she thinks it sucks, but is also a *little* funny.

"I actually am cotton candy now. I have become one with the fluff."

"And I can't believe Demon Dad signed up too! What are the odds?"

"Oh, he wasn't signed up." I shake my head.

"Wait, what?" She stops walking and faces me, so I stop too.

"No, he just offered to help," I say, then realize I have precious information. I raise my hands over my head, purse my lips. "Guess who is the infamous cotton candy dad from last year?!"

Celeste's mouth drops open. "No way! The one who dumped that bin of sugar on that fourth-grade dad? That was *him*? I can't believe it!"

"Right? Crazy. I kind of thought he was an urban legend."

We resume walking. Up ahead, the kids have stopped to wait

for us before they cross the street. I am filled up, and almost choked up, as I watch them, dancing in circles in a luminous spotlight. So pumped to be out at night. Childhood abandon. I love my friend. I love my kids. In many ways, I like my life. If only I could get this job—maybe I could even afford to relax and enjoy it a little more. Maybe there would be room for more.

"That was kind of nice of Demon Dad to help though," Celeste is saying, as I snap back to attention. "Especially after last year's debacle."

"Sort of." I toggle my head. "I think he was triggered by my ineptitude."

Celeste raises an eyebrow at me, which I act like I don't notice. "Maybe," she says, the contours of her skeptical expression emphasized by shadow. I can't pretend away the moment when I wanted to jump his bones tonight, but I have already rationalized it nicely: I am starved for attention, sex-deprived. What wouldn't get my motor running?

"Jesus," says Celeste. "Why is he so damn familiar to me?"

"I don't know. He wasn't to me. And he says we actually met years ago."

"It's driving me nuts!"

I shrug. "Maybe he made you a cotton candy last year?"

"I do like cotton candy." She nods. "That must be it."

On Sunday morning, when I tell the kids about my upcoming trip, they're sitting on the floor playing a memory game in which they must pair adorable forest animals. Bart wears only dinosaur underwear (his favorite outfit). Nettie is in a nightgown and, inexplicably, nylon gym shorts. Both have full bedhead.

"Squirrel," says Nettie, examining the board. "And . . . ugh! That chipmunk again. Damn you, chipmunk!"

She shakes a fist in the air. Bart cracks up like she's Sarah Silverman doing a set. He jumps up, arms in the air. "Go away, chippy!"

I sit down on the couch. "Hey, guys, can you pause your game for a sec?" After I ask three more times, they finally stop and look at me expectantly. I am not sure how they'll react.

I explain. Work trip. Three nights. Turks and Caicos.

They have some questions and I supply answers: Yes, that's a place with beaches. No, I cannot bring whole coconuts back. Yes, I can bring home coconut candy.

"Wait," says Nettie. "So, we're going to sleep over at Henry's house for the whole time?"

I nod, holding my breath as I watch the information settle in her brain. Bart watches her too, to determine how he should react.

"Yes!" she celebrates, jumping up and dancing in a circle. She is getting older. All gangly arms and legs.

"Yes!" Bart mimics, also dancing around, his body still pillowy in places where hers is long.

"I'm so glad you guys are excited." I really am. It alleviates some of the stress.

Nettie stops and looks at me like I'm being absurd. "Of course we are, Mom! We get to sleep at our best friend's house. Right, Bart?"

"Right!"

"And anyway, Mom." She walks over to where I'm sitting and places a hand on my arm. "You deserve this."

I will never adjust to how she ping-pongs between forty-five and eight years old. Celeste calls her "our old soul." I don't know where she has learned this, but I look away as my eyes flood with tears.

"Fox," says Bart, who has settled back down to play the game. "And . . . chipmunk! Damn you, chipmunk!" I'm pretty sure he has picked the chipmunk on purpose this time. But he's achieved the desired effect. Both kids crack up again.

I spend the rest of the week, when they're back in school, co-ordinating the video shoot. As the producer, I'll be responsible for organizing all of the elements in advance—and arranging contingencies—and then, during the actual trip, guiding the crew as they capture behind-the-scenes footage of both the property and the still photo shoot, as it's happening. Very meta.

I've been in touch with the general manager of the property to organize the schedule, crew meals, transportation.

The hotel's owner turns out to be Martin Bernard, a retired actor and hundred millionaire, who has brought in many notable celebrity and CEO investors. He will feature prominently in the story, of course. I am in touch with his publicist in advance since she won't be on-site. She is deeply inscrutable, which is either for the sake of discretion or a symptom of being heavily medicated.

"Thank you so much for your help, Barbara," I say. "Anything else I should know about Martin?"

There is a long pause.

"Hello?"

"Yes, that's it, darling." Everything out of her mouth sounds screen-siren breathy, like she's lying in silk sheets from dawn till dusk.

I connect with Charlie, the photographer, and Peter, the cameraman. I try to nail down logistics with Stephanie, who has conceived this whole spread and will be writing the accompanying story, but mostly she wants to know whether I like Aperol spritzes and am open to powder drugs in the era of fentanyl. The answer is: a lot. And not at all.

I'm spending copious time in a giant Dropbox folder, scouring scouting images of the hotel itself. And it is spectacular. Escape porn at its best. The first time I look at them, I literally gasp, covering my mouth with my hand. *I get to go here?*

Infinity pools with sharp edges blink in the sunlight before collapsing into the ocean's waiting arms. Rustic, yet immaculate, barn buildings radiate zen in a rainbow of muted neutrals. Who knew there were so many shades of sandstone? Organic vegetable gardens are laid out in perfect geometric lines. In communal spaces, hand-woven pillows and blankets—created by a local women's collective—offer pops of color, walking a fine line, but ultimately leaning chic. The spa building could double as a Goop store.

I'm excited and nervous. And Wednesday arrives too slow and too fast.

The kids have continued to celebrate their extended sleepover with Henry, creating a list on lined notebook paper about what they're looking forward to most. Bart wants to play tag in their brownstone backyard; Nettie wants to compare Pokémon cards. Apparently, Jamie's famous butter popcorn tops the list too—though Bart only refers to him as "Henry's dad." (The kids are crossing their fingers for a weekday movie night.)

But when I put Bart to bed on Tuesday night, his resolve wavers.

"Mommy," he says. "Who will give us dinner?"

"Celeste and Jamie, Bonk."

"How will they know what we like?"

"Well, I've told them. And you can tell them too. And, if you need, you know Nettie will help you."

He considers this for a moment. "Who will give us breakfast?"

"Cutie, Celeste and Jamie will. They'll give you all your meals and snacks. And I'm actually going to the grocery store after drop-off at school tomorrow morning to get some of your favorite things and bring them over to Henry's house."

"You'll get Cheerios? And Crispix?"

"I will."

He grins, rubbing his eyes with his fists. Sleepy. I know he's only minutes from dropping off to dreamland. "Yay! I love Cheerios."

"I know you do, cutie. And I love *you*!"

I push myself to standing.

"Mommy, you'll be home by Halloween?" Bart asks.

Nettie has asked me this multiple times too. Halloween is a big deal in our house. And I'm set to get home the night before, which gives me just enough time to prep everyone's costumes the next day and head out to trick-or-treating.

"Yes! I would not miss Halloween with you for the world."

"Promise?"

"Cross my heart and hope to . . . yes, promise."

I bend back down and give him kisses on his cheeks and head and belly until he giggles and wriggles. He smells like apples and milk. He is scrumptious. I think we're good—at least I hope we are. As I stand up and begin to pull the door closed behind me, he says, "Mommy, why do you deserve this?"

I pause in the doorway. "What?"

"Nettie said that. 'You deserve this.' What does *deserve* mean?"

Sometimes I forget he is so young.

"*Deserve* means that you've earned something."

"Is that good or bad?"

"Actually, it depends. It can be either."

"Did Nettie mean it in a good or bad way?"

"A good one, cutie. She was being kind to me. She was saying I've earned a fun trip. For me."

Bart thinks about this for a moment. "I think Nettie is right," he says, turning on his side and cuddling his Elmo stuffy close. "You're the best mommy."

The words settle over me like snowflakes. I close the door softly before I burst into tears.

On our way to drop-off in a cold drizzle, I know we're late because Redhead Mom's dog is leading the charge. And even he looks stressed. She is attempting to carry an umbrella and push a stroller at the same time, which I know from experience to be an impossibility. Her youngest child is in a bubble gum–pink raincoat with a face to match. She is wailing at top volume in the carriage.

Nettie sees what I see and knows what it means. She gasps. "Mom, I don't want to be late!" she says, speed walking ahead. This is not how I wanted to say goodbye to my kids.

I am able to hug and kiss both of them before rushing them off into the recesses of the school. I take that as a win. And when they disappear and I look up and down the sidewalk, there are almost no parents to be seen. It's deserted as if drop-off never happened. Even the usual procrastination crew who lingers on the corner has disbanded.

I head quickly to the supermarket before I plan to return home, close my suitcase and leave for the airport. Inside, it's a cozy refuge from the storm, the dim lights and familiar stock of past-due produce, a hug.

My phone rings and I fumble for it, stuffing old-school earbuds (with wires) into my ears and repeating "hello" fifty times like I've lost my hold on reality. I've given up on the wireless ones. They always fall out. Celeste says I have abnormally small ear canals. I think everyone else has abnormally large ones.

Of course, it is my mom. Of course, on FaceTime. I tuck myself in a corner by the cold beverages.

"Mom, hi."

She's calling me from bed this time. Maybe she has just woken up, which is odd because she is generally an early riser. She's leaning back against patterned pillows. It's not a flattering angle—chin foremost.

"Hi!" she says. "How are you?"

"I'm fine."

She narrows her eyes. "You look weird."

"You should talk."

"What?"

"Nothing, Mom." I slip my raincoat's hood off. "I love being told I look weird before nine a.m."

"Sorry." She shrugs, not sorry.

I give myself the once-over in the FaceTime window. My hair is a little worse for wear, but everything else appears to be in place. I always thought I looked cute in this coat. It's army green and so are my eyes. But . . . maybe not.

"I'm at the supermarket"—I sigh—"grabbing some last-minute items before I leave for the airport."

"The airport?!" my mother says, furrowing her brow. "Where are you going?"

This is a surprising question for multiple reasons: (1) She knows I'm going away because I asked my parents to watch the kids before I discovered they were busy. (2) We have discussed my trip multiple times, including when we debated the name of that one sunblock we both like that doesn't clog our pores and when she told me that taking care of myself doesn't make me a bad parent. (3) Five seconds ago, I assumed she was calling to wish me safe travels.

"Mom," I say, trying not to panic. "I'm going to that private island in Turks and Caicos, remember? For the magazine shoot?"

"Oh, right," she says in a tone that is not at all convincing. I try to ignore the worry strumming though me.

"Why are you still in bed? Is your neck bothering you again?"

"No. Just a lazy morning. Actually, my neck has been feeling way better ever since I started taking this new medication. Thank God Carol recommended her doctor."

"Oh, great. I'm so glad!"

Not that I'm not enjoying the chitchat, but my local supermarket has narrow aisles and I've already had to smoosh myself against the chilly shelving twice to let people pass through to the apples, potatoes and tomatoes.

"So . . . ," I say, inspecting and rejecting a container of overpriced blackberries as I weave my way past bruised kiwis. I stop to contemplate the cotton candy grapes, then decide they're triggering. Cotton candy. Too soon.

"So . . ."

"Mom, not to rush off, but did you call for a specific reason?"

"Hmm. Good question. I can't remember!"

I close my eyes. Take a deep breath. *It's going to be okay.*

"Oh," I say, trying to modulate my voice to an approximation of normal. "Well, I'm not leaving for a couple of hours. I'm around if it comes back to you."

I slip into the cereal aisle. I grab a box of Cheerios from the bottom shelf, then start scanning for Crispix.

"Ron, why did I call again?" my mother is asking my father.

"Dad is there?" I say. That man is always hiding in plain sight.

I glance down at the phone, as she lets it tilt to the side. There is my dad, lying beside her in his reading glasses.

I'm so distracted that I manage to get my earbud cord tangled on the buckle of my bag strap. My free hand is holding a shopping basket, so I can't tug it off. So I am contorted into some bizarre yogic pose, trying to yank myself loose, when another customer behind me clears his throat, hoping to get through. My supermarket. Again, with the world's narrowest aisles.

"Sorry, sorry," I say, as I whirl around and flatten myself against the shelves. I look up and find myself face-to-face with Demon Dad. Of course. I've only seen him in passing since Monster's Ball, though I'm unsettled by how often he's been popping up in my head. Now, his face is just inches from mine. His hair is damp. He clearly got caught in the downpour without an umbrella. And, in the most annoying way, wet looks really good on him. My chest flutters.

"You're wet," I say like a full moron.

"Wet?" says my mom. "Why, wet?"

Right. I'm on the phone with my parents.

He is on a call too. "Yes," he says to the person on the other end, adjusting his AirPods. "That makes sense." He nods hello to me. Shrugs that he is, indeed, wet.

Mortified, I move to let him pass, but he gestures toward the shelves like he is also shopping for cereal. I have no choice but to turn around and stand shoulder-to-shoulder with him while I continue looking for Crispix.

I finally spot the cereal. Of course it's on the highest shelf. Way out of reach. Kind of like my self-respect.

"I have no idea why you called Sasha," my dad says to my mom as I stand on tiptoe, pretending like that extra inch is going to make up for the footlong deficit between me and that blue box.

An arm appears above my head. I watch as a strong hand plucks the box effortlessly from its resting place.

"That's fine as long as we're not compromising our vision to appease him," Ethan is saying as he hands me the Crispix, which was a benign breakfast product seconds ago and now feels radioactive.

"Who's that I hear?" my mom says. "Is that Celeste?"

"That's a man, not Celeste!" my dad says.

"She's very tall," counters my mom.

"So she sounds like a man?"

Ethan gives me a thumbs-up. I guess I look confused because he mutes his call and says, "That's the goods." He is talking about the Crispix.

I nod. "It's in regular rotation," I mouth. I have no idea if he understands.

I suddenly have a sensation like I've fallen through a wormhole into a silent movie. Only there are no captions and I can't follow the thread.

"It's for Bart," I whisper. "I'm going out of town." This makes no sense without context, which I assume is why he looks at me with legitimate confusion. But there's no time to find out what he's thinking. Because there are at least four conversations happening at once. Possibly five. And my cord is now caught on my sleeve. And the aisle is so narrow that I'm practically pressed up against Ethan's damp chest. And I'm starting to seriously overheat. And I can't stop staring at a drop of rain that is trailing its way down his neck.

I'm suddenly thirsty.

So I do the only thing I can. I salute him. *Salute him?* Then back down the aisle a few steps and turn to walk away, cheeks blazing.

"You know what, sweetie?" my mom says. "We should go. This isn't a good time for us to talk. We've got to start our day."

"Mom. You called me!"

"Did I? I don't think so."

I suppress rising panic—and put a pin in it until I get home.

DEMON DAD

I can't decide if something's wrong with me or if she's the problem. Either way, Sasha and I are incapable of having a normal interaction.

When I see her in the cereal aisle, she's tangled in her earbuds and I'm dripping wet (as she points out with a scrunched nose). But, in my defense, what adult owns a raincoat? She does. That's who. And it's weirdly good on her. Green like her eyes, which widen in what looks a lot like horror when she sees me.

I don't know what's up, but she was clearly not thrilled about running into me.

And here I thought we had bonded over cotton candy. Which makes me think I've way misread things. Which is not excellent. My stomach drops. But the train has left the station. So, here's hoping for the best.

TO-DO

- Finish call.
- Finish grocery shopping.
- Put the box of cereal back once Sasha is definitely gone since I never needed cereal in the first place.
- Stop making up pathetic excuses to be near her when you see her.
- Figure out why you're making up pathetic excuses to be near someone who salutes you. (I'm pretty sure that's not a sign of sexual attraction, by the way.)

21 | Under Where?

KAITLIN

At pick-up, I'm running the clothing drive outside the gates. Other schools in the district are doing jacket and coat drives, but most people don't know that refugees and unhoused people need underthings above all else. So we're doing it right, collecting tags-on underwear and socks.

The truth is, I thought it might make me feel good to do something for people less fortunate, but I am still a storm cloud. If anything, I'm tamping down extra irritation as it prickles under my skin. I feel assaulted by Lisa's garlic breath. I am flooded with venom for parents who walk by without contributing. And I am furious that I've dedicated so much time to this damn school that I'm down to the dregs of my own underwear drawer, deeply behind on laundry. The only options left this morning—a painfully irrelevant fishnet La Perla G-string and two stretched-to-the-limit Hanky Panky thongs from 2004—were clearly mocking me.

During a lull, I scroll to social. I have lost three followers in the last three days. And I'm becoming obsessed with finding out who—and why. Lisa swears it's because they're all bots anyway. But I'm not so sure.

That's when I notice Celeste's husband, lingering nearby, waiting for their son to emerge. He's a giant man in an army jacket and way too much facial hair, if you ask me. But no one does. If it was up to me, every man in a ten-mile radius would be stripped of his "Brooklyn beard." When I think about what must get stuck in them . . . ugh.

He's otherwise attractive enough, I think. It's hard to tell. But I assume Celeste chose him not because of his looks but because of his remarkably sunny disposition, which seems weirdly absent today.

Today, he does not say hello to me. When he drops by a package of Fruit of the Loom tube socks, he catches my eye and looks away.

Did I do something? Snub him in some way? Did he hear something bad about me? Did he hear what I *did*?

Did he see me adjusting my last-resort panties in a literal bunch beneath my jeans?

Usually, there is no cheerier parent. You can't help but smile back when he flashes you his teeth (or what I assume are his teeth behind his "chin pubes"). Like me, he remembers people's names.

I try to imagine him and Celeste meeting and falling for each other. Was it in college, when a kind of softness and lack of ambition was still passable? When "chill" had value? Was it in their early twenties, when a motorcycle alone might have been enough to do the trick? He looks like the type who rode a motorcycle. Was it at work, when he once had authority, which he surrendered—to her chagrin? Joy? Ambivalence?—when her career took a stratospheric turn? Had they always known he'd be the stay-at-home dad? Certainly, she was never going to be a stay-at-home mom. I've heard her ask for a reminder about drop-off and pick-up times twice since school started just this semester! It's been four years! She should know by now.

Lisa hands me a few more pairs of wool socks to add to the cold-weather box, the same brand my husband wears. What did I like about him when I met him? What did I expect? Can I remember?

Certainly, he was good-looking. He always has been though, of course, he's gotten better with age while I have begun to shrivel in the image of my great-aunt Leslie. Soon, I will double as the crypt-keeper. Or, conversely, I'll join the ranks of the injected, adopting raised eyebrows and swollen cheekbones until my age is indeterminant, somewhere between thirty and seventy-five.

My husband had a cool job when I met him. I know I liked that. I got to go as his date to elaborate events that spawned Getty

Images reels, their logo obfuscating the pictures, denying entry like a red-carpet rope.

Early on, I think we both liked how we appeared to the world as a unit, me as a native New Yorker and him an up-and-coming out-of-towner. In those days, we still thought people were looking. And we were good at climbing. We liked the mixology cocktails and the late nights, the career momentum and Hamptons weekends with friends who inherited their way into higher tax brackets and vanity clothing lines. We liked the B-list celebrities, who treated us as insiders. I wore navy-blue shift dresses and neutral sandals, my legs bare and Pilates-toned. Unlike at those sceney high school parties, I felt like I made sense in this world, posh and polished. A little uptight. Maybe that was the first time—the only time?—I almost felt like enough. I almost felt in control.

If I hadn't gotten pregnant, would we have ended up married? Or would we have just been a twentysomething chapter? A romantic lesson learned? I always tell myself we were headed down that committed path, regardless, but, in my worst moments, I do wonder.

Because then he lost interest. Not in me, but in being seen. Had he grown up or grown complacent?

He stopped caring about the pretty picture we created, leaving me with crumpled *Us Weekly* magazines on my lap at corner manicure spots when we had sitters, while he headed to play poker or see baseball games (and not in a box) with regular friends. Average friends. Run-of-the-mill friends, who invited us to basic Super Bowl parties and family-friendly game nights instead of to movie premieres. We moved to a barely fashionable neighborhood in an outer borough.

Soon, the babysitters seemed like too much trouble to book. The twinkly events became obligations, where he'd make an appearance alone and head home by 9:00 p.m. The good life lost its shine.

Was that it? Had I become less shiny too? How come I didn't get a vote?

Is that what happened with Sasha and Cliff? Had she lost her luster in his eyes? Or was it the other way around?

The kids come filing out now. Celeste's husband plasters a smile on for Henry, but his face still has a grayish cast that I recognize from the mirror. He waves goodbye to the teacher and walks up the sidewalk with his son and both of Sasha's kids too.

My daughter, Ruby, loves Henry. She keeps begging me to make plans with his family. But it never feels like the right time to ask. Why does organizing a playdate make rage bubble up inside me? Do the children even like her or is Ruby trying to hang with the cool kids? Are these the new velvet ropes?

22 | The Voodoo That You Do

SASHA

There is a plane without legroom. A duty-free catalog. A safety demonstration that no one watches. There is a choice between pretzels and cookies. A flight attendant in dangly shell earrings. A toddler running up and down the aisles followed by bleary-eyed parents muttering, "*Sorry, sorry, sorry.*"

There is a view out the righthand window of sea foam and turquoise water, drippings of white sandbars and gargantuan hotels that look like miniatures. There is a wait on the tarmac while the gate frees up. There is an indoor-outdoor baggage claim area that smells like island and runs on island time. It is balmy and sunny and delicious.

And this is all expected. But what is less expected is the drive in a van that smells like diesel fuel to a private jet airport and a transfer to a private flight, a sea plane that takes off from the ocean's surface. A plane that can walk on water.

Derek, the managing editor, flew ahead yesterday, so I share the six-seater with Stephanie, Peter, Jackie and a pilot, a local man in a classic airplane captain's cap and a yellow T-shirt that reads "Turks & Caicos: Beautiful by Nature!" His name tag reads "Jimmy Baptiste" and his wide smile is contagious.

I feel like I'm buckled into the jump seat in an old-school checkered cab. Not exactly stable. But I push my fears away before going to that *What will happen to Nettie and Bart if I die?* place. I will not sabotage this experience for myself.

The plane flies so low and the water is so clear that, out the porthole, I can literally see stingrays gliding in slo-mo beneath the surface like I'm watching a nature documentary from above. Like I'm *in* a nature documentary! I can see tiny sand islets topped with toupees of greenery that shrink when the tide is high. Out the left side of the plane, Jackie spots a creature with a fin.

"Is that—?!" she says with alarm.

"It's a gray reef shark!" the pilot Jimmy proclaims gleefully, like it's a special breed of puppy.

Jackie is wide-eyed. "Are they—?!"

"They're not aggressive," he says. "Attacks are rare."

"Rare is not never," she murmurs to herself like a mantra.

"But what a way to go!" Stephanie exclaims from behind rose-gold aviator sunglasses, her feet propped up on the empty seat in front of her. Not a care in the world.

Peter, our cameraman, is green and has not spoken for the duration of the journey, except when he efficiently handled accounting for our vast array of production equipment at baggage claim. Now, he is hunched over, his hands clasped tightly in prayer or restraint.

"Are you okay?" I whisper to him.

"I do not like planes," he says. "I especially do not like small planes."

"Peter is afraid of flying!" Stephanie announces, swatting his worries away with her manicured hand like one would a gnat. Phobias are a drag.

"But what a way to go!" she says again.

Looking around at my fellow passengers, I can safely say we would all prefer not to "go" no matter what the way, however arresting the landscape. Jackie is shaking her head like she has not signed up for this.

Soon enough, we teeter toward a tiny airstrip on what looks like a mostly untamed island. We bounce and rebound upon landing. And, when we hit the ground, Peter holds his head in his hands, shouting, "Oh Lord!" But we ease to a safe stop. He stays in that position for minutes afterward. We give him grace to recover.

As soon as we're told it's okay, the rest of us unbuckle our seat belts (as if they served a purpose) and, with Jimmy's assistance, climb one by one out onto a portable step stool on the tarmac.

I step down to solid ground and look around. There is no other sign of life. At first, it's just us on this alien planet, surrounded by dry earth, savage shrubbery and the embrace of that humid tropical air. There is only the back of a large white Georgian-style house ahead of us that I assume is the reception center. It has heather-gray asphalt shingles on the roof and teal shutters.

I close my eyes for a moment and breathe it all in, feeling my shoulders drop. I am here for work. The stakes are high. I need this job. But I might as well enjoy it.

As we begin to walk as a group toward the entrance, a tiny lizard skitters past. *Cute! Wildlife!* But, as we reach the door, framed by brush and strategical palm trees, the lizard's much larger cousin lumbers across our path. *Welcome to Citrine Cay!* Peter and Jackie both shriek, taken by surprise. Jackie actually skitters away herself. But she returns, quickly, catching her breath with a hand to her chest.

"I wasn't expecting that," she says to me.

I nod with understanding.

"I wasn't expecting that," she says to Jimmy the pilot, who laughs heartily.

Inside, this is like no hotel reception area I have ever seen. It's like a home in heaven. Everything is white. Everything is plush. The space is entirely indoor-outdoor with a seductive breeze blowing through. Below a bamboo ceiling fan with palm frond–shaped blades, I am led to a wicker couch that cradles the world's cushiest cushions. There, I am handed a glass of bright red rum punch with an umbrella and a chunk of sweet pineapple in it. It tastes like vacation.

So this is how the other half lives.

I pretend it's all normal to me. An average day. Stephanie is chatting up a manager who has come to greet us. Peter, recovering on the couch beside me, seems grateful for the alcohol. Jackie is already checking out a rack of organic cotton caftans in a gift shop off the main room.

I take out my phone to snap a few photos—a portrait of my drink sitting poised atop the rattan coffee table. I sign release forms, delivered on a clipboard directly to my lap, promising not to smoke in or otherwise destroy my room. Then, just as I'm signing into the hotel's Wi-Fi so my phone will work, an older white man in a starched uniform and a name tag that reads "Michael O'Connor" approaches to say he'll take me to my room. In the distance, I can see that my luggage has already been loaded into a golf cart that's nicer than any car I've ever owned.

"See you at dinner!" Stephanie chirps, winking as I'm led away. In that moment, I have a sensation like I'm back in middle school playing truth or dare, being led into a bedroom by some boy. What might happen next? I am a lamb to the slaughter, and I am cool with it.

That's when my phone starts *binging* as my texts populate.

"Ah, so sorry," I say, fumbling with my purse latch to try to extract and silence the noise pollution.

I pull my phone out: there's a text from Celeste. I quickly click on it in case it's about the kids.

> Sash! Code red!

I have a small heart attack.

> I finally realized why Demon Dad looks so familiar to me!

In that moment, sensing an energetic shift in the room, someone new and important entering the vortex, I glance up. And there is Ethan, standing in front of me. *Ethan*. On this deserted island. Looking drop-dead. In shorts. I drop my phone.

"Hi, Sasha," he says, like it's the most normal thing in the world. Us both being here, on a private island, with all the lizards.

Michael scrambles to grab my phone off the ground, dusting it off and handing it back to me. I take it numbly and murmur thank you. What planet am I on? Am I dead? And, if so, is this heaven or hell?

"What are you doing here?" I ask.

Michael looks confused. "Showing you to your room, miss?"

"What am *I* doing here?" Ethan asks, pointing to himself.

"Yes."

"Me?"

Michael's gaze ping-pongs between us.

"Yes! That's what I asked: What are *you* doing here?"

Derek walks up before Ethan can respond. He is also in shorts and a T-shirt, only it's all black and somehow incongruous. Like his resort wear is in mourning.

"Oh, good!" he says. "You've met! I came here from my room all ready to do charming introductions."

"Well, don't let us stop you." Ethan smirks, slipping his hands in his pockets and rocking back on his heels. Like he could do this all day.

"Okay! Ethan, this is Sasha Rubinstein. The amazing video producer I've been raving about, who has swept in at the last minute to save us all." He turns toward me, squinting through his glasses against the sun. "Sasha, this is Ethan Jones. Our incomparable newish editor in chief, who will guide us all toward manifesting a remarkable shoot and lifting the magazine from the ashes! We worked together before at another publication too, so I know his excellence to be fact."

My mouth drops open. My phone *bing*s with a text from Celeste. I look down dumbly.

> He's the new EIC at ESCAPADE! I totally styled for him when he was creative director at another magazine!"

I look up at Ethan's grill.

"Nice to see you," he says, grinning.

I stare at him, dead-faced. "Seriously?"

Derek senses something is up. Probably because it is deeply obvious. "Do you guys already know each other?"

"A bit," says Ethan. "Our kids are in school together. I recently gave Sasha some jogging tips in the park. So, I guess I'm kind of like her running coach."

"That is definitely not accurate," I counter.

Derek looks from Ethan to me, then exhales sharply. We are clearly stressing him out.

"Rum punch?" offers a waitress who has approached with a flower behind one ear.

Derek takes a glass and chugs its entire contents, then returns it to the tray. I have known him for no time and know this is out of character. He is about PowerPoint proposals, not piña coladas.

Why is he so tense?

"Excuse me for a second," he says, then heads off to anywhere else. Even Michael has inched farther and farther away until he is safely situated in the driver's seat of my golf cart. Ethan and I sure know how to clear a room.

Now, he and I are alone, for all intents and purposes. I run a hand down my cheek and sigh, unable to right myself. "I'm so confused. What is happening? Is this a coincidence?" But I know it's not. Because Ethan doesn't seem remotely surprised. I am the one off-kilter. I am the one off my game.

"No." He shrugs. "I heard you were a good producer, so I suggested that Derek take a meeting with you when we realized we needed someone."

I give him an impatient look.

"Seriously! I looked you up. I saw what you do. I asked around. It was perfect. The timing felt fated."

Fated? "But why didn't you say anything? Once you knew I was hired for the shoot?"

"Honestly? I thought you knew. Who applies for a magazine job and doesn't look up the name of the editor?"

Me! *Me.* That's who. Someone who needs the job so badly that she doesn't care. I feel like the world's biggest idiot. And I can't help but feel like Ethan designed it this way.

Suddenly, our cotton candy bonding session feels null and void. I am hoodie-era frustrated all over again.

"Didn't you think it was odd that I never mentioned it?" I say.

"Yes, a little. But I figured you were trying to keep your professional and personal lives separate."

"But I didn't see you at my interview—at the *Escapade* offices!"

"Oh. Yeah, I was kind of locked in my office on calls."

Yet another humiliating scene flashes before my eyes. I cover them with my hand as if I can stop from seeing it. "When I saw you at the supermarket, I told you I was going on a trip! Like you didn't know!"

"That did seem weird. But, honestly, that whole interaction was weird. I mean, you saluted me, so."

So he noticed that. A part of me dies.

I drop my hand. He holds my gaze for a beat. I sip my rum punch, resigned. I'm experiencing a cocktail of emotions, but, above all else, I'm confused.

I am not the only one.

"You really didn't know? That it was me?" Ethan seems almost disappointed. He thought I knew and still came. Could he have *wanted* me to come? I can't begin to unpack that.

"I really didn't know," I manage. "I thought we were strictly in the Monster's Ball zone. Celeste thought you looked familiar, but . . ."

"Who's Celeste?"

"Celeste Alameddine? Tall, statuesque, beautiful? I'm always with her at PS421 events? You've worked with her as a set stylist, I think?"

He racks his brain, then begins to nod. "Oh! Celeste! Of course. She's fantastic. I didn't even know she was a parent at the school."

"How is that even possible?" I ask. But I know.

"Well, I never did drop-off really until six months ago. I still don't do pick-up. I haven't been around."

And that makes me angry all over again. I don't even know why. Because he's a man? Because I have to do both?

"Hi, Sash," says Stephanie, who has appeared at my side bearing the gift of a new nickname. She leans her elbow on my shoulder, tilting her head toward me. "So, I see you've met *Ethan*. Our fearless leader! Isn't he the greatest?" This is the first time in my life I have actually seen someone flutter their eyelashes.

"The greatest," I say.

"Ms. Rubinstein?" prods Michael, who has left the golf cart and bravely crept closer again. "Should we take you to your room? You're going to love it!"

I look at him adoringly, like he is a saint for getting me out of this. And I think he knows because he widens his eyes and then winks at me.

"Thanks, Michael," I say, tearing my eyes away from Ethan. "Yes! Sorry to keep you waiting."

I turn to leave and don't look back. We hop in the getaway car and make our escape.

23 | Paradise City

DEMON-IN-CHIEF

Shit. *Shit, shit, shit.*

I should have mentioned the trip. Of course I should have. I see that now. But it's not like Sasha and I talk regularly. And I truly figured she knew.

I thought we both knew. Which would have been a very different scenario.

But she definitely didn't know. Not today and not when I was hiding in my office, giving them space to interview her without my bias. And, by the look on her face, this is not Sasha's idea of a welcome surprise.

Now I'm *that* guy.

Derek is pissed at me too. He's glaring at me from across the living room in his villa. But at least he's letting me hide here. Leaning back against the modernist peach sofa, looking out onto teal water, I take a swig of my beer and let my forehead drop into my free hand.

"Derek. I told you I knew her."

"No. You told me you heard she was good. Not that you *knew* her."

"I don't *know* her."

"Well, your face looked like you want to *know* her."

"What I want is for this shoot to go well."

"Good," he says, sitting in a chair across from me. "Then we're in agreement. Just keep it professional, be standard by-the-book Ethan and everything will be fine."

I nod. *Sure.* Bite my lip.

Derek isn't usually the person I'd confide in about this kind of thing, but he's who's here—and at least I can count on him to be discreet and a voice of reason.

I risk a glance up at him: "But do you think she . . . ?"

He looks to the ceiling for outraged commiseration. "Ethan! I don't know what she thinks."

"But she *seemed* . . . ?"

"Surprised, to say the least," he says. "And mad. *Really* mad."

I nod. She's often really mad. At me, at least. " 'Surprised' like she doesn't want to *know* me or . . . ?"

Derek sighs, deflating. "Surprised like maybe she does want to *know* you but doesn't want to want to *know* you. That might be why she's so pissed and disconcerted."

I'm bolstered by this but also realize I need to give her space. I need to let Sasha do her job, stay out of her way, follow her lead.

"I've never seen you like this and the timing is not great," Derek says. "You're usually so uptight. I like you better that way."

I try to shrug off his words, but I can't even fake it. "Yeah," I groan, swigging from my beer hopelessly. "I know."

TO-DO

- Go back in time and mention the trip to Sasha beforehand.
- Fire up the flux capacitor and tell her about the job opening before putting her up for it.
- ~~Hide for the rest of the trip.~~
- Keep things all business for the rest of the trip.

24 | Couch Surfing

KAITLIN

The rain is coming down in sheets. It's been pouring since this morning. And I cannot get down to business.

Instead of working, I am lying on the couch, scrolling through Sasha's pictures again. Wondering why I keep looking to the past for answers about the future. But doing it anyway.

Rewinding back to high school hasn't worked well for me thus far; it basically combusted my life. And yet I persist.

I've seen this image of Sasha and Bart stuffing their cheeks with popcorn at the Bronx Zoo at least five times. She almost never posts. I don't know why I keep checking for new ones.

Sometimes her ex-husband's feed is fun. A bevy of humble brags and bullshit gratitude. Occasionally, there is Ryan Reynolds.

But then, as if I had manifested it, magically a picture appears in stories—some kind of tropical cocktail with a pineapple skewer. *Lucky, Sasha.* The caption is nothing but sun and sunglasses emojis.

I do *not* click like.

"Mom!" my daughter barks like she's already said it four times.

She turns on the light in the living room, and it's only then, as I squint against the assaultive brightness, that I realize I've been lying in the dark.

"Ruby. What?!"

"I'm hungry. Can you get off your phone?"

Like she's the parent.

She's right, of course. It's getting late. And I have given no thought to food.

"Coming, coming," I say, pushing myself up off the couch. I put my phone aside, for now.

25 | Island Dreams

SASHA

Michael is not wrong. The resort is spectacular. And I do love it. It's so arresting, in fact, that I momentarily *almost* forget my jumbled feelings. At least I try.

I take three deep breaths, shaking off my startle.

As we approach the beach, bucking along the dirt road, I see ten perfect villas set back from the shore, before a wide-open expanse of sand. Each has its own palm tree and landscaped trim of scraggy brush. Though the roofs are pointed and bear the same heather-gray shingles as the reception house, their silhouettes feel almost Japanese, low and flat with sharp symmetrical lines. The white exterior is in stark contrast to black-tinted windows. A play of dark and light.

I've seen the pictures, but, in person, this place is next level. I can't believe I get to stay here.

Michael brings the golf cart to a stop, helps me out and leads me into the villa via a slatted white door, framed by cacti in porcelain planters. Inside is a burst of energy. It gifts me my own burst of joy, despite my pounding heart. Beneath a lofted ceiling is an enormous open-floor-plan living room and kitchen. Though the fundamentals are neutral—couch, rug, granite side tables and countertops—the accents are unapologetic and lively: electric orange wall prints, French blue–striped throw blankets, yellow Acapulco chairs, Mad Hatter shelves of incongruous heights that are lit from within, illuminating artisan vases and figurines.

Michael points out the fancy espresso machine, the remote-control shades, the giant flat-screen TV, the stainless steel refrigerator stocked with complimentary drinks. A bottle of wine is positioned on the kitchen counter beside a lavish tray of sliced tropical fruit, from papaya to kiwi, chocolate truffles, crackers and cheese.

I am Alice and this is Wonderland. I don't belong here, but I'll take it. I will shrink and grow to fit. A wonderfully wrong dream.

Two walls of the villa are entirely windowed so that sunlight falls across the floor. It makes me want to curl up like Larry the cat. Maybe tuck myself in a corner and hide from reality, given the situation with Ethan. I honestly don't know whether to feel flattered or humiliated. I am vibrating with both. So I try to push my worries aside for the moment.

There are three bedrooms off this main room: one alone by the entrance and two side by side off the far wall. Michael leads me to one of these far ones, opening its door and then stepping aside so that I might be the first to walk in and experience my sanctuary for the coming days.

I can't help but smile big. Much like the living room, it is bright and airy with mile-high ceilings and transparent shades that filter in a lemony haze. The bed is king-size with an embarrassment of plush pillows. I want to collapse into it and make snow angels. But Michael still has much to show me, and he is serious about his job.

"This room can be adjoining with the one next to it, if guests prefer," he explains, gesturing toward a closed door beside the closet. "It's perfect for families with small children."

"Darn it. I've left mine at home," I joke. "I knew I forgot something."

"We can supply anything you've forgotten," he says. "Within reason." He raises his eyebrows. Michael is funny!

He takes me through the lighting system, which looks like a motherboard in a James Bond movie. I know I will never retain any of what I am told about how it works and will instead press every conceivable button and pray.

In the bathroom, the walls are a mosaic of iridescent metallic tiles. It feels *fancy*. The bath products are scented like lemongrass and basil. And there is a tube of sunblock that I uncap and sniff. It smells like abandon.

He references a sundry drawer, lit from within, which I peek in as he moves on: organic cotton balls, a recyclable shower cap, bamboo Q-tips, aloe after-sun gel, neon pink earplugs, orange blossom and neroli essential oil pillow spray—even the condoms are hipster and fair trade! Some brand called RAW.

I squeal internally, then rush to catch up.

Guiltily, I realize how thrilled I am to have a beautiful space that's mine and mine alone for a few days. Where no one will leave their dirty socks on the floor or smudges of bubble gum toothpaste on the wall.

"There's also an outdoor shower shared by all the guests in this villa," Michael explains, "but the entrance is at the back of the common room."

"An outdoor shower!" I exclaim, startling the poor man. "My favorite!" I really love an outdoor shower.

"Now, if you have everything you need, I'll leave you to get settled," he says. But he demurs when I offer money.

"This is a no-tipping hotel," he says proudly. "We're paid full salaries." The subtext is clear: this is not your mama's resort. We're not in Kansas anymore. Or even Saint Thomas.

Unable to show my appreciation in cash, I thank him profusely, probably embarrassingly, as he escapes, leaving me to my bliss.

I close the door to my bedroom behind him and take stock. By some miracle, I use the appropriate remote and raise the shades on the floor-to-ceiling front window. They glide upward to reveal a layer cake of boundless sky, aqua sea, white sand and chlorinated crystal. There is a David Hockney–blue pool, minus the humans, and, beyond it, the ocean, tie-dyed with teal where plant life and coral reefs sway beneath the surface. Below a crisp umbrella, two minimalist loungers are sharply angled, an obligatory invitation.

Nothing is round here. Everything is too beautiful to touch.

On my honeymoon with Cliff, we went to Costa Rica. It still seemed a bit wild in those days. The nicest hotel we stayed at was a former Smithsonian observatory, overlooking an active volcano in the midst of the largest eruption in fifty years. At night, after Cliff passed out, I would lie—propped up by a similar abundance of fluffy white pillows—and watch molten lava race downward in fits of neon orange. I am both reminded of that place and time now and struck by the difference, in the setting but also in me. That was stunning in its unpredictability. Frightening like a dare. It matched our bravado and our rapport—even our attraction. Agitated, frenzied, rushed.

This place is so calming; it feels like the antidote to my current angst. Like what I need. And, of course, there is no Cliff, which is always a win. I am almost afraid to ruin the view with the less precise curves of my human form, but I've got to take a closer look to believe it's real. And I don't have much time before cocktails and dinner.

When I slip out my door a few minutes later, I am wearing a tank top, jean shorts and my jaunty straw hat. I'm not surprised to see Stephanie lounging on the couch in a Natalie Martin muumuu. Living the bohemian dream. Her bare feet are propped up on the coffee table, and she's drinking a generous glass of that complimentary wine. This woman isn't afraid to take up space. I look around for Jackie, likely our third roommate, but she has not yet arrived.

"Oh, hi!" Stephanie says, at once upbeat and lazy. "Where you headed in that cute hat?"

"Just down to the water. Wanna come dip your toes?" I hope she does not want to come dip her toes, but I'm being friendly.

No offense to Stephanie. I actually think she seems fun. I like anyone who's that enthusiastic about hanging out with me. The more time I spend around her, the more I'm impressed by the way she moves around the world without apology. But I need a second to wrap my mind around my current circumstances. The Demon Dad of it all. I need to walk down to the beach. Feel sand between my toes. Try not to lose my shit.

"Nah," she yawns. "I think I'll dip my whole body in the pool instead. Come!"

"I think I don't have time to swim, then make my hair presentable."

"Oh, keratin treatment, baby!" She tosses her hair from side to side like a L'Oréal Paris model, and it does look smooth despite the humidity. "Remind me to send you the info. I got a guy."

I don't doubt it.

I step out the front—and I'm a bit like Lawrence of Arabia trekking through the desert. The stretch from our villa to the shore is farther than I thought. But the sand is warm and malleable beneath my feet, and it's been ages since I felt that sensation, that give. I sigh. Whatever else is happening, this is a giant gift.

As I near the water's edge, I realize that, impossibly, it's as clear from this vantage point as it was from up above in the plane. There's barely a ripple on the surface. Definitely no waves. Tiny yellow fish swim by in schools. I give them an A-plus. I test the temperature with my toes, and it is bathtub warm. Suddenly, I'm regretting not wearing my bathing suit. Who cares about my hair?

I wade in to just above my knees. And, for a moment, I stand there, basking in the beauty of my surroundings. For one thing, it is as silent as any place I have ever been. Since the resort hasn't opened yet, the island's entire population is comprised of our small crew and the hotel staff. The photographer, Charlie, is arriving late tonight. There are no cruise ships, no sailboats, no rowboats or kayaks. No additional hotels. There are no swimmers, no surfers, no children splashing or collecting shells. There are no cars, no musicians, no playlists playing, no shouts or laughs between friends. This might be the quietest moment of my waking life.

Unfortunately, that means I can hear my thoughts loud and clear. And they come rushing in, anything but subdued. About my mom's memory, about the kids, about money—or lack thereof.

Most of all, about Ethan.

Just when I was entertaining the idea that he is decent, I am hating him again. I have to ask myself: Why am I so thrown off?

Arguably, he did me an enormous favor. He searched me out, gave me a shot, got me hired on this incredible job. And yet, I want to grab him by his tan neck and throttle him.

Part of me knows I am feeling foolish. One-upped. Like my upper hand got handed to me. But there is something else too, insidious and nagging: I thought I *earned* this job. I thought they chose me on my merit. On my charming disposition. On the really cute, yet responsible, Rachel Comey sample sale sweater I wore to our meeting. Now, I feel like I'm getting a handout. Did he force them to hire me? Do the others believe that? That thought makes me want to hide under my hotel bed in embarrassment. Which is challenging because it's a platform.

But also, I feel tricked. Why didn't he mention he was putting me up for a job? Why didn't he ask me if I was interested before he went ahead and did it? Why did he take ownership over my life without my permission? How dare him! How dare all the men!

I swore, after Cliff, that I would never let a partner shape my world so entirely. No matter how gradually and insidiously he accomplished it. No matter what his apparent intentions. I will not shift into default mode.

But, I realize, my biggest anxiety of all is about the full-time job: now that I know Ethan would be my boss, even if not my direct supervisor, can I still reasonably consider applying? Would they even consider hiring me? If this goes well, can I work for him? Can we work *together*?

The word *together* in reference to anything about me and Ethan makes me deeply uncomfortable and more than a little nauseous. And I am summoning the courage to ask myself the truly terrifying question of why, when I feel a sensation like butterfly wings against my shin.

I've been so in my head that I've forgotten to even see through my eyes. To remember where I am standing. In this spectacular place. I look down now with alarm to find a small stingray—maybe a baby?—swimming in circles around my legs. I gasp, unsure of what to do. I try not to move for fear of scaring it off. What is this magic? This place of wonder! Am I on the edge of the world? Am I in *Moana*?

All my worries of the moment before take a back seat. My first urge is to share this miraculous moment. I turn my head—and only my head—to look for another being, but of course I am alone. And that is a bit of a theme. It doesn't matter. I have been handed a hefty dose of perspective. How fortunate I am to be on this planet, in this place, in this moment, right now!

My stingray buddy brushes past me three more times, her fins like velvet gliding against my skin. I'm reminded of Larry the cat, brushing up against me to beg for treats, and I stifle a laugh at the thought of his grumpy face.

Too soon, my baby stingray swims away, disappearing into the darkening distance. She is lost forever in the shadows of the coral and seaweed. The sun has begun to set. It turns the bellies of the clouds gray. The sky blushes fiery orange, then blurs to yellow. As the sun dips lower, I watch it transform from an amorphous glow into a true circle, a point of light.

It is suddenly growing quite dark. Gratitude swells inside me. And, if I'm honest, so does fear that the stingray has some shark friends following close behind. With a squeal, I jog out of the water and start up toward the villa.

Up toward the villa. That's a nice phrase to get to think. This experience—and the opportunity—is too special to let some dude mess it up. The same dude who laid it in my lap. The complications of that swirl inside my brain. I am not evolved enough to untangle it.

So, I land on this: Forget Ethan and all his annoying perfect T-shirts and shoes. His nice hair. His crinkly eyes. His broad shoulders and muscular back. I can be professional. I can be polite. I can have nice hair too! (Well, sort of. The humidity is a challenge.)

I can avoid him and the topic altogether.

I can wow the whole team with my incredible work ethic and

superlative skills. I can make it impossible for them not to hire me. And I can enjoy the process while I do it. I can multitask.

After all, I am a woman.

Ethan is, of course, wearing another perfect T-shirt. This one is slate gray, and I don't notice how nicely it fits his lean frame and highlights his biceps. Because I don't see hotness. I am a *professional*.

I am in a good headspace, I tell myself. I've got swagger. Because I showered for as long as I wanted, with no kids to interrupt, for what felt like the first time in years. Because my floral nap dress looks cool with my sandals and frosted pink lip (and not in fact "influencer-y" as I feared). Because I texted with Celeste before I left the room and confirmed that my children are alive and thriving. (I will FaceTime with them tomorrow.) And, most of all, because I am now friends with a stingray. Beat that!

Our small team is mingling by a tasteful tiki bar, under a short thatched awning and atop bamboo stools. I seem to be the last to arrive. When I crest the top of the stone steps, Stephanie shouts my name like we're doing a production of *A Streetcar Named Desire*. "Sashaaaa!"

Not that I notice because Professional Sasha doesn't care, but, in my peripheral vision, I see Ethan do a double take when he spots me, and I realize he's never seen me dressed as an actual person before, only for school drop-off or a park run. His eyes linger on my face, then track down my body, before he remembers himself.

Take that, sucker!

His gaze warms me up like a heat lamp. But I am choosing to ignore that fact for now and feel smug instead. After all, I am triumphant! Remember?

There is a new member of our group who I recognize as the resort's owner, Martin Bernard. Of course I've seen him in a million classic Mafia movies, largely during my film school years. Cliff's favorites. Or the favorites he claims in interviews now. Oddly, I have never read an article in which he mentions his deep love of *Porky's Revenge!*.

Stephanie, who is wearing enormous gold hoop earrings and a heavy cat eye to line her eyelash extensions, grabs me by the hand and drags me over to Martin. He is probably mid-sixties, leathery from sun but still handsome in an imposing way. Instead of smaller and bigheaded like most celebrities, he is larger in life.

"You must meet Martin! Martin, this is Sasha! *Escapade's* brilliant new video producer." I like being characterized this way. I am in the club and I am brilliant! Stephanie is fast becoming my new favorite person.

Martin turns his penetrative gaze on me. I shift under it.

Taking his time, as if he's used to people letting him set the pace, Martin lifts his hand and takes mine in his own. His palm is warm and coarse. He opens his mouth so slowly that we all lean in, concerned that he has frozen in place and might never form words again. "A pleasure," he says finally. "Welcome. To. Paradise."

I have never heard a human being annunciate so sharply. Those *p*'s! Each word is a glass of Riesling with a crisp finish. I'm so entranced by the strange way his mouth moves that I forget to respond. Stephanie elbows me. And I bolt up straight, my power switch flipped back on.

"Th-thank you for having me!" I smile. "What a magical place you've created."

He takes his time, scanning the expanse of the open-air restaurant—with its twinkle lights, intricate stonework, Moroccan tiles and tiki torches—and the surrounding landscape, as if he has not seen it a million times before. As if he never saw the blueprints, green-lit the plans. "It is," he pronounces finally. "Magical. You've chosen the perfect word."

"This afternoon, I waded into the water and saw a stingray!" I say, then look around at the others for emphasis. "It swam around me in circles!"

There are murmurs of "Oh, really?" and "That's cool," but no one seems super enthralled. I am a newbie. Mental note: I must learn to be more chic and jaded.

"There are a multitude of exquisite creatures on the island," says Martin, landing hard on that final *d*. "And now . . . there is one more." He smiles down at me—apparently an *exquisite creature*. "That's one of the many wonders that attracted me here and helped me envision the kind of transcendent destination it could become—with my Midas touch, of course."

Speaking of his touch, he is still holding my hand in his sausage fingers. And I kind of want it back. I peek as subtly as possible to my left and right for help, but everyone is too busy hanging on his every word to receive my SOS.

On the contrary. "Such incredible vision!" oozes Stephanie, clasping her hands and raising her shoulders in apparent wonder. But Martin's eyes stay trained on me.

"I'll show you more wonders tomorrow, as your personal guide," he says to me. "I can tell you'd *especially* appreciate them."

"Oh, um—hmm," I say. Always with the big words.

I barely know these people. It's my first day. The last thing I want to do is offend the owner, blow things up and get us all kicked out before work has begun. But I am not loving this exchange. And I'd like my hand back.

Am I overreacting?

"Actually," says a disembodied low voice to my left, "she's going to be quite busy working on producing our video content for the website and social tomorrow."

If Martin hears this, the only indicator is a slight raise of one eyebrow. But I glance over to see Ethan, now standing close by, watching. His face is relaxed, his expression impassive; he takes a casual sip of his drink. But his free hand is balled in a fist.

I've got to speak up for myself. Establish boundaries! It's the only way to subvert this patriarchal mash-up.

"It's true," I say. "I expect to be tied up all day."

Poor choice of words. Martin's eyes go round. Now he thinks I'm flirting back. If anything, he tightens his vise grip on my hand. "I'd like to see that." He spits a bit on the final *t*.

I am no longer confused about his publicist's silence and sighs.

"Speaking of seeing things: Martin, would you mind showing me around the restaurant before dinner begins?" Ethan presses. "I'd love to get a full understanding of the design process."

"Maybe later."

Enough is enough. I don't want to offend this guy, but did he nap through #metoo? Also, his hands are starting to sweat, and it's triggering my gag reflex. I'd rather not puke on his mandals.

"Oops!" I say, then drop my clutch. I yank my hand from his grip, as I bend down to pick my bag up. I do it in that order, reacting *before* I've dropped it, which is why Martin is an actor and I am not.

He doesn't seem to notice. It is inconceivable to him that I would want to escape. He probably thinks that, after his blessed touch, I'll run off and have my hand bronzed. I'd rather have it fumigated.

"I better go show the big editor in chief around," he says, nodding his chin at Ethan perhaps in subtle mockery or rather to underline the importance of men's work to me. "God forbid we risk a poor review." He laughs. Any unfavorable critique is also inconceivable.

The two men head off together to talk sconces and limestone.

I exhale, then turn to find the bathroom so I can loofah all the skin off my hand.

"Wow, girl," says Stephanie, before I can leave. She squeezes my forearm, affectionately. "I thought you seemed on the tame side, but look at you scoring the white whale—he's yours for the taking!"

For a brief irrational second, I think she means Ethan. My cheeks grow hot, and I am about to protest. Though I have to admit, he was the lone person to pick up my signal and try to help me. But then I realize she means Martin, like attracting that man is a win. And I am rendered speechless. I can't tell if she's joking. But I am saved by the bell: she looks down at the thawing ice cube in her glass. "I need another drink! Do you need a drink? You do! I'll go get us some. Their ginger mojito is to die!" Off she runs.

It is novel, I suppose, getting hit on by a movie star, albeit a gross one.

Recently, as a mother, I can barely conceive of myself as a sexual being. That piece of my identity feels twice removed, like a character in a movie I once watched and found both cringey and entertaining. Like most women my age, these days, I often get ignored walking down the street. I am not yet fully invisible but am beginning to disappear like the siblings in the *Back to the Future* Polaroid. Only in this photo, my tits and ass vanish first.

Actually, in my tiny neighborhood in Brooklyn—populated largely by retired firefighters, plumbers and hairstylists of grandparent age and then distracted parents like me—there is no one to check me out, anyway. But it's funny to think of someone else seeing me that way—dateable, "exquisite," even fuckable—when I don't myself.

When dinner is served and we go to sit down, I am the object of Martin's attention again. Lord help me.

"Come sit by me." Martin winks, patting the empty chair to his right. "Seat of honor."

It occurs to me that he might see me as "age-appropriate" and I am even more deeply offended.

Before I can demur, Derek steps in. "Unfortunately, I think you're stuck with me instead. I have some boring details to review with you before tomorrow and, sadly, it can't wait!"

Martin frowns, but he accepts this fate with decorum. "Tomorrow, then," he says, with a flourish. "Tomorrow and tomorrow and tomorrow . . ." His hopeful tone makes me think he hasn't done a lot of Shakespeare, unless he's intentionally lamenting the futility of existence.

As everyone begins to settle in, I whisper to Derek: "Thank you."

He nods barely perceptibly, as if we're undercover. "Anytime."

It is Derek's job to put out fires. He won't let his team get burned.

"Sit here!" says Jackie, a much more welcome invitation.

I settle next to her with relief, placing my glass beside the place setting proprietarily.

"Well," she says, raising her eyebrows.

"Indeed," I say, matching her look.

That is the extent of our conversation about Martin. Enough said. But I have come away with some fairly obvious intel: famous actor plus bazillionaire equals entitled asshole.

Luckily, there is plenty to distract me from both Martin and Ethan, who I am studiously avoiding for very different reasons: I let myself get lost in the family-style spread of fresh fish tacos with mango slaw and an island hot sauce that is not for the timid. Ignoring the sound of Demon Dad's laugh behind me, I focus intently on Jackie, who grew up in Alabama as the daughter of a preacher and now lives in Washington Heights. I learn that she just broke up with her long-term girlfriend but has a new short-term boyfriend. That, when she's not working as a set stylist, she solders her own jewelry for her Etsy store (all of which I want).

Basically, she's one hundred times more clued in than me.

But then most of this crew is more in-the-know than I am. I'm at least ten years older than both she and Peter (who eats quietly and then excuses himself early, still a bit green from the plane). So, I resist the urge to show them pictures of my kids, though I am tempted. It will only make me seem more ancient. Save that for night two.

After inhaling a tub of Meyer lemon crème brûlée, I am next to excuse myself. I can only keep my back to Ethan for so long.

"I'm sorry to break up the party," I say, rising from my seat. "I've got to get sleep if I want to be functional tomorrow. Early call time!"

"Boo!" jeers Stephanie with a good-natured grin. She has moved to sit by Martin, and they both look toasted. "Have another drink! Drink! Drink!"

I am suddenly reminded of nights out in high school, when, saddled with a stricter curfew than the others, I was always the first to leave. My friends' heckles and hisses followed me as I receded down the sidewalk or, if it was really late, down the broken white lines that divided traffic, so no one could jump out at me from behind a parked car. I haven't thought about that in ages. Another lifetime.

"I can't!" I shrug now. "I'm sorry!"

In the old days, I never apologized. I acted like I was leaving by choice.

"Ms. Sasha." Michael, always standing by, hands me a miniature lantern, and I'm delighted.

"Really?" I say.

"It's quite dark," he says. "No lights at all on the path, to preserve authenticity and avoid interruption to the lizards' migration path. This will help you find your way."

Am I finding my way? This place continues to surprise me.

"I'll walk with you," says Ethan, pushing his chair back from the table.

"Oh, I'm okay," I say.

"Well, I need to go anyway. I have work to finish."

There is no way out. Despite the flutters in my stomach at the thought of being alone with him. Despite the cold shoulder I am trying to give. Unless I want to bicker with Ethan in front of everyone. And Professional Sasha doesn't do that.

The brief pause before I respond is making Derek squirm. He leans forward in his chair, watching our every move, poised to intervene. He has sussed us out as potential problem children.

"Okay," I sigh, as if we will be walking to our sure deaths instead of down a secluded beach in paradise. "Let's go."

As we start down the steps, I catch a glimpse of the ocean, cast in borrowed glow from the restaurant's lights. It is almost entirely still, except where small fish bubble below the surface. *Hello, baby stingray!*

I'm happy, I realize. At least, I would be if I was with almost anyone else. And I am walking what I acknowledge to be bizarrely far away from Ethan.

"Do you want me to carry the lantern?" he asks.

"I'm good," I say.

Michael wasn't kidding. It is extremely dark. Without the lantern, we'd be lost.

"Look, Sasha," Ethan says. "I want—"

"No need," I stop him, without looking back. "We're good." I wish he would quit saying my name. Something about the way he does sends tingles through me—or, I assure myself, maybe it's just the evening breeze.

"Okay. I'm glad you're good," he says. "But I'd really like to expl—"

"That's all right! You do you!"

"What does that even m—?"

"I'm good. You're good. We're good!"

"Oh my God!" he exclaims, stopping on the path, hands on his head. "Will you just let me talk?"

I shoot him a dirty look, but I do stop and turn to face him.

"I'm sorry," he says. "But you are a maddening human."

"Is this part of your apology?"

"No?"

I rotate my hand, gesturing for him to get on with it. He steps closer to me. And, suddenly, I'm aware of my dress clinging to my body in the heat.

"I'm sorry that I put you up for a job without telling you. In retrospect, that was a weird thing to do."

"Yes." I nod. "It was weird. *You're* weird."

"Okay." His eyes narrow. "Don't get carried away."

My plan had been to avoid talking to Ethan, but, as long as he's in front of me, I go ahead and ask, "But why did you do it?"

He runs a hand through his hair, so his T-shirt rises just the slightest bit above his perfect cotton slacks, revealing the top of boxer briefs and a strip of tan skin that, horribly, I flash to running my fingers along. He's close enough for me to touch. A warmth travels through me.

What am I thinking?

I restrain one hand with the other and will my stubborn eyes up back to his face. Luckily, he's too consumed with his own neurosis to notice. Luckily, it's pitch dark and I'm holding the lantern, so he can't see my beet-red face.

I squeeze my thighs together, fusing them shut. *Get a grip.*

"I think I felt bad about the hoodie thing and the after-school drama," he's saying.

"What drama? There was no drama." I am not at all defensive. And my underwear is not damp.

"No. Like, after-school drama *class*."

"Oh. I see."

"And I wanted to give you something—be helpful—since I had inadvertently taken something away. But I figured if I asked you about the job, you'd say no. You would have said no, right?"

"I would have said no."

He sweeps his hand to the side like *There you go*.

Irritation rises in me. "But, Ethan, you don't get it! If I wanted to say no, that was my prerogative. I should have had that option: the chance to make a decision for myself with all the relevant information available to me."

I've been blind too many times before. I need to make informed decisions. I cannot live by someone else's will. That's how I wound up here—solo parenting, with only a semblance of the career I envisioned, no time for myself, being eaten alive by financial worry.

He bites his lip. Slowly nods. I have gotten through to him. Somehow, in the midst of a disagreement, he has heard me. I can tell by the way he hangs his head.

I have to admit, I'm a little impressed. Admitting you're wrong in the middle of an argument? Now, *that's* my idea of sexy.

"Sasha," he says, sending another wave thrumming through me. "Of course you should have had that right. I thought I was being helpful, but . . . I totally fucked up." He takes another step toward me so that he can't be more than a foot away. He is trying to see my face in the dark when he says, "I'm really sorry."

I can tell he is. And our eyes are glued to each other when I rasp, "I know."

There's a beat as we absorb this.

"For what it's worth, once you took the job, I really did think you knew I was the editor," he says hesitantly, swallowing hard. "I thought you knew and were choosing to come . . . with that knowledge."

The subtext of what he's saying hits me like a freight train. He thought I had agreed to come, knowing he'd be here. That we'd be on this island . . . together. It's an acknowledgment of something I've been studiously ignoring—every time I've rationalized trying to catch a glimpse of him at drop-off or revisited Cotton Candy Gate in my head.

Maybe since the hoodie showdown. Maybe since we spoke on the park loop. Definitely since Monster's Ball.

I might hate this guy, but I also love to hate him.

Now, we stand staring at each other wordlessly, in the dim glow of the lantern light.

I can see his chest rise and fall. So close. I know this is a bad idea, but my mind is at odds with my body—and, currently, my body is in charge. Blame the balmy breeze. Blame the ginger mojitos. Blame my years of sexual sabbatical. But, despite what my mouth has been saying, I've got tunnel vision for his full lips—and, before I know it, I'm rising up on my toes, leaning in, closing the gap between us until we are only centimeters apart. I can feel his breath on my skin.

His heavy gaze drops to my lips. He is a statue, still, like he is afraid to startle me away.

He hesitates. Waiting for my whistle to blow.

I give up. I give *in*.

I lean closer, so a whisper separates us. We've come too far to turn back. Time is suspended. The air crackles.

I forge ahead. Close the gap. Press my lips against his as he responds. And, for an electric instant, heat sears through me in a way that shocks me senseless, melting any remaining resolve to syrup. Place and propriety are no longer a thing. There is just his mouth and mine as we fall deeper.

But then, just as quickly, a sharp sound startles us from our shared stupor. Stephanie's throaty laugh, carried on the breeze.

We break apart. I take a step back. Disoriented. Bring a hand to my lips.

What the hell am I doing?

My whole body is tingling. With embarrassment, with possibility, with . . . him. It's been a while since I had a first kiss, but I remember enough to know they don't usually feel like that. And we'd barely even gotten started.

Which is going to make everything harder.

Damn.

"W-we should go to bed," I say, looking anywhere else.

Why am I incapable of phrasing anything in a benign way? And why can't I stick to my own rules with this man?

"I mean *I* should get to bed," I mumble, starting down the path again in front of him and away from what almost happened. "You can do whatever you want in your bed. I mean, obviously."

I am dying on the vine.

"I'd like to go to bed," Ethan says. "But I'm all tied up."

Ugh! I storm ahead. "Funny!"

"I thought so."

"Look," I say, whipping around to face him as we arrive at my villa's front door. I take a step back so we're far apart enough for me to trust myself. "I'm trying to be professional! This job . . . it's actually an important opportunity for me."

After a beat, he nods, reorganizing his face into a serious expression. "Fair enough. You're right. Of course. I promise to respect that. It's important to me too."

"Good." I turn to bolt inside.

"Hey, one thing," he says.

I pause and force myself to look back at him, though I can barely make eye contact.

"Did you really see a stingray? While you were just standing out there?"

"Oh." I exhale. "Yeah. I did."

"That sounds incredible."

If this is designed to disarm me, it works.

"It was the most amazing thing."

"I bet." There's not a drop of cynicism in his voice.

A moment of silence.

"It's so beautiful here," I say finally.

"It is," he agrees. But he is looking at me.

"Hey," I say, holding out the lantern. "Don't you need this to get to your villa?"

His brow furrows; he parts his lips—the ones I just had my mouth on.

But then "Boo!" Stephanie appears out of the darkness, making me jump. "Hi, guys!"

My hand comes to rest on my pounding chest. I have reached my quota for surprises today. "What happened to drinks?" I manage.

"Eh, everyone wanted to be 'responsible,' and Martin was too pickled to continue, so . . . here I am with my two roomies."

"Two roomies?" I say, realization beginning to dawn.

"Yeah!" she says. "The three of us are sharing the villa!" She slips past me, scans her key card and pushes the door open.

"Oh," I say, struck dumb again. "I thought we were with Jackie."

"No." She shakes her head. "I organized the room assignments. This is the *fun* house! They can be all tidy and proper over there!"

My eyes slide to Ethan's. He holds his hands up like it's a stickup. *It wasn't me.*

Stephanie crosses to the counter and pours herself another glass of wine. I follow her inside, and Ethan trails behind me. There is no way I can look at his face now. He'll see too much in mine.

Without passing go, I cross to my room and rest my hand on the doorknob, desperate to disappear. To be polite and "normal," I turn back, posture proper. "Good night!" I chirp, too brightly. Stephanie waves, mid sip.

Ethan is standing just feet from me, his hand on the doorknob of the room next to mine. My *adjoining* room. I cannot even think about the interior door that separates us. What is *with* me?

Trying to be brave, I meet his eyes and, honestly, I'm too jumbled up myself to read his expression.

"Good night," he coughs, as he enters his suite.

"Sleep tight!" I reply. And die of embarrassment.

26 | That Guy

EDITOR IN CHIEF

I strip off my clothes, toss them on the chair 'cause tonight I can't be bothered and collapse into bed, willing myself not to think about Sasha doing the same on the other side of the thin wall. I will not think about her pulling that flowery dress up over her head. Past freckled shoulders and the pink bra that snuck out from underneath the straps.

I will not think about her hair, messy from the sea air. The arch of her neck, when she threw her head back to laugh at dinner.

How much I wanted to punch Martin when he wouldn't let her go.

I throw a forearm over my eyes and groan.

I will not think about what would have happened if Stephanie hadn't come along.

The shadowy lantern light. The beach. Sasha smelling like honey-suckle. Her eyes reflecting my own urgency back to me. Her lips parted as she leaned in. The push and pull of her lips against mine for that brief moment, sending shock waves through me.

I'm only fucking human.

So, I didn't stop it. But I let her take the lead. That's something, right?

I think about the way we have a kind of silent communication, like I never had with my ex. With Sasha, it feels like I've known her forever, even though it's basically only been weeks.

But it seems like maybe Derek was right, though I don't plan to tell him. Whatever she's feeling, she doesn't want to give in. And I've got to respect that. I *will* respect that.

Even if it's torture.

The last thing I want to do is stand between her and this opportunity. The last thing I want to do is be *that guy*.

TO-DO

- Make sure Sasha knows I didn't orchestrate the room assignments.
- Focus on the shoot. Work. Remember that?
- Speaking of: email corporate an update.
- Stop wondering what her shiny pink lips would have tasted like, given more time.
- Stop thinking about that second when I almost knew.
- Go the hell to sleep.

27 | Snack Attack

KAITLIN

Sasha is nowhere to be found.

Judging by the photo she posted, she's still somewhere tropical. Meanwhile, I am down two more followers.

That's the big news in my life.

She isn't at drop-off. She isn't at pick-up. I know because I am at both.

You know who else is at both? Celeste. And it is both pleasing and strange to see her arrive harried at 3 p.m., answering the kids' demands in place of greetings with a dip into her tote for whatever snacks she grabbed as she rushed out the door.

Of course, her tote is still Goyard. I'm wearing a faded canvas giveaway from a health food store in the Berkshires. Until this moment, I thought it was kind of cool. Cool *enough*.

The kids emerge.

Celeste takes the little one's backpack. Sasha's youngest, Bart. By all appearances, he is the world's cutest five-year-old and easy as hell. Of course he is. He dances at Celeste's feet, cheering his strawberry fruit roll-up like he has won the lottery.

In some ways, Nettie already embodies the Sasha I first met. She is pretty, precocious, too cool, with eyes that miss nothing. But she has a seriousness that her mother never had; she is not carefree.

Maybe our children don't have that luxury. To trust the ground they stand on so entirely. Not like we did.

Not that I was ever carefree.

My own daughter, Ruby, has begun having panic attacks. No

mystery there. So much change. If she understood what worried her, it would help, but instead she projects outward. She worries that a movie will be too scary; that she'll feel awkward at a birthday party; that her goldfish might die (he will). Even if we're out, she must say good night to both parents each evening before bed. For the first time in years, she has requested a night-light.

There's a part of me that wants a night-light too.

But the demons in my darkness are not under my bed. They live in my head (and, apparently, in my underwear drawer on laundry days). They live on my phone. They come in the form of looped memories, of relitigated poor choices I cannot change, of revisited relationships that don't serve me, of past slights that still feel like indignities, of other people's self-celebratory posts I scroll through when the insomnia wins. They echo with phrases like, *How did I get here?* and *What am I doing wrong?* and *Is this really me? Is this really* it?

Ruby will make better choices. I've put all of my eggs in that basket. *This is just a blip,* I tell myself. The world is in a tough place. It simply has to rebound. Right?

But Bart is still small enough to be chipper, jogging to keep up with Nettie and Henry as they run ahead down the sidewalk, stopping now and then to tightrope walk the brick borders around dogwood trees. He reminds me of simpler days. Days that overwhelmed before I knew what that meant.

28 | Oh, Shoot

SASHA

For some stupid reason, I set my alarm for a 6:30 a.m. run.

Sunrise sounded way more worthwhile the night before. Now, my memory foam pillows are giving the spectacle a run for its money.

I have two children. I never get to sleep in! Why am I voluntarily getting up earlier than I have to now?

But I'm up! And it's warm out! And when I step outside in my sports bra, loose tank and throwback velour gym shorts, the air is thick and dreamy. The dark is just beginning to lift.

As far as I can tell, there is only one path where I am guaranteed not to get lost and eaten by a giant iguana, a winding dirt thing that weaves its way behind the villas, up the hill through brush, around toward the activity shed (which is less a shed and more a giant lofted barn decked out with pristine bicycles, paddleboards, kayaks and neon life jackets) and back past the restaurant and spa.

As the dark dissipates and light eases its way forward, a dimmer in reverse, everything from the scraggy vegetation to the sporadic palms and jagged rocks are bathed in a diffuse golden luster. Even me.

There is a stillness to this hour, to this place, that is not the stuff of everyday life. It is reserved for these few stolen minutes. *I have done something right to wind up in this moment*, I tell myself. Not every choice has been wrong.

It's so quiet that I decide to embrace it and run without music, at least to start. And I'm feeling this new zen me: the rhythm of my breath, the light breeze smelling of algae and sea, the crisscrossed grooves—golf cart tracks—that emerge in the shadows below my feet as darkness lifts. It's settled: I am transcendent. At one with the universe!

Until, a thumping behind me gets louder and louder—the giant iguana?—and I whip around just in time to see, really *feel*, Ethan zoom past in a blur. Up the hill ahead, he turns around to face me, puts his hands up to correct my arm position, and then turns and continues on his way.

Just like that, my enlightenment is snuffed. I swear, at that exact moment, the sun blasts out the last hint of dawn, rendering the moment obsolete.

Dammit! Can I not get a moment of peace? More important, can I reasonably deny *almost* kissing him last night? Even in my own head?

I turn on my music—a shuffle of Taylor Swift songs about how much boys suck. *Word, Taylor. Word.*

This path is not long, and so it's really a matter of time before Ethan laps me again. I resolve to act normal when he does. Smile politely. Nod. I will not make this a thing.

I spend the whole rest of my run tensed for his return, but he never comes. Maybe that lap was his last.

When I finish my three miles—not a step more—and stroll back, sweaty and flushed, Demon Dad is somehow already showered and changed (perfect army-green tee). He is reclining in a lounger by the pool like some *GQ* model, reading on his phone and drinking coffee from the fancy machine. Which he of course knows how to work.

He looks up. Like he's expecting me. Which, of course, he is. "Good run?"

He is completely relaxed—or doing a tour de force performance of it. Like last night is not a thing.

That's good, I guess. He's letting it drop. But he could at least have the decency to lust after me.

"Yup," I say, hands on my hips as I catch my breath fully.

"Did your thing where you stop abruptly before the loop ends?"

"Abruptness is subjective."

"How long do you run again?"

"Three miles. Why? How many did you run?"

"Six."

I frown. "That's excessive. Like, objectively."

"I like to push myself."

I would like to push his smug ass too. Into a ravine. Or at least the pool.

He considers me for a beat. "You know, they make earbuds without cords now."

"You don't say."

"Yup. They're called AirPods and you don't get tangled in them at the supermarket."

My cheeks no doubt flush redder at the thought of the cereal aisle. Ethan salutes me. And I consider burrowing my way into the ground.

"It's so weird," I say, instead. "It's almost like I'm an adult human who lives in the world, knows stuff and makes conscious choices for myself."

"Sure." He shrugs, dropping his gaze back to his phone. "Just questionable ones."

I almost lunge for him. A tiny black lizard shoots out from under a bush and stops in front of me, offering a frank look. It seems to favor a measured approach.

"It's too early for this," I grumble as I head toward the villa entrance.

"I'm kidding," says Ethan as I walk away. "I know you're on top of things."

I roll my eyes but also can't help but smirk. With my back to him, he'll never know.

I am all mixed emotions. I hate this—*right?*

"I'm so screwed," I whisper, and walk inside.

The day goes off without a hitch. Give or take eight thousand hitches.

The shoot is meant to begin at one of the unoccupied villas down the row, toward the most secluded end. This space looks a lot like ours, only more expansive—same neutrals accented with pops of unapologetic color. Martin is to be the subject in this primary location, both for the glossy print spread and digital components for the website. Much of the other imagery will depict wild expanses of earth and ocean, uninterrupted vistas, indoor-outdoor spaces, where nature comes in but always wipes her feet at the door. The accompanying feature Stephanie is writing for the magazine is called "Paradise Found," and it's all about how new luxury is not about ostentatious glitz and glamour. It's about unspoiled nature, true quiet and solitude, an intimate place that only, like, three people will ever experience. An Eden that will remain mostly immaculate. Like everything else in high-end editorial, at its core, it's about wish fulfillment.

The concept that Stephanie has conceived for our supporting video footage is a behind-the-scenes look at this far-flung spot, a true deserted island, before it's been seen or touched by even the most elite jet-setters. Essentially, we're filming the print shoot itself, as it's happening.

Inside the villa, Peter is busy setting up lights and sorting out sound. Jackie is styling the space to her liking, adding and subtracting objects and shifting furniture by inches, then standing back to inspect the larger picture.

The photographer is here too now, taking test shots to get a sense of the lighting. From the back, I can see that he's wearing an old-school Jane's Addiction T-shirt. But, like, a nice one. More men in perfect tees.

"Charlie," he says when I approach and introduce myself, extending his hand to give mine a firm shake. "Good to finally meet you in person."

This man is ridiculously handsome. He almost puts Ethan to shame. Hazel eyes and dark skin. Tall. Lean. And I am surprised by his friendliness. Almost alarmed. He was lovely over email and phone too, but I'm accustomed to fashion photographers who pose more than their subjects. This guy is pretension-free.

"From what Ethan has told me, I'm in great hands." Charlie smiles.

"Oh. Definitely don't trust what Ethan has told you."

"Are you sure?" He cocks his head. "'Cause he thinks you're pretty great."

I pretend to study my clipboard as I try not to blush.

I'm confirming that everything is copasetic, checking and re-checking my list and debating the best spot for our video setup with Peter, when Ethan makes an appearance. He saunters over to Charlie and gives him a pound and a bro hug, which makes me super glad I'm not a dude and I get to give people normal hugs. They chat for a minute, then he surveys the room and, apparently finding it acceptable, makes his way over to me.

"You've got everything you need?"

"I think we're in bizarrely good shape." I nod. The truth is, when you're planning a shoot on a deserted island, you really have to consider every contingency before you arrive. You can't be running to the store for safety pins and duct tape when the lone shop sells only sunblock and terry cloth beach cover-ups. "Even the photographer is in great shape."

Ethan gives me side-eye. "He's in 'great shape'? And by that you mean . . . ?"

"He's got everything under control." I shrug. "And he's so nice too."

"By 'so nice,' do you mean, 'so nice-looking'?"

I turn and glare at him. "What is wrong with you?"

How dare he! I am Professional Sasha. I don't notice super beautiful photographers! Sorry. Beautiful and *tall*.

"I'm just saying, the women, and men, tend to like Charlie. Maybe he's your type too?"

He stuffs his hands in his pockets, all casual, like my answer couldn't matter less. But the way he bites his lip suggests something else.

It's too easy to mess with him.

"And if he is? My type? What do you care?"

"Just making conversation." Ethan shrugs. Flustered, he rubs the back of his neck.

Whatever game we're playing, in this instance, I am winning! Not that Professional Sasha cares.

"Whatever," Ethan says. "Anyway, we play basketball together."

"Oh yeah?" I say. "Did you box him out one too many times?"

"What?"

"Foul him too hard?"

"Sorry?"

"Dunk on him and then assuage your guilt by offering him a job?"

"Ah, I see," says Ethan, rolling his eyes. "Like you think I did for you. Job opportunities in exchange for guilt. Very funny."

"I am funny."

"Sometimes unintentionally."

I shoot him a death stare. Why is he standing right next to me? Is it warm in here? I can't focus. It's not helping that he smells good, like that mowed-grass cologne. I pull my (literally rose-colored) sunglasses down over my eyes. *Boundaries.*

From across the room, I see Derek watching us and wringing his hands. *What is he so worried about?*

"Interesting though," Ethan says.

"What's interesting?" I say.

"You look at me and you think I can dunk." He flexes his tricept.

"Oh *Lord.*"

That's when Stephanie walks in. Finally. She is definitely wearing dark sunglasses and all that implies. But she's here, and she's got coffee in her hand. She spots us and raises her cup in cheers.

I wave.

An hour—and many random requests of the hotel staff—later, we're all set up and good to go, only Martin is nowhere to be found. One contingency for which we did not plan. An egomaniacal retired movie star with a probable drinking problem.

Stephanie volunteers to set off with his staff—mainly Michael—and try to rouse him. Forty-five minutes later, once we are officially behind for the day, Stephanie and Martin pull up in a golf cart together with matching nauseated expressions.

The dust outside literally settles.

"It's that last glass of wine that gets you," Stephanie is saying to me, as the makeup artist begins prepping Martin. "It's always that last glass of wine."

We need to get Martin ready quickly. Charlie keeps checking his watch and looking at the sky out the windowed doors. His assistant, a local from Provo—the most bustling of the Turks and Caicos islands—keeps checking and rechecking the setup. But Martin is in no mood. He growls at everyone who approaches. The makeup artist, who is on staff at the hotel spa, is barely holding back tears.

"What's wrong with you?!" I hear Martin yelp; we all hear him. "I look like a two-bit hooker!" I think he means *sex worker*.

Normally, we handle photography first, as the main event, then capture the behind-the-scenes video footage as unobtrusively as possible during and afterward, but Charlie, Peter and I huddle up and decide to reverse the order and try to get Martin warmed up first. Maybe he'll be more amenable after his coffee has had time to work its magic.

Once I've talked the makeup artist down from the brink of quitting, Peter asks permission to mic Martin and begins tossing him softball questions for starters.

"Had you spent time in Turks and Caicos before finding this spot?"

"Why build this here and not closer to LA, in Hawaii or Mexico, for example?"

The legendary star of the silver screen is not having it. Armed with more formal questions that Stephanie has created for us, everyone tries to no avail. Everyone. Even Ethan. Martin won't budge. He is noncompliant. A toddler gone limp in his mother's arms.

By design, I am last up. I am our clutch hitter. Sure, I'm a seasoned producer. But, more important, I have weathered two small children by myself, even during the lost Elmo debacle of 2021. There is no irrational baby I can't lull.

I pull an Eames-style chair up in front of the man, who is still wearing his sunglasses. He folds his hairy arms over his giant chest. He looks like an obstinate tree stump.

"Martin, hi. How *are* you?"

He sniffs at me. "I didn't realize you cared. You've left me to all these amateurs! Aren't you supposed to be running the show?"

"I apologize, Martin." I frown sympathetically. "Of course, you deserve the very best and also my personal focus. I've been making sure the shoot itself runs smoothly. But I'm here, with you, now."

He huffs, but I can see his shoulders relax as I explain that we're basically getting behind-the-scenes footage and want him to be the star. "No one knows this property, this place, like you do," I say. "No one can talk about it with the same depth of understanding and evocative language."

I basically throw up in my mouth as I say this, but it's part of the job when dealing with difficult talent. I am equal parts organizer and mediator.

"Well, that's true," he harrumphs. "But I'm not going to describe it to some Neanderthal cameraman!"

Peter went to Vassar. He is definitely not a Neanderthal.

"I understand," I say. "It's you and me now."

He raises an overgrown eyebrow at that. Tilts his head to one side and narrows his gaze. "Alone at last."

I fear this is his *come hither* look. And I am not going anywhere near hither.

Surreptitiously, I signal to Peter to start filming. He signals everyone else to go quiet.

"Martin," I say, "as such an iconic actor, you've no doubt had the opportunity to visit incredible places all over the world. What drew you here, in particular, and inspired you to create this unique property? When you first saw the island, what did you think?"

"I didn't think," he snaps. "That's entirely the point. I *felt*. I believe in that above all else—trusting how something feels. As it enters your body."

The way he is petting the arm of his chair is more than a little disturbing. He reminds me of a cartoon supervillain. Which he kind of is. A megalomaniac with nefarious intentions.

"Of course, a deserted island is a kind of trope or . . . a *fantasy*," I continue, cringing as soon as I use the word. I have played into his trap. I see him react, eyebrows raised, but I soldier on. "In your mind, what makes this particular island unique?"

"This island is truly . . . virginal," he purrs. I think he's going to say more about the privilege of deflowering something untouched, but he has said his piece. Thank God.

Our interview goes on like that. Revolting innuendos woven throughout. My hope is that, edited and without context, his words will be usable.

At the end, I throw him a final easy question about the locals, a chance to talk up the property's green initiatives and collaborations with makers collectives. "I know you and your team of designers and architects have put a lot of thought into protecting the environment here and indigenous species like the charcoal lizard. Not only is this property sustainable, but it's LEED certified. Why was the environmental element important to you? What about the culture here? How are you involving the locals?"

"Oh, I love the people here!" he says. "And they love me!"

I steal a glance at the local makeup artist, who has finally stopped hyperventilating.

"They're very welcoming and thrilled to have us. Especially since we have made it our personal mission to protect their land, keeping it groomed, fertile and succulent. Working with these people is much easier than navigating Hollywood, for example." He leans in, covering his mic, and whispers so the sound won't catch it: "The Jews."

I freeze. I cannot have heard him right.

"Sorry—what?"

"The *Jews.* You know how it is."

I stand up. This is my limit. "I am literally Jewish," I say.

He scans me from top to bottom. "It's okay," he says.

"No," I shake my head. "It is absolutely not."

So ends our love affair.

We get the footage we need, and Charlie gets his initial photos for print, which look vibrant and luminous. If Martin ends up looking terrible (physically and fundamentally), then there is justice in the world. I wonder if Ethan has qualms about what a shit bag this guy is.

The rest of the day is mercifully Martin-free. He retires to his residence on the other side of the island, and we break for lunch. A buffet—an embarrassment of multicolored riches on rows of tables adorned with tropical flowers—is waiting at the restaurant.

Beside me on the buffet line, Ethan readies to take a plate of food back to the villa, grumbling about work to catch up on. Of course he takes only the salads and fruit. Not a fritter on his plate. In contrast, mine is a culinary revelation: fried food, ten ways.

He looks from my plate to his. Raises his eyebrows. Says nothing.

Wise man. But it's also sort of unlike him to pass up a prime opportunity to give me shit.

I surreptitiously study his face. His brow is creased. He looks stressed. During the shoot, I'd noticed him hammering away on his phone off to the side. I'm tempted to ask him what's up, but it feels like none of my beeswax.

He grabs a utensil-napkin roll-up and turns to head out. I shouldn't care that he's leaving. His absence can only make life less complicated for me. I can eat my lunch in peace. And yet I'm a bit bummed to see him go. Who else am I going to mock and heckle?

"You ditching us plebes?" I say, as he starts toward the stairs.

"No choice," he says, without breaking stride. "I'm all tied up."

Point, Demon Dad. I will be hearing this for the rest of my life. Or at least whenever in his presence.

The rest of the crew piles a cornucopia of tropical fruit, conch fritters, coconut shrimp and papaya salad onto plates. There is a gluttonous sweet and sour sauce, a thin hot pepper marinade that stains the plate orange and a vinegar-and-lime dressing with pickled pink onions that I consider mainlining.

We've got a mandated hour break and, though we are still a bit behind, I'm glad for it. I need to decompress post-Martin. I'm still considering whether to bring up what he said with the *Escapade* staff, since I'm not sure if any of them heard. On one hand, it was unacceptable. On the other, I don't want to blow up this whole project and risk losing the larger opportunity. If I tell my coworkers and they do nothing, where does that leave me—with them but also with my own moral compass?

I sit down at a table, shaded by a large umbrella, with Jackie, Derek and Stephanie, then order a passion fruit iced tea. Make it a double. It arrives adorned with sprigs of fresh green mint. Heaven.

Martin is a scumbag, but the place is special.

"Do you mind if I join you?" asks Charlie, approaching our table with a more measured plate of food than mine.

We all hustle to make room. Because we are courteous. And also he is not unhot. Not that Professional Sasha cares.

"It's so good to finally meet you in person," I tell him as he settles next to me. "Have you guys all worked together before?"

"Actually, I don't think so," says Charlie, surveying the group.

"You'd remember," says Stephanie, sliding a chunk of pineapple off a toothpick with her teeth.

"I'm sure that's true." He laughs.

"Where has Ethan been hiding you?" she asks.

"It's not his fault, actually. I spent a bunch of years working with mostly dive magazines. Lots of underwater and on-the-water stuff.

So, I've been here in Turks and Caicos many times, but never with *Escapade*."

"So, you scuba dive?" Derek asks.

"Whenever I can."

"And you know Ethan from some basketball game?" I say.

"Well, partially, yes. A weekly game. But I've also worked with him on editorial before. And we've become good friends."

We all nod agreeably, and Charlie thinks he finally has a window to pick up his fork and go to town on his lunch, when I say: "So, what kind of basketball player is he? Shit talker? Enforcer? Ball hog?"

I look up from my plate.

They're all staring at me like I'm out-of-bounds (okay, fine, pun intended). I hope they're thinking I know a bizarre amount of basketball lingo and not that I'm overly curious about Ethan.

Which I am *not*. This is purely for research purposes.

"Wow," says Charlie, now fully grinning. "I won't mess with you on the court! No, he's a great athlete and, okay, also a shit talker. But you know that, right? Aren't you guys running buddies?"

This catches me off guard, and I feel like I'm denying something torrid when I say, "Us? Me and Ethan? No. Like not at all. Not even a little bit. Like, no." I shove something giant, fried and round into my mouth to stop myself from talking.

"Oh, my bad. I thought I saw you guys coming in from a run on the way to my room this morning."

I am shaking my head but am rendered speechless by the enormous amount of food I am trying to chew. I wish to God they would all look away, so I could spit it out. I gesture with my hand in a way that communicates nothing. "Mmm—negh, nmph," I try. "NO!" I finally manage, a hand covering my mouth, so no one has to witness the atrocity.

Jackie giggles, her hoop earrings winnowing. I kick her playfully under the table.

"But you do run?"

"Yes," I say, once I have finally swallowed, thank goodness. "I'm not a real runner though. I'm like, Runner Lite. Ethan seems pretty serious."

The whole table is nodding.

"He is definitely intense about the running," says Derek, with a meaningful look.

"OMG with the running! Don't even get me started!" Stephanie rolls her eyes. "Ever since he wrote that feature about the barefoot runners in Kenya, it's like stride cadence, stride length, heart rate blah blah blah." She mimes nodding off.

"He's always trying to recruit people too," Jackie says. "Like, why is it necessary to proselytize? You do you! I'll stick to Pilates. I want to keep my knees."

Now they're all starting to snicker.

"Oh, wow. This is edifying," I say. "I ran into him at the park once and he tried to give me some tip about how to hold my arms and, ever since, he won't let it go!"

I have hit on something true. Because now they're all fully cracking up. Even Derek quakes silently, tears streaming from his eyes. And the funny thing is you can feel the fondness. All I can think as they roast him is, *They love this man.*

Charlie is shaking his head and grinning. "Oh, man. I feel like a traitor right now. But it's so true!"

As the laugher devolves into sighs, we return to our food. I'm practicing taking small bites now, traumatized by Fritter-Gate. Maybe I'm done with lunch. Maybe the dessert table—with its chocolate parfaits and mini key lime pies—is calling my name.

"In Ethan's defense though," says Charlie, as I'm about to stand up, "I think he was dealing with some difficult stuff around that same time as the Kenya article. Seems like the running helps him cope."

I am going nowhere. Glued to my seat. First of all, I relate to this. Second, who needs dessert when there's dish?

"True." Derek nods solemnly.

"Mmm," Jackie agrees.

"Is that right?" Stephanie cocks her head to the side. "Was that the same time? It feels like he's been at the magazine forever, but I guess it hasn't been that long."

I am intrigued. And also clueless.

"Was what at the same time?"

"Oh, you know," says Jackie. "The challenges. Which coincided with Ethan coming on as editor. And the running article."

"Challenges?"

"With *her*."

Oh, now I'm getting it.

"That witch," says Stephanie.

And now I'm really getting it.

"We probably shouldn't . . . ," says Derek.

"And yet, we are," says Stephanie. "She understands," she continues, leaning in toward Charlie. "She's divorced too."

This she is me. And now all eyes are on her. Me.

"I am," I say. "It's true. Divorced as charged." Jazz hands.

Derek raises his eyebrows. "I assumed you were married," he blurts out. He looks relieved. Why does he look relieved? "Because of the kids. Sorry."

"Oh. No. Well, I mean, I was married. And now I am happily *un*married."

I hate this. When people get awkward around the *d* word. It makes me want to say what my kids call "the *f* word."

Despite the umbrella and the lovely breeze, it's pretty hot at the height of the day. The sun is lording over the sky, threatening to scorch us. My thighs are suctioned to my seat.

And they're all looking at me with sympathetic—yet curious—expressions. Except Stephanie. She is leaning in without apology.

"Was he an asshole too?" she says. "Your husband?"

"Too?"

"Like the nightmare Ethan divorced."

Honestly, thank God for this woman. Filterless Stephanie. She just says the thing.

I let out a sharp laugh. "Oh, right. Yes. Mine was an asshole too. *Is* an asshole. Continues to be. On an ongoing basis."

Sometimes I make excuses for Cliff. I say things like, "He does what he can. He does his best. He's a complicated person. He's not a bad man." Not today, Cliff. Not today.

Something about Stephanie is freeing me up.

She presses a manicured hand to my forearm. "Isn't he some sort of bigwig screenwriter? About to direct some huge Ryan Reynolds project? I keep hearing about it."

I am stunned out of my reverie. Someone has done her homework.

"What?" says Stephanie, as Derek shoots her a chiding look. "Am I the only one who googled her?"

Her is me again.

"He cheated on you also, right?"

"You don't have to answer that," says Charlie, his nose scrunched in distaste. But he is looking at me like he'd kind of like to know.

Normally, any reference to the Golden Globes or that seat filler makes me want to hide. I'm not big on public displays of humiliation. But I am way too intrigued now by the word *also* to care.

"It's fine," I say, taking a sip of my iced tea. "We were really already over by the time my ex . . . did whatever he did. At least, as far as I know. Why? Did Ethan's ex-wife cheat on him?"

This is surprising to me. Very surprising. I'm not sure why. Maybe because he seems like a keeper. Maybe because of how he looks in a T-shirt or all wet in a supermarket aisle. Maybe because he doesn't seem disposable, the way—I realize in this moment—maybe I feel.

When I pictured his wife, I envisioned a woman who was quietly angry, resenting the way he didn't help. Not a philanderer.

"Yup. She cheated. With some guy she dated in high school! One of those fucked-up stories you hear about reconnecting on social. Emotional affair turns real. Midlife crisis. So basic. You know the drill."

Do I? I guess so. I know the trope anyway. But that is so not how I pictured Ethan's broken marriage. I pictured flirting turned to bickering turned to sniping turned to separate lives. Maybe separate beds? I pictured values changing, clashing parenting styles, the quiet desperation of figuring out what to make for dinner. Every. Single. Night.

I have more questions. Many. And I am about to ask them when Jackie lets out a bloodcurdling scream. By the time my eyes catch up to the action, she is standing on her chair, holding on to the sun umbrella like a life preserver.

A gargantuan lizard is staring up at her with interest. It ticks its head back and forth between her and the ground like an automaton.

"It ran over my foot!" she yelps.

In her defense, it is the grand master of lizards. It is enormous. And it's taking a special interest in her like when cats snuggle up to someone who is allergic. In its defense, her behavior could be considered alarming to a creature unfamiliar with human neurosis.

"Ah," says Michael, approaching as if from nowhere. "You have met one of our friends from the iguana sanctuary. They're endangered, and Mr. Bernard is helping to protect them."

Jackie looks like she'd like to finish the species off. "Can you please make it leave?"

I look at my phone. Shoot. I need to make us leave too. It's time to get back to work.

Our next setup is at the pimped-out spa and that, plus the absence of Martin, makes the work more chill. After that, we'll shoot back at the restaurant and the activity shed.

The weather and lighting cooperates. Derek—who apparently has a heavily trafficked Instagram platform chronicling his and his husband's baking endeavors—has been charged with taking some vertical videos for the magazine's social platforms. They come out pretty cool.

Charlie is pleased with the photos for the official glossy spread, after a cursory look through them. Unfortunately, Peter and I are less jazzed about the video content. Somehow, the very thing that makes this place so beautiful—how minimal and neutral and stripped down it feels—isn't coming across. It just looks flat and barren. And about as flavorful as Whole Foods–prepared foods. It feels like featuring negative space.

Though the still photos work without models, our footage doesn't.

Peter, Stephanie, Derek and I are huddled around the camera's playback, shaking our heads, biting our lips and sighing.

"It lacks life," I say.

"We could shoot some footage of the iguanas," suggests Peter.

Jackie shudders.

"This is the problem with shooting on a deserted island," I say. "You've only got what you've got."

"Anyone got a couple models on them?" asks Stephanie. She has plucked a rose quartz roller from the spa boutique's beauty display and is running it back and forth across her forehead.

"No supermodels in my pocket, sadly," I say.

"Okay. Fine. Catalog models, then."

"I've done some modeling," says Peter.

"Hilarious!" says Stephanie, and I grin too. But he doesn't crack a smile.

"Oh," says Stephanie, rearranging her face. "Of course you have."

"Steph, put that away," says Derek, pointing to the crystal roller. "Those are for guests to buy. We're not meant to sample them."

She rolls her eyes. But, sheepish, she puts the beauty tool back in its velvet case for some unsuspecting future guest to purchase. And that's when I have my light bulb moment.

"Okay, I might have an idea. Hear me out."

All eyes are on me. I am grateful that at least Ethan is staying out of it, leaning against a wall at the back, on his phone.

He's doing work, I think. He has his email face on. It's one of many of his expressions I'm coming to learn. I shake my head clear.

"The whole crux of what makes this place—and our ability to

feature it—special is that it's as yet unspoiled by the very spoiled. Right? We're here first! Even before the one percent."

"Okay?" says Stephanie. "And?"

"And everyone loves a glimpse behind the curtain. So, what if we give the viewers one? What if, for the video and digital element, we mess around a little and feature Stephanie using that gua sha and lounging in the infrared sauna? Jackie sneaking a cocktail at the bar? Derek at the dessert buffet? And on from there?"

Jackie scrunches up her nose. "Would anyone want to see that?"

"Of course they would!" Stephanie says, tossing her hair over her shoulder. Joking, not joking.

"I think it might work," Derek agrees. "Just the whole aspirational element of getting to fuck around in this super swanky place. It could be kind of addictive to watch. In the vein of unboxing videos?"

"It's kind of our only option. And the worst thing that happens is that it looks bad, so we fall back on the other B-roll footage and chop it up into bite-size chunks to make it feel more dynamic."

Everyone is nodding. I am way less confident than I seem. What if it's a disaster? What if I fail at this one shot to impress the team?

To impress . . . Ethan?

As makeup begins touching up Stephanie for the spa shoot, I feel half like Ms. Marvel and half like Miss Muffet. Am I a hero? Or a colossal fraud?

Time will tell.

At least Stephanie looks at home reclining in her plush white robe, her frizz-free hair framing her face. And she does a great job of hamming it up. The footage is strong. Hopefully everyone will be this good.

After the spa shoot, when we ready to move on to the restaurant, she heads out to go conduct her big interview with Martin at his home for the article.

"Text me if you need *anything*," I tell her as she packs up her tote. She insists on being alone with him so he'll "open up." I think he's likely harmless, but I still don't love it.

"I got this," she says, winking.

Soon after she leaves, my phone vibrates in my pocket. I duck out to answer, blinking as my eyes adjust to the sun.

"Hello?"

"Hi, love!"

It's Martin's publicist, Barbara. I recognize this ploy. I am definitely "love" because she's drawing a blank on my name—just like I'm "Mom" at school pick-up.

"Hi, *Barbara*," I can't help but say pointedly. "How are you?"

"Remarkable! You? I wanted to check in."

"I'm okay. Look, this is awkward, but you should know that Martin made some very offensive anti-Semitic remarks to me earlier."

"Yes, yes," she says.

"And he's pretty inappropriate with the ladies too."

"Right, yes."

This is not the response I expected. Or what makes sense conversationally. So I say, "Does that surprise you to hear?"

After a beat of silence, Barbara says, "It'sss . . ." She trails off, a balloon deflating. It takes me a minute to realize her thought will not be completed.

"Um," I say into the deafening silence. "Well, we did complete his portion of the photo shoot and video interview today and hopefully got what we need."

"Wonderful," Barbara breathes. "Well, I better run! Enjoy, love!"

And then she is gone. I stare at my phone, but it's not at fault. This is how people get away with horrible behavior. This is how it continues unchecked. Everyone is afraid to rock the boat.

The restaurant is surrounded on three sides by ocean. At night, it was too dark to see much and, during the day, I've been too busy to notice. Now, I stare at the horizon and lose myself in turquoise water as it glimmers and swells, hoping for an epiphany. Some people find this meditative. It just makes me crave a blue raspberry Blow Pop.

An iguana creeps out from behind a nearby banquette. Are they really endangered? It feels like there are four million of them! This one scurries up onto the seat. It is spectacular in all its prehistoric glory against the tangerine cushion. A miniature Godzilla. Jackie would be horrified, but I kind of like this guy. I think Nettie and Bart would too.

I snap a quick picture. Then, we connect for a moment, eyeing each other in interspecies communion. I lose our staring contest. After all, there is work to be done. Work this iguana won't ever see or understand, unless he's into oxygen facials.

I have an irrational urge to play Turks and Caicos geography with this guy. Maybe he knows my stingray. But then Derek calls me back inside.

At the end of the day, you can stick a fork in me. I am toast. Which you don't even eat with a fork. Whatever. Suffice it to say, I am very tired.

We are still a bit behind, but we are losing light. So, at 5:30 p.m., I confer with Charlie and then call it.

A bunch of the others are heading to the bar for a much-needed margarita. Even Peter agrees to join. I do love a post-shoot download and the restaurant's guacamole—which I know comes with pome-granate seeds—is calling to me. But it will have to wait. I've got a hot FaceTime date with my kids, and I miss their sloppy faces.

When I leave to head back to the villa, there is no one to boo me, though Jackie makes a sad face at my departure, then waves in slo-mo. Derek shoots me a warm smile, all the more appreciated for its rarity. Stephanie has been absent since she left for her interview with Martin. If she doesn't materialize soon, I might organize a search party.

It's still warm out, of course, but the light is settling once we've broken all the equipment down and said our goodbyes. I push my sunglasses off my face and perch them on my head so I can see the true colors. It's an exceptional thing to walk "home" from work barefoot on slatted wooden walkways dusted with sand. The still-damp shore has been hung out to dry as the tide recedes. Only a bit more than a day in, I am growing used to a world without the roar of engines and car stereos; without strangers and overheard snippets of conversation; where the only abrasion is the grains of sand exfoliating the bottom of your feet.

Through the window of our villa, I can see the light glowing yellow. There is a moment when the outside grows darker than in, and I am there to witness it. It's not fall here. Not in the way I know it, anyway. There are no browning leaves or crisp breezes with edges that cut. There are certainly no knit hats and gloves. But something about this time of day feels autumnal. It's nostalgic though I've never lived it before. And from somewhere, probably the outdoor barbecue pit by the restaurant, the smell of fireplace wafts and seduces. Oh, right. Michael mentioned something about "island-inspired" s'mores.

When I step inside, I discover Ethan sitting in one of the deep armchairs, his laptop on his lap. He is wearing reading glasses I've never seen before. And he is frowning at his screen. I didn't expect to find him still here, but, when he looks up and meets my eyes, it feels familiar. Natural. Good. He shoots me a small smile.

"Nice glasses," I say.

He frowns again, takes this as an insult. Which I guess I intended. But the truth is, I like them.

And, against my better judgment, maybe him?

He takes off the glasses and inspects them like an alien intruder. Like they just showed up on his face of their own volition. "Yeah. I finally gave in."

"That's wise. Rather than being blind."

"I guess so," he grunts. "You guys wrapped?"

"We did," I say, taking my sunglasses off my head and my bag off my shoulder and resting both on the kitchen island. "We're a little behind, but I think we'll catch up tomorrow."

"And?"

"And what?"

"How do you think it went?"

I am not accustomed to downloads like this. I live with two small children and one oversize cat. There are no adults around to ask me about my day. And, before that, I got used to Cliff's disinterest in anything beyond himself. He was not the sort of man who asked after my day. Of course, Ethan is being thoughtful and also looking after the project. These are normal things to do. But I am momentarily stymied by the crushing realization that I have spent too many years on my own or playing second fiddle. I have let too many years pass with my head down. I've gone too many evenings without anyone asking me about me.

It is so obvious. And everyone who loves me has tried to tell me. My parents. Celeste. Even Nettie, who recently asked me for the first time why I "never get crushes." But it is in this moment, as I lower myself into the corner of this immaculate linen sectional beside Ethan's chair, that the knowledge actually roots. In this moment, I believe it.

Which is why I forget to speak. And glance up to find Ethan studying me intently. "Are you okay?"

"Yes! Sorry," I say. "I think it went well."

"Okay, good. You're sure you're okay?"

"Positive," I say, softened by his concern. "Just tired." I lean back against the sofa and sigh to put some distance between us. I will stay strong. Glasses be damned.

"And you're still liking working with Charlie?"

"Charlie? Totally. He's amazing!"

"Amazing," Ethan repeats.

"Why?"

"No reason." Ethan shrugs. "Charlie is great."

"Yup," I agree, widening my eyes. Ethan is being weird, so I make it weirder. "He said you also think I'm *great*."

Ethan's cheeks flush. He looks caught. For once, I am not the one off-balance. He shakes his head and shrugs simultaneously. "I mean, whatever. You know. I mean . . . your work is good."

"Don't you mean *great*?"

What is more fun than making this man uncomfortable? My new favorite hobby.

"Yeah. Fine. Great."

I can't help myself, I nudge his foot with my own. "So, you just meant my work?"

He looks up, catches my eye. Smirks. "Well, I didn't mean your cotton candy."

We eye each other for a beat. For self-preservation, why didn't I sit farther away?

Ethan clears his throat, resets. I think for my benefit. He is also trying to behave. "You didn't want to grab dinner with the others?"

"I need to call my kids."

"Ah. Me too. Soon." Ethan closes his laptop and stands up, stretching. I catch a glimpse of his abs, which will haunt my loins for eternity. "I think I'm going to grab a beer. Do you want one? Or a glass of wine . . . if Stephanie left any?"

"I think she killed the bottle."

"I meant if she left any in the whole resort."

That makes me laugh. Which makes me relax. Which makes me realize how tense I was today during the shoot.

"I'll take a beer," I say. "Sure. Thank you."

I lay out cork coasters, and he returns with the drinks, something local called Turk's Head with colorful labels. It all feels very domestic.

"To Stephanie leaving us some wine next time," he toasts.

"To Stephanie getting a good interview and then never having to talk to Martin again!" I say.

Ethan shakes his head like, *That guy.* We swig in tandem.

"There was one minor snafu today," I admit, once I've swallowed my sip. The beer tastes cool and fresh.

"Yeah? What happened?" He props his bare feet up on a nearby ottoman.

Goddammit. The man even has nice feet.

One of the glass doors is propped open and, between the gentle wind and the subtle coconut scent they pump through the vents here, I feel for a moment like I'm on vacation. With Ethan. Which kick-starts butterflies in my stomach.

"Peter and I thought the video was looking a bit . . . flat," I stumble, "but I think we found a solution."

Ethan smiles. "You mean *you* found a solution."

"How did you—?"

"I was there. I saw it go down. You should take credit for your own ideas. You took the initiative."

"Yeah, okay. I know. Fine. Thanks for the tip. What did you do, write a feature about workplace assertiveness too?"

He scrunches up his nose. "What's that supposed to mean?"

"They told me all about how you wrote an article about running and now you can't stop yourself from dispensing advice. I thought it was regular old mansplaining, but I guess giving tips is kind of your job."

He narrows his eyes. "Who told you? Who is *they*?"

"You know, Jackie, Derek, Stephanie, Charlie . . ."

"Oh Lord," he says, running a hand along his stubbled cheek. "What else did they tell you?"

"Nothing," I say quickly. *Certainly not the details of your failed marriage.*

I am the world's worst liar. He is onto me immediately.

"Oh, fuck. Seriously—what did they say? It's obviously something bad. Look at you! Your cheeks don't lie."

I slap a hand to either side of my face. "You don't know. Maybe it's an allergy! Alcohol makes me flushed."

"I watched you down an entire flask of bourbon at Monster's Ball and nothing."

"Hey! You drank half of that too!"

"A third, maybe. Maybe a third."

The reminder of our shared home turf feels somehow comforting, like an inside joke. We are grinning at each other. Why are we grinning? I take another swig off my beer. It's sweet and bitter on my tongue. For a moment, I let it sit and fizzle.

"No, seriously. What did they say?" he repeats, dropping his feet to the floor and leaning forward on his thighs.

I try to ignore the hint of a tan line where his shorts ride up on his upper leg. I am in his confidence. He is dangerously close to me. And there go those pheromones again.

"I need to know. It's only fair."

"Fair?"

"Yes. I have to know what they told you about me. Otherwise, our conversation is . . . imbalanced."

"That's not a thing."

"It is actually."

"Well, then, some would argue the imbalance already exists because you're kind of, like, my boss."

"You think I'm your *boss*?" He cringes.

"No. I know this is Steph and Derek's baby. But you're *their* boss!" J'accuse! "So, by the transitive property . . ."

Ethan tilts his head to one side. "Hey, Sasha," he says.

Oh, fuck. I wish he'd stop saying my name. It sends something unseemly ping-ponging through me. I cross my legs. Ignore all the tingles.

"Yes?" I manage.

"What is the transitive property?"

"I have no idea. But I still think I'm right."

"Of course you do," he says. It sounds damning, but his eyes, fixed on me, spell something else. He holds my gaze. I know I should, but I can't look away.

Suddenly, the silence is supercharged. The air that separates has texture. Can magnets attract and repel at once? I feel like I should speak, but I can't find my voice. I feel like I should move, but I am a statue. He licks his lips. I am riveted.

I flash to the fleeting feel of his lips against mine last night, and I want to relive it.

Just like that, I am leaning in again as if in a trance and, as I do, he follows suit. Little by little until we're close enough for me to notice the inkiness of his lashes, the way his eyes actually have gradations of color, hold multitudes. I am ready to fall headfirst into their depths.

His gaze drops to my chest, then sears its way back up to my lips, all lava. And that's it for me. My brain may be a holdout, but my body is in. And I am closing my eyes against reality and saying screw it, when an alarm goes off. It takes me a moment to realize it's not in my head. That there is an actual alarm sounding from Ethan's phone. We dart back to our corners. Again. And this pattern is starting to feel painfully familiar.

As he goes to grab his phone, I exhale. Shaky. What is happening here? I'm unsure. Or maybe I want to be unsure. Actually, it seems pretty damn clear.

"It's six thirty," he says, running a hand through his hair so it stands on end. "I've got to call my daughter."

"Oh, shit!" I say, shooting to standing. "I have to call my kids too."

I grab my bag from the counter and, as we cross to our adjoining rooms, we almost smash into each other, my hands landing flat on his chest.

"Sorry, sorry!" I say as I snatch them back. I am the platonic ideal of out of sorts. If that could be a platonic ideal.

The nothing that has happened is more awkward than something.

Inside my room with the door safely closed, head in my hands, I mouth a string of obscenities. I am literally vibrating. Then, I flop onto my bed, steady myself, and pull my phone out of my purse. But, just as I'm starting to dial, there's a knock at the door. Ethan pops his head in. Demon Dad. In my *bedroom*.

I sit up straight.

"Hey," he says. I have an impulse to cover up, I guess because I'm sitting on my bed, but I am fully clothed and wearing the same tank top and jean shorts I was wearing one minute before in the living room with him. "Meet you back out there afterward and we'll order room service?"

"Room service?"

"Yes. Food. That they deliver to your room. Because we skipped the group dinner. You must be hungry?"

It's true that I have eaten mostly taffy and plantain chips since lunch, since that's what we had for craft service. I realize underneath the panic and the other thing I refuse to name (let's call it "Bob"), I am ravenous. "Yes," I say. "Hungry, I am."

Have I turned into Yoda? Ethan looks at me like I've lost it.

"I think maybe I should place the order now, so we don't have to wait, actually," he says. "Any idea what you might want?"

"A burger, maybe?"

"A burger, for sure?"

"A burger, for sure."

He closes the door, shaking his head.

And, as I push the memory of the feel of his chiseled chest under my palms out of my mind, trying to ignore "Bob," I realize I am in a definite pickle.

29 | Demon Pickle

ETHAN

This woman is my kryptonite. I'm losing my damn mind.

Even after a whole day on set—where she killed it, by the way—she comes in flushed and glowing. And, in those shorts, all legs.

Then she sits down to hang out, and it's like we do this every day. She's just natural, cool. I mean, she's also totally impossible. But I like that too. And I realize, this ease—and spark, if I'm honest—is exactly what I never had with my ex-wife. We had mutual respect, even similarities. But not this.

When Sasha walks in a room, I wake up. Stand at attention in all the ways. I could talk to her for hours. For*ever*.

Then she nudges my foot, pretends she's not gawking at my legs—sorry, but it was so damn obvious. She leans in toward me, her shirt gaping in a way I barely have the willpower to ignore. And her catlike eyes go hooded when she moves to kiss me—'*cause she was about to kiss me again, right?*—and there's no way I'm saying no.

I know she said to keep it professional. I know Derek warned me too. But the saying and the doing are not matching up. And, honestly, maybe it's bad, but I couldn't be happier about it.

Charlie is the one person I confided in besides Derek.

"When was the last time you liked someone this much?" he asked, as he unpacked his suitcase. "I say go for it."

I don't want to blow this for her. I *can't* blow this for my team at the magazine. But I don't want to blow off what's brewing between us either.

Anyway, it's dinnertime. And I'm fucking starving.

TO-DO

- ~~Kill Charlie for telling Sasha I was talking about her.~~
- Thank Charlie for telling Sasha I was talking about her—maybe it worked to my advantage?
- Get out of the middle school zone and start talking to *her* about her like an actual man.
- Finish that kiss.

30 | Indecent Potatoes

SASHA

With the door safely closed again, I dial Celeste. And when she takes shape on the screen, she looks a bit harried. At least by Celeste standards. She is standing at the kitchen counter, the phone propped up, while she chops cucumbers for dinner. The universal symbol for vegetable a child will eat. Her hair is piled atop her head and, not that she ever needs a lot of makeup, but she's wearing none. Her Joan Jett T-shirt has a bloodred stain down the front.

"Celeste. Hi!"

"Hi, Sash!"

"How are things?"

"Good, good. Everything is good."

That was one too many goods to be true. I tilt my head like maybe a new perspective will give me better insight.

"That doesn't sound good."

"It is . . . good!"

"Okay, then. Good."

We eye each other for a moment. Who will break first?

It's me! Of course, it's me.

"Celeste! Be honest: Are my kids being horrible? You can tell me."

"Oh God, no. Not at all. Imagine having a child who does homework without being told!"

Nettie. She is good that way. I can take no credit. She arrived with batteries included. I want to be her when I grow up.

"I think she's actually having a good influence on Henry!"

"How about Bart?"

"He's having the time of his life. He discovered Henry's old stash of *Jurassic Park* LEGOs. He may never leave."

"Is he eating food?"

"Do pretzels count as food?"

"While I'm away? Sure!"

"Then yes! He is packed with food."

"And you're okay, otherwise?" I ask. I'm no dummy. I can tell when my bestie is off her game.

"I'm okay." She lets her smile drop.

I narrow my eyes, silently asking what's up.

"I'll tell you all about it when you get home."

This is mom code for *the kids can hear me* and/or *this is a longer story than I can squeeze in right now* and/or, finally, *if I tell you now, I will lose it, and I can't afford to lose it, so can I tell you and lose it at a designated future time?* Whatever is going on, Celeste can't go there right now.

"Got it." Message received.

In her defense, I'm not sharing the details of my dicey situation either.

"Is that my mom?" I hear a little voice say off-screen.

"It is!" says Celeste. "Here, Bart, let me set you up with my phone in your bedroom, okay? So you can talk to her!"

"Which one is my bedroom again?" he asks. Classic. I drop my head in my hands, cracking up.

"Nettie! Nettie! Mommy's on the phone!" he calls.

"Oh, okay. One second," comes the much more distracted disembodied voice of my eight-year-old.

I am treated to some trippy visuals as the phone is carried into Celeste's guest room and propped against what I imagine is a stack of books atop the side table. Bart's face comes into view. Or at least a section of it does.

"Mommy!"

"Hi, Bonk!" I say. I want to eat him. "How are you?"

"Good," he says, settling down on the bed across from the phone. He's already wearing his favorite wild-animal pajamas. He grabs Elmo and cuddles the raggedy red thing.

"How was school today? Did you do anything special?"

"Um, I forget." He looks at the ceiling while he thinks. "Oh, I played zombie fighters with Chris and Palmetto!"

"Palmetto? Who is Palmetto?"

"Mom! You know! In my class. He sits at the red table."

"There's a kid in your class named Palmetto?"

How have I missed this deeply Brooklyn detail?

"Yeah. At least, I think that's his name."

"I'm sure it is."

This mom version of me, I can do. This me, I understand.

From afar, I see Nettie walk in and close the door behind her. She's wearing a black sweater and bell-bottom jeans we just bought a few weeks ago. Is it possible she looks older and more beautiful than two days before?

"Hi, Mom!" She grins.

"Are you having fun, Net?"

"Totally. It's a blast!"

"Getting along with Henry?"

"Oh, totally. Also, remember I told you about that small-moments writing unit we started? Guess who got theirs read aloud by the teacher?!"

"Nettie did!" Bart exclaims.

"Ugh, Bart!" she growls, turning to him. "I was trying to tell Mommy. That was my news to share!"

Bart shrugs. "Oops."

She rolls her eyes. "Anyway. As I was saying before I was so rudely interrupted . . ."

Until I had Bart, I never understood when parents complained that they could never get their kids to share about their school days. Nettie has always shared every detail. And I mean—Every. Single. Detail. Which is to say that she spends the next ten minutes delivering a monologue about the poor behavior of the boys in her class, the kickball game she rocked at recess and the drama between two of her girlfriends over jobs for a babysitters club they're starting (not that they have any clients). She is about to tell me the entire plot of the animated otter movie she, Bart and Henry just watched when Celeste pops her head in and tells the kids dinner is ready.

"We should go!" says Nettie, already getting up. "C'mon, Bart."

"Wait, one thing," I say. "Have you gotten to do any of the fun things on your list? Have you had Jamie's famous popcorn?"

"No, actually," says Nettie, frowning. "We haven't seen Jamie at all since he picked us up on the first day. I guess he's away or something." Then she leans down toward the phone, makes her eyes wide and whispers, "It's a bit weird."

Alarm bells are going off in my head, but I've got to respect Celeste's boundaries. At least for today.

"Okay," I say. "Hey, Nettie. Be easy with Celeste, okay?"

"Of course, Mom! I know how hard it is," she says, shrugging.

"How hard what is?"

"To be a woman alone!" she says. "Love you!"

With that mic drop, she goes off to find Henry, leaving Bart behind. He smiles at me and lumbers toward the phone, mischief in his eyes. I know that look. He is aching to press the red button (a.k.a. hang up on me).

"I love you, Bart!" I say, before he cuts me off.

"Love you, too, Mommy! Oh," he says, his finger hovering above the button. "I forgot to ask—"

"Yes?"

"Are you having a good trip?"

I melt. I am a puddle. It's too much cuteness to bear. It occurs to me that I have underestimated my children. In fact, for the past few years, I have not been so entirely alone.

• • • •

I get off the phone and text Celeste.

> I love you. Thank you. I hope you have a wipe nearby to clean Bart's grimy fingerprints off your phone. Who knows where they've been. And, when you're ready to share, I'm here to talk.

All I get is a thumbs-up.

That will have to be enough for now.

When I get up the courage and emerge from my room, the food has already arrived. I am hungry like the wolf. Ethan—well, more likely Michael, who has come and gone—has spread our dinner out elegantly on the patio table.

"I thought it might be nice to eat outside." Ethan gestures toward the setup.

"Very nice," I say.

Too nice, I think.

There are twinkle lights and sea breezes. The lingering smell of sunscreen. Island flora abounds. We are literally eating under a palm frond. Once I sit down, I kick my shoes off and bury my toes in the now cool sand. I'm just waiting for a cartoon iguana to pop its head out and serenade us.

It is, in a word, *romantic*.

Luckily, if anyone knows how to destroy a mood, it's me.

"They sent a pitcher of rum punch," Ethan says, as he sits down. "Do you want some?"

"Yes," I say. "No," I say. "Yes," I say again.

It seems like a bad idea. So bad, it's good.

"You're going to have to translate that response."

"Yes. Thank you. I would love some rum punch."

As he pours the red stuff into my glass, ice clinking cheerfully against the sides, I take the metal lid off my room service dish. The burger is enormous, thank God, but it comes with a salad. *Salad?* I wilt like day-old lettuce. Ethan reads me instantly.

"I got us a side of fries to share too." He uncovers another metal dish at center to reveal enough french fries for an army—or just me. *Voilà!*

My hero.

I figure he'll be eating something heart-healthy like wild-caught salmon and ready myself for a lecture on the environmental impact of greenhouse emissions from beef, not to mention the clogging of essential arteries, but he has actually ordered the same thing.

"The way you're looking at that burger kind of scares me," Ethan says. "But also brings me joy."

"Pleasure and pain. Two sides of the same coin."

I take a large sip of my rum punch. It is not weak.

"Do you mind if I . . . ?" I say, crouched at the starting line ready to dig in.

"Not at all."

And we're off! The next few minutes are depraved and borderline indecent. I eat the fuck out of that burger.

When I come up for air, Ethan is watching me, smirking. "Wow."

"What?"

"Nothing. I'm just impressed, that's all."

"Don't shame me!"

"I wouldn't dare! I just know the real deal when I see it."

"Oh, please," I scoff, waving his comment away with my hand. "You haven't even seen me attack the french fries yet."

"I look forward to it."

"As do I."

I drink some more rum punch. And some more. This stuff is dangerous. It's sweet but strong. Like me, I think, and crack myself up. This is the first sign that I am in trouble.

"How was your daughter?" I ask, semi-soberly.

Should I be asking? My buzz is making me reckless. I've literally never asked him a single question about his kid. Not her class. Not her name. And, though it's been an unconscious choice, I realize suddenly it's because I want to keep things separate. Our time here. Our complicated lives at home. As soon as I know details, I can't unknow them.

"Fine." Ethan smiles easily, the twinkle lights illuminating the dreamy angles of his face. It's a really nice face. "I talk to her every day when I'm away."

"Do you travel a lot?" See how I switch gears? Rum makes me crafty. I'm workshopping that theory.

"Less now. I used to travel all the time. And have work events most evenings."

"You *had* to slow down or you *chose* to slow down?"

"I think both," he says, staring at his hands. "I just never said no to a flashy party or trip back in the day."

"I bet your wife loved that. Out every night." I point a finger at him. "I bet you never did pick-up."

"I still never do pick-up. But at least now I do drop-off." He frowns sheepishly. "If I'm honest, in retrospect, I think I may have been trying to escape my marriage. Now that things have shifted and I'm around more, I realize how unbalanced it was. And what I was missing."

"So much mac and cheese."

"Excuse me?"

"That's what you were missing. Primarily. At least, that's what my ex-husband misses at our house." I am trying to lighten the mood, but it is interesting to hear his perspective—a reformed workaholic dad.

"I like mac and cheese," he says.

"You know," I say, "for what it's worth, we all think we don't have it as parents sometimes. We all feel like we're doing it wrong."

"I think that all the time," he says, nodding. "But then I remember that my friend Bruiser from college has kids and I think: *How bad can I be?*"

I laugh. We smile at each other. And, looking across the table at him, I have to admit to myself that, yes, he's hot as hell. But it's not just that. I kind of love talking to him. It's so comfortable, but also entertaining.

"In all seriousness," I say, "it's hard to give up your freedom. To stop going out and having those kinds of adventures."

"It is. But I've become more of a homebody in my old age."

The same is true for me. And yet I can't help but think about the difference between me and Ethan, despite the apparent similarities in our circumstances and in our worldview. I realize—even as we chat easily about the challenges of being away from our kids, about the way that having a kid changes you, even as he nods in understanding—that he has no real idea what I mean. Whether or not he travels is a choice; it's not a circumstance. I gave up my "freedom" the moment Nettie was born. He had to get there. And getting there is "growth." I can tell his career always took precedence in his household by the way he talks about *opting* to stay home more often.

Even now, his ex-wife—cheater or no—takes his kid when he goes away. His daughter's biggest disruption while he's gone is her parents switching custodial days. She sleeps in her regular bed, among her own things, eats her broccoli prepared per usual and the usual array of snacks. Ethan likely is not responsible for organizing anything at all before he leaves—no childcare, no meals, no reminders or schedules for school assignments. No procuring socks for major events like Silly Sock Day. Even divorced, he has someone to carry the bulk of his mental load. This is a gender thing, but it's also the chasm created by my particular deadbeat-ex predicament.

As if in hallelujah, my phone *bings* with a text. I look down and, with a start, realize it's from Cliff, of all people. His ears must be burning! His stupid oversize ears. Twice in one week. To what do I owe this glorious gift?

"Ugh!" I groan more loudly and obviously than I would have before all the rum punch.

"What is it?" Ethan asks.

"My ex . . ."

"What does he want?"

"What *doesn't* he want?"

"To parent?" says Ethan, who is also clearly a little tipsy.

"So true! Shall I read it aloud?"

"Please do."

"'Sash! Baby!'" I read, as I mime gagging. "'Are you per chance on some Caribbean island with Martin Bernard?'"

"Ugh. How does he know?" I ask Ethan.

He shrugs. Beats him. "Does he talk to any of your friends . . . per chance?"

I shake my head, giggling. I got the friends in the divorce. The good ones, anyway.

> I am indeed on an island. How did you know?

The dots appear instantly. He is a greyhound on the star-fucking scent. Cliff doesn't miss a chance to "network."

> I follow ESCAPADE on IG. They posted a pic from there and you're in it. How come?

> I'm producing some content for them.

> Wow. Sash. So cool! We're actually thinking of casting Martin Bernard in the Ryan Reynolds project. He's looking to resurrect his career and . . .

I look up at Ethan, who is waiting patiently. "I actually need to put this away before I throw my phone into the ocean."

"Fair enough," he says. "I'll put mine away too."

We both set our devices in the middle of the table, face down. Like it's a poker bet. I take a moment to appreciate where I am. I tip my head back. The warm wind feels like a new start on my skin.

When was the last time I felt this relaxed?

"Your ex-husband seems like a piece of"—Ethan hesitates—"work." He almost says *shit*. That would have been more accurate.

"Oh, he is! He sucks." I nod, throwing up my hands. "He's a no good, irresponsible, cheesy cheater. But you know how that is."

I don't realize the faux pas until it has slipped from my lips. *Damn you, rum!* I clap a hand over my mouth, though we both know it's too late.

"Aha!" says Ethan, rising out of his seat to point at me. "I knew they told you more!"

I shrug sheepishly. "Are you mad?"

"Nah." He shakes his head, sitting back down.

I can tell he's not.

It occurs to me that he is objectively adorable, in a total way. His eyes, heavier now. His smile crooked with our inside jokes, his single dimple showing. Not that Professional Sasha cares. Although Professional Sasha just drank a gallon of liquor. She is out-of-office. Apologies for the delay in her responses. For urgent matters, please contact anyone else.

Shit. I think maybe I really like him. Do I? The fact that I've almost kissed him twice seems like a possible indicator. But whatever, I mean, everyone *likes* him. It doesn't have to mean anything.

"For what it's worth, they really seem to like working for you," I say.

"This job is by far the best one I've ever had." Ethan smiles, but then his forehead creases with worry. "And it's a big step in my career. I just hope I get to keep it."

"What do you mean?"

"Oh, it's nothing," he says, rubbing at his forehead.

"It seems like something." Before I can think, I reach out and touch his other hand, as it sits palm down on the table. I want to bring relaxed Ethan back. "Tell me what's up."

He looks slowly from my face to my hand, which I yank back. There is a moment of silence as we eye each other. Like it or not, there's a fireworks show ricocheting through me.

Does he feel the same?

"You were saying?"

"Right," he says, clearing his throat. "The magazine has just been bought out by a new publisher, and corporate is making decisions in the coming weeks about who stays and who goes. I feel pretty confident that my staff will remain regardless, though I still want to make sure and protect them, but my job is less secure. I'm still relatively new, and they have to like the direction I'm taking things."

Ahh. So much makes sense now. Derek's anxiety. Ethan's stress. "So it's contingent on . . . ?"

"This feature and shoot potentially. I mean, everything is a factor, but this is the lead story, and I get the sense that they're waiting to see what we come up with here. And if we can pull in readers."

"Which is why you came on the shoot. To oversee. Even though you've been traveling less lately."

"Well"—he swivels his head to look at the surroundings and then levels his gaze, hot and heavy, on me—"in part."

I shift in my seat, his look like a laser shooting through me, reducing me to flickering embers. I take this in, consider how much hangs in the balance for him. And yet he still took a chance on me.

Why? *What are we doing here?* By design, I'm now too tipsy to truly dissect that, so I take a sip of my punch instead. Opt to remain squarely in the fuzzy zone.

"Anyway, none of this explains why my people dished all my dirt to you." Ethan rolls his eyes.

"If it's any consolation, they made you sound like the injured party."

"Well, that's kind. But, as you said in the schoolyard, it's complicated. A million reasons why marriages don't work out."

Huh. I had forgotten that I said that. But he hadn't.

"Okay," I say, staring him down. "Name one."

"What?"

"Name one. What was one reason your marriage failed?"

"Damn," he says. "*Failed* seems like a harsh word."

"Okay," I say, leaning in. "Name one reason why your marriage amicably combusted."

"Way better," he sighs, running a hand through his hair.

I do not notice the way his bicep flexes 'cause I care about his *words. What was he saying again?*

"You really want to talk about this?" he says. "They always say not to talk about this."

"Who is they? And when? And to whom?"

"I don't know."

"You don't ever talk about this?"

"I try not to burden people."

"Uh-huh." I rest my chin in my hand. "And by 'burden people' you mean talk about your feelings?"

"Tomato, tom*a*to."

"I mean, I guess you're not meant to talk about divorce on first dates," I ramble. "But this isn't a first date! It's not a date at all."

He looks at me, long and hard. Shakes his head. Then sighs again. "Right. Okay. One reason, then." He shifts in his seat, taking a beat to consider. "I think she felt like I wasn't interested in her anymore. And she was right. I don't mean, like, physically. I mean fundamentally. We didn't care about the same things—or like the same things. When I found out that she was cheating on me, I was pissed because it felt disrespectful—not just to me, but to our kid, our whole life together. But I didn't really *care*. That's when I knew."

"That's when you knew what?"

"That it was over."

We sit with that for a minute. Let the immensity of it settle.

"When did you know it was over for you?" he asks.

"When he stopped coming home."

Ethan presses his lips together; I shrug. Then we bust out laughing—hard.

"Pretty decisive!" I say, through tears.

"Um, yes," he snorts.

And it feels good to laugh about it with someone, my dumpster fire of a marriage. It beats the eggshells people usually walk on.

Eventually, our outburst stems to a trickle and a wheeze. I wipe my cheeks with the back of my hand—my misery so very amusing.

"What did he like so much about LA, anyway?" Ethan asks, like he does not like LA to the same degree.

"Oh, he said the weather, the sushi, the In-N-Out, the canyon hikes."

"Can't blame him for the In-N-Out."

"No. You can't. Though he claims their french fries are decent. And they're really not."

"They're indecent?"

"Indecent potatoes. They're an affront to root vegetables everywhere."

Crickets—or some such island insects—have begun chirping in the background. I am reminded that we're outside. It's gotten too dark to see beyond the pool.

"Strong words," Ethan is saying, "about a starch."

"I really like potatoes. I will defend them to the death."

"Clearly." He nudges my toe with his under the table, sending another wave of heat through me. And something else: maybe affection? Damn. I have definitely had too much punch.

"Seriously: Why do you think he really liked it?" Ethan asks. "LA. Not the fries."

I take a breath, trying not to react to the intimate way his foot grazes mine. "Because he didn't have to be a parent."

Ethan sits back and lets out a low whistle. "Damn. I mean, I get that it's challenging, but . . ."

"I mean, it wasn't just that. He liked feeling successful. He liked the borrowed power from being in the orbit of stars. In Hollywood, he found his people. His fellow opportunists and immoralists. He found a scene where he looked like a comparatively decent human being. Where he didn't have to feel bad about bailing on us or putting himself first because he was 'living his truth.'"

I watch Ethan turn that over in his head. "I get that to an extent. I used to care about those things too, I guess. But then you grow up, produce a few shoots and realize stars are overrated." Suddenly, his eyes go wide. He leans in. "Wait! Speaking of, I have a genius idea!"

"Speaking of poor ethics and bad taste?"

"No! Speaking of stars! Let's take our lantern down to the water and go look at some constellations. The sky is spectacular here, and we haven't even checked it out!" He is puppy-dog adorable when he's excited. It's contagious. There is no saying no. I have no *no*.

Plus, I do love a night sky.

We have killed the pitcher of punch. I take a final watery sip from my glass of melted ice, then stand and throw my hands up. "Let's do it!"

Ethan runs inside and turns off the villa lights before we go. There is something touching about his need to do this—a sense of responsibility, of care, of age-old dadness. I endure only a short lecture about wasting electricity.

A minute later, barefoot, with the lantern in tow, we make our way down toward the water. It is dark. Not like city dark or suburban dark or even rural-road dark, where there are still occasional streetlights or passing high beams to guide you. It is dark like a blackout. Black like our windowless upstairs bathroom at home, where Nettie and Bart go behind closed doors to see their phosphorescent toys glow. Blind like the middle of the night.

The moon is a slim crescent. A sliver off a wheel of cheese. The farther we get from the villa, the inkier the night becomes. Soon, I can sense more than see Ethan next to me, plodding through the sand, telling our story in footprints. I can smell his grassy cologne and it ignites something deep inside me. Something that I'd rather not name. The dark protects me from seeing it. From him seeing me see it. I wonder if he's thinking the same.

"Ow!" he yelps. "Dammit!"

Apparently not.

"Are you okay?" I ask in his general direction.

"Yeah, fine. I think I tripped on a rock and then stepped on a shell."

"You should keep your hands up when you walk," I say. "To protect yourself. In case you eat it."

"Good point. See? Some people *can* take constructive criticism."

"Yes. People who need it."

He doesn't respond, but I know he's shooting daggers at me.

"Want to turn on that lantern until we get to the water, so we don't kill ourselves?"

"Oh, sure," I say. "If *you* need it."

I switch on the light. It radiates only a soft glow. I hold it up toward our faces. Ethan is indeed rolling his eyes at me. "Do you want to look at your foot to see if there's a cut? I think I have a *Frozen 2* Band-Aid in my bag back at the room."

"No. We've come this far. If there's a cut, I'll just risk sepsis."

"Wow. True heroism."

I hold the lantern low and in front of us to avoid further mishaps. We are so busy watching our step that when we reach the edge of the water, our destination, we're both surprised. The tide laps at my feet.

"This is it, I guess."

"Wait!" Ethan says, grabbing my forearm. The flesh to flesh contact sparks its own celestial event in my body. "Don't look up yet."

In the lantern light, it's like we're telling fireside ghost stories. And Ethan has a good one.

"Why?"

"Because we need to turn off the lantern first to get the full effect. And then we need to look up at the exact same time. To maximize impact."

He is dead serious. This game is no game. I sense I am seeing a glimpse of him as a kid and I am positive he is an older brother. No younger child was ever that bossy.

"Fine," I agree, as he drops his hand. I fight the urge to grab his palm and put it back on my arm. "Ready?"

"Born ready."

I switch off the lantern, and we are invisible to each other again. Somewhere not too far off, a frog croaks. I am tempted to remind it to say "Excuse me," but I can tell Ethan will not be amused if I ruin his moment.

"Okay," he says. "Should we sit?"

"Sure?"

We make our way down onto the drier sand. At least I do and I assume he does. I hear him moving.

"Are you looking up?" he checks.

"No."

"Are you lying?"

"Oh my God! You're like the stargazing nazi!"

"Okay, okay. But are you? Be honest."

"No!"

Then, suddenly, I can feel him settle in next to me and it's like we're seated side by side at the planetarium. The edge of his T-shirt sleeve brushes my bare arm, his elbow bumps my knee, and a shiver pulses through me despite the warm air. Is there such a thing as a warm chill? Maybe that idea about one sense being heightened in the absence of others is real. 'Cause I can feel *everything*.

"Sorry," he says.

"It's fine," I squeak, the words catching in my throat, then tripping out.

"Okay. On the count of three. Look up. One, two—"

I am tempted to make a joke, but when I look up on three, I am rendered speechless. I hear a sigh escape his lips.

I like the sound of it.

But I can't dwell because I have never seen so many stars. Clusters of them and lone wolves. Planets like freckles on the face of the galaxy.

The sound of the ocean feels magnified. The smell of the sea. Or is it the sky?

"This is even better than I expected," Ethan says finally.

I have no words.

"Are you still with us?"

"Oh, yeah," I say. "I am definitely with you."

I can't even be self-conscious about how that sounds.

I expect him to tell me about the various constellations, and I am all ready to share my theory about how their names could double for sexual positions—the Big Dipper, Ursa Major, the Plow—but he stays silent, just taking it in. So, I do too.

Settling in, I rest my palm down in the soft sand between us, accidentally overlapping Ethan's hand. A shot of electricity courses through me. "Sorry," I say, moving an inch away.

"I don't mind," he says, his voice lower by an octave. "Now I know where you are." He shifts his hand, so it is pressing up against mine.

I hold my breath.

For a full moment, I am in bliss. I shine as bright as the stars. Joy rises in me like its own high tide. This place, with its strange beasts and empty spaces, has uncorked something inside of me. Away from the chaos of home, I am becoming someone new. Someone I might actually like . . . sitting beside someone I might like too. Not that I want to admit it. That I haven't liked someone like this in eons. And with that recognition, slowly, surely, the worries creep into the quiet as litter. First one, then two, then a garbage truck's worth of anxieties. All dumped on my shore.

I'm drunk. He's drunk. We work together. We have an early morning. Someone might see us. Someone might think things. There's a job at stake. A job I need. A job he needs well done. A job my kids need. What am I doing?

Who is this guy anyway? How do I know he's not just another Cliff, putting his best foot forward before revealing his true nature?

Anyway, I'm an old lady! Not some sexy young thing. This part of me has long been on layaway, payments delinquent and gone to collections.

And yet things are changing. I'm changing. I can feel it. And I am powerless to stop it. *Where are the brakes on this thing?*

"What time is it?" I say finally. My heart is racing.

We have left our cell phones face down on the table, forgotten. The last time I did that was likely a different decade. I have no clue how much time has passed.

Ethan groans. "Probably time to pack it in, sadly." He moves his hand away.

"Totally," I say, all casual, as if I'm not freaking the fuck out. As if I don't miss the pressure of his hand. "Morning waits for no man. Woman. Person. Whatever."

"You are truly so weird."

"Gee, thanks."

"So, are we going?" he says.

I hear him rustle to standing, brushing sand from the back of his shorts.

If I search my soul, I'm sad. Though I have instigated it, I don't want to leave. Worries aside, I'm having fun.

"Yup," I say. "Let's go."

Then we both wait. I am stymied by ambivalence.

"Sasha," he says softly. "The lantern."

Or maybe we are stymied by me.

"Oh, right!" At that precise point, I realize I have misplaced the lantern.

"What are you doing?" he asks, as I bend down and begin feeling around in the sand.

"Nothing, nothing!"

Like so many unread tea leaves, the grains tell me nothing. My hands find something like the root of a plant. Then I realize it's Ethan's toe.

"Oops."

"Sasha. Seriously. What is happening?"

I exhale. "I kind of . . . dropped the lantern."

"What?"

"When I saw the stars, I think I was just overcome and . . . I sort of forgot about it. I let it go."

This is what happens when I stop being vigilant. I bite my lip and wait for him to be mad. Instead, he chuckles. "Always on top of things . . ."

"And now we're screwed."

"Nah, nothing as bad as that. It has to be here somewhere."

Now we are both on hands and knees feeling blindly, disrupting sand crabs from their slumber.

"This is actually a really strange experience," I say.

"It's like on Halloween when they blindfold you, put your hands in a bowl of spaghetti and tell you it's brains."

"Um. Who does that?"

"Um, everyone."

"Maybe if you grew up in a cult."

"No! It's a thing," he insists. "My family did it every year at our annual Halloween party when I was a kid. Spaghetti as brains. And grapes are eyeballs."

"In my family, we just ate our grapes."

"Oh, I think I got— No. Just a rock. Oh God. I hope it's a rock. It sort of feels like it's moving."

This strikes me as hilarious, and I begin to giggle. Maybe I'm overtired. Maybe the temporary disaster has disengaged me from my paralyzing fears. Maybe the rum is still working its magic.

"Oh, that's funny? That I maybe just squashed a hermit crab?!"

Now, I'm laughing even harder. "S-sorry!" I sputter, as I crawl around. "I feel like I'm playing some horrible improv theater game."

"Yes and . . . ?" Ethan starts to snicker too. "This is quite the move, by the way—ditching the lantern. If you wanted to spend the night on the beach with me, you could have just said so."

What? This will not be pinned on me!

"You're the one who dragged us down here to gaze at the stars! What's next? Piña coladas and getting caught in the rain?"

"In my defense, I didn't realize you'd lose our one light source. Dim lights are romantic. A total blackout is apocalyptic."

"Well, welcome to the end of the world!" I say cheerfully.

"Happy to be here!"

In that moment, I come into contact with something hard. And, gratefully, made of metal.

"I got it!" I exclaim, holding the lantern over my head. "Victory!"

After some fumbling, I switch on the light. And I am caught by surprise. We both are. Because as it turns out, we are sitting face-to-face on our knees, only inches from each other.

Our laughter stops dead.

"Hi," he says.

"Hi," I say. After a beat, I add: "So, that's your face."

"Keen observation."

"It's not so bad," I murmur, my gaze dropping to his lips, then locking on his eyes.

"A ringing endorsement."

As we watch each other, his eyes turn molten. "Charlie was right," he says finally.

"About what?"

"About you being great. About *me* thinking you're great."

A warmth swells in my chest. I smile, look up at him through my lashes. "You think I'm great?"

"I do."

"Me? Not just my work?"

"Nope. Not just your work. You."

And I know in that moment, I really like him too. *Damn.*

There is a heavy pause.

"What now?" I ask.

I watch as if in a trance as he lifts his hand to my face, runs a thumb along my jawline, leaving trails in its wake. "We're screwed, remember?"

I set the lantern down. The air between us sparks and sizzles. We both lean in. Our lips are millimeters apart. There is no space for thoughts. He smells like sea and that damn cologne. The sounds of the ocean and his breath sync up in my head.

I decide to give in. Why fight it? It's just a kiss. Our lips, parted, brush each other. A tease. A drive-by. It leaves me hungry for more. Every inch of me lit up.

He circles back for a lengthier visit. His lips press against mine, softly at first, and then harder—and it's like a feverish release. Like I've been waiting all my life. I nip his bottom lip, pull away slightly to let him chase for more. Run a hand down the bicep I *wasn't* eyeing before. His skin is warm, firm. He pulls me close, his fingers lacing through my hair at the back of my neck. I grind into him, heat rising to the surface as he drags his hand slowly down my side, all the way to my waist. He kisses me deeper.

"Sasha," he says, pulling back for a moment. "Damn."

I know what he means.

I'm seeing stars, but now they're behind my lids. I slip my arms around his neck and pull him back in for another kiss. He tastes like rum punch and promise, and everything in my body needs this. My worries from before have been subsumed into a tornado of want. I am lost in him. Nothing else matters.

Is sex on the beach as sandy as it sounds?

I'm ready to find out.

As he nuzzles my neck, I feel Ethan's fingers creep up my thigh, and I am here for it.

Works for me.

I glance down for a visual. His big hand on my bare thigh. But it's not Ethan's palm on my skin. Instead, I see a giant iguana mounting my leg like a jungle gym.

I scream at the top of my lungs. We all jump a mile.

"What the hell!"

Darkness.

My heart is thumping. I am breathless. I can't be sure why. There are so many possibilities.

Afterward, I will wonder if the intruder was my iguana friend. The one I met at the restaurant banquette. Arriving on the scene to save me from myself.

Regardless, he has broken the spell. The tsunami of real life has rushed in.

The iguana scampers away. Ethan—disoriented, with his hair and T-shirt ruffled adorably—is looking at me for a cue. I am on my ass in the sand.

"I guess we should go," I manage.

He parts his lips, then closes them again.

Once I grab the lantern again, Ethan and I plod back to the villa in silence. I want to speak, to fall back into our comfortable banter, but I can't think of what to say. I am too haunted by the push of his pillowy lips against mine, his hand grazing my side-boob, to think straight about anything else.

It keeps *almost* happening. Maybe it's not meant to be.

When we reach the villa, he feels around on the wall for the outdoor light switch. It turns on like a floodlight, that dreaded reality check when the bar is closed. Sighing, he picks both our phones up off the table, still strewn with the remnants of our debauched dinner, and hands me mine. Real life rears its scaly head. I'm reminded of the dumb text from Cliff, asking me to put in a good word with Martin. So many levels of fat chance.

There's a new text from my mom. A picture of both my parents at their literacy conference, holding up copies of banned books with glee. But I'm slammed with a wave of worry. Does she remember where I am? That I'm not in Brooklyn?

There is no colder shower.

Once inside, I head straight toward my room, as Ethan crosses to the kitchen to pour a sensible glass of water. I want one too, but I can't face him.

I know the grown-up thing would be to talk. But I am not feeling my most evolved.

"Goodnight," I say, as I open my door.

"Night," he says.

Then, I turn back around. "Hey, in all seriousness, should we be worried about Stephanie? She hasn't come back from Martin's. And he really does seem like a creep."

Ethan shakes his head. "I checked in with her a few hours ago. The interview went fine. He behaved himself. I'm sure she's grabbing drinks with the others."

I nod. I'm glad he made sure she was safe. And that he did it of his own volition. But does he share my misgivings about bolstering this man's image? And, if so, is the new job too important to risk? For him and for me? So many thoughts ping-ponging inside my rum-soaked head.

"Okay, well," I say. "Later, dude." I do not sound casual. I sound deranged.

Even with my back turned, I can feel him shake his head. "Sasha," he says softly, like he knows what it does to me. "Sleep well."

As if I'll be able to sleep.

31 | Pardon the Interruption

ETHAN

It's like whiplash.

One minute, she's pressed up against me, her tongue finally down my throat, the next she's searching out the lantern and trudging up the beach like nothing happened.

Like we're acquaintances. Like we didn't just have a night for the books.

I'm trying to keep up, but Sasha's head is like a rickety roller-coaster ride—crazy fun but also has me praying for solid ground. Hoping that I make it out alive.

She obviously freaked out. So I'll just keep retreating. Keep giving her space.

I'm not going to try to convince her. She's got to want this.

In the meantime, I am tossing and turning. There is no comfortable position, no way to close my eyes and see anything but her.

I'm doomed anyway. Work starts early tomorrow. It's a pivotal day. And I drank too much. I can already feel throbbing in my head.

I should get some sleep. But all I can think about is the small groan that escaped her lips when the kiss got real. I think about it till dawn.

TO-DO
- Keep your eye on the prize. Mind on work.
- See which way the wind blows.

32 | Go Blue!

KAITLIN

It turns out that the absence of Sasha is more annoying than her presence. No Sasha at drop-off. No Sasha at pick-up. It's as if seeing her gave me an outlet for my dissatisfaction. In a twisted way, it was something to which I could look forward. That deep irritation.

I have that feeling I remember from elementary and middle school, when having a crush makes you excited to go to class and then that drops away. Only it's not a crush I have. It's something else.

Now I am left to sit in it. My phone tells me my screen time is at an all-time high. I turn off the tracking.

Lisa says Sasha is on a work trip. So she probably is. Lisa does get all the good dirt.

Today was unseasonably cold, the wind slapping us as a reminder that winter is close behind. A wake-up call. *Snap out of it!* But to what end? I know what's coming will be brutal, snow, ice and gray, but it's part of the life I chose. Back when New York's extra effort seemed like a fair trade-off. Not like my sister, who absconded to California and is always trying to convince me to move West too. She has an orange orchard and goats. She treats earthquakes like sneezes.

I don't mind the cold, usually. I'm used to it. I went to college in Michigan in search of convention and football players. *Go Blue!* Currently, I am wearing a Wolverines hat and scarf and working the sign-up booth for our winter book-drive outside. Some other PTA folks said they'd deal with it, Lisa included, but I have a few things to handle in the administrative office, anyway. Some fliers to print for the book fair. Also, if I'm honest, this is my time out of the house today and I need some air.

In early motherhood, my part-time work for the market research firm that once employed me full-time was ideal, flexible and rarely demanding. But, lately, the home demands are fewer, too, by half at least. And I am numb as I slog my way through rote emails, half listening on never-ending Zooms. I spend more time catching up on *Real Housewives* reruns than I do logging work hours. My world has shrunk until it no longer fits. Kind of like my favorite jeans (only they didn't shrink; I grew). The quiet desperation might explain some of my more questionable choices over the last year or two. But why dwell on that? Especially when you can dwell on more interesting things.

Celeste comes to school every day, twice a day now. She looks like she's being pummeled. I've never seen her this frequently, and I think maybe her beauty dulls a bit with oversaturation. Regardless, she is a poor substitute for Sasha, as she is less likely to act out. It's harder to mock or disdain her. She does not wear her emotions on her sleeve. Rather, she keeps them in her tote. But she will have to do.

At drop-off today, Celeste has not showered. Her outfit is not cute. Her cool-kid Joan Jett T-shirt, which peaks out from beneath her camel-colored cashmere trench, has a red stain down the front and looks slept in.

She ushers the children inside, waves goodbye with a smile plastered on her face, then heaves a sigh of relief once they're out of view. Or maybe it's not relief. Maybe that sigh is something else. Something more defeated. She looks up the block like it's the rest of her day. Like it will be endless—an uphill battle. Like she's Sisyphus.

But she can't be Sisyphus. Because I am. And her legs are too long.

She begins her trudge toward home and, when she passes me, she actually turns and offers a small wave. "Hi, Kaitlin," she says.

She knows my name?

"Hi," I respond a moment late, like a robot. I am that shocked by her acknowledgment.

I almost feel guilty. But then I don't.

33 | Wake-Up Call

SASHA

The morning is a double rum punch to the gut. In every way.

I wake up hungover—physically and existentially—and to multiple texts from Celeste. Apparently, today Nettie's class has a big field trip to the Museum of the City of New York and I never signed her permission slip. Of course, I didn't. Her teacher emailed both me and Celeste in a tizzy this morning. If the office doesn't have the form by 8:30 a.m., when school begins, Nettie will have to stay back and miss the excursion.

My mouth is dry and my head is dryer as I wrap my mind around that potential disaster. I swear I never received a paper permission form in Nettie's folder. I never received a reminder email. I can just feel the school administrators' evil eye on me from afar.

By some miracle, the teacher manages to email me the form, I manage to sign it digitally and Celeste manages to print it for me at her house. Just having a printer work on the first try seems like divine intervention. Toner cartridges firing on all cylinders! Thank goodness for these other women. I am broken at the thought of Nettie sitting in that administrative office alone again, eating a sad doughnut while her friends are playing rock, paper, scissors on the bus.

I feel like I've already waded through a day's worth of adrenaline by 8:00 a.m.—and pre-coffee!

I run my rain shower, step underneath the stream and lather myself in coconut milk soap. The water pelts me like a tap on the shoulder, a nudge. The metallic walls glitter and shine. Like stars.

So, of course, my mind wanders to Ethan from last night. To his lips on my lips. His lips on my ear, my neck, my collarbone, the places they never got to tour. The water is suddenly warmer on my naked skin, the steam thick. I am wide awake and borderline desperate.

Why did I walk away again?

No! I won't go there! I will chalk up the incredible kiss to rum punch and constellations, my lack of willpower to latent libido. A vagina too long under wraps. After all, everyone looks like a good idea in the right lighting. Once upon a time, I thought Cliff was the beginning and the end. Lust is not my friend. I strap on a mental chastity belt, pushing—no, shoving!—men of all stripes from my mind.

My phone's trill penetrates my shower haze. At least something is getting action. And, because of the morning's Nettie debacle (and, okay, my primed flight response), I jump to attention, scurrying out and jogging naked to the bedside table to grab the call. I press the green button without thinking, afraid I might otherwise be too late.

It's my Mom. On FaceTime.

"Oh Lord!" I shriek at the sight of my naked self in the video window, then toss the phone onto the unmade bed and run to grab a towel. *For fuck's sake.* Once it's wrapped around me, I return, heart maxing out, and pick the phone up. My hair is soaking wet, dripping in cold rivulets down my back.

She is back on the couch in her reading glasses, which means they flew home from the conference last night, but this time she's got some dense theory book sitting next to her and she's wearing sweatpants. *Sweatpants?* My mother? That's new.

"Hi, Mom."

"Why are you naked?"

"Well, for one thing, I don't usually shower in clothing."

"What?"

"I was in the shower."

I try not to watch myself in the FaceTime window. My bedraggled hair like a wet dog's. I am all too aware of the gray cast to my skin, from last night, and the way my jawline is losing elasticity, from life.

"Oh," she says, furrowing her brow. "You shouldn't answer video calls without clothing on."

I press my lips together, practicing patience. "Sage advice."

She looks at her watch, which she has worn my whole life. It's gold and belonged to my grandmother. The fanciest thing she owns, since she's not a believer in flashy objects or superficial people. In retrospect, that's one reason she never liked Cliff. The human embodiment of an overdetermined watch—that needs a new battery. The Rolex of social climbers. "Isn't it a bit late?" she's saying. "Don't the kids need to get to school?"

I am at first annoyed and then something else. Something worse. Nausea descends. Does she *really* not know where I am? After all of our conversations about my trip?

"Mom," I say. "I'm in Turks and Caicos. For work. Remember?"

I study her for signs—of what, I don't know.

"Oh. Oh, okay," she says. But, heartbreakingly, I'm not sure if she does.

My stomach flips. Belly flops. Lands on its face.

"Hey, Mom, are you okay? You're wearing . . . sweatpants."

"They're performance joggers," she sighs. "My other pants felt too tight."

I decide to be honest. "I've told you I was coming here multiple times. Do you really . . . not remember?"

"Maybe I do, vaguely," she says, toggling her head. "I actually wanted to call you while your father was out, so we could talk about this exact issue."

I don't have a ton of time. I am running late for call time. And I have a sinking feeling. But this is too important to rush. I settle on the edge of the bed. On the edge, full stop.

"What's going on?"

"I feel like I'm forgetting things." She frowns, bringing a hand to her head like she might hold the thoughts inside. "It's like, I can't hang on to an idea. It's not just normal signs of aging, 'senior moments' like walking into a room and not knowing why I'm there—"

"Yeah, I think that's normal. Even I do that all the time. It's the stuff of multitasking."

"Right. It's more than that. It's like I'm getting *confused*." She blinks.

This is a woman who has run entire institutions. Testified about literacy before Congress. A rock.

My insides are agitating like a washing machine on heavy duty, but, outwardly, I am intent on standing my ground. I will not heighten her anxiety with my own free fall. But I won't pretend it's not happening either. "Have you talked to Dad?"

"A little bit, but I think he'd rather not acknowledge the issue. It makes him panicked too."

I nod. "Well, it sounds like you should call your doctor. Maybe set up some cognitive tests? An MRI or brain scan? I'm not sure what they do. But, that way, you don't have to guess at what's happening or figure this out alone. If something really is wrong, I'm sure there's medicine you can take at least to slow down the progression."

She shakes her head. Like she can't believe we're having this conversation. I can't either. At least she's wearing clothing. Some of us are in the nude. "Right. I should do that. I'll do it today. You're right. I'm writing it down."

I exhale, bring a hand to my forehead. I realize it is likely a mannerism inherited from my mom, a mirror of what I watched her do minutes before. I need to hold it together. That is priority number one. Everything feels so high stakes, the dial turned up. I am suddenly nostalgic for my peaceful rut of the past years. A safe space baseline of low-grade depression and ambivalence instead of ping-ponging between panic and hope.

"Mom," I say, "how are you feeling otherwise?"

She brightens a little at this question. "Actually, I'm on this new neck medicine, and I think it's working really well. I barely feel pain anymore."

"Good news!" I exclaim. It turns out this is a relative term. "Listen, I'm home tomorrow evening. Are you guys grabbing the kids from Celeste in the afternoon, as planned?" I hold my breath. Does she remember?

"Yes! We're so looking forward to it. Your father got the kids those rainbow cookies they like."

"Okay, great," I nod. "Once the kids have gone to bed, let's talk more and make a plan for figuring this out. Who knows: maybe it's just stress?"

"Maybe," she says. "I am stressed. But that's because I can't remember anything."

"Vicious circle," I say.

"Life," she says, putting her reading glasses back on. She's still beautiful, my mom. "Let's plan to talk then. Have a wonderful time! And take pictures!"

"I will, Mom. Although there will be professional pictures too."

"Not the same."

"Right."

"One last thing, sweetie," she says, as I stand to cross back into the bathroom. "There's a man standing behind you."

I gasp, then slowly twist to peer over my shoulder. I have accidentally left the shades up. Michael is standing on the other side of the glass with his back to me, like he is guarding my room and my reputation.

"Thanks, Mom."

We hang up. I close the shades. And I am gutted.

Despite my semi-horrible headspace, I function fine for the first half of the day. I manage to avoid running into Ethan in the morning. Instead, when I emerge, I find Stephanie in the living room in her requisite dark glasses. Her hair is in an unbrushed ponytail and she's wearing her sundress from yesterday. Wait. Did she *really* sleep with Martin? It's not that I judge her. To each her own. It's just that Stephanie is pretty amazing. She could do a lot better than that giant rawhide poof of a human being.

"Morning," I say.

She shoots me a peace sign. Otherwise keeps her body still. I know that feeling. Trying not to upset the balance—or puke.

"Rough night?"

"You could say that. Rough in all the right ways. You?"

I choose my words carefully. "It was quiet." That's true!

She pushes her sunglasses on top of her head, then fixes me with an appraising look. I think I detect a glimmer in her eye, about what I am unsure. Then, she stretches her arms above her head and yawns with gusto. "Okay. I gotta motivate."

"Sounds good. I'm heading out."

"Ethan just left for a jog," she says, crossing to her room. "I can't believe he went running again this morning. Except I can."

"Except of course he did." I laugh. Knowing what I do, I'm even more surprised (and not surprised) than Stephanie. I didn't take down that pitcher of rum punch alone.

Last night, when I climbed into my fluffy cloud bed, I hadn't come down so easily from the night. And I'm not just talking about the fact that I was peeing every fifteen minutes. That's simply what you do when you've had two children and two liters of alcohol. No. I'm talking about something much more insidious: images of Ethan flashing through my head, spiraling me into equal parts embarrassment and longing. His finger tracing my jaw. Trailing down my neck. The roughness of his five-o'clock shadow against my cheeks. His muscles flexing under my palms, giving new meaning to the term *dad bod*. His other hand encircling my waist with untempered urgency, tugging me toward him, before the iguana made its untoward advances up my thigh.

Whether I wanted to admit it or not, drunk me obviously wanted to sex him up. I couldn't think about his lips searching mine, the taste of punch on his tongue, without dying a little. But, first of all, that didn't mean a tryst—even what promised to be a great one—was worth complicating the job opportunity. And, second of all, maybe more important, if I'm honest with myself, what happened last night didn't mean he was all in either. Maybe he had his own reservations. Once the iguana interrupted, it's not like he made a move to resume or tried to convince me to stay. He didn't invite me into his room when we got back to the house or even kiss me goodnight. Instead, he got really quiet.

Yes, so he was clearly attracted to me in that brief moment on the beach. He said I was great—when he was drunk. But the reality of a deserted island is that there's not a lot of competition. How would he see the idea of "us" in the real world? Was he currently lying in his own bed on the other side of the wall, spiraling with regret?

Plus, this shoot is important for him, too. His job hangs in the balance. Maybe, like me, he has misgivings about getting distracted from the task at hand.

By the time I fell asleep, I was convinced that we were both under the influence of vacation goggles. Once we got home to our kids and his ex and school drop-offs and pick-ups, this would all fade away into something otherworldly, a moment in the recesses of our minds colored by a sense of escape. When we got home, the way he wore his perfect T-shirts, the way they rode up, offering a glimpse of tanned skin that made me wonder what lay beyond, would be just like seeing any other neutered Brooklyn dad with his Park Slope Food Coop tote bag and slumped shoulders. (Tote bags are a real libido killer.)

Today, we're shooting outdoors. I plod over to the set holding my sandals in my hand. I am soaking up every sensation, all too aware that tomorrow I head back to reality. *So soon?* Peter, Jackie and Derek are already at the yoga pavilion, which sits on a short rocky cliff jutting out over the water. And it is arresting. The sky is almost indiscernible from the water at present, a mass of blue and green with a clarity I could only dream of possessing.

Since Charlie hasn't yet arrived and we are basically set up, Jackie and I decide to put the branded mats to good use and do some sun salutations before we get started. It feels amazing to stretch. We are in mountain pose; we reach for the sky; we hang down to the ground; we are in plank, in up dog. And all the time, the water glistens against the horizon. Another magic moment. A "rose" in our day as Bart and Nettie would call it.

It's not until I'm upside down, in downward-facing dog, that I spot Ethan between my legs. He and Charlie have walked up together, bathed in sunshine, a couple of J.Crew models with matching sustainable water bottles out for a stroll. And, for all intents and purposes, I am currently sticking my ass in their faces.

Today's T-shirt is white. *Fuck.* It is my kryptonite. I know it the moment I see it. Salted caramel sauce, books that make you laugh, TV shows about teen love, last-minute tickets to any play, a hot dog with mustard at a sporting event, candy at a movie, chips and salsa after a day at the beach, any cocktail with foam, well-built men in perfect white T-shirts. These are the things I cannot resist. I will spend the day trying to look anywhere else.

I break my pose and come down to my knees. "Oh, good! Charlie's here," I say, intent on diverting my own attention. "We can start!"

He waves, crossing to check in with his assistant.

I stretch my neck from side to side.

"You injure yourself?" Ethan asks.

"No," I say, giving myself permission to glance at him. Just for a second, I swear. "I've got a kink."

As I hear it come out of my mouth, I realize I've done it again.

"A kink," he says, eyeing me. "Good to know."

Jackie giggles.

I glance around, worried that the others might suspect something happened between us. But it's business as usual. Because he's casual, relaxed. A hand in his pocket. Like last night never happened. Or like it happened and he's good with it. *No big deal.*

Fine. I too can feign chill.

"Okay, people," Derek intervenes, always on task. It's a lucky reminder to stop staring. "Are we ready to start?"

"Peter," I say, standing up from my mat. Professional Sasha is back. "Who did we choose to shoot for this location? For the yoga sequence?"

He shrugs. "I already got you and Jackie, and it looks great."

My face flushes hot. "Me? But I wasn't supposed to be featured!"

"You guys did make it look good," says Derek. "Against the horizon, it's like—infinity yoga."

"Ooh," says Jackie. "Good term."

"But I'm not even *Escapade* staff!" I protest.

Jackie nudges me. "Not *yet*."

But I'm too distressed to fully appreciate what she's implying. I am strictly behind the camera.

"Can you crop me out and just use Jackie?"

Peter shakes his head. It's all or nothing. "Just come see."

As Peter and I huddle together to watch the playback, Ethan comes up behind us to check it out too. I hold my breath and try to ignore what his proximity does to me. The heat I can sense coming off his body like I'm a snake and he's my prey. I am so aware of him that my body practically vibrates. The way my bottom is nearly pressed up against his front. The way his cheek, when he leans in to see, is inches from my own. I am unraveling.

And dammit, the footage does look good.

"But I'm not wearing yoga clothes!" It's my last attempt to avoid being featured. I look down at my black tank top and jean shorts with doubt. "Do you think it matters?"

Quietly, from behind me, Ethan says, "I think you look great."

His words—low and loaded—travel through me like contrast dye before an MRI, coursing down tributaries, marking territory, before pooling into a bubbling geyser. I can feel his breath on my neck. I shudder.

And I am undone. I want to lie down and die.

Or turn around and jump him.

What is wrong with me today? My defenses are down, I reason. I'm upset about my mom. Stressed about my kids and the snafus I somehow can't stop from interrupting their experiences at school. The way that it feels like failing. Away from home and everything that anchors me. I am not *actually* invested in Ethan. I don't have actual feelings. It's only a little natural chemistry. And I am just more susceptible to him than usual. I have an Ethan predisposition, but that doesn't mean my feelings ever have to become full-blown.

Full-blown. Now everything sounds dirty.

I just need to keep my distance.

Only that will prove hard. Because, after Charlie's shoot wraps up at the pavilion, we are breaking for lunch, changing into bathing suits and shipping out to a small sandbar, a "baby cay" as they call the tiny islands here, for the final shoot of the day. Via the hotel, I have chartered a small boat for this purpose and, of course, a captain to helm. And, now that Stephanie has arrived on the scene and watched the yoga footage, she wants it to feature Ethan . . . and me.

"It'll look amazing!" she says. She is drinking murky green juice.

"You look like you recovered quickly." I smile at her.

"Oh, yeah," she says, toasting the air with her drink. "Hair of the dog."

Just the idea of a splash of vodka in her spinach, kale and ginger juice brings my own hangover back. I try not to gag.

At lunch, I am seated at the same delightful table under the umbrella with Derek, Jackie, Stephanie and Charlie. Today, Charlie ambles up with a robust plate of food.

"Hungry?" asks Stephanie, arching her brow.

"Oh, yeah." Charlie grins. "Today, I've worked up an appetite."

He digs into his hearts of palm salad and plantains, caramelized to perfection. I need to go back to the buffet and grab some of my own.

Derek shifts in his seat, uncomfortable, and keeps checking his phone like it's a tick. I wish I knew why. He seems to pick up on everything, and I pick up on nothing.

"Steph," says Jackie. "How was the interview with Martin yesterday?"

"Oh, perfect." says Stephanie. "It could not have gone better. The whole night was a win."

"He said all the things?"

"He said all the things!"

"He did all the things?"

"He did *all* the things!" She winks.

Gross. "But he's kind of a pig," I say before I think. All eyes are on me, as I immediately regret my outburst. "No?"

"Completely." Steph grins.

I guess that's how she likes them. Smarmy and leathery. As long as she's happy.

I already know she slept at his villa. I recognize a walk of shame (without shame) when I see one. And I saw one this morning.

I'm dying to ask the rest of them if they have any reservations about running this story, knowing that Martin is so terrible. But I'm still weighing the pros and cons carefully before I do. Does protecting job security for the people employed at this property take precedence? Does *my* need for this job—and Ethan's need for this shoot to turn out well to keep his staff safe—trump the rest?

Derek's phone vibrates, and he quickly responds. "Sorry, guys. I know. No phones at the table."

"This is work," says Stephanie. "You don't need to follow Eric rules."

Eric is Derek's husband. Eric and Derek. "And, yes. I know it rhymes," he said when he revealed this during a Zoom meeting before we left.

"What are 'Eric rules'?" I ask.

"We don't need to—" Derek starts.

But Stephanie bulldozes over him. "What aren't Eric rules? Eric is so high-strung, he makes Derek seem chill."

I look at Derek, who smiles sheepishly. If Eric is uptight, Derek doesn't mind. "He just believes in creating boundaries. Something that *some of us* don't have."

"*Boundary* is just another word for 'wall,'" says Stephanie. "And I don't believe in limitations."

"And she means *any*," Jackie giggles.

From there, the conversation turns to marriage. Jackie is not ready to settle down with anyone and is curious about ethical non-monogamy. Stephanie hasn't found the right guy. Charlie just got out of a three-year relationship. Only Derek has tied the knot, and his marriage sounds like a kind of nuptial bliss.

"Well," I say, "it sounds like we represent the spectrum. And only Derek knows the secret to lasting love."

We all look at him expectantly.

"What?" he says, looking up from his Pellegrino.

"We're waiting on your wisdom," says Charlie. "So we can get wise."

"Oh, I don't have any wisdom." He laughs. "What am I going to say? All the clichés? Don't go to bed angry? Never stop laughing? Whatever other trite things they say in wedding speeches? I mean, it's pretty basic: the most important thing is making each other feel heard and seen. Keeping the other person's priorities on the same level with your own. Feeling invisible is the kiss of death. But I think Sasha knows—actually all of you know from past relationships—that none of those things matter unless the rest works."

"The rest?" says Jackie, leaning in.

"The rest. Compatibility. It's just right or it's not right," he says, shrugging. "But it's never convenient."

Derek may think he has no wisdom, but he has just schooled us.

We all sit with that for a moment, as a breeze worries the napkins under our tumblers. Jackie gazes down at her food. Charlie nods. Stephanie bites her lip. I exhale.

"Well, that's enough truth for one day, I think," says Stephanie, tossing her napkin on top of her plate, and we all smile. She pulls out her lipstick to reapply.

"Where did you meet Eric, by the way?" I ask Derek.

"At work." He smiles but then frowns. "But don't anyone get any ideas."

I am dressed in a sarong. It's not mine. It's Stephanie's. Because I am not the kind of person who owns sarongs. But I am also not the kind of person who is willing to appear on video in only a bathing suit.

Thank goodness, no one has glitched on my black one-piece underneath. A bikini was a nonstarter. These are the only bathing suits I wear. Because they have actual cups for your boobs, boy-short bottoms, and 007 ruching to disguise the rest. Basically, I am an optical illusion.

While we were getting changed after lunch, Stephanie asked me again about what I did last night. I'm not sure what she's getting at—surely she didn't see me and Ethan together on the beach? We could barely see each other! The truth is, there was mostly nothing to see, anyway. Unless she can see inside my head. But, if anyone can do that, my money is on Derek.

Demon Dad (who I no longer think of as such) is, of course, in his perfect white T-shirt with perfect slate-gray board shorts. His sunglasses are old-school Wayfarers. So are mine.

"Twins!" Stephanie giggles, and I hope my hat shades my shade.

He looks me up and down, languidly, from behind his glasses. "Not exactly."

I still can't get a read on how he feels about what happened on the beach last night. Indifferent maybe? He's been friendly enough but has kept his distance. Up until this moment, he has been Professional Ethan.

And that's good. That's what I asked him to be.

Only, if I'm honest—which I have no interest in being—I'm fiending for more.

What's going on in that stupidly handsome head of his?

Even if we're a bad idea, I still want him to want me. That's twisted, but it's reality. Feigning boredom, I reach up over my head and rest my hands on the top of my hat, stick my chest out a bit. Strike a pose.

In my peripheral vision, I see him swallow, hard. I can't even see his eyes, but I feel them boring into me. *Interesting.*

Professional Sasha does not feel lit up. Professional Sasha is *not* trying to get his attention.

In the nick of time, Michael motions to us that the boat is ready, so I turn toward the dock.

"Sasha! Wait up!" I swivel back around at the sound of my name, stupidly hopeful. But it's not Ethan. It's Charlie calling me.

I wait as he jogs up the beach toward me.

"Hey." He shoots me a smile too wide not to be calculated. I have too much experience with cute manipulators to be fooled. My antenna is up. He wants something.

"So, before we get on the boat, can we quickly try something?"

"Something like?"

"Let me show you."

Minutes later, we're standing with the rest of the crew staring at a hammock suspended between two palm trees down toward the ocean.

"I just feel like it screams 'desert paradise,'" he is saying. "And I don't want us to miss having a shot of it."

He's not wrong. It's dreamy as hell.

"Okay," I say. "As long as you think we can be quick, so we don't lose light, it's fine with me."

"Great!" Charlie says. But he doesn't exhale.

Okay. Out with it. "Charlie, what's the catch?"

"So, since you're already dressed for the other shoot, I'd like this to feature—you."

This is not my favorite development, but I begin to wrap my mind around it, when, gaze focused anywhere but on me, he mumbles, "And Ethan."

My eyes surely bug out of my head. I am a Beanie Boo. And, before I can stop myself, I blurt out, "Together?!"

I say it and I say it loud.

Now everyone is staring at me. Especially Ethan, who has removed his sunglasses and looks either mortified, hurt or ready to commit me to an institution. Maybe all three.

"Um," says Charlie. "Yes? I know it's a bit unorthodox."

He locks eyes momentarily with Stephanie. She nods ever so slightly. And now I suspect she's behind this subterfuge.

But why?

I can contemplate the answer and her demise later. Right now, I need to pick my chin up off the floor and act like a big girl.

I force my face into what I'm sure is a terrifying fake smile. "Okay! Great! Let's do it! Can't wait!"

The rest of the team remains where they're standing, looking at me like they're unsure whether to approach. Like I'm a rabid skunk.

"Now!"

Everyone jumps into action, setting up quick-and-dirty reflectors and styling the hammock just so. Brushing sand and dust from surrounding rocks and fronds.

Charlie wants to get a wide shot, to create the effect of us floating above the water, so he will shoot from a distance away. But, first, he walks down the beach to the hammock itself and gestures me and Ethan over. I approach like the condemned. I'm trying to keep my cool, but it is long gone. It's bad enough that I'm having confusing feelings about Ethan, bad enough that we kissed last night and haven't even acknowledged it, but now we have to get up close and personal in front of an audience.

"So, I want it to feel like you guys are a real couple on vacation together," Charlie is saying. "Like just super relaxed. No need for posing or smiling at camera. I just want you guys to climb in and chill—like you're blissfully alone at the farthest recesses of the world."

Ethan nods, studiously listening—and maybe avoiding my eyes. At least that's what he projects. He is the good pupil; I am the troublemaker.

"Chill! Perfect! Sounds good!" I say too abruptly. Like a drill sergeant on amphetamines.

Ethan and Charlie glance at me like I've lost it. They exchange a look I can't read.

"We'll get into position," says Ethan, ignoring me. Charlie takes this cue to walk back up the beach and check in with Jackie. As usual, we've cleared the area.

Ethan takes a step toward me and dips his face close to mine, so I am shielded from prying eyes. He is trying to give us privacy, but it ratchets my stress up a level. He is sharing my personal space. Part of me wants to take a step toward him. The other part wants to run away. But staying where I am feels like torture.

"Are you okay?" he whispers. "If you feel uncomfortable, you don't have to do this."

"I'm good!" I try.

"Sasha," he says. "C'mon."

This diffuses me. I exhale, gathering myself. I was surprised by the request, but I can handle this. I can be close to Ethan and not fall apart. Even with his breath on my neck.

"No, it's okay," I say. "I'm okay."

"Okay. Well, then we should . . ." He gestures toward the hammock. "I'll get in first, so I can steady it for you."

He falls effortless against the ropes, his tan forearms flexing as he shifts his body to make space on the near side for me. He lies back. And he is a vision. As sparkly as the sun. Lightly rocking, he puts his hands behind his head in full relaxation and sighs. "This is actually amazing."

There are shadows of palm fronds playing across his handsome face. His hair is adorably shaggy, like the vacation has won. He looks up at me and offers a genuine, almost vulnerable smile—a little crooked in the best way. One-thousand watts and counting. "You coming?"

I am. I am coming. If I can just catch my breath. I grasp the rough hammock in one hand and, for a second, I'm distracted by the mechanics of climbing in without displacing the sarong around my

waist and my bathing suit top. There is no graceful version of this—
at least not for me. I opt to go butt first and, by the grace of God, I'm
able to shimmy on and into position, so that we are head to foot, my
knees bent so that my feet are in line with his thighs.

But my bliss at having succeeded is short-lived.

Ethan lifts his head, peering at me curiously from the other end.
"Um. I think Charlie intended for us to be lying in the same direction."

"What? No! Why?"

"Well, because we're supposed to be a couple on a honeymoon,
not two twelve-year-old Boy Scouts sharing a tent."

I see his point. Of course, I do. If I'm honest, I saw it from the out-
set. I was just hoping no one would notice I was nowhere near him.

I try for one last out: "How do you know that's what he wants?"

We both look up the beach to where Stephanie is gesturing
wildly in circular motions for me to switch positions. *Damn.*

"Ugh. I just got on successfully. Now I have to move?"

Ethan doesn't even speak. He just looks at me with one eyebrow
cocked like, *Are you kidding me?*

"Fine, fine." I begin my struggle to get up so I can reapproach from
the other side.

"You don't have to do that," he says. "Just climb over."

Climb? I mean, this is getting worse by the minute. But what
choice do I have? He's right. This is the easier way. I flip around onto
all fours, so now I'm facing Demon Dad cleavage first, crawling toward him like a chick from some eighties metal video.

I will not fall off. That is my one promise to myself. I don't care if
I have to cling for dear life upside down, if the thing flips. I will not,
under any circumstances, hit the ground.

I begin to crawl unsteadily toward the other end, where Ethan
is now propped up on his elbows watching me inch closer. And I'm
doing just fine until I get cocky and speed up. I'm too close to the
outer edge, and the hammock begins to teeter and tip, threatening to
spill me onto the sand. Not on my watch!

To steady myself, I throw a hand toward the middle, making contact not with rope as intended but with something hard and warm. Ethan and I both turn toward my hand, which is resting on his substantial upper thigh. In a panic, I draw my palm back sharply, causing the whole apparatus to sway perilously.

"No!" I yelp.

"I got you," Ethan says, grabbing my hand and pulling me up toward him so I won't fall off the side. I don't. But the momentum, and the feel of his hand on mine, throws off my balance in the other direction, and I land flat on top of him, chest to chest, hips on hips.

Instinctively, his hands come up around my rib cage, protecting me, as the hammock reverberates. And, for a stunned moment, we are frozen in that position. Him holding me against him. *Fuck.* He fits just right under me. Like the world's most sinewy Tempur-Pedic mattress. And all my body wants is to snuggle in closer. My hands are itching to run their way over whatever bare skin they can reach. Luckily, my brain has the sense to flee.

When the hammock slows, I roll off of Ethan and lie, humiliated—but also buzzing—beside him. Sardines in a can.

"Well," he says after a beat. "That was . . ."

"Graceful?"

"Hey, guys!" Stephanie shouts from the upper beach. "We're just about ready, but we're low on time. Can you get into a workable position? Ethan, maybe an arm around her? Sasha, put your head on his shoulder! Remember: you're in *love!*"

Ethan turns to me. We're so close that we're practically nose to nose. I can't help but notice his lips, remember how they felt last night. It would be so easy to lean over and kiss them again.

"Hey," he says quietly. "Are you sure you're okay with this?"

I nod. I truly am. I am a grown woman. I can put whatever messy feelings aside for the sake of everyone involved. For the sake of their jobs and mine. This is Ethan. And, even though I haven't known him long, I know I'm safe.

I raise my head, as he slides his arm under me, careful not to pull my hair. And I turn my head into him. Because that's what I'm supposed to do. I'm acting! I am most certainly not soaking in the scent of his hyper manly deodorant mixed with the smell of . . . well, him. He brings his hand to rest on my outer arm and squeezes lightly, affectionately. And I really can for a moment almost imagine that we're that couple, on vacation without a care in the world.

"Great!" Charlie calls, cupping his hands like a megaphone so we'll hear him. "But Sasha, can you turn your body so that you're half facing him? I want the body language to feel intimate."

Intimate. Right. I shift my body toward Ethan, so I'm facing him on my side. Then, throwing caution to the wind, I rest my hand on his chest and inch my thigh over his. Because that's what someone in a couple would do. And also, now that I've had a quick taste, I'm curious about how the rest of his body feels. I want another taste.

"Sasha," he sighs.

Ending me as always. I snuggle in closer, sigh back at him. His grip on my arm gets a little firmer.

"Perfect!" Charlie says. "Just like that."

Now, I'm really in character. My heart is racing as I apply a little more pressure, moving my thigh farther onto his hip, toward his groin. Now that I suspect he's a boob man, I let my arm fall against my chest, emphasizing my cleavage.

"Sasha," he whispers, stealing a glimpse down at me. "We should stop."

But I don't. 'Cause I don't wanna. I slide my stomach and chest all the way flush against him, my thigh all the way across his body. His hip presses firmly between my legs.

"Sasha, seriously," he pleads. "I can't take it. Not here."

"Oh! You want me to move?" I tease, moving my leg against him. And that's when I feel him get hard against my inner thigh.

"Oh. OH!" I say.

He throws his free hand over his eyes. "Fuck. I'm so sorry."

But I'm not. I mean, I am. 'Cause if he can't think of something distracting, this is going to be embarrassing and it's definitely my fault. I should have taken him seriously. But I'm also a little flattered, if I'm honest. At least now I know he's definitely attracted to me, even sober. Not that I know what to do with that information.

I am a new kind of mystical creature—half horny, half hesitant.

"It's okay," I whisper. "No one can see. They're far away." I shift my leg mostly off him and edge backward a bit. "I can fix this! I'll distract you. Think about benign things. Whatever comes to mind: um, rum punch, hamburgers, stars."

He looks down at me, humor in his eyes even under the awkward circumstances. "Maybe something that doesn't remind me of last night."

"Right! Sorry. That was top of mind." I rack my brain. "Custody agreements!"

He frowns.

"Did that work?"

"Maybe too well."

Ten minutes later, when we climb out of the hammock, it should be uncomfortable, but it's not. It's like it got so awkward that the tension got diffused. He helps me up like it's all okay, and then crosses the beach to Charlie to check in on the next location.

I watch him retreat as Stephanie jogs down the beach toward me. "Wait till you see those photos," she says. "Charlie is a genius. They're incredible!"

"Oh, I'm glad," I say. And I am.

But then she fixes me with a wicked grin as we start toward the boat. "You guys looked pretty cozy canoodling in that thing." She winks, hip-checking me.

And, suddenly, I am once again seeing all of this through other people's eyes. This job is my chance to show what I'm capable of, and I'm spending it dry humping the person in charge.

Ugh. Why can't I stay focused on work? What do I think I'm doing? That's it. I need to exercise some serious willpower.

Only I am obviously not able to behave in Ethan's presence. So, there's only one other sure-fire tactic: avoidance.

Which will prove basically impossible.

On the boat ride, I sit at a distance and resist glancing over, though Ethan tries subtly to catch my eye. But even when I look down, his legs are in my view, and I can't avoid noticing the masterpieces that are his calves. Someone could compose an opera about them. But not me. Because I am Professional Sasha, who doesn't care about calves. And also I hate opera.

Eventually, I do manage to get distracted. Because this is an incredible ride. The wind is a microfiber blanket against my skin, the sun is a modulated heat lamp, the spray of the water is a mister, the boat rocks like a cradle. It's heaven. I am lulled into a stupendous stupor. But the truly amazing part is what you can see below the water. As we skim along the surface, fish, stingrays and all manner of coral swirl beneath. Our captain is the pilot, Jimmy, from our small plane—apparently, there is nothing he can't do. He has traded his captain's hat for a floppy fisherman's cap, and he acts as naturalist from under its brim, telling us what we're seeing all around us. He says we might see sharks! And, with the exception of Jackie, who is dubious, and Peter, who is poised to leap lest our equipment fly out of the boat, we all want to be the A-plus student who sees one first, so our eyes are trained on the water.

No sharks. But, when we pull up to the island, we are all breathless. It is like no place I have ever seen before. It's literally a sandbar with ellipsis-like archipelagos in the middle of the damn ocean, surrounded on all sides by shallow turquoise.

Our pilot helps us all out and, when I step from the boat and he releases my hand, I turn right around in the sand and absorb the view. We have traveled far enough from Citrine that we can see no other land at all. It is truly like we are marooned.

I feel humble and small.

The only objects breaking up the landscape are giant intact conch shells, the likes of which I have only ever seen shellacked in gift shops. These seem impossibly vibrant, a spiral of textured white and orange. A shock of pink. I walk over, pick one up and hold it to my ear. Sure enough, I am treated to the sounds of the rushing ocean. Only there is no rushing in this sea. Only calm, collected water. This ocean takes its time.

But this is a swanky island resort, not some *Gilligan's Island* fantasy (or nightmare). This is a shoot for an important glossy magazine. So someone—multiple someones—have been here first. I picture Michael and his uniformed friends on the staff stealing away back to the hotel before we spotted them.

There are eight bleached-out beach chairs with shaded overhangs immaculately aligned along one edge of the cay. The sharp lines feel alien here.

The boat has a secret compartment—probably secret only to me—out of which our pilot pulls coolers of cold beer, soda, coconut water and more of that lethal rum punch. I eye it like it might attack me. That rum and I cannot be trusted. A second cooler is stocked with sandwiches, fruit and cookies to sustain us while we play castaway.

Charlie is anxious to get started before the tides change dramatically. With the exception of his assistant, armed with a broom to smooth the sand, we all stay silent and out of the way, afraid our presence will blemish its flawless complexion. Even Stephanie goes quiet. Watching Charlie in this environment, with his pants cuffed up to his knees, as he dodges between shadows and tributaries streaming with water, is like witnessing some kind of performance art. He stands tall. Crouches low.

From a distance, Derek and Peter capture snippets of it on camera.

Sensing eyes on me, I turn and catch Ethan watching me watch Charlie. His expression is quizzical. For self-preservation, I quickly look away.

Maybe he's tense about the shoot going well? Or feels awkward about what happened in the hammock? In this idyllic setting, it's easy to forget how much is riding on this.

Then the still photoshoot is done and Charlie returns, happily accepting a beer and a beach chair.

"Okay, people!" says Stephanie. "Let's get the video segment wrapped, so we can hang out and let loose."

Ethan and I step forward. I'm still trying not to look at him.

"I'm thinking we should have you guys walk way out into the distance to the farthest tip of the sandbar," Stephanie says. "Sasha, you can stop freaking out about being featured because, that way, it'll only be your back. And, I think, if Peter and I have worked this out right, it will all be backlit in silhouette."

"Just to the edge?" I ask.

"Yes," says Stephanie. "Just the tip."

Unlike my gaffs, her implication is very intentional. She winks, then stalks back to Peter to discuss logistics. Once again, I envy her brashness.

"Shall we?" says Ethan.

"Sure," I say, without looking up. For reasons I can't confront, I am vibrating with nerves. I wish I had a minute to step away and get my head on straight.

"Okay!" says Peter. "Action!"

We start to walk, slowly, out on the narrowing sandbar into the ocean. The strip of island gets slimmer and slimmer, until we can't help but walk side by side.

"I feel like we should talk," Ethan says quietly.

"Sure!" I say with too much pep. "Happy to talk."

"Right. But it feels a little like now you're avoiding me."

"Me?"

"No. The other woman on this peninsula, walking as far away from me as possible."

"Oh, good," I say. "As long as it's not me."

"Sasha."

Ugh. With the name. My resolve liquefies.

"Ethan," I say, "I am not avoiding you." My nose grows.

How can I explain how conflicted I feel when I don't understand it myself?

We are nearing the end of nature's runway. And, at the very edge, we will have no choice but to stand directly beside each other, pressed together in order to fit. Of course this is Stephanie's design—to create a cozy picture of romance for the viewers. Only, we are not a couple. And the hammock was confusing. And so is my brain—and vagina. And my heart is beating faster and faster as my legs move slower and slower, so maybe what Peter will actually capture on film is me having a heart attack.

"Can you at least look at me?"

No. Yes. Fine.

I have no choice. I have no excuse. I slowly turn my gaze up to meet Ethan's, and the first thing I see are flecks in his eyes that I haven't noticed before. Fireworks against an amber sky.

The second thing I see is a twinge of hurt that takes me down in a whole other way.

"I'm sorry if I made you uncomfortable yesterday or just now in the hammock," he says.

Oh God. This is the last thing I want him to think. That he is some junior Martin, making unwanted advances. He barely advanced! And nothing was unwanted. If anything, I spurred the hammock incident. I feel awful.

"Ethan, you didn't make me uncomfortable. Not even a little bit."

"Okay, because, I had fun with you last night."

I swallow hard. "I . . . had fun too."

"And I don't mean to complicate things, but I think there's something—"

But it is in this moment that we reach the narrowest part of the spit, and our bodies are suddenly flush together again, my upper arm to his lower arm, my thigh to his thigh. His skin is warm, solid. I can't take any more of this push and pull today. And my body is flooded with a jolt of electricity that throws me off course, literally and figuratively.

Before I know what's happening, I'm catapulting sideways and landing on my ass in the water. Splat.

". . . here," says Ethan, finishing his sentence.

I can see he is trying to hold back laughter, and who can blame him? But I can't handle all the things happening in my head at this moment and, when he extends his hand to help me up, I turn to flee instead. Like a child, I dunk my head under the water and swim away.

The ocean is not deep here and, even when I swim farther out, I am still able to stand, the water not cresting my shoulders.

"Sasha! Come back!"

I should. I should go back. For all the reasons. This is not Professional Sasha's most shining moment. And I am about to get my shit together and swim back to the spit, when I realize something vibrant and floral is now floating several feet away, being swept up by the current.

"Shoot!" I yelp. "The sarong!" I swim after Stephanie's cover-up, trying to grab it, but it keeps slipping farther from my grasp. And just as I clasp it in my hands, I see an unidentifiable sea creature venture near me. This one is not my friend. I know it right away. It looks at me like I'm an intruder in its house. Within moments, searing pain radiates from my thigh as I yelp at the top of my lungs. And all the while I'm thinking, this is not how I wanted this to go. Not at all.

In a split second, Ethan is next to me, scooping me and the sarong up and carrying us both to the shore. All in a single bound.

Even the pain and shock can't obscure the heat I feel with his hands on my wet body, palms pressed to my upper arm and thigh. Even the mushroom cloud of embarrassment gets pushed to the back burner with his abs against my side. His strong arms encircling my ribs, inches below my chest. There is so much bare skin against skin. I'm lucky there are other people around to stop whatever wild impulses might take over.

He lies me down on the sand.

His perfect white T-shirt is now soaking wet and clinging to his body. He's got supermarket rain hair. This spells true disaster for me. I am a goner. Either from the poisonous bite or from his hotness. Whatever kills me first. I am a chalk outline waiting to happen.

"Where does it hurt?" he asks.

Nowhere. Everywhere. Only the actual bite is on my inner thigh, and I can't even show him without feeling like I'm giving him a money shot.

I level him with a look. His eyes track down my body to where a big pink welt is forming inches below my bikini line.

He opens his mouth to speak. Closes it again.

He is saved by the bell, as Jimmy rushes up. "Are you okay, miss?"

"I think I just got stung by something," I manage.

"Yes," he says. "I suspect you have met one of our minor predators, the thimble jellyfish. They usually come in groups, but I've not seen one here for many months. Quite an unusual sighting."

He says this like perhaps I will be thrilled. Take a photo of my contusion. Put it in a scrapbook.

"Okay," I say, breathing as the stinging sensation worsens. "What now?"

"Unfortunately, miss, we'll need to get you back to Citrine. It's not serious, but you do need some medicine and should have the doctor look at it." He turns to Ethan. "Perhaps some ointment?"

Is there a less sexy word than *ointment*?

"It's not far," Jimmy continues. "I can take you back and give the others time to relax here, then return for them."

Stephanie and Jackie rush up, and now I've drawn a crowd. "Are you okay?" Jackie asks. "Was it a lizard? I don't trust those motherfuckers."

"Jackie!" Stephanie rolls her eyes. "WTF! The lizards are harmless. And not in the middle of the ocean! What is your deal? Were you attacked by a dinosaur in a past life?"

"Maybe!"

As Stephanie and Jackie squabble, Ethan and Jimmy help me to standing and, as best as I can, I limp toward the boat. With absolutely no grace, I climb in. Ethan follows behind, taking a seat beside me.

"What are you doing?" I ask him, too shrilly.

"I'm coming with you."

"What? Why? No! You should stay here and enjoy the rest of the afternoon."

"No way." He shakes his head. "I'm not sending you back alone. Anyway, it's a liability. I can't have you die on us. The magazine might get sued."

"I'm not planning to expire."

"Best-laid plans . . ."

He's joking, but I realize he's not going to budge. There's legit concern in his eyes. For me, I think. Not the magazine. I have other concerns.

"But—"

"No buts," he says. "Even if that's your kink."

I drop my head in my hands. Oy. I will never live this down. Any of it.

For the record, I am not a clumsy person. This man just throws me off-balance.

The boat's engine sputters then purrs. As we're pulling away, I turn back to the beach. "Stephanie!" I shout. "I'm sorry I got your sarong wet!"

"No worries," she shouts back. "I think you put it to good use, ya damsel."

I pull my hat down to obscure my red face.

On the boat ride back, Ethan asks if I'm okay so many times that eventually Jimmy lays a gentle hand on his shoulder and says, "Mr. Ethan. This is not a life-threatening injury."

In truth, though the site of the bite is throbbing, the pain isn't extreme. Jimmy has given me an ice pack from the boat's first aid kit, which is slumping on my upper thigh (let's just say crotch and call a spade a spade). As long as I lean back, keep my thighs apart and my leg outstretched like a cowboy in a saloon, it's really okay. I try not to consider the visual.

It's really the humiliation of the past hour that's searing an irrevocable hole in my being. What is *wrong* with me? I am an adult woman. I have two children. A career. Friends. People who trust and respect my opinion. Yet, even now, with a giant welt swelling on my thigh, I am distracted by this man's proximity to me like some hormonal teenager. By the memory of how it felt to snuggle in close to his shoulder and side. By the way he runs a hand through his hair when he's stressed. By the way he's looking at me now with full brown eyes.

Was I ever this infatuated with Cliff? If so, I can't remember.

Oh no. *I am infatuated.*

To be clear, Ethan is not gazing at me with lust or affection. It's more like I'm his dumbest and most pathetic child. Like he's wondering, is she okay? And, also, how does she get herself into these messes? And, lastly, will she still be living in my basement when I'm retired?

When we reach the shores of Citrine, Jimmy anchors and ties off the boat, then helps ease me up onto the small wooden dock. Ethan is either too wise to me, afraid of me or horrified by me to be my crutch on the way to the villa, so I lean on our captain as I limp to the door.

"I'll be back with medical!" says Jimmy, once we're inside. Like this is *Baywatch* and I have almost drowned in my own hotness. Only if this were *Baywatch*, my hair would be blown out in perfect beach waves instead of knotted into a rat's nest from the wind. He hurries outside to the golf cart and jumps in like it goes more than fifteen miles per hour.

Gingerly, I lie down on the couch, a throw pillow under my head, and continue to ice my wound.

Ethan brings me a glass of water and sets it down on the table. Of course he uses a coaster. *Damn.* This man is perfection.

I'll raise you one ex-wife who says different.

The warring sides of my brain. I am reminded to be wary.

"So," says Ethan.

"So," I respond.

"That was . . ."

"I think the word you're looking for is *exciting.*"

"That's definitely not the word I had in mind."

"You're the editor," I say with a shrug. I rest my forearm over my eyes. If I can't see him, will I also turn invisible?

This makes me think of Bart, who subscribed wholeheartedly to this belief when he was a toddler. "Oh, damn!" I curse, sitting up. "I was hoping to grab conch shells for my kids! And I forgot to take pictures!"

"Do you want a picture now?"

"Of me lying on the couch? With an ice pack on my . . . ? No, thank you. I would not like to memorialize this moment."

Ugh. The outing was an epic fail on every level.

"Is that even environmentally sound?" Ethan says, eyes narrowed in thought. "Taking the conch shells out of their ecosystem? I think they might be endangered."

I lift up just high enough on my elbows to shoot him a dirty look, then plop back down.

"I don't know why you're annoyed with me. It feels like I'm the one who should be mad."

My heart plummets along with my full-time job prospects. "Because I ruined the video shoot?"

"No, I'm not worried about that." Ethan shakes his adorable head. "If someone (and by 'someone' I mean me) leaks the footage, it will definitely go viral. One for the blooper reel. That fall was digital gold."

I snatch the pillow from behind my head and whip it at his face. It misses him by a mile. I really need to work on my aim. He watches it arc and hit a bookshelf. Ball four.

Unfortunately, now I have no pillow for my head, so my neck is contorted in an awkward position against the ridge of the sofa. I adjust. Readjust. Then readjust again.

"For the love of God!" Ethan exclaims. He grabs a throw pillow from an armchair beside him and hands it to me. I tuck it behind my neck, haughty with what little self-respect I have left.

It occurs to me that maybe Professional Sasha has personnel problems beyond being attracted to her would-be employer. Like throwing foreign objects at him.

"Why should you be mad, then?" I ask. "It's not like *you* got stung by a jellyfish. You don't look injured!"

On the contrary. He looks A-plus. Of course. The boat ride has dried us a bit, but his T-shirt is still damp and fused to his chest and shoulders. Shoulders so broad they have no business belonging to a magazine editor.

"Actually, my ego is pretty bruised," he says, his arms raised to the sides with palms up, as if to present himself. "I can't say I've ever had a woman jump into jellyfish-infested waters to avoid talking to me before."

"I was saving the sarong!" I protest.

"How heroic. You'll be a top contender for the Medal of Honor. Save the Sarong!"

"Sarong rights are human rights," I deadpan.

He groans. Collapses into a chair. Buries his head in his hands in frustration.

I am torn. On one hand, I am impressed by my own ability to drive other humans, especially this one, bonkers. On the other, the man is only trying to help. I nearly humiliated him on the hammock—and then I was in fact avoiding him. And yet he just gave up a dreamy, perhaps once-in-a-lifetime afternoon on a deserted sandbar with free-flowing food, booze and good company to come back here and watch me ice my loins.

When was the last time someone did something like that for me? Took care of me? Prioritized me?

"Ethan," I say softly.

He deigns to look up at me, peering from above his hands.

"Thank you for coming back with me. For caring how I'm feeling. And for making sure that I'm okay."

He drops his hands. Shoots me a small shy smile, more killer even than his higher-watt ones. Then looks down, pleased. I have given him at least a taste of what he wants.

"You're welcome," he says. "I'm glad you're okay."

He drags his eyes back up, finding mine. My heart flips, the newest cast member of Cirque du Soleil. The Vegas show. And all that implies.

"Look," he says, "can we have an actual honest conversation, or are you going to throw yourself headfirst into the coffee table?"

He is overestimating my maturity. Just saying an earnest thank-you was my idea of a big step. I can't let him say the thing, whatever it is. Because I can't handle it. Because I'm worried it won't work out. Because I'm worried it will work out. Because, the truth is, I want him badly. Because I actually like him. Because I've been here before and it didn't end well. Because I really need this job and I can't let this crush cannibalize it.

I'm about to ask for a rain check or pretend to pass out from pain, when there's a knock at the door.

Jimmy is back with the doctor, an older woman in a lab coat and daisy sundress who he introduces as Dr. Marie—and, surprisingly, his cousin. "Twice removed," he explains.

She smiles warmly, then presses the back of her hand to my forehead with authority. I realize in that moment how much I want my mommy. But it's not the sting making me feel vulnerable.

Why can't I handle my life?

Jimmy leaves to make sure the abandoned film crew on the sandbar hasn't been eaten by an eight-eyed sea monster, and Ethan slips on his flip-flops too.

"It looks like you're in good hands." He smiles at me and Dr. Marie, though there's a kind of resignation in his eyes. "I'm going to go grab some food since I missed lunch and take care of a few work things, let you rest. I'll be back later to check in. Do you want anything?"

I have too many answers, so I shake my head. "Just rest."

And, with a sigh, he leaves.

Despite my misgivings, I realize I'm sad he's gone. I like him around me as much as I fear my own impulses. In truth, I want him to sit down on the couch, so I can rest my head in his lap. My imagination is straying into dangerous hammock territory again, so I pinch my own leg to snap myself out of it.

"He's handsome," says Dr. Marie as soon as the door clicks shut. "Maybe he wants to meet my daughter."

"Maybe," I say. "Does she like to run?"

"Run? From what?"

"No, I mean like jog," I say, miming with my hands.

"Oh! Like exercise? No. Not unless Costco on Provo is having a sale."

Dr. Marie gives me an antihistamine to quell the swelling and Advil for the pain. Then, she swabs the red area with white vinegar. "It's the best remedy to mitigate the venom."

She leaves me with hydrocortisone cream to apply morning and night for the next few days.

Once she's gone, I plod into my bedroom and lie down under a throw blanket for a few minutes while the medicine takes effect. I FaceTime Celeste to say hi to Nettie and Bart—there's early dismissal today, so I figure I might reach them. But they're at the Prospect Park Zoo—ambitious plan—and the sea lion show is about to begin. They wave to me though.

"We can't wait to see you tomorrow!" Nettie says.

"It's almost Halloween!" Bart tells me.

This I know. And I can't wait to see them too. Tomorrow morning, we have one final outdoor shoot and then I'll fly home in the early evening. I'll have the following morning back in Brooklyn to decompress and shop for last-minute costume elements and treats for our small gathering, before the trick-or-treating begins.

Still, once we've hung up the phone, even the memory of my kids' faces can't distract me from my current obsession. The pain of the sting is basically gone. But adrenaline courses through me at the thought of what Ethan was about to say before Jimmy returned with the doctor. The can of worms he was about to open. What might have wriggled out.

There won't always be a Dr. Marie to interrupt us. So, I just have to stay the course for one more night. Because I can't sacrifice my plans for a guy—not again.

At home back in Brooklyn, Ethan can go back to being someone I nod to or chat briefly with at drop-off. Or, in an ideal world, if I get this job, maybe he'll become my coworker, who I pass in the halls when I'm not working remotely. Who I see mostly at large meetings with the rest of the staff.

And, yet, I know delusion when I see it. Even my own. Because how am I ever going to stand in close proximity to that man and not feel tempted to run a hand down his chest? To graze his stubble with my fingertips? To stand on tiptoe and press my lips against his? Basically, I will always want to hump him.

Ugh! Lying here without other stimulation is not helping my cause. The book I'm reading can't hold my focus. I can't concentrate on the word games on my phone. I open my email, but there's not even pressing work to steal my attention. Just a text from Jackie making sure I'm okay.

"I'm all better!" I write. But it's a lie. I am far from fine.

What I need is a cold shower.

And that's when I have an epiphany. I'm leaving tomorrow and have yet to use—or even see—the outdoor shower. No one loves an outdoor shower like I do. *Brilliant!*

I grab a towel and shiver through the too-air-conditioned living room en route to the back entrance. Outside, on the periphery of the house, I spot what looks like a tall wooden slatted fence, painted white, with its own door. Behind it, what I discover is even better than I imagined! It is transformative. I might have been on a nice work trip before, I might have been stressing, but now, for these minutes, I am on vacation—from all the things.

I feel like I can breathe again!

The top and bottom are open like the world's poshest outdoor bathroom stall, larger than my bedroom at home. The walls that aren't wooden are sporadically decorated in oversize green tea and cream-colored Moroccan tiles. The floor is a masterpiece of stonework in various gradations from white to gray, small smooth rocks embedded in plaster. In the far corner is a collection of large green potted plants in white ceramic planters, seemingly in conversation with each other. Perhaps chatting about how dope this place is.

It's hot today. Steamier than it's been. The air has a kind of weight to it, a density. Like I'm swimming through it. And, in light of that, this shower feels like the most ingenious idea I have ever had. This is the thing I need. To wash away my troubles. And also the sand that worked its way into unspeakable crevices during the jellyfish-versus-sarong battle.

I step inside the stall and close the door behind me, slipping off my plastic Birkenstocks and hanging my towel on a hook. Then I pad in my bathing suit over to the shower fixtures. A rain shower like this one, with all its handheld attachments and settings, is above my pay grade. There's no planet on which I will figure out how to use this properly. So, I just mess with the nobs until water shoots from the overhead nozzle. I find the perfect temperature, the perfect pressure.

Perfect. I sigh.

The water unlocks something. The scent of the frangipani flowers, like a Caribbean honeysuckle, rises with the steam, intensifying into something intoxicating. An iridescent hummingbird flits in through the gap at the top and flits back out. I am in full Cinderella mode! Communing with animals! I hum "Whistle While You Work" and "A Dream Is a Wish Your Heart Makes"—a medley!—as I step under the stream, close my eyes and moan. It's heaven. And I have almost—*almost*—forgotten about Ethan.

But just thinking about forgetting him sends a flash of hot and bothered through me, radiating all the way down my chest, stomach, arms and legs to my bare fingertips and toes. They seem to alight with extra sensation. I am a live wire.

I try to push him out of mind, as I untie the halter top from around my neck and peel it down to my waist, let the water cascade over me. Prickles hit my skin like tiny wake-up calls. It is frankly not helping to distract me.

"Oh, shit!" says a voice from behind me, startling me from my compulsion. It takes me a split second to realize it's not in my head.

I whip around, hands flying to cover up my chest on instinct. And there he is in the flesh. Standing in the doorway, wearing only a towel around his waist. Like I manifested him.

Ethan.

Adrenaline thrums through me. This *really* isn't helping.

I am not naked. Not fully. Each of my hands covers one of my boobs. But I sure feel exposed, standing under that stream of water with my straps dangling from my waist, tickling my thighs as they sway.

A breeze passes over the fence, and through its cracks, whispering past my skin. Every nerve ending is open for business.

And the problem is, I like it.

Ethan is staring pointedly down at the ground. But he has not left. And if I thought the white T-shirt would be my undoing, his bare upper body has officially ended me.

He is chiseled but lean—not bulky. A jagged scar down one arm adds an unexpected bad-boy dimension. And reason has left the building. Professional Sasha is hogtied in a basement somewhere. I just don't give a fuck anymore.

It will be just this once, I tell myself. Or just this trip. Or whatever it needs to be. But I am done fighting it. I want this. Behind my hands, my body has a mind of its own.

"Sorry," Ethan is saying to the ground. "I didn't know you were in here."

"I'm in here," I say. "And, now, so are you."

"What happened to resting?"

"I couldn't rest. I'm rest*less.*"

He runs a hand through his hair, shifts his weight, like he can barely contain himself. "Tell me about it."

"I thought I just did—want me to tell you more?" It comes out breathy and more loaded than I intended. Anticipation flutters in my chest. There are a lot of things I'd like to tell him right now. Things I'd like to show him.

He bites his lip. And I feel territorial. Almost mad that he's doing it for me.

"Okay," he says, pointing a thumb behind him. Hitchhiking to a less charged place. "Well, I'll go form a single file line outside and wait my turn." He turns to leave, and I am not having it.

All the pent-up chemistry of the past weeks has come calling and it won't be denied.

"Oh, but, see, I think that's a bad idea," I say, stepping toward him before he can go. I am out of the stream, goose bumps rising on my skin, but water still drips down my body.

Surprised, he chances a glance up at me. My bathing suit is still partially up, after all. Though his eyes drift to where it threatens to fall farther.

"You do?"

"I do. Because the thing is, I love an outdoor shower."

"Who doesn't?" He is trying so hard to stare at anything other than my hands cupping my chest—my face, my neck, my rib cage, my belly, my legs—but it's a challenge.

The naked need in his eyes makes me want to skip the pleasantries. But I'm not quite done toying with him.

"If I know you're waiting outside, I'll feel rushed," I continue. "And I really don't feel like rushing."

"You don't?" He swallows hard, his voice hoarse.

"No," I say, taking another step forward, so I've narrowed the gap between us even more. "I feel like taking my time."

He exhales a shuddered breath. I can practically see his heart pounding. Mine has also joined a drum circle.

"So, what do you propose?" he asks, his hand resting where his towel meets his hip. I'm suddenly aware of how easily it might drop. "Should I go back to my room, to my regular shower?" His heart is definitely not in that offer.

"Hmm," I say, tipping my head toward one shoulder. "That seems sort of unfair."

He nods, now on board for whatever this is. "I think so."

"So, I guess maybe you have to *stay*."

He holds my gaze, his eyes darkening as my message fully computes. "Maybe I have to stay."

"Maybe we're just . . . screwed?"

I shrug. Drop my hands.

His eyes pan over me slowly. Reverently. Like a tracking shot. And I am the landscape. Shoulders. Breasts. Stomach. Thighs. Water drips down my body from my hair and neck, down my chest, past my bellybutton and into the recesses of my suit's bottom. We both watch it disappear.

He licks his lips.

I take a final step forward, so we're as close as we could possibly be without touching. I can see every nook and cranny of his upper body, the chiseled lines of his pecs, abs, arms. The slightest move, a microscopic tilt forward, and my bare chest will be pressed against his. My breath hitches. I don't know if the anticipation is going to kill me or if it's keeping me alive. He smells like tropical sunscreen and escape. I can feel the heat from his body like flying too close to the sun—or maybe it's mine.

"Sasha," he says, his voice rugged with gravel. If my insides weren't already molten, they are now. "Are you sure?"

And I am. I want this too much to stop. In my mind, I have already taken the plunge.

I am wet, and I am wet.

I look him hard in the eyes. Once we go there, we cannot turn back. Whatever passes between us in that moment communicates more than all the words.

"Positive."

That seals the deal. Ethan shoves the door closed behind him with his elbow without glancing back. It clicks into place. Decisive. Like a foregone conclusion. His eyes are locked on mine. Finally, *finally*, I lift a hand and dare to run it along his collarbone, then down his stomach, his skin warm to the touch. His ab muscles clench beneath my fingers. There is a sharp intake of breath in which I read multitudes.

Everything in me feels pulled taut.

This. Is. Happening.

We stand there, zeroed in on each other, for a beat. My whole body buzzing.

"You wanted to talk earlier," I rasp, barely able to catch my breath. "Still need to now?"

"Nope," he says, eyes fierce and boring into my own. Vaguely threatening. Like I'm the burger now. "I'm good."

But there is the smallest something glitching in his expression.

"So, what's the problem?"

He blinks, nods toward the shower, which we are far from under. "You're wasting water."

As I groan in irritation, Ethan takes me by the wrist with one hand and the waist with the other and backs me against the wall.

I look up into his face, inches from my own. "So, are you giving a TED talk about conservation or are we . . . ?"

I don't get to finish the sentence. He kisses me hard up against the slats, shutting me up. And I'm more than good with it. His lips are soft at first, then less patient, his stubble delightfully rough. He tastes like dragon fruit and salty sea. His body feels both new to me and like it's already mine. And, as he slips his tongue into my mouth, he changes the tone of my groan.

If I thought the kiss on the beach last night was full-on, this is next level, frantic with need.

And this time there are no interruptions.

There's nothing calm or languid about what happens next. It's a full-court press. That's just fine with me. I've been waiting too long to wait longer. We're flush against each other, his hips pinning mine, our hands on their own personal journeys. I cannot get close enough. Pressure is already building inside me. His deep kiss gets deeper, rougher, as he picks me up, his strong hands cupping my ass. My legs wrap around him. Like I'm a python and might end us both. Entangled, he carries me under the shower stream, where we tear our lips apart for an instant, staring into each other's faces.

His lids are heavy. We're both out of breath. I shake my head, laugh.

"Better?" I ask.

"Better," he agrees.

My body bumps and grinds against his chest and six-pack, slick and wet, as he slowly slides me back onto my own two feet. From my new vantage point, I watch water drip down his cheeks from his wet supermarket hair, down his toned body. *Fine*. I admit it. I guess all that running is *kinda* worth it.

And it's all mine to touch. I can choose my own adventure.

Under the scruff is that dimple I admired before. I reach up and trace it now with my fingertip, then drag my finger across his plump bottom lip. Because I can.

"Hi," he says, from an inch away.

"Whattup," I say back.

I glance past him at the huddle of plants in the corner. "I feel like I'm being watched."

He rakes his eyes down my body, leaving prickles in his wake. Head to breasts to tippy toes. "That's because you are."

That does me in. Enough talk. I slide my fingers up into his hair at the back of his neck, then reach around and tease his ear with my teeth. He growls, then urges my head back up with his chin, capturing my lips and kissing me properly again. Only there is nothing proper about it. Proper is for amateurs. His hands come to my ass as I dig my fingers into the backs of his wide shoulders, pulling him toward me as if there's anywhere left to go. We're in so deep, we might fuse.

His thigh presses between my legs. I gasp. I can feel him hard against me.

His lips trail from my face down the side of my neck, to my shoulder, my collarbone, shooting me full of chills. He cups my breasts as I arch against him.

"Keep your hands up," I mumble. "Don't let them drop."

"Don't worry," he grunts, his teeth against my neck. "I've got this."

"All right," I sigh. "As long as you're on top of things."

He pauses to look up with a raised eyebrow. "Maybe for *part* of the time."

"Maybe for *all* of the time."

"You're impossible," he whispers against my ear, shaking his head. "But also really hot."

I'll take it.

Just like that, we're grinding against each other with the urgency of teens with a time limit and parents downstairs.

And that's when his towel drops. A sopping white terrycloth heap on the rocky floor. We both look down at it and back up at each other. He laughs. Shyly. Adorably.

Only, there is nothing to be bashful about. More like something to shout from the rooftops.

I can work with this. And I take it as an invitation. I raise my hand way up and, starting at the top of his head, trace the path of water down his body, past his shoulders, his chest, the place where his lower back slopes into his ass. I lick a droplet from his chest.

"Fuck," he groans.

I like it when Demon Dad curses.

He grabs my hips with authority—running isn't the only thing he knows how to do—and slips his thumbs inside my bathing suit on either side, teasing it slowly down. He pauses there.

"What's the holdup?" I ask, pursing my lips.

He looks at me sideways, then yanks it the rest of the way down, so it drops with a smack, pooling at my ankles.

"No holdup."

I am fully naked. In all the ways.

We stare at each other like a dare.

He calls my bluff first, backing me toward the shower wall again in a cloud of steam. Apparently, the water preservation will have to wait. I am also a finite resource. My shoulder blades press against the wood, as he pins my hands to the wall.

He takes a beat to look me up and down. "You're so fucking beautiful," he murmurs. And it's like I've been waiting for this my whole life instead of a few weeks.

My breath catches as he drags his palm down my arm and side to my hip. He makes a pilgrimage across my upper thigh and slips his hand between my legs. *Finally.* He just barely touches me. I claw at his back. He gives me more.

If my jellyfish sting still hurts, I'm in too much of a fugue state to know or care. I am no longer a solid. I am liquid mercury, shiny and illusory. No, I am a vapor! I am weightless. I am one of the constellations we saw looking down on us from the sky.

And I want it all. I am prepared to beg.

That's when it occurs to me. There's a hitch in my plan. *Damn.*

"Condom," I mutter, like it's the name of someone I hate.

He breaks away, his brow furrowed like he's never heard of such a thing. Like it's a foreign object. "Condom?" Then, "Oh, shit. Condom."

We're old married folk. Well, at least we were recently. People who either had weekly sex without constraint or never bumped uglies at all. Why would we think to carry such things? And it's not like we're in New York City. Like there's a corner bodega or a twenty-four-hour pharmacy with blinking fluorescents advertising carnal convenience. This is a deserted island. Literally. A five-star wasteland. And, unless we can MacGyver a contraceptive device out of Turkish towels and key chains from the gift shop, we're out of luck.

Now, we might *actually* be screwed.

But my fiery loins aren't having it. Not with his wet skin pressed against mine. We must not be stopped.

I silently brainstorm; I can see Ethan's wheels turning too. Stephanie surely has a stash. But we can't go there. There's no planet on which she doesn't ask questions. There's no way to ask Michael if I ever want to face him again.

That's it! The thought of my favorite Citrine staff member reminds me of his tour and suddenly I have all the answers.

"The sundry drawer!" I shout, like I've got the most popular answer on *Family Feud*. Like 98 percent of the people they polled during sex said "sundry drawer!"

Still gripping my body, Ethan looks at me like I've lost it. "Sorry?"

Then I remember that he is a man. He does not use cotton balls. He does not use shower caps. He does not think about after sun gel.

"In the bathroom," I say. "With the Q-tips."

I watch realization dawn on his lovable face. "They have condoms in there?"

We bolt apart, throw on our towels and flip-flops and, pausing momentarily to make out against the back door to the main house, scurry through the villa like semi-naked burglars. Once in my room, I am on a mission. Clutching my towel to my chest, I slip into the sparkly bathroom, open the drawer with a prayer—and there are my RAW fair-trade condoms, hip to be square and backlit like the Holy Grail!

Thanking the gods, I turn back to Ethan, who is standing by the bed, a pained but hopeful look on his face.

"Are they there? Please tell me they're there."

I hold up the package like a winning ticket. And, in doing so, drop my towel. I don't pick it up. He throws his head back and grins. And I'm on him before three.

Luckily, this time, the shades are drawn.

We topple onto the fluffy cloud bed and, in an instant, he flips me underneath him. He settles in like he's my favorite weighted blanket. And I don't ever want to get up. He leans down and nips my bottom lip. Then, pressing kisses against my overheated skin, he works his way from my jaw down. Neck. Collarbone. Breasts. Rib cage. Waist. Hip.

I feel like I'm about to burst I'm so impatient.

I close my eyes. Flash to all the times I've tried to push my feelings for him aside—stealing glances at his body in the park, the hot shock of his hand grazing mine in the schoolyard, his thigh between my legs on the hammock, his rum punch lips and tongue entangled with mine on the pitch-dark beach. His warm hand running slowly, appreciatively, down the side of my body, sending shivers through me. Every adorable smile and playful smirk. And I am overwhelmed with how much I want him.

It's when he reaches my inner thigh, and stays for a while, that I call it.

I appreciate the gesture, but I can't wait anymore. I need his bigger body between my legs. His chest to my chest. I need my hands on his back, him pressed into me. No air between us.

"It's time," I say.

"Time?"

I nod, holding up the condom. "To bang."

He shakes his head, laughs. "Such a way with words." But he doesn't hesitate before he reaches for it.

I get to watch him, like a preview of what's to come, as he rips the package open. The boyish angles of his face. His furrowed brow as he concentrates. His muscular forearms. He is a thing of beauty.

Then, not soon enough, he is hovering over me, his rapacious eyes fixed on mine. This man wants me too.

I wrap my legs around his hips and hold on tight; he is so hard against me.

"Sasha," he says gruffly. My *name*.

I am already undone.

"Ethan. *Please*."

He shoots me one of those crooked half smiles, like he likes that I'm tortured for him.

"Since you asked nicely," he says. Then he finally thrusts inside me—first slow, deep, then harder as I demand it.

And that's when I lose all cogent thought, all hell breaking loose in the best possible way. The best *laid* plans. (God help me and the puns.)

34 | The Deed

ETHAN

Finally.

I swear I didn't mean to walk in on her in the shower. I tried to work, barely ate lunch, then went back there looking to find relief, some distraction, from obsessing about her, about the hammock, about how good she looked in that goddam bathing suit. But I'm definitely not sorry about the mix-up.

Best mistake ever.

And then she told me to stay. Standing there, half naked, with water trailing down her insane body. Like a fucking reprieve.

I already thought Sasha was hot. Objectively, she is. But she's so much more—she's a supernova. And when she looks up at me from the bed, her green eyes blazing, hair tangled and wet against the white comforter, cheeks flushed, her naked body forcing me to admit that her three-mile runs are more than plenty, I wonder if there's anything I don't like about her.

I like when she's throwing down over a hoodie, I like when she's scowling at me, I like when she takes control on set, and I definitely like when she shoots me a wicked smile now on the heels of a stupid condom joke.

I like her ski jump nose. The birthmark on her hip. The fact that she's ticklish around her ribs.

I definitely like her naked and pressed up against me. Though I *will* hold out.

I like her. And now I'm gonna show her how much.

TO-DO

- Sasha.

35 | Postproduction

SASHA

We are reliving the sarong saga. Again. At least, Ethan is. The more he rehashes it, the funnier the story becomes to him. I am lying in my bed next to him, glowering. Grumpy Smurf.

Apparently, now that he knows I like him enough for naked stuff, his ego is less fragile. He is no longer worried about pissing me off. *Typical.*

Luckily he is an appealing sight. A late-afternoon fairy-tale light glows through the shades, dusting us with happy endings—of all kinds. His brown eyes are lazy, easy, even as they spell mischief. The Demon Dad, the runner, the editor in chief, has gone out of them. He's just him.

Surrounded by cumulus bedding, his skin looks especially taut and tan. His chest is exposed at the top; one leg pokes out from beneath the comforter. I trace the scar that meanders down his left forearm, taking its time before dead ending at his wrist. When he got it in a skateboarding accident at sixteen, you could see bone. His mother almost threw up, even though she's a surgeon. These are just some of the things I've learned in the past hours, as we swapped stories and fluids. I am getting an Ethan education.

"And you just careened into the water!" He laughs now. "Why didn't you break your fall? With your hands?!"

I tilt my head and glare at him, pointedly. Because obviously he is about to tell me to keep my hands up. I beat him to the punch, grabbing *his* hands and pinning them to his chest before he can make the move.

He doesn't even need to say it. He just dissolves into laughter again, the bed quaking and me quaking with it. Needless to say, I have never seen him lose it like this before, and I would love it more than anything. If it wasn't at *me*.

"Maybe it was all a ploy," I say, releasing his wrists and flipping haughtily onto my back like I'm a noblewoman sleeping with a stable boy. As if I have the upper hand. Which I clearly do not.

He raises an eyebrow. "A ploy to . . . ?"

"Seduce you."

"That was definitely not necessary." He rolls over and kisses my bare shoulder, a large hand palming my thigh.

"Well, whatever! I still think the incident with the jellyfish cemented things."

"Actually, oddly, I don't usually think of pratfalls as foreplay."

I grab an extra pillow off the bed, where the duvet is in blissful disarray, and hit him in the head with it. It's easier to make contact at close range.

"Oh, hell no," he says. All authority is lost, as his voice is muffled absurdly by the pillow. "You messed with the wrong man!"

He tosses it aside and flips me on my side so he's pressed up behind me, kissing down my neck and the middle of my back, making me giggle. We are so cute.

He stops, lying on his side, and I roll onto my back. For a moment, I'm overwhelmed by how much I like him. He exhales, maybe having a similar thought, and brushes my hair from my face. "In all seriousness, I would have been on board no matter how many times you tried to save that sarong."

"Well, I'm about to question *my* choices if you bring it up again."

"Okay, okay." He raises a hand in surrender, then lies back and sighs. "Thank God this finally happened. I was losing my fucking mind."

This, I like to hear. I roll over to face him now, resting my chin on his chest and tracing the lines of his collarbone with my finger. No perfect T-shirt to cover it up. Now that I get to touch Ethan, I will never stop. Well, at least not today. I push the concept of timelines from my head.

Not today!

"Tell me more about how much you wanted me," I say.

He shakes his head and smiles.

I have basically had at least one point of contact with Ethan since we absconded, damp and dangerous, from location A (the shower) to location B (my bedroom), and made a mess of location C (my bed). If I thought I liked outdoor showers before, now they've eclipsed all other fauceted environments forever. Bathrooms, mudrooms, hammams, kitchens (even the Nancy Meyers kind).

"Honestly, I kind of have that effect on people," I joke. "Make them lose their minds."

"I'm sure you do."

I tip my head onto his shoulder, throw my thigh over his. The thigh without the sting. His skin is warm. His leg flexes under mine.

I might make a map of his muscles. I'm starting to learn his terrain.

I can't figure out if I forgot how much I like sex, or if it's never actually been this good before. And I'm contemplating going again as research, when his expression turns earnest. "Seriously, I think this is probably obvious, but"—he glances down, unsure, then back up to meet my eyes—"I've liked you since I met you. Even if you don't remember."

I shoot him a doubtful look. "Um. That's a little hard to swallow."

There I go again. Innuendo o'clock. He opens his mouth to call me out, but I cover it with my hand. He bites my finger lightly. I want to bite him back.

"It's true!" he says.

"Really? Even at the school merch stand? As I contemplated your demise? And we almost became one of those salacious headlines: 'Murder by Sweatshirt!'"

"Especially then. I thought, *Now, there's a pain in the ass . . . with a really nice ass.*"

I swat him again. "Takes one to know one." I pinch his firm butt. He nudges me, flirty.

"Seriously, though. I even liked you when you yelled at me on the steps outside of school. I was afraid of you. But I liked you. And now I like you even more."

I have no clue if he's for real about having liked me way back then, but it sounds nice. I'm flattered, for sure. "If that's true, why did you go mute the other night on the beach after we . . . you know?"

"Kissed?" He sighs, then stretches his arms up behind his head, like he's sunbathing. Fair enough. I am surely emanating heat as I watch him. "I was following your lead. First of all, you also clammed up. And then you shut things down instead of laughing it off or signaling that you wanted more. Plus, earlier you'd been insistent that our dinner wasn't a date. I wasn't going to force things."

"It wasn't a date! I would never eat a burger that way on a date!"

"Well, that's just a shame."

He grins at me. I roll my eyes.

"But also"—he clears his throat, looks away—"I thought maybe you were into Charlie." He chances a glance at me, like he might still be wondering.

Ah. The idea is absurd. Charlie is a beautiful specimen, but he is so very young. And, anyway, I've been too busy trying not to fall for Ethan to notice anyone else. But, as soon as Ethan says it, some puzzle pieces slide into place.

"Wait!" I sit up against my pillow and, as the sheet slips down to my waist, I watch him notice. "Is that why you keep asking if I like working with him? Lord. Men may get older, but they do not get smoother."

He sits up on his pillow too, dropping his arms. "Excuse me. I resent that. I can be plenty smooth. I saved you from a sarong!"

I look at him sideways. Is that really what happened? We share a sardonic stare.

"No, but seriously. It's just . . ." His gaze flits down again, his nervous tell, and his lashes are dark against his cheeks. "I haven't liked anyone like this in a long time . . . for some reason."

Well, that was *almost* a compliment. "For some reason?"

"Yes. Despite all the obvious issues."

I prop myself up on my elbow. "What is this? *Pride and Prejudice?* What obvious issues? My family isn't embarrassing. Well, if they are, you don't know it yet. And I'm definitely as well-bred as you. After all, *I'm* the one who's originally from New York."

"Oh Lord. I'm going to ignore that. No, I mean the other issues." He counts on his fingers. For the umpteenth time that day, I think, *He's got great hands.* "Your terrible running form, your terrible attitude (especially when you think someone snakes something from your kid), the fact that you generally avoid me as much as possible . . ."

I smile, but, at the same time, I glitch for a second on his finger, which has a subtle tan line from years of wearing a ring. I recognize that particular type of branding. I have it too. An indentation on my finger. Mine is less pronounced. Fewer years married. More years passed.

I love hearing about how much Ethan likes me, of course. Even if it can't amount to anything because we will have to return to real life soon. Maybe one day I'll get up the guts to tell him that too—that I haven't felt this way in a long time either. Maybe *ever.* The thought makes my chest tighten. But, in that moment, I am reminded that Ethan is also someone's baggage. For someone else, he is Cliff. More reliable, of course, and a way better dad, a better listener, a more quality human, but still the source of frustration, anger, disappointment. I feel panic rise and settle in my chest. Will he be that for me, too? How do I know he's not just another shitty father on a good streak?

I exhale, working to calm myself down.

He studies my face with suspicion. "What's happening here?" he asks, waving a palm to encompass my expression. Perhaps to make it magically disappear. "Something bad just happened in your head."

"I'm good," I squeak, pulling the covers up higher over my chest.

I close my eyes for a split second, reminding myself of how much better the last two hours have been than most of my last two years (time with my beautiful children aside).

Ethan shoots me a doubtful look. Why does he read me so well? Is this the problem with sleeping with an editor? Is he always going to see my errors? Proofread me? Correct my flaws? Catch my dangling participles?

"To be clear, in case I freaked you out, I was kidding about your issues," he is saying. "Except for the running thing. That's real. You should maybe see a coach." The fact that I don't roll my eyes or swat him seems to worry him more. His expression grows serious. "For what it's worth . . . this, with us, isn't something I do a lot."

Wow. Oddly, because I live like a nineteenth-century nun, it hasn't even occurred to me to wonder about Ethan's love life beyond his ex. This momentarily diverts my panic away from the word *us*. Suggests an alternate route on my neural pathways—self-destructive curiosity!

"Wait, do you, like, date?"

He shifts, uncomfortable. Pulls the sheet a little higher on his chest too. "I have . . . a little."

"You have a little? So *a lot*. Tell the truth: Do you actually have a condom in your wallet, after all? 'Cause if you held out on me . . .'"

"I do not."

"Because you don't believe in contraception?"

"Because I haven't been having sex with random strangers."

"What about less random strangers?"

He shoots me an impatient look.

I let that one go, but I press on—because now I need to know: "Are you, like, on apps?"

"Not yet."

"Not *yet*?"

"That isn't what I meant. That sounded wrong."

"Yeah," I agree. "It sure did."

"I just meant: people—some buddies of mine—have been trying

to convince me to use them, but I haven't. It doesn't seem like a good fit for me."

I nod my head like, *Yeah, it better not be*. I don't know why, since two minutes ago I was panicking about the possibility of a future with him. A future in which I get hurt. Or he cramps my style.

I am all over the map. No compass in sight. No idea how to use a compass anyway.

What do I want? Do I even know? And can I even have it?

"What about you?" he asks.

I shake my head. "No apps."

"Have you been set up by friends?"

"Recently? No setups."

"Have you dated anyone at all since you broke up with Cliff?"

I toggle my head. "I briefly considered marrying my exterminator after the water bug debacle of summer 2022. But we don't speak of that."

"Sasha!"

"Ethan!"

He gives me his best *Cut the shit* look. It reminds me of when I was little and my mom came into my room with an empty marshmallow bag and a knowing look. The marshmallow debacle of summer 1985.

"No," I admit. "Not really. I dated one guy. For one month. But then he wore the ugliest shoes, and I just couldn't."

"Ah." He nods knowingly. "Well, at least your values are intact."

"Look. Attraction is attraction, man. And I can't date a guy in Tevas."

"Teva actually brought on new creative directors," he says. "The shoes aren't terrible."

I stare at him for a beat. "Oh, okay. My bad. You're right." I point my thumb over my shoulder. "You want me to go find that guy I was dating? Give him a second chance?"

"No." Ethan shakes his head, hands up. "I'm good." He rolls over and runs a hand down my arm, props his head on his other hand.

"What about your wife?" I say. Just like that, he rolls away from me back onto his back.

"*Ex*-wife."

"Right."

"Is this when that never-talk-about-an-ex-on-a-date rule kicks in?"

"This is still not a date."

"What is this, then? An all-hands meeting?"

"Ethan! Does she date? Your ex?"

He sighs. "Kaitlin? Well, I assume you mean aside from the guy she had the affair with?"

Everything stops.

If Ethan continues talking, I don't know, because there is a roaring in my ears like a conch shell hooked up to an amp. I am dizzy with horror. Did he just say *Kaitlin*?

Ethan is repeating my name. "*Sasha. Sasha. Are you okay?*"

It finally jolts me out of my k-hole.

"Ethan," I finally manage, sitting bolt upright. Even the light outside has darkened, the sun ducking behind a cloud. "Your ex-wife is . . . Kaitlin? Like Kaitlin Lafferty?"

"I mean, technically, she changed her name to Jones when we got married," he rambles, oblivious, "but she never really used it, and I'm sure she's not using it now." Only then does he look at my face. Like really look at it. "Wait. Did you not know that Kaitlin was my ex?"

I drop my head into my hands and shake my head. What the fuck have I done? Am I *that* mom? How could I have assumed that I could somehow keep this thing with Ethan separate from real life? That there would be no repercussions?

"You really are the world's worst cyberstalker. Can you even use a computer?" He's joking, but my mood has changed.

"Sasha, it's okay," he says. "It's not like you guys are close friends."

"I know," I mumble into my hands. "But I know her! Or I knew her. A little bit. And she's a VIM!"

"What's a VIM?"

"Never mind."

"So you knew each other as kids—who cares? It's not like you're friends now."

I look up at that. Ethan genuinely appears unconcerned, leaning back against the headboard. He glistens. Not a care in the world.

"You *know*? That we know each other from growing up? And you never mentioned anything?"

This is starting to feel like a trend to me. And the dark clouds in my head are moving in like a storm front. He didn't mention the job opportunity. He didn't mention that I once had sleepover parties with his ex-wife! What else isn't he mentioning?

"Honestly, Sasha, I assumed you knew."

Ethan is not wrong. Like the *Escapade* editor in chief details, this information was easily accessible. On some level, I chose not to look. But I still feel defensive.

"It's a big school! I don't know who belongs to who! I've avoided getting too engaged for this exact reason!"

"You were afraid you'd have sex with all the dads?"

I shoot him my best death stare. "No, Ethan," I say through gritted teeth. "But my divorce from Cliff, his Golden Globes antics, turned really public. Everyone at school knew. It was humiliating! So, I like to keep things separate. Private."

"Understandable." He shrugs a shoulder.

"And, by your own account, you were never around. No pick-up. Not even drop-off. How could I have known? It's not like Kaitlin and I hang out."

He is shaking his head, confounded. "But, Sasha," he says quietly. "We *met*."

"I know. You said that. But I don't remember everyone I meet in passing!"

He presses his lips together, clearly bothered. "It wasn't in passing."

I am stopped dead in my tracks. Brakes screeching. All aboard the home-wrecker train. "It wasn't?"

Ethan looks legitimately hurt. His eyes are downcast, and he's fiddling with a loose string on the comforter's seam. And that sears a hole in me.

"Ethan. Tell me."

"You really don't remember at all?" I shake my head. "The girls, Ruby and Nettie, had a playdate once at the park when they were small. Kaitlin had to leave, so you and I stayed alone together. We met. We *talked*. For hours. About real things."

"We talked," I repeat. To no one in particular. Myself. Ethan. The cheerful yellow lampshade on my bedside table which, in this tense moment, is looking for a reason to excuse itself.

How could I have spaced on talking to this amazing man? Granted, I was a mess in those days. Cliff was disappearing, and I had tunnel vision, trying to navigate caring for the kids on my own. But still. Was this willful denial on my part? Did I not know because I didn't want to? All those times I never asked Ethan about his daughter, never asked Ruby's name. Was I avoiding an inconvenient truth? On some unconscious level, had Ethan simply enabled my myopia?

What already felt complicated now seems like a Rubik's Cube. Perhaps solvable for some, but not for me. Suddenly, I am just so naked under the covers, my skin nervy against the cotton sheets. I pull my bare thigh back underneath.

"I'm just trying to process this," I say. "It's not your fault."

Ethan nods. But, by the way he's looking at me, I can tell he doesn't totally understand why this is a big deal, never mind why I forgot him. I get it. It's not that Kaitlin and I are tight. We're absolutely not. I know nothing about her, as evidenced by this current shocker. And I knew his wife was a mother at the school. It's not surprising that I know her a little or have seen her around. But things have just gotten real. I have fallen back down to earth. And, as is my style, I have landed like a sack of potatoes.

"Sasha, I'm sorry you didn't realize. But this doesn't have to change anything. This," he says, referencing the room, the messy bed, the cool-kid condom wrappers, us, "was great. *Is* great."

I nod. Fair enough. I concede. It was great.

But that just confounds me more. What seems so good turns sour as soon as it hits the air outside this room.

"Please don't freak out," he continues, leaning in, a hand resting on my cheek. "You haven't betrayed anyone. Kaitlin and I were all wrong. As she clearly demonstrated."

"By telling you she was unhappy?"

"No. By fucking someone else for like a year."

"Oh, that. Yeah. Right."

"But you and I . . ." He exhales, dragging a hand through his hair. "I think maybe there's something that's really right here. Something—"

Before Ethan can continue, the front door to the villa slams. We both hear it. And, though I can't be in his body, I think it gets us both in the gut. Winds us. We listen as Stephanie, presumably, kicks off her flip-flops and pads across the living room floor.

"Damn," he whispers. "Reality."

"It's a bitch." I nod.

It's not that I'm afraid of being caught. I mean, I don't want to be outed. But I don't think that's what it is for Ethan either. As we look at each other, wordlessly, it's easy to read the uncertainty in our expressions. What is this thing? What just happened? What does it mean for our actual lives? Anything? And is it going to happen again? Should it not, for all the reasons? And, if so, is it worth the complication?

We are definitely not getting a chance to sort any of that out right now.

"I guess I should go," Ethan says. But he doesn't move.

The blanket has slipped lower on his lap, revealing the indentations below his abs. I don't want this to be the last time I'm privy to that sight. The last time I get to hoard him for myself.

Tomorrow, after the short morning shoot, I fly home. The rest of the staff stays on for one more night to do pick-ups. Tie up loose ends. We arranged it that way, so there was no way I'd miss Halloween.

I didn't realize the loose ends would be us.

"I wish we had more time," he says. In some ways, we have all the time in the world. We live in the same neighborhood. Run into each other daily. Bump into each other amid Crispix and tangled earbuds. But I know what he means. More time to figure this out. To concretize it. To make it something or nothing before the number of players expands. Before we go home, get stressed, and most likely pretend this never happened.

The thought makes me so sad. Most of all because it feels impossible.

"Me too," I sigh.

But it's time. Not just because Stephanie is back or because we're due at drinks and dinner soon. But because he's got his daughter to call. I've got my kids to FaceTime. We've got work we ignored and text chains we abandoned. News stories to read and photos to post. We've got to return to the world. The world, which includes his ex-wife. *Kaitlin.*

Slowly, surely, he peels back the blanket and climbs out of bed. It feels lighter with him gone in a way I hate. He is backlit against the sheer window shades, the muted sun setting behind him. Despite my guilt and agita, I enjoy the view. Both views.

He wraps a towel around his hips again. Shrugs at me with that small crooked smile, like he's not sure why he's bothering to cover up, then crosses to the door connecting our rooms. At the last minute, he reconsiders, turns around, and comes back to my bedside. He leans over me, his breath soft on my face, and kisses me slowly, firmly. For a long time. Like a promise. Now, he takes his time.

I am tempted to pull him back down as it escalates, wrap my arms and legs around him and start from the beginning, but I know I can't. For so many reasons. Instead, eventually, *regretfully*, we break apart. He takes a last look at me before he leaves.

"Please don't freak out," he says.

It's so weird to think that he once belonged to someone else. Who was he then? Who was she? Is there a world in which he gets to be mine?

But there's little time for thought. As he disappears beyond the other side of the connecting door, he takes the languid pace with him. If the clock moved at half speed for the last dreamy hours, now it plays catch-up.

It's time to get dressed for dinner. Begrudgingly, I get up too, throw on my robe. I "showered" before. But now I have to shower.

As soon as I'm up, there's a knock at the door. Not the one to Ethan's sex den (its new name). The main one. To the living room.

"Hello?" Stephanie calls. "Sasha? Are you alive in there?"

Will she see what just happened all over my face?

I walk over and open the door. "Hey, Steph."

She's the picture of post-beach day bliss. Her wide-brimmed straw hat is still perched on her head, her hair below it a tangle of salt-water strands, even with the keratin. Her cheeks bear just the slightest hint of pink. She looks relaxed and happy.

Having spent the day swimming and lolling in the sea, she is wearing less makeup than she usually does. And, honestly, it looks better. She's kind of glowing. I realize, at the sight of her smile, that I really like her.

"She lives!" Stephanie says. "I just wanted to see how you're feeling."

How I'm feeling? I don't know. The best and worst I've felt in ages! The most I've felt in years. I look at her in confusion. How does she know?

"Post-sting," she clarifies.

The sting. *Right.* So much has happened since then. My jellyfish beef seems like the least of the issue.

"Aw, thanks." I smile back. "It's not bad at all. The doctor came and gave me some meds, and now I barely know it's there."

She raises her eyebrows. "Good meds?"

"How do you feel about ointment?"

"Not great."

"Not good meds, then."

"Ahh." She shrugs. "Well, I'm glad you're better but so bummed that you missed the afternoon!"

"Me too!" I smile-frown. "I'm so sorry I messed up the shot when I fell, by the way. That probably wasn't exactly what you envisioned."

"Oh." She crinkles her brow, shakes her head. "Don't even go there! You didn't ruin the shot at all. We already had everything we needed."

Phew. The reality is I'm working for Stephanie too. I need her to be pleased. Also, it's nice to feel like less of a loser. Even if she's just being kind.

"Where's Ethan?" she asks.

"Ethan?!" I say, like I've never heard of him. *Ethan? Condom? Wife?*

"Yeah. You know the guy. Tall. Handsome. Has more rules than a casino."

"Ah. *That* Ethan." As the world's worst liar, I decide it's safest to tell some version of the truth. "He waited until the doctor came and then went to catch up on some stuff."

She leans against the doorframe. "Ah, damn. I thought you might get some time alone together." She wiggles her eyebrows suggestively.

"Alone? Together?" I tighten my robe around my waist, a jolt of panic strumming through me.

"Yeah, *alone together.* I mean, it seems like you guys are a chemistry set, if you know what I mean. He obviously digs you. I've been trying to give you some *space.*" She extends the last word for effect.

I am completely thrown. My words are lost. Have we really been that obvious?

"Y-you have?" I manage. "Like, that's why you stayed out last night?"

She shrugs. "In part."

"But . . . he's a coworker."

"Eh. Sort of."

"But this is work."

Stephanie takes off her hat, shakes out her hair. "Look, I care about Ethan, and I like you. It seems like you both could use a little . . . fun. The rest will work itself out. It always does."

"Right." I wish I could be so confident.

I almost want to tell her what happened, to reward her hard work. Her heart is clearly in the right place (between our legs?). But I know I can't.

She shrugs, throwing up her hands. "Oh well! You can lead a horse to water, but . . . you can't make it bone. I should go change. I might check out that outdoor shower! Have you tried it?"

I grunt noncommittally and shut the door before she can see me flush from forehead to toes.

Just before it clicks shut, she calls out: "Oh, by the way, have you peeped tomorrow's weather? Looks nasty!"

My heart drops.

Damn. That's not even an option on my radar. Bad weather is going to ruin tomorrow morning's final shoot. Man, when it rains, it pours. Literally. I grab my phone off the bedside table, where Ethan's water glass still sits as a reminder of our hours together—mostly of how much he hydrates—and launch the weather app.

Stephanie is right. The forecast predicts thunderstorms from 8:00 a.m. through most of the day. This is the Caribbean, of course, which means the weather is changeable. It could be fine, but this does not look good.

Right away, I go into producer mode, considering contingencies. This isn't the first time I've had to improvise in bad weather. I once ran a shoot in the Bahamas where I made the crew wrap cameras in plastic bags to protect them from rain and pitch glamping tents to keep out the wind. I spent the whole day terrified that, at any moment, tens of thousands of dollars' worth of equipment would be destroyed on my watch. Not an experience I want to revisit.

But that won't work here, even if I could survive that stress again. Not unless Charlie doesn't mind changing up the whole aesthetic of his spread. The final shoot is right here on the beach, and it's meant to look placid and clear, in keeping with the rest of the images from the trip—sunshine for days. He intended this for the lede.

Which means the shoot has to push until the weather improves.

Which means I have a problem. Because I need to get home by to-morrow evening or I will miss Halloween. I already know there's no early enough flight out the following day.

My chest is tight. I'm working hard not to envision the look on Bart's and Nettie's faces if I don't make it back. His wobbly chin. Her watery eyes. And, even though I know it's irrational, it's hard for me not to feel like this is karmic. Like this is what I get for giving in to the pull I feel toward Ethan. For making the irresponsible choice and indulging my base impulses. This is what I get for taking my eye off the ball.

Ever since Cliff left, I have put every ounce of energy I could muster into being as good a mother as I can be. That's why the con-stant screwups and blunders at school have been so maddening. Be-cause, with the carnage of my marriage, I feel like I have already given my kids an extra hill to climb. I won't let it become a mountain.

But now I'm on what, if I'm honest, has felt a lot like a vacation. I've left them at home while I went off to pursue an opportunity that, if I'm real, I have just jeopardized. No. That's the wrong word. I have just obliterated. I can't work for Ethan *now*!

I text Celeste.

> Fuck.

> Is that a good fuck or a bad fuck?

> It's an I'm-worried-I-could-get-stuck-here fuck.

> Oh. Fuck.

There's a pause. A few seconds pass. Then she writes:

> Hey, it will be okay. I'm obviously taking Henry trick-or-treating. The kids can always stay one more night.

She is a lifesaver. Thank God for her. She's doing her best. But something is up with her too. I can't ignore the fact that she just said "I" instead of "we." Where is Jamie?

I can't take advantage. And, I know in that instant, there is no way I'm doing that to my kids or to her.

> You know what? I'll be there. No matter what.

> Are you sure? Work is work. You know I get that.

> I'm sure. I'll be there. With zombie makeup on. Good chance I might not need the makeup.

> Hey! Zombie Mom is *my* costume. Don't steal my thunder.

> Twins! Anyway, I'm flying home tomorrow come hell or high water.

It's a bird. It's a plane . . .
It's a train wreck.

36 | Time After Time

ETHAN

She's going to freak out. Obviously.

She's already freaking out. Otherwise she wouldn't be Sasha.

I needed more time. *We* needed more time. To adjust, figure shit out, lock it down.

Especially after she connected the dots about me and Kaitlin. Honestly, how the hell did she *not* know?

As I shave before dinner, I think about what I said earlier—and what I didn't. I told Sasha it had been awhile since I liked someone like this. What I didn't say: I can't remember *ever* feeling this way about anyone, especially this quickly.

Never mind how I can't keep my hands off her. I would have fucking loved to climb back into bed with her instead of kissing her goodbye.

Maybe that's why the fact that Sasha has completely blocked out meeting me still stings. Maybe it's more than just a blow to my ego.

Giving myself a no-bullshit once-over in the mirror now, I know that's the whole truth.

But I'm not going to let some hurt feelings get in the way.

With Kaitlin, things worked on paper. We looked right. We worked right—for a while. We were a decent team. She liked lists as much as I do.

At first, when I had just arrived in New York, she seemed classy and confident, a native city kid who knew the ropes. We had fun in the beginning. But we were never right.

What she wanted had more to do with what things looked like

than how they actually were. And when it turned out I didn't really give a shit about Page Six mentions and South Beach white parties, she took it personally. Like I had gone back on a promise.

From then on, the marriage was like going through the motions. And the more she griped at me, the more I retreated.

I would have stayed though. For Ruby. And, honestly, because it never occurred to me that I could leave.

In some ways, I should be grateful to Kaitlin for cheating. Because, otherwise, we would have gone on like that—in a joyless relationship—for God knows how long. Maybe forever.

Even then, I was hurt by her betrayal but more relieved. I didn't realize how trapped I'd felt until the gates opened.

She could have picked less of a dirtbag though. For someone with high-status standards, she really dumpster dived. Whatever he had been like in high school, the guy had turned into a bottom-feeder. Way beneath her. I can even say that now. After everything.

Made me wonder about how she sees herself.

I throw on my T-shirt and slacks. Take a deep breath before I leave my room. Put on my game face. But no one is in the living area when I leave, and I can hear water still running in Sasha's room. Long shower.

Is she wasting water again?

What the hell is wrong with me?

I have tonight. To talk to her. To stem her panic. To hatch some kind of plan with her before she leaves for the airport in the morning and, faced with reality, doubles down on her doubts.

Here we go.

TO-DO

- Keep it chill at dinner.
- Get Sasha alone and convince her this is viable.
- Test out my bed this time.

37 | The O.K. Corral

SASHA

When I finally emerge from my room, the villa feels empty. The quiet is deep. Ethan and Stephanie have left, already en route to dinner.

I am staying calm. By which I mean that I am telling myself I am calm, but my body is a blender on chop. I am pushing mental images out of my mind of Bart with orange makeup running down his face and onto his furry pumpkin costume; of Nettie's mouth dropping open as she absorbs another disappointment and pulls further into herself. Me, spending the rest of my career making videos of Larry the cat in Do It Furr Fashion.

I have a plan: I will talk to Stephanie and the rest of the group about the situation and see what we can figure out. Hopefully, there's some reasonable solution. A way for me to avoid failing everyone at once.

I grab my clutch and head up toward the restaurant, too anxious to truly appreciate the sun setting this one last time over the horizon, a laser pointer finding focus until it dips out of view. The world's most gorgeous eye exam. "This one?" it asks. "Or this one?"

Stephanie's laughter rings out, greeting me before I arrive. And, as I crest the steps, I see that everyone is already taking their seats at the long outdoor dining table. I expect to find Martin in the seat of honor at the head, but he's nowhere in sight. I wonder if Stephanie is disappointed or if she's already gathered enough intel for a lifetime of salacious dinner-party stories.

Too late, I realize: I am freaking out so much about the weather that I have forgotten to have postcoital panic. This is the first time

I am seeing Ethan after doing the deed. I should be feeling preteen awkward. I should have run out of things to say before I began. I don't know if it's the other pressing issues, the man himself or my blossoming maturity (it's not this), but, instead, when I spot him, I just feel warm inside.

Damn. I like this man. Like, *like* him, like him.

Tonight, Ethan's PT (it's time I make these perfect T-shirts an official thing) is navy blue and it's a fantastic color on him. His hair is just disheveled enough; his stubble is freshly trimmed. His skin is sun-kissed. His trousers hug his butt like I would if no one was around. Having gone there has not quelled my desire to go there again.

Not even my Kaitlin guilt—or fear of widespread VIM hatred—can stave off the horn dog in me when it comes to Ethan.

For a second, when I see him see me, when he looks up from conversation and a hundred-watt smile spreads across his face, I forget how fucking unhinged I am. How close to the edge. I just want to walk over to him, like he's not my damn employer, and tuck myself under his arm, bury my face in his chest. And then I want to live there forever.

I feel like he's mine.

I smile back. Until I remember. He's not.

He is not my boyfriend. This is not the prom. We will not be slow dancing to "November Rain." And that is a damn shame.

He is the boss. His ex-wife is a woman I know, who I will have to see daily at pick-up. I am a grown woman. I have a job to do. My kids need me at home tomorrow. And I've got to find a way to get to them while remaining Professional Sasha with the others. I've got to be in two places at once, like a million mothers before me. I need to split and duplicate like a cell.

Maybe the full-time job is a pipe dream now that we've complicated our relationship, but I can still leave Derek, Stephanie, Charlie and Jackie with a good impression of me. They can still be great references, who think of me for other projects. I won't dwell on the opportunity I traded for a tryst.

Ethan watches my face fall, and his follows mine off the cliff. His brow furrows in silent communication. He tilts his head. *Are you okay?*

There's more than I can say with my face. I open my mouth, but nothing comes out. I frown. And then Jackie is grabbing my arm and ushering me over to the table.

"There you are! I feel like I haven't seen you all day! How's your crotch? Those jellyfish are monsters! Clearly in league with the lizards."

"Crotch is well," I say, as I arrive at the table, recovering enough to present as normal. "And it thanks you for asking."

Ethan's hand is on the back of the chair beside him like he's expecting me to sit there. Like we're a *thing*. A normal couple, out to dinner, with friends. But he's across the table, and there's no inconspicuous way for me to walk the perimeter and get to him.

Some lovers move heaven and earth. I am foiled by a dining table.

Also, I'm not sure I would go there even if I could. I don't like how lifted I felt when I saw his face, how—for the first time in years—I had the impulse to lean on a man for comfort. I don't like how hungry I am to get him to myself again. That does not feel safe. Or wise. I am leaving tomorrow no matter what. I am back to real life. To my kids. To my mom and her faltering memory. To my practiced balancing act. I will not make the same mistakes I made with Cliff. When I return home, this thing between us goes away. *Poof.* So, maybe there's no point in prolonging the pain.

Wait, pain? Will I feel pain? Heat blooms at the back of my neck, flowering into full panic.

But I have no time to assess because I am the last one standing. I quickly settle into a seat between Stephanie and Jackie, with Ethan, Derek and Charlie across from us.

"It's boys against girls!" Stephanie giggles, pointing out the gender divide on either side of the table. "Can you guys handle it?"

Charlie raises an eyebrow. "I'm down to try."

Under the table, Ethan nudges my foot with his own, shoots me a secret smile.

Maybe this is high school prom, after all.

I do my best to smile back, but my heart isn't in it. The world is leaden on my shoulders. I busy myself spreading my napkin on my lap.

"What's with you?" Jackie asks, concerned.

The vibe of this crew is light and airy tonight. They're effervescing around each other, on the brink of completing a job well-done. They're eating bread and sipping fizzy drinks. I am a lone dark cloud.

"Is it the medicine?" Stephanie asks.

"The ointment?" I say.

"Oh, right. Damn shame they didn't give you anything better."

"It's fine," I try, but then confess because I have come to trust these women: "I'm just stressed."

"Is everything okay at home?" Ethan asks, breaking into our huddle. The genuine concern in his voice breaks my heart.

I wasn't planning on bringing this up at the start of dinner, but I guess I have passive aggressively ushered the issue in with my mood.

"I'm just worried about the weather tomorrow. And the shoot."

"Oh!" says Stephanie. "No worries. It looks like it's supposed to clear up in the late afternoon. We can just bump everything to later in the day or even the following morning."

But what a way to go.

I feel my shoulders tighten. "The problem is, I'm supposed to leave tomorrow late morning."

"Oh," says Ethan, waving away my concerns. "Don't even worry. You'll just stay another day. We can change your flight to ours." He smiles. Is even delighted. "Extra time. On the island, I mean." He clears his throat. "For work."

Smooth.

They are all nodding—*Yes! More time!*—and I know they mean well. They have no idea that a tornado is swirling inside my brain. But I am suddenly struck by a loneliness and alienation so intense that it threatens to bury me. None of them understand.

I am a single parent. I don't function as they do.

"The thing is, I can't," I say, careful not to let my voice wobble.

I am worried I'm about to cry and there is no way on God's green earth that I am letting that happen.

"Why not?" asks Charlie.

He means it in the most good-natured, innocent way, but I have to work to keep the frustration out of my voice.

"Because Sunday is Halloween," I say. This explanation has no impact on my listeners. They are all waiting for more. "I need to get back to my kids." I direct this to Ethan, knowing that he's the only parent, the one most likely to get it.

"Oh," he says, brow crinkled. "Well, they're with Celeste, right? Is she able to take them trick-or-treating?"

Maybe it's irrational. Maybe it's unfair. But the disappointment that floods my body at his words penetrates to my soul. And, once there, it begins to crystalize into anger. *So typical. They're all the same. The injustice!*

"I promised them I'd be there," I say, with forced calm.

"I'm sure they'll understand." He shrugs. "It's Halloween. Kids are psyched as long as they're plied with candy. We do need you here."

"I like those mini 100 Grand bars," Charlie is saying. "I steal those from my nephew."

The others begin debating the merits of Almond Joy versus Snickers and questioning the point of Now and Laters, in general, as the storm inside me continues to wail. I need to resolve this thing, but I don't want to come across too intense.

Only Derek sees me. Like really sees me. With those assessing eyes.

"Sasha, have you checked into alternate flight options that would still get you home in time?" he asks, cutting across the chatter.

"I know from when I originally booked flights that there isn't one."

"Okay. So, what can we do?"

"I'm not sure," I say. "I don't want to leave you guys in the lurch. I was thinking about contingencies I've used for inclement weather before and they might work if we try to move ahead in the morning, but I can't guarantee it will have the aesthetic effect Charlie wants."

Derek is nodding. And now Stephanie is on board too. "Girl, don't worry," she says, laying a manicured hand on my forearm. "We got this. We really need you more for the video content anyway. You've already organized every last element for the photo shoot. Your attention to detail is so good, it's frankly a little concerning. We've done a bunch of shoots here now. We're pros. Maybe you and Peter can just get up early and try to capture the video footage before the storm hits?"

"Do what, now?" says Peter, from down the table. He has stopped pretending to participate and is reading a book.

Stephanie explains and he nods.

"Oh, sure. I'm down. Whatever. I can also handle it myself probably if you have to go."

"Thank you guys so much," I say, exhaling. I am beyond relieved by how relaxed they're being. Like my absence is not a big deal. "I would never want to be unprofessional or let anyone down. I hate the idea of not finishing a job."

"Then finish," says Ethan, shrugging like it's a no-brainer, his tone bordering on harsh. "Stay here. Finish. Your kids will be fine. *Relax.*"

I don't know if he realizes his voice is dripping with condescension, but I am fully drenched. How dare he blow up my spot! Especially when everyone else is respecting my needs.

This is the man I squandered my dream job for?

"How do *you* know they'll be fine?" I bite back, before I think to stop myself.

"Because I have a kid too. And I know."

"Oh yeah? Who's watching your kid right now?"

He shrugs. "My ex-wife."

"Who is also . . . ?"

"Who is also what?"

"Who is also their *mother!*" Now I'm making a scene. All eyes are on us. The mention of Kaitlin has upped the tension exponentially.

"So?"

"So, I am the only parent to my kids! The only one. And when I don't show up for them, it means no one does."

Ethan looks a bit taken aback. "I think you're being too hard on yourself—"

"I'm not being hard on myself. It's you being hard on me! I'm their mother, and I take that seriously. I need to get back and keep my promise."

He leans in and narrows his eyes, angry now. "Oh, so, I don't take being a parent seriously? Because I keep my work commitments? You're here to do a job. A job we were expecting you to complete. There's a lot riding on this!"

My mouth drops open. I could catch flies.

Derek puts up his hands, palms out, like he's breaking up a fight. And he is looking at both of us like he knew this would happen. Like we are two kids he's been trying to keep from murdering each other this whole time. Speaking of parenting.

"Okay. Okay," he says. "Everyone is great at their job. Everyone is great at parenting. All the kids are thriving. The kids are all right. The magazine is all right. And everything is *fine*."

But nothing is fine. Ethan's face is flushed. I'm sure mine is too. And I can't help but think it's in painfully stark contrast to just hours before, when our faces were flushed for different reasons.

Derek maintains pointed eye contact with me, as if reprogramming my brain into a state of calm. "The shoot has gone beautifully," he says. "You've done an amazing job. It will not be a problem. With your prep in place, we are more than equipped to handle one tiny shoot. If you and Peter can manage to shoot the video before the storm hits tomorrow morning, fantastic. If not, we got you, so you can be with your kids. Because we *all* understand how important that is."

He shoots Ethan a meaningful look.

Then, slowly, without taking his eyes off us, he retracts his arms. Like he's making sure the bomb is fully defused.

There's a deep, prolonged silence as Ethan and I glower at each other, awash in equal parts rage and humiliation.

"Well, that was awkward!" says Stephanie with a grin, peering around for a waiter. "Can I get another drink over here?"

Jackie squeezes my knee under the table in solidarity.

After that, the conversation slowly returns to normal. And, as my pulse follows suit, I studiously ignore Ethan, focusing my gaze anywhere but across the table. Anywhere but on his perfect T-shirt and perfectly imperfect face.

I eat dinner as quickly as I can, barely tasting my chicken and rice, and then excuse myself early to go pack. And, when I leave, I'm sure everyone is relieved. I am officially a drag. I am so frustrated. Frustrated that my position and Ethan's are so different. That being "the divorced dad" means everyone thinks he's a god if he manages to throw an apple in a lunch box, while I feel criticized for every missed Silly Sock Day. Frustrated that he thinks I can just *choose* to stay. Frustrated that he thinks I make choices instead of compromises— like a man. That, despite all that, I still want him. That nothing is ever simple.

As I walk down the steps with my lantern toward the villas, I hear a sound behind me like footsteps. I turn expecting to find Ethan, standing there contrite and wanting to talk, come to a resolution. But he is nowhere to be found. It is just an iguana. It stares me down like I am the alien and then scurries away.

Maybe it's right.

38 | Smash Hit

THE MAN

Well, that sucked.

Lying in bed after dinner, I want to smash down the door between our rooms. Or maybe just smash something.

I don't even know if I want to Hulk a path to Sasha or bring down the whole building in frustration.

By 2:00 a.m., when I still can't find a comfortable position, I decide I'm done trying to convince her. If she's this set on fighting what we could have, then maybe I should let her win.

TO-DO
- Get any sleep at all.
- Surrender.

39 | The Fame Game

KAITLIN

I'm losing sleep.

An idea is starting to form in my head. One that I don't like at all. The days are ticking by, with no relief.

I'm with Ruby full-time while Ethan is away, which should fill more empty hours in my day. But I'm distracted, half there.

I think I catch sight of Sasha at Vanderbilt Playground, but it's a different small honey-headed brunette. Her hips are too wide. Her jeans are too Gap.

I think I see her down the dairy aisle at the supermarket, shivering in front of the almond milk display, but she's gone before I can confirm or deny.

I think I see her at the Italian meat market, but, when she turns around, it's not her at all but an older woman, a neighborhood local, carrying aluminum tins of meatballs and chicken Parmesan. I am seeing her everywhere and nowhere. And it's hard for me to think about anything else.

So, I am back online. Looking out for a single post.

Is she back in town or still away? Is she living it up somewhere while the rest of us stay mired in misery? Why does she have this divorced life so figured out?

Is she missing Halloween with her kids?

At one costume party when we were teenagers, back when I was still with Hugo, he and I were sitting in a banquette playing a game we called "being famous," where we pretended that everyone around us wanted to look at us, be us. Because we were stars.

I loved that game. It was fun. It came with confidence. It changed the way I felt in the space.

"Why is that girl always bored?" Hugo asked, nodding toward Sasha. She was across the room, sitting on the arm of a quilted purple velvet couch and staring at the ceiling. Her friends were all beside her—convening, bopping, aping—but she seemed thoroughly disengaged. Actually, now that I think of it, she wasn't dressed up in a costume then either.

"Who, Sasha?" I shrugged, pretending not to care. "Maybe she's too cool. Or maybe she's just dumb as dirt."

Hugo shook his head beneath his Knicks cap, eyes glued to her. "I don't think she's dumb."

Had he been watching Sasha? More than just tonight?

I laid my hand on his arm, bare beneath his oversize Danücht T-shirt. I scratched him affectionately with my long nails. "Anyway, who gives a shit? Why should we care? We're famous." I leaned my head on his shoulder, pursing my lips and feeling cool. Lifted and sipped my hot-pink cosmo.

"Yeah." Hugo grinned, dragging on his cigarette. "She should be looking at *us*."

I couldn't have agreed more.

But, even as he said it, he kept his eyes trained on her. He couldn't pull them away.

40 | Just Deserts

SASHA

Because life is cruel, when I wake up at six the next morning, I am awash in spectacular sunlight.

The storm they expected to hit us has passed somewhere out in the ocean, upsetting only a few fish. And yet its hypothetical has sent irreparable reverberations through my life.

I have stressed out Celeste. Pissed off Ethan. Irritated Derek. Weirded out the others. Spent a sleepless night alone. The meteorologists only shrug and aim to nail it next time. Expectations of accuracy are low. Meanwhile, I am waiting for aftershocks.

Just in case, Peter and I still meet early and knock out the video footage, which turns out to be fortuitous. This last shoot is without a human subject. I have certainly had enough of the limelight. And, whether because of the storm or the predawn hour, the birds turn out in full force as the shadows lift. We capture footage of a brown pelican diving for fish, two green herons communing on a villa rooftop and a prehistoric beast that we decide, after copious googling, is a yellow-crowned night heron perched on a pool lounger like some kind of diva. It's peaceful and kind of lovely, working just the two of us. At least in the moments when I can ignore the nagging shame of having brawled publicly with the guy I kind of work for and sometimes want to bone.

I finally can't bear the stress of what's circling in my head alone. I've got to give it oxygen.

"That was bad last night, huh?" I say to Peter as he is kneeling down, packing up a camera in its armored black box. I am half hoping he won't know what I mean.

He squints up at me, the sun behind my head bright. "It wasn't great."

Well, there you have it. I have not exaggerated the exchange. Even Peter was put off by it, and I thought he'd been busy reading. What else needs to be said?

But then, as I bend to hide my face and help pack up a tripod with my back to him, he adds: "But I had a single mother. And I think what you're doing for your kids is really nice."

I turn to look at him, surprised. "Thank you, Peter."

"They'll remember," he says, then he goes back to work.

I hold back tears.

Then the others appear. One by one, they trudge through white sand toward us.

The others, that is, except Ethan, who is notably absent. His perfect T-shirt of the day still packed in his suitcase or worn behind closed doors. I am part relieved and part sad. This is easier, I tell myself as I tear my eyes away from our villa for the eight hundredth time.

Stephanie arrives next to me, holding out a fresh cup of coffee. I take it gratefully. "That didn't go how I expected at all with you guys," she says, following my gaze. "My radar is usually so on point." Then she shakes her head and walks away.

I want to agree. I want to say, *Me either*. I want to ask her why she thinks Ethan didn't text to check in last night or this morning. Why he didn't try to make up or talk things through, even though I know I might have told him it was pointless. I want to tell her how I stared at that door separating our rooms as I lay on my side in bed the night before, a portal to a different outcome, thinking about how we could have at least made use of it for one last night. Maybe? If we hadn't imploded.

But I don't. Because, though I haven't maintained my countenance at all times, I am now Professional Sasha, for real. And PS doesn't freak out over a PT. Or, in this case, the absence of one.

I am able to oversee the entire final shoot before it's time to leave. That's the good news. By noon, I have hugged all those in attendance goodbye (no Martin, no Ethan). I am on that small plane again, hovering over the transparent sea with Jimmy and the head of housekeeping, who is taking a day off on Provo to celebrate her sister's birthday.

By 3:43 p.m., I am on a flight to JFK, surrounded by strangers. I am no one special. I no longer have a villa or remote-control shades. I no longer can depend on Michael and his golf cart. I no longer have an outdoor shower—or anyone to defile me in it.

The more time passes, the bluer I feel and I can't sort out which part is bugging me most: Am I disappointed or angry? Am I upset about my argument with Ethan or about its lack of resolution? About getting my hopes up or having them dashed? About glimpsing something I hadn't in years or the fall from grace when it fell apart? About sleeping with someone else's ex-husband or about caring too much what others might think? Or am I most mad at myself for trashing this career opportunity?

Last night, when Ethan and I clashed, was my rage about my stress? About the way life is unfair? About how his cavalier attitude reminded me of Cliff? About how it's different in amicable divorces? About the fact that I—and not Ethan—have to choose between my responsibilities and my freedom?

About how I'm afraid?

Or was it about being called out in front of people? Being portrayed as overprotective and matronly? Having my worries reduced to hysterical womanhood?

I have none of the answers. What I do have is a job well-done, at least. A week or so to work with the editor to deliver the finished footage, which I think will be strong. And two kids at home, equally excited to both see me and, the following day, to count the number of Sour Skittles pouches in their stuffed jack-o'-lanterns. And that is a lot.

• • • •

When I turn my keys in the door at home, they cheer. Before I even see their little faces, I have to smile. I always miss them most when I return.

Nettie swings the door wide open, almost smacking Bart in the face inadvertently.

"Mommy!" she yelps. She throws her arms around my waist and sighs. Bart is the baby. I worry about him. But, of course, as grown up as she seems, Nettie needs me too. Parroting his sister, Bart runs up a few seconds late and wraps his arms around one of my legs. The one with the jellyfish bite. There is pain involved.

I grin up through the hurt at my mom and dad, who picked the kids up from Celeste's this afternoon and returned them home.

"Hi, guys!" I say. "I can't walk."

"All right, all right," my mom says, as she holds open the door, which has come to rest against my foot. "Give the woman some space! Let her inside."

Nettie gives me the deets on everything that happened while I was away, including the field trip she almost missed, which turned out to be so fun. When she comes up for air, I turn to Bart.

"How about you? What did you do while I was gone?"

He thinks for a minute, and then he shrugs. "I don't know!" But then he pulls seven thousand crumpled drawings out of his backpack to show me. Mostly of spooky ghosts.

I show them pictures of the lizards and tell them about my stingray.

By the time the kids are fed and in bed, I am beyond exhausted. It's been a transportation triathlon. I feel like I trekked home from the Caribbean instead of flew.

"We're going to go," my mom says as she and my father slip on their coats. She can read me like a book.

"But we never got to talk," I say, even as I yawn.

"Next time," she says, wrapping a gray cashmere scarf around her neck. "Get some rest."

I feel bad. I want to help her. I want to solve what's ailing her. But I am truly toast.

She and my dad kiss me on the cheek, pat me on the head and send me off to bed. I realize I'm happy to be home, even with the plastic game pieces scattered on the floor and the recycling that needs to go out. And I am about to put on my own pajamas and pass out when Bart calls my name from behind his closed door. I pad back into his room.

"What's up, Bonk?" I say, the door cracked.

He pokes his head up from behind his headboard, illuminated in a slice of light. "I forgot to ask," he says. "Did you get what you deserved?"

It takes me a minute to remember what he means. What Nettie said. That I deserved the trip.

"I think unfortunately maybe I did." I sigh.

I am a blob of uncertainty.

I kiss him good night again on his smoosh of a cheek and then put myself to bed. And I am surely fast asleep before my parents' taxi makes it home.

The next afternoon, on Halloween, Celeste and I meet at the corner of Sherman and Tenth Avenue. Only I'm not me. I'm a zombie in my regular clothing (a.k.a. I drew a few drops of blood dripping near my mouth). And she is not her, she is full-fledged Princess Leia. Henry is Luke Skywalker, naturally. I have never had the energy for family costumes, or sometimes costumes at all, but they always do.

"Luke," I say in my best Darth Vader timbre, which is truly horrible. "Where is your father?"

"In the woods," Henry says, as he corrals my kids and begins leading us all down the street toward the first brownstone stoop.

Nettie, as a gothic sorceress (really just an excuse for purple eyeshadow and black lipstick) follows close behind, clutching Bart's fluffy pumpkin paw. It is crowded, so I've instructed them to stick together.

There's something heavy about the day. Something damp and incisive in the air. I notice Redhead Mom standing a few feet to my left in mouse ears and a blackened nose, waiting for her kids. She and her dog both look cold and haunted. She barely nods to me.

Our neighborhood does not mess around on Halloween, which is part of why my kids are so obsessed. When I was growing up, we lived in a prewar apartment building in Manhattan. So we traveled from door to door and up back staircases inside, ringing bells and hoping doors might open. Too often, in those crunchy Upper Left Side days, we were rewarded with apples and raisins or just a cranky "Go away!" shouted through the deadbolted door. We weren't allowed to eat anything unwrapped, so not only were these "treats" disappointing, they were forbidden. Any candy bars we received had to be cut in half too for fear of poisoned needles and razor blades stuffed inside. (Not a thing. Like literally ever.)

Once I hit high school and went out with my friends on Halloween, the situation didn't improve. What had been lackluster became dangerous—and not in a fun and spooky way. Not that I have ever been one for horror movies and Ouija boards anyway. Things to avoid on All Hallows' Eve: Gangs of teens with eggs. Gangs of teens without eggs. Drunken cabdrivers. Drunken lunatics. The park at night. The subway at all costs. Drugs laced with worse drugs. Intact candy bars and apples. (That didn't stop just because we got older!)

Basically, as a result, I hate Halloween. I resist dressing up. But in this idyllic Brooklyn enclave, one step removed from the suburbs, I am the only one—except maybe for a few other New York City natives of my generation. Here, my kids anticipate the same decorations, resurrected outside the same row houses and brownstones every year, with unbridled excitement. Giant stuffed spiders creep down three-story webs. Candy is shot from the roof to the sidewalk down giant tubes. Images of cackling pumpkins and adorable flying ghosts are projected on building exteriors.

We have moved ten feet, and the kids have already run into school friends. So they're distracted enough for me to turn to Celeste and say, "In the *woods*?"

She sighs. "I'm afraid so."

"That's accurate? I was hoping it was a *Star Wars* reference I didn't get. Since I don't get *Star Wars* references. Or *Star Wars*, full stop."

"No. No." Celeste shakes her head, a bun on each side. "That was literal."

"Celeste, what's going on?" I ask with deep foreboding.

As we turn the corner, bedlam envelops us. The street is crowded like New Year's Eve in Times Square. Minus the drunk Jersey bros.

"Hey, guys!" she says to the kids. "Stay together and, if you lose us, meet us at the bottom of this block, on the corner. Do not cross a street under any circumstances."

They seem to have heard us. At least, they nodded at the right intervals. But we both keep an eye on them anyway as we talk, weaving past people as we inch our way downhill.

"So I only understand so much," Celeste begins. And as she unburdens herself, her true level of exhaustion registers on her face. Her eyes are puffy. Her cheeks are drawn. She looks weathered. Celeste never looks weathered. The day she's lost her glow is the day it's over for us all. "Basically, Jamie started acting strange. I don't even know how long it's been—maybe six weeks ago? It was slow. Started small."

"Okay? Is he sick?"

"No, nothing like that. Well"—she toggles her head, smiling faintly—"not physically, anyway."

A tiny witch runs up and grabs my leg. Calls me "Mommy." I am not her mommy. She looks up, realizes this, says "Oops!" and runs over to her actual mom.

She is embarrassed. We are unfazed.

"You were saying?"

"Yeah, so. He just seemed really blue. Depressed. Way less gung ho. You know how Jamie usually is. Or was. He's always been the parent with boundless energy!"

"Did he acknowledge the change or say why?"

"Not at first. He just seemed grumpy and was grumbling about my work hours, which he's never done before. So, I started trying to pick up more slack, cut back on client dinners and that kind of thing. But then it seemed like the more I did, the angrier and more disengaged he became. Like, by helping out, I was upsetting his system."

I am truly surprised by this story. It doesn't match with the Jamie I have known up until now. But then again, that's outward-facing Jamie.

"Ugh. I'm so sorry." My heart aches for my friend.

"Yeah." She nods, rubbing a hand over her eyes, maybe to change the view. "Thanks. Anyway, Henry started to ask questions, so I confronted Jamie about everything, and he just exploded. He said he was 'sick of being married to Wonder Woman.'"

My mouth dropped open. "Wonder Woman?"

"I always thought of myself as more of a Catwoman type."

"I totally agree."

"He said he feels invisible! That I saddle him with all the grunt work and take him for granted, while everyone fawns over me." Celeste weaves through the crowd toward a grandmotherly woman in a Raggedy Ann wig, holding a basket of Starburst, and sticks out her hand. "Trick-or-treat."

The woman gives her an odd look, being that our children are nowhere nearby, but drops a few candies in her palm. My friend is beyond giving a fuck. She unwraps a red, pink and yellow and pops them all in her mouth at once. Like she is a squirrel.

"Imagine! A middle-aged man saying that to a middle-aged woman with no sense of irony!" she says around the lump of candy. "Like I'm not literally disappearing before his eyes! And so he announces that he needs time to figure out who he is. Without us. To figure out what he has to contribute."

I knew Jamie wasn't acting like himself, but I am in shock, though I'm trying not to register it. You never know what's going on in other people's houses. In other people's heads.

"You know, I never asked for this!" Celeste is saying, her gestures growing more emphatic with each passing word. "I didn't ask him to be a stay-at-home dad, if it didn't feel good to him. In fact, I asked if he was sure he wanted that job about three million times! But he argued it would be good for our family." She throws her elegant hands up in the air like an umpire calling a foul ball. "Oh, yeah? How's that going, dude? How's *that* going?"

Celeste is usually so chill. She's careful about what she shares. I'm the one who is the basket case. So, I have literally never seen her like this. I feel terrible that she has to go through this. But I am also kind of loving this less controlled version of her.

"So, now he's in the woods?"

"Yup! Now he has Airbnb-ed a log cabin. Apparently, he's working the fucking land."

"Oy."

"Oy, indeed. And you want to know the worst part?"

"What?" I say.

She stops abruptly, turns to face me, eyes now brimming. She parts her lips twice before she speaks. "He's right."

A tear tracks down her cheek.

"Celeste. I'm sure he's not—"

"No," she rasps. "He is. I have been taking him for granted. I've started treating him more like my assistant than my partner. I think I was trying so hard not to turn into my mom that I turned into my dad. And now I'm scared that I can't salvage things."

With Celeste, I am ride-or-die. What she says goes. I will not contradict her. Instead, I take her hand and squeeze.

We are nearing the bottom of the block. I can see our kids up ahead, sitting cross-legged on the sidewalk and comparing their spoils in the middle of pedestrian traffic, oblivious to the logjam they're causing.

"Celeste. I'm so sorry."

"Me too," she sighs. "I miss him. We've been together for so long. Why couldn't we melt down together?"

I don't say it, but I wonder if maybe that's the problem. I have been on my own for long enough that I live on the other end of the spectrum. I protect my solitude. But maybe there is a point at which you need to prove that you can still function autonomously, even when you have a serviceable partner in crime. That you are someone, alone. That you exist without your appendages—your spouse or even your kids. Outside your well-behaved grown-up life. Your routine. That you can still come back to yourself.

There is nothing good to say. I want to tell Celeste they'll work it out. That if anyone can make it, it's them. But I know too much to know if that's true. So I just stop Celeste and give her a giant hug. We hang on extra long. I ignore the bun in my face.

"Thanks," she says, when we let go. Her eyes are flooded.

"Let's get this trick-or-treating nonsense over with and get back to my house," I say. "I've got a giant duty-free thank-you bottle of rum for you and a tote bag full of shit nobody needs from the Caribbean, including chocolate-covered coconut patties."

"Rum sounds great," she says. "I hope you have an IV."

I have not stopped thinking about my conversation with Celeste.

When we got back to my place, I made us passable rum punch. We ate pizza, watched *A Series of Unfortunate Events* and pretended not to notice how much candy the kids were inhaling. I did not mention Ethan. I wouldn't know what to say anyway.

We did not speak of her mountain man husband again, except at the very end of the night, when Bart asked if Jimmy was in the bathroom—as if he'd only just noticed that Henry's dad was missing. Even Celeste had to laugh at that.

But what I can't stop thinking about is the one-eighty. The fact that Jamie was the poster child for "ideal dad" until the moment he lost patience and a sense of his own autonomy. I guess I am not alone in feeling tapped out sometimes. Turns out parenting is hard. And so is being a person. I love Jamie. But it never seemed like Celeste had picked the sexiest, coolest or funniest husband. She had picked the most lovable and loving. The handiest. The best sport. She had made a smart choice. But, as it turns out, he is also a human. He needs space for an identity outside granola bars and Goldfish.

As solid as he is, he is still changing.

Maybe there is no smart choice. Maybe, as Derek said, relationships are never convenient. No one is ever one thing. There is no perfect. Except perfect T-shirts, of course.

Does this mean I need to cut *everyone* more slack? All the moms and the dads? Even . . .

It is this thought that's passing through my head as I stare blankly into space at my makeshift desk at the kitchen table the following afternoon. I have left my probiotic soda unsipped and my sad cucumber-and-turkey sandwich untouched. I am subsisting solely on self-sabotage. I have only an hour before I need to leave for pickup, and yet I cannot focus on completing a single email. My work remains undone.

My brain has become a land mine, filled with flashes of Ethan's eyes, shoulders, chest, dappled in sweat. His hands on me. My hands on him. Him gazing down at me from above in my bed at Citrine Cay. I know what happens with these types of memories. We try to preserve them. Wrap them in tissue paper, careful not to crumple them. Close the cardboard box and stow them away, pulling them out with wonder about ourselves at a different time. They become a way to keep ourselves afloat. A kiss that lasted three to five minutes. A memory to return to for a lifetime.

Is that all Ethan will be to me? A memory? If so, why won't he stop haunting my thoughts?

The buzzer blares. And I am a jack-in-the-box. Answering the door for UPS is valid procrastination.

I jump up and cross the living room to the intercom. Press the button with the key and listen to it unlock and buzz. Wait to hear a package drop in the hallway outside.

But it is oddly quiet.

Until the buzzer blares again. This time, in my ear.

"Holy shit!" I yelp, my hand to the side of my head. Then I sigh and press the key button again to let the offender in.

This time, there are footsteps. They come to a stop outside my apartment. The doorbell rings. *Ah.* The Fed-Ex person wants my autograph. More excuses to avoid work!

Combing my fingers through my bedhead and sweeping my hair into a quick ponytail, I swing the door open. Only it is not a delivery person. It is not a mail carrier. It is not even my upstairs neighbor, Bonnie, dropping off leftover cinnamon buns for my kids.

My polite smile drops.

Ethan is standing in front of me. And it's like I forgot that he existed in this New York dimension and not just on repeat in my brain. For a moment, I am confused about how he can exist in both planes. In Brooklyn, he is wearing a perfect jacket over his perfect T-shirt. And, as always, he is a tall drink of water.

"It's you," I say. Because I am the most articulate.

He ignores my genius observation. Narrows his eyes at me. Says instead, "You just buzzed me in without asking who I am."

"I know who you are."

"Yes, but you didn't when I rang the buzzer."

"I figured it was the mailman."

"It wasn't. And this is New York City. Which is why you need to ask people to identify themselves before you buzz a potential murderer into your building. Especially when you live on the first floor!"

"Oh. Are you a murderer?" I put a hand on my hip.

"Would I tell you if I was?"

"No. Which is why asking you to identify yourself is null. You'd be like, 'Amazon delivery.' And I'd be like, 'Cool! Come in!' And the rest is a crime scene."

He brings a hand to his head like he might literally pull his hair out in tufts. Only he won't. Because he and I both know his hair is too good to waste.

"What about your neighbors? What about protecting them?"

"From you?"

"Apparently from yourself!"

I want to know what he's doing here, but I also want to drop kick him. I can't decide which impulse is stronger. I decide just to stare him down. He bites his lip under my gaze, rethinking his entrance. And damn if my eyes don't linger on his mouth.

Only then do I think to wonder if my *Back to the Future* shirt is see-through—or rather *how* see-through. It's a super-thin oldie that I don't generally wear in public.

Oh well. Too late.

"So, um, to recap, yeah, it's me," he says finally. He's a bit nervous. I can tell because his eyes keep flitting to the floor.

"You know where I live?"

"Oh, is this your house?"

I tilt my head, impatient. At least, I think I'm impatient. I have so many feelings about him being here that I can't unscramble them. That's it! I am scrambled.

"Yes," he says. "By some miracle, I found a class list."

"Go figure."

"Go figure."

"Found it in an old email?" I ask, calling his bluff.

"Um. Found it at the school office where they took pity on me?" He shrugs, sheepish. "Kaitlin was always in there helping with PTA mailers and stuff. I got to know the ladies."

If I'm honest, I'm impressed. Not by the school office staff, who should not be handing out private information willy-nilly, but, by this man, who has gone out of his way to sleuth me out.

But why didn't he just check my HR file at *Escapade*? Then I realize.

"Derek said no?"

"Derek said no."

I lean against the doorframe, thickened with countless coats of paint, the ghosts of tenants past. "And yet you're here, against his better judgment. Stalking me."

"Mm." He cracks a smile, his one-sided dimple making an appearance. "This is light stalking at most. A person can only loiter in the Crispix aisle hoping to run into you for so long."

"If you say so."

A silence hangs between us as I wait for him to speak.

"I know I could have called," he says finally, running a hand over his five-o'clock shadow. "But I just got back, and I wanted to find you."

I am not sure how I feel about this. On one hand, even when I'm angry, I crush hard on this man. Just the sight of him sends something untoward rocketing through me. Am I even angry anymore? Or more ambivalent? Unsure? *Afraid?*

Ethan looks as good as always, his contrite expression a welcome accessory. The wall-mounted mirror behind him reflects his angles from all angles. And, I realize, he is carrying a white canvas bag from Citrine's resort gift shop.

I take it back. Some men can wear totes.

On the other hand, this man disappeared on me. We had a disagreement, and he ghosted. He didn't even emerge from his room to say goodbye.

"You didn't say goodbye," I say. Because I have no impulse control.

"Neither did you."

"I guess that's true. But you also didn't show up at the shoot. I figured I'd see you there at least. And you didn't wish me a safe flight. What if I had died in a plane crash?"

"That's statistically unlikely. Planes rarely crash."

"Okay. What if the person in the seat next to me was an assassin and put poison in my ginger ale? Is that likely enough for you?"

"Then I would have been very sad. And also confused about why someone would need to assassinate you. I mean, you're frustrating, but . . ."

"Probably for the same reason a murderer would break into the building," I deadpan. There's a weighty pause. "You still haven't explained why you disappeared."

"I needed a minute to think."

"About?"

"About how angry you got at me when I asked you to stay."

My mouth drops open. This is not what I expect him to say. Nor is it the way I would have characterized what happened that night in paradise. "Asked me to *stay*?"

"Yes! I realize now that what I saw as a chance for us to have one more day away together seemed to you like me putting you in a bad position with your kids—"

He thought he was asking me to stay—with *him*?

I shake my head clear. "And in front of coworkers!" I blurt out.

"Yes. Although, I can't take all the credit for ratcheting things up in front of the entire *Escapade* staff at dinner. You got so pissed."

I roll my eyes. Fine. Maybe I was somewhat complicit. Not as complicit as he is.

"Anyway." He takes a step closer to me, so, if I had the guts and the gall, I could easily reach out and touch his face, his arms, that dimple.

I restrain one hand with the other behind my back, using my shoulder to prop the door.

"After you left, I felt horrible," he continues. "I didn't want to call because that just seemed cheap. So, this is me, apologizing in person for not getting it. For not getting *you*. And also for letting my fears about the shoot failing without you guide my response. I'm just so stressed out about this story turning out well, about losing my job or losing *their* jobs. I let my desire to spend time with you, and capitalize on your expertise, get in the way of listening. Please forgive me."

Wanting to spend time with me? Listening? Capitalize on my expertise? Ethan thinks I'm good at my job! I know it's wrong, but I'm flattered. Apparently, it doesn't take much.

So he hadn't been questioning my choices, calling me a "helicopter parent" or doubting my work ethic? He just wanted another go in the outdoor shower? He wanted to make sure we finished the project strong?

Damn. If only I had realized instead of jumping to conclusions. If only we had communicated better. We could have had that last night. Made use of that adjoining door. I never even saw his sex den. I mean, room.

I am so lost in this reverie, at sea in his eyes, awash in memories of the shower stream, that I forget to respond.

He shifts on his feet. "So, is that a good blank stare or a bad blank stare?"

"Why didn't you tell me you were so stressed?"

He shrugs. "I tried to, but I couldn't spell it out in front of the others. They don't totally know what's at stake. Derek mostly does. But the others don't at all. And then I didn't realize exactly what had happened until you were gone. I know. It was stupid."

He looks truly defeated.

The truth is, I can hardly fault someone else for not knowing their mind. I'm too absorbed in the ping-pong match in my own head to even construct a basic email.

"Okay," I say. "I accept that this was a misunderstanding. And maybe I overreacted."

"Maybe?" He scrunches his nose.

"Yes!" I say. "Maybe." We smile at each other for a beat.

"So," I say.

"So," he says. He is looking at me expectantly.

"Oh, sorry! Do you want to come in?"

"Yeah. That would be great."

Ethan steps over the threshold, and I close the door behind him. Click. Suddenly, Demon Dad is in my house. Alone. A fresh wave of sparks shimmers through me.

I look around at the living room, seeing it through his editorial eyes. There is a basket of unfolded clean laundry by the couch. There's a Nerf football on the rug. It could be worse. It could be better.

I look down at myself too. My threadbare T-shirt (yes, fully transparent, but it's too late to remedy), soft gray joggers, bare feet. At least I still have my Turks and Caicos pedicure.

"Sorry," I say, with a general sweep of my arm toward the room and myself. "I wasn't expecting company."

"It's perfect," he says, but he's looking at me, not the decor.

Heat prickles up my spine.

"What's in the bag?" I say abruptly, changing the subject. "Scuba gear for the Harvest Festival raffle?"

"How is there already another school festival?"

"There is *always* another school festival."

"No. This is for you, actually," he says, handing me the bag. "Well, for your kids."

"Really?" I take the package and look inside. "Tissue paper! My cat Larry will love it. So thoughtful."

"Where is Larry anyway?"

"Downstairs. Larry doesn't just make appearances when you drop in. You need to *earn* his trust."

"Noted," Ethan says. "Anyway, it's conch shells. From the beach. Found already empty of creature hosts, so ecologically sound. I know you wanted your kids to have some and weren't able to grab them the day . . . you got stung."

The day I got stung. The day I got laid. The day I got mad. Big day.

This is extremely kind. I am wowed by the gesture. Touched. Because it's for me. But it's also for my kids. He understands how much I hate to disappoint them. This must be another thing magazine editors know how to do—gift.

"Thank you so much," I say, meaning it, as I peer down at the tissue paper. "Truly. They're going to be so psyched! This is really thoughtful."

"Well, you know," he says, kicking at the fringe on my rug, his hands in his front pockets. "I'm a thoughtful kind of guy."

"And humble."

"That too."

We smile at each other.

"Anyway," he says, "I just wanted to say, after I thought about things . . ."

"Things in the outdoor shower?"

"Well, *definitely* the outdoor shower." His eyes flare in a way that I'm sure makes me blush. "But, no, things more globally. I realized I was partially afraid of our bubble bursting when we got home. Of losing the simplicity of that one perfect afternoon. But then I realized, it's fine. Things will be different here. But it can be good different. Indoor showers, for example. They're underrated."

And that's when it dawns on me what he's saying. And how differently we see our reality. Looking at Ethan, I am so tempted to give in. So tempted to fall into his arms and whatever else he is offering up.

But I have been down this road before, and a good apology does not equal a good match. Saying sorry is not the same as delivering. It is not a guarantee. I don't have the space to gamble.

"Ethan," I say, as carefully as I can. "The trip was amazing. You're so great. I really . . . like you. But there is no 'different here' for me."

And I feel like I'm breaking both our hearts—but at least not as badly as they'd be shattered later on.

He tilts his head, like maybe if he changes his visual perspective, I'll start to make sense. "What do you mean?"

"We can't actually *do* this. I have kids. And work. And family. And a sad shower that needs to be retiled. And we don't even get along."

"We do get along!" he insists.

I raise my eyebrows and he exhales.

"When you're making sense."

"I'm making sense now."

"No." He leans in. "What you're doing right now is throwing away something good, something rare with real potential, because change is scary."

"I'm not afraid of change," I say. "I just don't have the luxury of it."

"Luxury?!"

"You seem frustrated."

"I *am* frustrated."

Even in this moment, as we square off in my real-life living room, what I really want to do is kiss him. Ethan, Demon Dad, whatever his name is. His lips are parted, his hair is a mess—in part because I'm driving him bonkers. He is wearing those perfect work boots and an irritated expression.

But I can't. And yet, part of me whispers . . . *can I?*

"What about Kaitlin?"

He sighs. There is true exhaustion in that sound. I get it. I really do. "The Kaitlin factor isn't ideal," he says. "I admit that. But you and I aren't doing anything wrong. If you can handle the scrutiny and gossip from other parents, I think it's worth it—for a chance to be happy."

"Happy? Pshh. That's way too high a bar," I joke.

But he doesn't smile.

I am already the subject of gossip. I know I can handle it. And I know it will eventually die down.

I feel myself waver as my conversation with Celeste comes top of mind again. Is it possible that I should also cut Ethan slack? And myself? That giving into what I want isn't necessarily irresponsible? That he and I deserve to have our own identities beyond parenthood? That we need that or we'll burn out? That it wasn't bad that he wanted more time with me? That the opportunity for happiness only comes around so often and, having trashed my chance at a new job, I should at least seize this? Take the win?

I try to wrap my mind around what I just acknowledged: that Ethan may be able to offer me happiness. *Long-term.*

Is it possible that one woman's Cliff is another woman's Jamie? Is it possible that Ethan is right and I'm just scared?

It hits me then: I really, *really* like this guy.

My expression must soften, or at least furrow in contemplation, because he senses me coming over to his side. Takes a step toward me.

I bring a finger to my mouth, tap as I think.

"Sasha."

My name.

The potential murderer takes another step toward me, sidestepping the football without a downward glance, like a parent pro. "I can't stop thinking about you. Can we please at least give this a shot? Otherwise, I should probably leave. Because your shirt is see-through and it's taken a Herculean effort not to look. Especially when you had your arms behind your back by the door."

Maybe it's the words coming out of his mouth. Maybe it's what I was going to do all along. Maybe I simply appreciate the way he navigated that Nerf toy and all that implies about who he is. Maybe it's because of the way he is unsuccessfully trying not to look at my boobs. But before my brain can fully synapse, my body is on his. And I have the fortunate realization, within seconds, that we don't need no outdoor shower.

If he's surprised by my attack, he hides it well. His lips catch mine, his stubble sandpapering my face as he pulls me closer—the world's dreamiest microdermabrasion. I part my lips as he slips his tongue in my mouth, threading his fingers into my hair, cupping the back of my head with his hands. Walking me backward, he pins me against the front door with his hips. He's good at this—and he knows it.

This isn't island Ethan, who smells like coconuts and sunshine. This is urban Ethan, who smells crisp and smoky. Who means business. And I am all about it.

This time, there's no pretense. Within seconds, my hands are traveling up his back, grasping at his firm muscles. His hands are up the front of my T-shirt, yanking down my bra, and we are grinding against each other.

He tugs my pony. I kiss him harder. Heat pours through me.

Behind me, through the closed door, I hear a rustle in the hall. My upstairs neighbors are collecting their mail. I pull away from Ethan, breathless.

"Just one sec," I whisper. "Don't go anywhere."

I mean that literally. I don't want him to move.

It takes everything in my power to rotate around to face the door, turn the lock. The outside world is not invited in.

But before I can turn back around, Ethan takes a step forward from behind me, pressing his body against mine, so I can feel him hard against my ass. He kisses down the nape of my neck; I sigh and arch back into him. Then, he reaches down and pulls my threadbare T-shirt over my head.

"I like this," he says.

"Me too," I agree.

"No, the T-shirt," he laughs. "But this too. Way more."

I giggle. But not for long.

Because then he unhooks my neon pink push-up bra and slips the straps off my shoulders, one by one. I let it drop to the floor with a shiver, as his warm hands take its place. I push my backside into his front.

The door is cold against my hands.

He takes the top of my pants and slides them down, so they fall to my ankles. *Three cheers for elastic waistbands!* I may be stripped almost bare, but he's fully clothed and his jeans are pleasantly rough against my back as his palm drifts down past my stomach and into the front of my underwear. We both groan.

Then I yelp. Not in a good way. The door handle has stabbed me in the side.

"It's fine," I gasp. "It's fine. Don't stop!"

"Couch," he says against my shoulder, gesturing with his chin toward the other side of the living room.

"What?" *No comprende.* I am not on this plane. I have taken leave.

"Couch," he says again, his eyes hot and heavy.

"Oh! Right. Couch." A piece of furniture for reclining. I know what that is.

I turn to face him, realizing in that moment that, this time, I get to undress him—get all up in that perfect tee. With his assistance, I wrestle his outer layer off, then ready to tear the T-shirt over his head.

It's just as soft as I imagined.

"Ooh. So buttery," I murmur, against his lips. "Seriously—what brand are these?"

He pulls away for a beat, raises an eyebrow. "Really? Now?"

"Fine. Keep your secrets. I'll find out. I have my ways."

Standing on my tiptoes, I manage to pull the shirt over his head and toss it on a chair. It seems too nice for the floor.

Ethan—now with those taut abs exposed—pulls me close again, so my breasts graze his naked skin. He gazes at me with those big brown eyes, shoots me a soft smile. Brushes my hair out of my face with one hand, and tucks it dotingly behind my ear.

"You're pretty," he says. "And I didn't like being in a fight with you."

"You didn't?" My heart squeezes.

"Nope." He shakes his head. "I was afraid . . ."

His voice trails off.

"Afraid of what?"

He shrugs, unsure. "Afraid that I wouldn't get to hang out with you anymore."

He is clearly hedging. Which just makes me want to pry.

"And? What else?" 'Cause there is definitely something he's not saying.

"Afraid that I'd lost you."

"And?"

"Afraid that I'd never eat your cotton candy again."

Now he's just making shit up. "Mmm. Doubtful." I purse my lips. "And?"

Ethan hesitates. Bites his lip. I wait. But I am not a patient woman.

"Out with it!" I say, shoving him lightly. "What else were you afraid of? Really this time!"

He looks down at the ground, then back up to meet my eyes. "I was afraid I'd never get to fuck you again."

That was not what I expected. Not from well-bred Ethan. With his reading glasses and running tips. I am stunned. And delighted. And now I need to jump his bones.

We never make it to the couch.

I dive-bomb his lips, as he picks me up—his hands under my ass and my thighs wrapped around him—and carries me over to the sideboard, setting me down on top. He steps in between my legs, as I grapple with the fly of his jeans and tug them down, revealing perfect boxer briefs. I pull him in close to me, feel him strain against my thin lace underwear.

Like a promise.

We go at it again. My hands scrape down his back; his cup my chest.

"I'm still wearing my boots," he mumbles against my neck as we make out furiously, mouths and hands everywhere.

"It's okay."

"This is clearly a no-shoes house."

"We'll make an exception."

"I should—"

"Ethan! Forget the stupid boots!"

He does. We keep at it until I can't take it anymore—grinding, touching, roaming. He teases my bottom lip with his teeth. Everything in my body is throbbing. I drag my hand down the front of his body to his briefs and try to tug them down.

"Condom," I pant.

"I have one," he says, like it's quarters for a vending machine.

I arch an eyebrow. "Why?"

"Why?"

"Yes, why do you have a condom with you?"

He smiles against my lips. "Optimism."

Fair enough.

Maybe it's because, for a small window, I thought this would never happen again, but I'm even more impatient this time. I shimmy out of my underwear, as he rifles through his wallet and takes care of business.

Then, he stands back up, steps between my legs—and I brace myself against the sideboard, its edges sharp beneath my thighs.

"Ready?" he asks.

"Me?" I scoff. "Born ready."

I wrap my arms around his neck as he brings his big hands under my ass, lifts and pushes inside me. Slowly first and then faster and harder, until I am dizzy with stars. Cursing, he slides one hand between us, then pulls me tighter to him with the other until there's nowhere left to go.

I am lost to everything else.

And, in the midst of it all, I realize I will never see this side table the same way again.

Afterward, Ethan removes his boots. And we do finally make it to horizontal. He is lying behind me on the couch, under a patterned throw blanket, with an arm draped over my waist.

I have put my underwear back on. He has pulled up his boxer briefs and jeans, though they remain unbuttoned. We want to be presentable in case Larry the cat shows up.

We were chatting, but now I'm so drowsy and content that I feel like I could fall asleep.

Then, with alarm, I realize Ethan has gone quiet for too long. What is he doing? I glance back to find him eyeing my bookshelf in wonder.

"What?"

"Are those DVDs?"

"Yes."

"You still have DVDs?"

"Apparently."

"But why?"

I shrug. "I like to own my favorite movies."

"You have the entire *Revenge of the Nerds* box set."

I swivel to face him. A moment of truth. "You don't like *Revenge of the Nerds*?"

It's not that liking that movie, which is admittedly deeply offensive, is a prerequisite to dating me. I mostly keep it for nostalgic reasons because I liked it as a kid. But I know what Cliff would say. He would feign disapproval, posturing to sound sophisticated, even though, in truth, he loves a guilty pleasure.

Ethan shakes his head. "No, I loved *Revenge of the Nerds* back in the day. It's a classic. At least the first one. I'm just amazed that you own all four. So many dimensions to you."

He seems more intrigued than judgmental. And I like how he nuzzles my neck. So I'll take it.

The truth is, I am happier than I can remember feeling in eons. And, this time, I am without postcoital angst. Something about being in my own home with Ethan . . . it feels real. *He* feels real.

I think he could, just maybe, be my future.

The buzzer blares at a deafening volume. I groan but force myself to standing, catching Ethan watching me from behind as I cross the living room.

"Who is it?" I call into the box.

"Amazon delivery!" a muffled voice responds.

I buzz the person in, hear a package drop in the hall and then the building's front door slam shut.

"Thank God you were here," I deadpan, "when the murderer came."

Ethan rolls his eyes at me. "It's a standard thing to ask who's at the door."

"Well, I am anything but standard."

"In this case, I'm not sure that's a plus."

I leap back onto the couch to give him a noogie but wind up straddling him instead, which starts us back up. Suddenly, we're making out again, fast and furious. Until, I look up for an instant and glitch on the laundry basket nearby. And that's when I remember: *pick-up!*

"Fuck!" I say, breathless.

"What?"

Damn, I don't want to leave.

"Pick-up," I choke, when I can find my voice.

"I don't do pick-up," he says.

"Yes. I know. But I do. And I'm late!"

He nods. First vaguely and then with more conviction, as reality comes crashing down on us. I try my best to pull my clothing back into place, throwing a nearby sweatshirt over the offending tee.

As Ethan gets dressed, I throw on my pants and sneakers, grab my sunglasses and keys and, in a minute, the front door of my building spits us out onto the sidewalk. The sunlight is a rude awakening.

It's daytime?

It's unclear how we're meant to say goodbye. We didn't have time to sort things out inside, and now we're out in the open, for all to see.

"I assume you're not coming . . . ?" I gesture toward the school.

"No," he says. "'Cause . . . no." He gestures to the bulge in his pants.

"Right," I nod. "Right. Good choice. I'll leave you to handle all that."

"Yup." He pulls a hand down his face.

"Well, thank you for the shells," I say. All formal. Like I should also curtsy. Or at least shake his hand.

He smirks. "You're welcome."

"Pleasure doing business with you. See you at the festival!" I call as I back down the block. I salute him. 'Cause that's my thing now.

"See you then," he says, shaking his head because it's odd to part ways like this when my tongue was down his throat five minutes ago. But what choice do we have?

He salutes me back, then drops his hand in front of his pants. Throws me a crooked smile. Then he pivots and walks slowly up the block, under the canopy of a dogwood tree. I have given myself per-mission to have this thing with him, whatever it winds up being. And, with that, comes a flood of recognition.

Is Demon Dad not a demon at all but rather the best person around? Maybe even *my* person?

As I watch him recede, I note his perfect jeans. On his perfect butt.

And I am on air.

41 | Pony Boy

THE BEST PERSON

TO-DO

- Make it home without running into any PS421 parents or scaring small children.
- Thank your lucky stars she accepted your apology.
- Ask her to wear that T-shirt and a ponytail next time too.

42 | Rabbit Holes

KAITLIN

I saw Sasha on Halloween. Huddled with Celeste. I saw her tiny tan, a dash of color in her cheeks. I saw the two women hug like they're—Just. So. Close. (Lisa reports that there is trouble in paradise for Celeste. She is a good lieutenant despite her constant Target plugs.) I saw their kids sitting dead center on the sidewalk, blocking street traffic like their needs trump everyone else's.

I saw Sasha at drop-off. Distracted. At pick-up, looking disheveled in a faded sweatshirt and sweatpants, her ponytail askew. A smile beaming from her face. Looking disgustingly refreshed. Invigorated.

She rushed past me even faster than usual.

I got what should have been my fix, but hating her has suddenly become boring too.

There is a dullness to my days. A gauzy film over my worldview. Sasha is back. My ex-husband is back. I should be back too.

But I am no further from the edge.

Solo parenting can be a slog. Even with an eight-year-old. Ruby doesn't need me to change her diapers anymore, but now she demands my focus in other ways. Her friends are fickle. Her teacher is unfair. Her after-school program is too long or too short or too babyish.

She wants me to engage. To be her sounding board. To remain attentive. The only option in the house. But I don't have it right now. The iPad is my babysitter. My phone is my frenemy.

So, when Ethan comes back from his trip and picks up Ruby, I am ready for a break. But then I only use the time to stare at Instagram and wait for nothing to happen. I stay up until almost 2:00 a.m.

going down a rabbit hole: a girl I knew from college became an influencer, got a Hollywood tune-up, and wrote a new decluttering book. Pictures of her at her Malibu house. Pictures of her wearing perfect neutrals. Pictures of her at her Hamptons book party, hosted by some socialite friend. Pictures of her appearance on *Good Morning America*. Pictures of her looking thrilled to be emaciated in one of those bikinis that shows under boob. "Compare and despair," she reminds us in one post about her "authentic truth"—in which she wears a scarf and looks out at the ocean.

Once, she was unremarkable. Once, even schlumpy. Once, she wore the same tie-dye sweatshirt for two weeks straight. My friends and I started counting the days.

But who can't be bothered to wash her sweatshirt now? What became of me?

Even when Sasha shows up wearing a crappy sweatshirt, of course, she somehow looks cool. I'm the worse divorced mom. Not even the good one.

I used to trace it all back to the beginning, like I was doomed to fail. Like retracing my steps back to Hugo, rekindling things with him, might help me find myself. Like, if I reconnected with my past, I could start over from scratch.

That failed, spectacularly. It upended my life. And maybe that was the point.

And I am thinking of this, while taking one last scroll through my newsfeed, when I am startled by a picture . . . of Sasha.

I sit up from my pillow. What's this? A unicorn?

But then I realize it's not on her account. It's on the *Escapade* account. I flash back to her post of the drink. And my brain explodes.

I am back.

43 | Harvest Time

SASHA

Isn't the fun of a festival contingent on it being special? I was once invited to a bluegrass festival in Colorado. That was fun. *Once*.

But I am not the PS421 event planner. I do not volunteer enough as it is. And, so, I cannot throw shade at the VIMs who have organized yet another gathering. It is Saturday. Crisp and overcast. We are headed to the schoolyard for yet another school-sponsored bonanza: the Harvest Hellscape! I mean, festival!

At least, we are spared wearing costumes, though Nettie has put a leaf on Bart's head and called him "deciduous." He's game to keep it there for as long as it's along for the ride. And for as long as it takes to him to figure out what the word means. His big sister is making him guess.

"Does it mean tall?"

"Nope."

"Yellow?"

"Nope."

"Good at balancing stuff on your head?"

"Nope."

We may be here for a while.

The kids are perfectly happy with our plans. I am more dubious. After all, they are off to play pirates with friends on the jungle gym, draw scenes with chalk on the asphalt, take a single sip of hot apple cider before realizing they hate it again. Maybe they will make leaf collages. Maybe they'll eat Rice Krispies Treats imbedded with candy corn and topped with autumnal sprinkles. Maybe, afterward, I'll be lazy and order pizza for dinner.

But I am nervous. And excited. But mostly nervous. Because I don't know what it will be like to be with Ethan here. We haven't been at school together since our cotton candy shift, and no labels have been established since he came to my house. Will we hang out or play it cool? Will I spend my time pretending not to scan the surroundings for him while I chat with other parents? And, then, when I do inevitably spot him, will I pretend I don't see him until he sees me? Will I look without looking? Long to stop longing?

It has been five days since he appeared in my doorway, then pressed me up against my door. Five days since he handed me conch shells and I jumped his bones.

It left me wanting more. I am still envisioning how we might've desecrated the couch if pick-up hadn't come so soon.

In those five days, Peter sent me and the editor the raw footage for the *Escapade* video content. I watched clips and sections and thought it was good. I watched as Ethan and I, as silhouettes, walked to the farthest point of the sand spit, then I stopped it before I watched myself fall.

I am not the better for the last five days. I am not less hooked on Demon Dad. I am replaying every second of my time on the island, pretending I am mining it for intel but really basking in its joy. How long can I ride this wave?

When I am supposed to be cooking dinner, playing Clue, watching *Clue*, doing work, in my mind, I flash to me and Ethan getting carried away en route from the outdoor shower to my villa room. My hand against his stomach. His rough against my hip. Our towels askew in all directions.

I have almost been able to push worry for my mother out of my head for a minute, worry for my dwindling bank account. As we near the school gate, I see Celeste waiting just inside. She waves. Looks pale. Jamie is still playing mountain man. I haven't seen her all week, except in passing. She has hired a sitter to help with pick-up. But I know enough to know he's not back.

Nettie, Bart and I head up the steps to the schoolyard. Inside, a few of the usual VIMs are sitting at a folding table with the school administrator standing beside them. Yes, *that* school administrator. A toy soldier.

They sure do love a folding table. Red Vest. Green Vest. *Kaitlin.*

Has he told her? If so, I think I would know. Ethan and I have been texting nonstop since he showed up at my house and changed the way I see my furniture forever. In fact, he has planned what he is calling our "non-first-date date" for tomorrow night. (We still do not agree about whether we had a date at Citrine.) And he is being secretive about where he's taking me.

I haven't been so excited about something for ages.

At the sight of Kaitlin, I bristle, inwardly. She has always creeped me out a bit. The intensity behind her hawkish eyes, especially when she talks about our shared past. But now I push those thoughts aside. She's just another mom. Another divorced mom, making it through the day.

I stop in front of Green Vest, a hand resting on each of my kids' shoulders.

"Hi," I say.

She opens her mouth to speak, but Kaitlin cuts in.

"Continue down this way to make space for others, please."

We do as we are told.

"Hi," I say again.

"Hello," Kaitlin says. She doesn't smile. Except her eyes. There's some amusement there.

"We'd like three entry tickets and two activity wristbands, please." I pull out my debit card.

She looks up at me, not down at the roll of red tickets. Her hands don't move. She is wearing a purple knit hat with a pom-pom on top. Her scarf is a match. There's nothing wrong with either. In fact, they look expensive. Pretty. Cashmere. But they are a set. Her blond highlighted hair sticks out the bottom, blown out. She doesn't look like she grew up here. She never did. Never quite fit.

"I'm afraid I can't help you," she says.

It takes a moment for me to absorb this. "Wait, what?"

"I can't sell you tickets."

"Um. Okay. Why not?" Was I meant to purchase tickets in advance? Did I miss yet another reminder?

"Because. Your kids' medical records are not up-to-date."

This is unexpected to say the least.

My heart starts pounding. Zero to sixty. The school administrator is giving me that look again. Patient but impatient. Like I'm here to complicate her day.

"Of course they are," I say. "We filled out the forms at the beginning of the year. They're still good. That was only two months ago."

Right? I'm sure that's right.

Kaitlin shakes her head. "Their vaccination records are not in the file."

"Mommy," says Nettie, looking up at me. "Are we not allowed in? Do we have to go home? Or get a shot?" She looks worried. The leaf floats off Bart's head and lands at our feet. Neither she nor Bart notices.

"Don't worry, Nettie," I say. "It will be just fine."

"Come over here to wait," says Celeste. She walks up and shares a meaningful look with me, then urges my kids off to the side, a hand on each of their backs.

"My kids are fully vaccinated," I say to Kaitlin. "For all the things."

"Are they though?" She crosses her arms, leans back in the folding chair like a Mafia king. "Unfortunately, unvaccinated children are not permitted at school functions. But perhaps you can clear this up before school on Monday. Or move to Florida." She shrugs like she's so sorry-not-sorry and then says, "Next!"

"No!" I yelp, as some dad steps up and then jumps back. I have had enough. Not just of this, but of the uphill battle that is existence. I know I should try to keep the peace with Ethan's ex for future's sake, but this is pushing it.

"First of all, they are vaccinated," I say. "Second of all, the school has the files. Third of all, how would you even know what's missing? Why are you rifling through my kids' files?"

Kaitlin purses her thin lips. "As class mom and PTA president, it is my responsibility to know all things and protect the student body."

"Excuse me, but as class mom and PTA president, it's your responsibility to organize bake sales, not invade my privacy!"

Kaitlin shrugs, unmoved. "I have earned special access. Something you wouldn't know about because you're so uninvolved with the school community."

I get it. I do. To an extent. Lisa—Mom Who Never Stops Talking—is standing nearby gaping and biting her nails. Even she won't speak up. I'm not surprised to get pushback from Kaitlin, though this is more psychotic than anticipated. But she knows. Ethan obviously told her. And she's mad. Why didn't he warn me?

"Look," I say. "Kaitlin. Is this about Ethan?"

If possible, her glare sparks with even more hatred. If her eyes were lasers, she would end me. "About Ethan how?"

And now I am trapped. Does she know or not? She is emanating a rage that suggests she does. Also, she is refusing my children entry to their own school. So, I'm going to bet on yes.

"About me . . . and Ethan. Being together." Sort of.

I swear, in that moment, the wind picks up. An oaktag sign blows off the popcorn stand and across the blacktop. Kids duck to avoid getting hit. The streamers and ornaments grumble and clash.

Kaitlin tilts her chin up at me and hisses, "I fucking knew it."

Ah. Okay, then. She didn't know. And now I have confirmed her suspicions.

I wish I could burrow into the ground. But there is no hole to be found.

Ethan said this wouldn't matter much. Kaitlin didn't want him anyway. The divorce was mutual. But, in this moment, she does not strike me as thrilled.

"But to be clear," she continues. "No. This isn't because you're bang-ing my leftovers . . . again. This is because of your lackluster parenting. Let's just say I checked the file because I had a sense you'd let certain details fall through the cracks and you'd feel entitled to a free pass. As usual, you aren't on top of things!"

And I am about to open my mouth, to protest this assault on my character, when suddenly those words echo through me. *On top of things. Again.* And, in that moment, so much clicks for me.

Those words. That became an inside joke between me and Ethan. The words he hurled at me outside the school when Ruby took Net-tie's drama club spot. They were unconsciously borrowed from his ex-wife. This phrase was no accident. It's something Kaitlin said about me at home. I could just picture her at the dinner table: "Nettie's mom is never on top of things."

But why? Why was she talking about me at all?

Maybe I don't understand the why, but I definitely understand the *what*. And I can hardly believe it.

Adrenaline ricochets through my body like a comet. It boomer-angs like a golden snitch. I have been catapulted into an alternate universe.

And all that comes out, as I point a shaking E.T. finger at her, is: "You!"

A smug smile creeps onto her face. Her eyes look hollow. Like she is not sleeping.

"Me what?"

"You. You're the reason I'm not getting the school updates. None of the reminders. Why I lost the after-school drama slot! And the hoodie—well, maybe not the hoodie. But kind of! You're the reason my information keeps getting erased from the system. Why I got cotton candy duty! You're doing this to me—on pur-pose!"

"Don't be ridiculous!" Even as Kaitlin laughs, she eyes me with triumph. She looks to Red Vest for commiseration, but her buddy is too rapt to notice.

"This predates anything with Ethan. So, why would you do this? What do you have against me?" I ask.

Her mouth drops open. "What do *I* have against you?" she repeats.

I have pushed the right button. Or maybe it's wrong. The nuclear one. It's clear from the way she pushes her camping chair back, scraping it against the blacktop, and stands up. She makes herself big like I'm a bear she is trying to scare off.

"Yes!" I press. "What's your *problem*?"

"What's my problem? What's *your* problem?" she spits. "You think you're so much better than everyone else! You always have. Waltzing up in your stupid leopard jackets and wide-leg jeans and high-tops, thinking you're so on trend!"

"Now my wardrobe is a problem? Is it also unvaccinated?"

We are making a scene. Especially here. In this quiet neighborhood with this quiet school. We are not at all quiet.

This feels like my new MO.

"You've always been this way!" she snaps, her face contorting with rage. "You've always been above it all. Always had it so fucking easy."

Always?

"Please watch your language!" says the school administrator. "There are children here."

But Kaitlin is well past listening. "You just take whatever you want and don't even care who you step on or ignore! Well, welcome to Earth, where you can't just treat others like shit."

I am pretty sure you can treat others like shit on Earth, unfortunately. And I cannot believe what I'm hearing. How long has this woman hated me? Is *hate* even a strong enough word? She's been actively working to make my life harder for months!

The part of me that isn't vibrating with fury is struck by the fact that she thinks my sheen stuck. The teenage sheen that dulled decades ago. This woman thinks I am still the person I was at sixteen years old. At twenty-two. At thirty. I am both horrified and compelled by this realization—and the chasm between how others see us and how we see ourselves.

"Fine," I say. "I'm not your favorite person. But why would you sabotage another woman? Other children? Another mom?"

"Oh. Like you're here to help other women? Or do you just take what's theirs? When I got divorced, you could have offered me commiseration. But you just ignored me as always!"

There it is. At least in part.

I exhale. "Kaitlin, I'm sorry if you feel like I've ignored you, but I really don't understand. You were fucking with my life before Ethan and I even met. What did I take from you?"

"What's going on?" booms a voice from behind me. A deep male one. With equal parts authority and shock. Demon Dad. I know without turning around. "What's happening?"

When I do swivel to look at him, disbelief is surely written all over my face. Eyes popping out of their sockets. He too looks alarmed. What she has been doing to me—to my kids—is mind-boggling!

I take a deep breath. I will remain calm. "What's happening is that your ex-wife has apparently been on a mission to ruin my life." I can't believe the words as they come out of my mouth. "I know it sounds bonkers, but it's true. And now she won't let my kids into the yard."

He closes his eyes, lets his chin fall to his chest. Exhales sharply. Like he wishes this wasn't happening, but it is within the realm of possibility. Then he approaches the table. "Kait," he says quietly. "What are you *doing*?"

Kaitlin brings a hand to her neck, perhaps the slightest bit chastened by Ethan seeing this go down in the light of day. She sticks her chin in the air, defiantly. "She did it to me with Hugo and now she's doing it with you."

"What did I do?" I ask.

"Who is Hugo again?" Green Vest asks Red Vest.

I'm wondering the same thing.

"Hugo! The guy she cheated on Ethan with," Red Vest stage whispers back. "Keep up!"

"Wait. That same guy from high school who she's always talking about?" I ask Red Vest. She nods until Kaitlin turns and glares at her.

Ethan looks beyond humiliated. Like he wishes he could disappear.

"I legitimately don't understand," I say to him. "Do you? What is she talking about?"

He exhales. Clears his throat. His shoulders slump. "She thinks you stole her boyfriend in high school."

"What? She does?" I look at Kaitlin. "You do?!"

"Yes! I do!" she shouts.

"Hugo—?"

"Reyes!" she finishes.

"I don't even remember him, really."

"Of course you don't," says Kaitlin. "You only care about yourself! You just make out with whoever the fuck you want!"

"But weren't you broken up?" I say, scrunching up my nose. I am trying so damn hard to remember. Kaitlin in those days. This random boy. One mediocre drunken kiss. One random night. Eons ago. And now this?

All I can come up with is my own heartbreak from that time. It obscures everything else. An encompassing fog through which I can only catch glimpses of objects. My high school boyfriend had recently cheated on me and then surprised me by dumping me instead of groveling when I found out and confronted him. He was sorry, he said, but he was out (though we would both come back for more punishment later). There was pressure from his friends; there were a lot of pretty girls who liked him. In his defense, he was essentially a child. But he left me desperate. And I went looking for absolution in flirtations with other boys in baggy jeans and backward baseball hats. Other boys who acted more grateful to have me around.

God, I feel old.

"Technically, yes!" Kaitlin is saying, her pom-pom bouncing as she talks. "But we only broke up the day before! And you were supposed to be my friend, even if you dumped me. And, I swear, everything has been shit from then on."

"You blame that incident for ruining your whole life?" I say, even as I silently recognize my own lingering abrasions. I'm not judging her for holding on to it. I'm legitimately trying to understand. "Like, this is why you hate me enough to punish my kids?"

She crosses her arms. "It was love. And, because of you, it was unfinished business."

Love. I turn to Ethan. Lower my voice. It is all starting to crystalize before my eyes. "And that's the man she cheated on you with? Like *recently*?"

He nods. Lips tight.

"Like she found him on Facebook or something?"

He nods again. *Jesus.* This is next level.

"Did you know she hated me this much?"

"Not *this* much," he says, destroyed. "She kind of hates everyone."

"I definitely hate you!" Kaitlin says to him.

I look at Red Vest. Green Vest. Lisa. They all nod like this is true. Why am I on a *Real Housewives* episode?

"Is this why you pursued me?" I ask Ethan, suddenly stricken. "Like, as revenge? To hurt her?"

"I didn't think I just pursued you. It seemed kind of mutual?"

"Ethan!"

"No. Of course not," he says gently. "I told you. I don't care what she does. I've never wanted revenge. Especially now. This is extreme. And worrisome." He brings a hand to his temple. Rubs like he's trying to reset his brain.

"Oh, sure!" says Kaitlin, who has clearly overheard. "But it's not extreme that she went after you?"

"Actually," I say, turning to her, "I didn't go after anyone! We didn't even know each other before, really. When you screwed up my life, you kind of forced us together. God! I should have known when your daughter *happened* to get that one after-school spot."

Ethan runs his hands through his hair. It is safe to say he is stressed out. "Obviously, I didn't know," he says to me. "I hope you realize that."

I look at Kaitlin, all red-faced and deranged. Red Vest, Green Vest and Lisa, staring wide-eyed. Celeste, her hands like one-sided ineffectual earmuffs on one of each of my kids' ears. The line of parents behind us, gaping as they wait to get in. Redhead Mom near the front, unblinking. I look at Ethan, a perfect barn jacket, over a perfect gray hoodie, over a perfect white T-shirt. The color drained from his face, creased with worry. And I cannot believe this is my life.

I'm not sure for whom I feel worst.

I turn back to the table. "You need to let my kids in now," I say. Red Vest and Green Vest stare down at the blacktop. They want no part in this, and I can't blame them.

"No," says Kaitlin.

"Let them in," I say.

"You're missing a form," she says. "And also you suck."

"Let them in, Kaitlin!" says Ethan. "This is not okay."

"No."

We are at an impasse. Except we are not.

"You. Will. Let. Them. In!" booms the school administrator, stepping up to the side of the table. My hero in a festive blazer and leafy necklace. "I don't know what's happening, but we will get to the bottom of it all. This is most certainly an abuse of your power."

Kaitlin opens her mouth to protest.

"Take a break!" the administrator says firmly before anyone can speak. She looks to Celeste. "Please walk the children in. They don't need tickets. It's on me."

Celeste hurries Nettie and Bart inside, hopefully not as traumatized as I feel.

The school administrator's eyes rest on me. The eyes I have so often felt were filled with judgment. "I will personally ensure that you are no longer left off school mailers and newsletters."

"Thank you," I say with a shuddered exhale. "I appreciate that."

In that moment, I realize I have been so busy complaining about being "Mom" at drop-off and pick-up, about having no name, that I

312 | NORA DAHLIA

never noticed that she didn't have one either. Maybe this woman also just wants to be seen.

Kaitlin throws her hat down, hair wiry with static, and storms off toward the bathrooms. Red Vest, Green Vest and Lisa do not follow. She is radioactive.

I take a few steps back now that my kids are in. Take a moment to collect myself. Ethan stands against the fence, shell-shocked. One hand white-knuckles the wire grid.

We are silent for a full minute. The ticket line begins to move again. Other parents file in, buy wristbands and join the throngs. Like nothing happened. Almost. Redhead Mom steals a look at me, then pretends she didn't. Hurries her kids inside. Our silent kinship is over. I have become *that* mom. I am flashing back to when the Golden Globes video of Cliff first surfaced, the way the others looked at me. I realize that at least now, faced with public humiliation again, I don't care nearly as much. Growth.

"Did you know—?" I ask Ethan, but I'm not even sure what to say. "Kaitlin was this troubled?"

He shakes his head.

"She wasn't always like this," he says.

I nod. Although I kind of think she was, to a degree. It's why I never got close to her when we were kids. I could feel the way she moved around the world with a scarcity mentality, like she always felt she'd somehow been shortchanged, even then. She seemed to experience other people's wins as her losses. Ethan may not have seen it. But sometimes people don't notice all the things. If they don't want to.

"I didn't steal her boyfriend," I say. "In 1995."

"Well, that's a relief."

"What's Hugo doing now, by the way?"

I figure Ethan has done his homework on the other man.

"You want to look him up too? Rekindle things?"

"I think I'll pass."

"He's a substitute doorman on the Upper East Side. And a 'music producer.' At least according to his social profile."

I nod. "That tracks."

"Tracks track." Ethan pauses. "I think maybe Kaitlin needs a vacation," he says, staring into space.

"It seems like it," I agree.

We stand together, watching the buzzing schoolyard for a beat. A group of fourth graders are competing in a Hula-Hoop competition and they are all terrible.

"Are you okay?" Ethan asks me finally. "I'm sorry you got dragged into all of this." He looks like he really is. He's the one who is likely not okay.

I care about him. Am almost moved to offer help. But there are red flags everywhere. And I've already been burned too many times. If age has taught me anything, it's to learn from my mistakes.

"You didn't know she was messing with my life," I say. "But you definitely knew she hated me. And you didn't warn me. You said this wouldn't be a big deal. But that was a lie of omission. And, to be honest, Ethan, this isn't the first thing you neglected to tell me."

"Sasha, I'm so sorry." His shoulders slump. "I never imagined it could get this bad. I didn't mean to ruin everything."

We both know this is a no-go now. We are a no-go. The non-first-date date is off. For good.

I want to cry. My stomach feels like a void. But, instead, I say, "On the upside, now I know, despite all the missed Silly Sock Days and permission forms, that I'm not losing my mind."

I force a smile. He can't really return it.

There isn't much left to say. Whatever ease existed between us has been blown sky-high. Life was certainly simpler on island time, where only the iguanas were thorny. Where's a baby stingray when you need one?

"I better go find Bart and Nettie," I say, tucking my hair behind my ear. "Assure them I'm not a hussy. Then explain what a hussy is."

He nods absently. "I should find Ruby too."

He doesn't move. A pall has settled over us. We are coated in sad. *Who are we now?* I wonder. *All of us. Besides hollowed-out versions of our former selves. Are we us from before? From three minutes ago? From three years ago? From thirty years ago? Who are the people we carry with us? Can we ever reclaim them or, conversely, let them go?*

As I walk away, Celeste spots me and runs up to give me a big hug, shaking her gorgeous head in shock and shoving a ginger cookie in my face. My heartbeat is only just returning to normal speed. And, when I look back, Ethan is still standing where I left him. By himself. Leaning against the chain-link fence. Perhaps trying to find himself in time.

44 | Ugh

ETHAN

TO-DO
- ???

45 | It's Me

KAITLIN

In the mirror in the bathroom off the cafeteria, I am just me—albeit with dark circles, bags, dull skin. But even I know I've turned into a monster.

I am furious that they're together, but also—of course they are.

Didn't I almost will it? Would he ever even have noticed her if I hadn't talked about her incessantly?

In the wake of the implosion, I am oddly calm.

The bathroom door wheezes open. A small child—maybe a first grader—walks in, crosses to a stall. Doesn't lock it.

For a second, I'm afraid she'll be scared of me. Then I remember that looks can be deceiving. To her, I am just another mom.

I turn on the faucet. The water is freezing cold, but I splash it on my cheeks anyway.

I need to get out of this place. Go home. I have blown up what was left of my life. And the stupid thing is, I don't even care about Sasha anymore.

In this moment, I can see what I've maybe wanted all along: confirmation that she's just as much of a mess as I am.

The little girl comes out of the stall.

"Don't forget to wash your hands," I say, drying my own on a brown paper towel. I hand her a dry one.

And then I go home, leaving out the school's front gates instead of the yard. I don't tell Lisa or Ruby or Ethan I'm leaving. And I don't go back for my hat.

46 | He's Going Down

SASHA

I am shaken.

How can I think about anything but what happened at the festival? Ever again?

When we return home, I escape to my room and sit on my bed, trying to make sense of the past few weeks. I put my head in my hands and let myself cry for two whole minutes before wiping my face clean of evidence and cooking up kale chips and organic chicken fingers. Because if they're organic, they're healthy, and I'm a good mom. Hussy or no.

Don't you dare tell me different.

For the rest of the rainy weekend, I am barely in my body, moving blindly through games of Sleeping Queens and UNO. I look up twice and realize I've lost. I am going through the motions.

Kaitlin imploded. And it was disturbing. My insides are roiling now too.

Why? Well, for one thing, now Ethan and I feel like an impossibility. Things have just become exponentially complicated and public. Everything I try to avoid. And, somehow, even though I haven't known him long, I really miss him. *A lot.*

It's hard for me to imagine life without him, even though I never had it with him.

I catch myself wondering what he's doing. I picture him in his reading glasses, staring intently into space while he considers how to word something. I picture him reading with Ruby. He said they just started *The Hobbit*. I picture him picturing me.

When I call to cancel my babysitter, since the non-date has become a nonstarter, the disappointment steals my breath. Like it's happening all over again.

I brace myself against the kitchen counter. I'm just sad.

I really thought this could be something.

And I'm wondering how long it will be before Ethan stops being the first thing I think of in the morning and the last thing at night.

For reasons I can't quite assimilate, I am also consumed with thinking about the other men in my past—ones who I thought were excited about me but who were actually excited about how we presented together. Josh, Cliff, others. Is that how a young Ethan felt about a young Kaitlin? Did they mistake a pretty picture for love? He said he used to care about those things—flashy parties, flashing lights. Image. Things my ex-husband prizes above even our children. Has that truly changed, or will Ethan regress? Where had things gone wrong? What drove Kaitlin to this brink? Because she didn't get there alone.

I think about the way Kaitlin saw me when we were teens. The way I made sure they all saw me. The way she sees me now.

Who I was. Who I am. The truth versus an idea.

How long have I been erecting walls to keep the world out? How much can we actually protect ourselves? To what extent does that have value?

I think mostly about their daughter, Ruby.

As an eight-year-old kid, what does she see and understand? Can she sense the unsettlement? Does the road feel bumpy or like every day? From how much can we really protect our kids? From how much should we?

I have spent a good deal of my time as a mother poised to shield Bart and Nettie from anything hurtful that comes their way, to be two parents at once for them, always present and available. I want them so badly to be happy, unscathed. But it occurs to me now, thinking about Ethan and Kaitlin and Jamie and Celeste, that even with two parents, you are not guaranteed such things. And maybe you shouldn't be. Maybe everyone needs a chance to be a person in order to be a parent. Maybe things never quite turn out as planned. Maybe that's okay.

And maybe, I am willing to admit, Ethan understood that better than I did when he suggested I skip Halloween. Maybe, thanks to the less pronounced pressures of being a dad versus a mom, he understood that being *there* isn't better than being happy, even if that means you're there a little less.

Definitely, Kaitlin needs a break. A real one. Maybe we're all just steps away from spiraling into that state.

On Monday morning, the video editor sends me a rough cut of the footage. Peter has done a spectacular job. His aversion to flying and people be damned. The reel is beautiful and funny and cool and, obviously I'm biased, but it definitely makes me want to frolic through Citrine Cay. They even managed to crop out my jellyfish sting. (There is a God. And that deity is a benevolent digital editor.)

Still, it's all a fantasy. That's what's enticing. The hotel is beautiful and unusual and otherworldly. The food is fresh and bright; the service is impeccable. There are no words for the softness of the sand or bumping into a stingray like a next door neighbor.

But the owner is a terrible person. And, as good as I feel about how the footage came out, I don't feel great about us giving him a pass. Do any of the rest of them care? Ethan? Derek? Jackie? Charlie? Certainly not Stephanie, who was still interested in hitting that. What is our responsibility to the world with regard to this man? And how much is it worth now that I know jobs hang in the balance?

On Monday evening, my mother calls. On FaceTime, of course. I am happy to see her face, but I feel an immediate pang of worry. My stomach tilts.

"I wanted to tell you, I sent you a text confirming Tuesday-night dinner with the kids at your place."

The whole point of a text is not having to call, but I don't even rib her about it. I'm worried that whatever is messing with her memory may also have done away with her sense of humor. It has certainly hampered mine.

I pull myself together to have my parents over for dinner on Tuesday. And, as planned, they show up. It's taco night! Which basically means I mix a packet of powdered orange MSG with ground beef, throw a bunch of toppings on the table and everyone goes to town. Old-school. Back to when preservatives were wholesome, dammit!

My mom stands beside me as sous chef, ostensibly helping to prepare the bowls full of tomatoes, onions, cheese, beans and such. But really she is just drinking a glass of red wine and inhaling an entire jumbo bag of organic tortilla chips.

Larry the cat stands beside her, pleading with his eyes. The injustice of her stuffing her face while he starves! That cat loves a chip.

"Mom." I smile. "You wanna leave a few of those for the kids?"

"Oh, sorry!" she says, stuffing another in her face. "Just ravenous lately."

I am trying to be gentle with her, not force things. After this evening, I plan to reach out to my dad separately to discuss her confusion. The things she forgets. The sweatpants.

It's time.

She is wearing them again, which, considering that my mom once informed me in no uncertain terms that yoga pants were not, in fact, pants, also feels like cause for concern.

What. Is. Happening?

After dinner, while the kids watch *Junior Bake Off* in the living room, there is a moment of calm. I am somewhat lulled by the sound of the TV: British children cooking "sponge" in the adjoining room. And by my father's occasional exclamations of "I love sticky toffee pudding!" and "Scrummy!"

I have taken a load off and am sitting at the kitchen table with my feet up on a nearby modernist chair.

"So," my mother says, settling beside me. "Should we talk about me losing it?"

My mother. Always with the subtlety.

"Yes, let's."

I drop my legs down and turn to face her. "So—what's new?"

She shrugs. "I mean, not much. Did I tell you we got a new toaster oven?"

I can't help but laugh. "Mom! I mean, has anything changed in your day-to-day that you think could have triggered a change in you?"

"You mean beyond getting old?" She frowns.

I smile at her. Tip my head onto her shoulder. She gives me a squeeze.

"You're not old, Mom," I say. "You're vintage couture."

She raises an eyebrow. Shoots me a look that I recognize from the mirror. "That's just another word for 'used.'"

"Yes. But a fancy word!"

Suddenly, her brow furrows. She looks distracted and stressed. She reaches over to the counter, grabs her black purse and sets it in front of her like she's about to dissect it. She unzips it and begins to rifle through. I have never seen so many pockets.

"What are you looking for?"

Instead of answering me, she begins muttering to herself. "Was it in the outside pocket? I could have sworn I put them in this left side pouch. Lord. I hope I didn't lose them again!"

"Mom. Lose what?"

Keys? Wallet? Obviously something essential.

"Aha!" she exclaims, startling me. She is holding a container of white Tic Tacs above her head like a championship belt. "There they are. Want one?"

Who is this woman? One minute she seems like my mother. A literacy advocate. Well-dressed. Haughty to a fault. The next she seems childlike, unhinged.

I shake my head.

"Suit yourself." She pops four in her mouth, as she points to a dish on my counter. "Can you grab that dark chocolate, too? It's a great combo."

"Really?"

"Yes."

Whatever is causing her mental shift is definitely messing with my mind too. A wave of nausea passes over me as I sit and stare at this stranger.

"Sasha! The chocolate!"

Right. I grab the bar and hand it to her; she rips into it. Emotional eating in style.

"Okay!" I say, with inappropriate gusto as I sit back down. "So, changes?"

But she is back in her bag, for the love of God. "I need my glasses." She starts taking objects out and placing them on the table. Pauses. "What am I looking for again?"

"Mom!" I say, unable to contain my anxiety. "Your glasses!"

"Oh, right."

How bad is this? I am beginning to envision the worst. Strings of doctor's visits, waning abilities, her forgetting my kids' names. My dad's broken heart. Me, a spinster, eating pasta with my parents at the assisted-living facility buffet. Where the marinara sauce is V8.

It's at moments like this that I wish I had a sibling.

"Let me," I say. I drag her bag over and plunge into its depths, excavating for her glasses. And that's when I notice. And stop dead in my tracks.

"Mom," I say, holding up a blue pill bottle. "What is *this*?"

She scrunches her nose. "That? Oh, it's nothing. Just the new medicine I'm taking for my neck."

There is a giant pot leaf insignia on the label. I dig inside her bag and find two more bottles.

I look at them. At her. Then back at them again. My mouth drops open.

"Mom," I say. "What doctor prescribed these to you?"

"I told you! Carol's guy."

"Carol's doctor?"

"No. I don't think he's a doctor exactly. Just a guy."

"A guy with what credentials?"

"I don't know," she says, as if my questions are beside the point.

"I only messaged with him online using some special app. Then he delivered the medicine."

"An encrypted app?"

"Maybe?" She shrugs, her gray bob brushing her shoulders.

I stare at her in disbelief. Then I begin to read the labels. There are two capsules and a tincture.

"Mom," I say. "Do you know that this is cannabis?"

She waves me off. "It's only CBD."

"It literally says THC right here!"

"What's THC?"

"Mom! It's pot."

"Right," she agrees. "But it's the marijuana with no psychotropic effects. It doesn't mess with your head."

I beg to differ.

"Mom," I say, with a patience that should earn me a Nobel Peace Prize nomination. "THC absolutely affects your mental state."

Her brow crinkles. "Are you sure? That's not what Carol said. Or Carol's guy."

"Well, Carol's guy is literally a drug dealer, so."

She looks at me in surprise, then begins to slowly nod.

"Huh. He did deliver the medication on his bike. But how convenient! Truly, you can get anything delivered in New York."

We are getting sidetracked. "Mom, how much of this are you taking a day?"

"Two capsules in the morning and two in the afternoon. And then some of the tincture at bedtime."

My eyes are popping out of my head. My hands are in fists. "Mom! You're taking twenty milligrams of THC twice a day, plus whatever this tincture is."

"Is that a lot?" she asks, stuffing chocolate squares in her mouth.

I cover my eyes with my palms, then look back up at her. "Mom. You're not losing your memory! You're high as a fucking kite!"

"High?" she says. She shakes her head. Purses her lips. "I don't think so."

"Mom, you're stoned! Doped up. Full *Pineapple Express*. Look! You literally have the munchies."

"No." She shakes her head. Stops. Looks down at the chocolate and Tic Tacs in her hand. At her elastic waistband. She sets the chocolate down. "Oh."

"Well, this explains the sweatpants. I thought you were falling into a depression!"

"No! Not at all. Just none of my other pants fit me!"

At once, my mom and I both look down at her waistband then up into each other's faces and dissolve into giggles. Full tears stream down my face.

I am so relieved. My mother is the third member of Cheech & Chong! Hallelujah!

It's as if an anvil has been lifted off my shoulders and I am now floating in the air, a helium balloon set free. (But not in a way that's bad for the planet.) My mother is not losing it. We get to keep her!

It makes everything that's been depressing me feel less heavy.

We laugh long and hard to the point where my dad gets curious about what's happened. He rises from the couch and crosses over to the table.

"What's so funny?" he asks.

"Mom is a pothead," I say. "She's applying to be the new editor of *High Times*."

"Really?" he says with genuine interest. "I haven't seen her smoke dope since the sixties."

And we start laughing again. I am in bliss.

After my mom promises to stop her massive daytime weed intake, I make tea, sit at the table with my parents and tell them all about my trip to Citrine Cay. About the stingray and the food and the tiny plane. About the shoots and even my jellyfish sting, though I leave out the racier and romantic details.

My mom looks at me thoughtfully. "Sounds like an incredible trip and like it could be an incredible job."

"I'm not sure." I frown. "It's a long story, but I think I might have hurt my chances."

"Why don't you talk to this Ethan person about it? Since he's also a parent at the school? Make sure he knows you want the position. He let you do your thing without intervening at all, even though his job is tenuous. He gave you a shot. It sounds like he trusts you."

She's right, I realize. He did trust me. He took a risk. Put my career aspirations on par with his. But, now, I'm not so sure. With all the complications, how can we trust each other? I know he was wrong in not telling me more, about the job opportunity, about his ex-wife. But I have to admit, if I'm honest with myself, he was mostly afraid of scaring me off. And he's not wrong. I do scare easily.

Thinking of him standing all alone in the schoolyard at the Harvest Festival after Kaitlin's meltdown, I am suddenly hit by a tsunami of regret. It steals my breath.

It's not that I think I did the wrong thing. I haven't heard from him, so I guess he's given up too. I just hate how it's all turned out. My heart is broken—for everyone involved.

Later, as they're leaving, my mom thanks me.

"It was nothing, Snoop," I say.

She smiles, though she surely has no idea what I mean, and lays a hand on my shoulder.

"You know, when I was worried I was losing my memory, I kept thinking, at least I have you and your dad. At least I'm not by myself."

"True." I am too happy that she's healthy to even be annoyed by the obvious implications. This is a huge weight off my shoulders, at least for now. Still, the lesson remains: life is short.

"I know you don't want to do those dating apps. I understand. It sounds like torture. But, the truth is, I worry about you being alone."

Same, woman. Same. But I worry about losing my autonomy too.

"I will try to remedy that," I say. But we both know it's an empty promise. I just came as close as I had in years, and where did that land me?

I am getting it from all sides. When I go into Nettie's room to tell her it's time to stop reading and go to sleep, she tells me she wants to do "true secrets." This is what we call sharing without fear of consequences or judgment.

"How do you know if you have a crush?" she asks, toying with the corner of her batiked duvet.

This is not what I was expecting. Usually, it's about how she argued with a friend at school or Bart stole candy without permission. (Like mother, like son.)

"Oh, well. I guess you just want to be around the person as much as possible. And maybe you get butterflies when they're around, like you're extra nervous or excited."

"Yup. Yup." She diagnoses herself. "I've got a crush." She groans, grabbing her giant penguin stuffy to cover her face.

"Who is it?" I ask.

"No comment!"

"Is it Henry?"

"What?!" she tosses the stuffed animal to the side and sits up straight in abject horror. "Henry is my *friend*!"

"Okay! Understood!" I hold my hands up in surrender. "Sometimes you can like someone in that way but also have them be a friend. Sometimes that's the best-case scenario."

Nettie lies back down and considers this. Her face is aglow, the moon to her pink reading light's sun. "Are you friends with Ruby's dad?"

I am not expecting this. I shift my position on her bed, buying time. On-the-fly parenting is not my strong suit.

Am I? I didn't act like it.

"Um," I say, scratching my neck, fidgeting. "Sort of? We work together."

That feels like the safe answer.

She nods and I cringe, wondering how much she overheard and understood at the Harvest Festival entrance. "I think he's handsome," she says. But then she scrunches up her nose. "For a dad."

Oh, boy. "Go to bed, kid!" I give her a thousand kisses, and she giggles like she did when she was five.

As I'm leaving, she calls out, "Don't tell Bart!"

"About what?"

"Mom! My crush!"

"Oh. Scout's honor," I say. "Not that he would understand."

"I think Bart has a crush on Elmo."

We both laugh.

Later, after my parents have left and the kids are done making excuses to pop out of bed, I know my job is officially done. The evening extends in front of me like a curse and a gift. My head is cluttered with debris.

I walk over to my mom's confiscated meds sitting on the counter, unscrew one cap and pop a capsule in my mouth. Life is complicated. Why should she have all the fun?

Celeste is at drop-off the next morning. I think I spot Ethan too, but as a retreating speck in the distance. I don't know what I'd say if I saw him anyway. But I guess I'm checking my corners. At least that's what I tell myself.

I haven't seen Kaitlin at school since the weekend. Not even at the bake sale booth or selling tickets to the winter carnival. Next week is Ugly Sweater Day and I actually received two fliers *and* an email reminder. I am back in the loop. As Bart and Nettie enter the schoolyard, I wave to the school administrator.

"Hi, Ms. Maureen," I say.

"Hi, Sasha. Have a good day!"

I am all excited to report about my drug-addled mother, but, in fact, it is Celeste who has the most important information to share.

Jamie has hung up his axe.

"He's home?!" I say. "That's great. Right? Is that great?"

She toggles her head as we wave to the crossing guard and start uphill past the charming brownstones on Sherman, toward the main commercial drag on Prospect Park West. She is headed to the F train for work. I'm headed to grab coffee and get home to my computer. I have shared the final edit with the *Escapade* team and am anxiously awaiting their responses. I see an email has come in from Stephanie, but I'm waiting to read it until I'm settled in front of my laptop with Larry at my side. Therapy cat. When he's in the mood.

"It's good that he's back," Celeste says. "Or at least a step in the right direction. We talked, and we're going to work together to figure out how to give him more agency and space. And make my work-life balance more . . . balanced. I'm going to try not to take him for granted so much."

"But at least the sabbatical is over?"

She nods. "We agreed, he needs to find a job. Something that makes him feel like he's contributing."

"Something manly, maybe?"

"Yes. Like a hacker. Or a blacksmith. Or a rodeo clown."

"Hmm. How does he feel about rubber chickens?"

"Jury's out! Anyway, at least he's home from the log cabin. All his laundry smells like fireplace and stew," she says, grimacing. "Why do men need to pretend to be in westerns in order to get their heads on straight? It's all one big remake of *City Slickers*. Only without the jokes."

"I don't know. You'll never find me in the woods alone. Anytime I'm in a cabin, I assume I'm seconds from being murdered by a deranged psychopath. Unless it's part of a quaint resort."

"Less woods. More Woodbury Commons."

"Outlet shopping, absolutely," I say. "Retail therapy is real!"

We stop at the top of the next block in front of our adorable neighborhood café. The smell of coffee and banana muffins wafts from the open doors.

"I should go," Celeste says. She still looks tortured.

"How are you actually feeling about it all? Jamie's mental state is on the upswing, but how is yours?"

"I guess time will tell," she sighs. "It just freaks me out how quickly things can change. It's a good reminder to appreciate what's in front of you. In the meantime, I have deadlines!" She turns to leave, adjusting her bag strap on her shoulder. "Wait, Sash. Any word from Ethan?"

After the scene at the festival, I had finally dished all the sordid details of my dalliance with Demon Dad. Celeste had been impressed by what she mockingly called my "wild side."

"No." I tie and retie my scarf around my neck. "I don't think I'll hear from him."

"Why not?"

"Because he lied to me." And possibly has sworn off women for life.

"He didn't reveal all the details, it's true." Celeste studies me for a beat. "Don't hate me, but I think maybe you should give him a break."

"You do?" There is an aching in my chest that releases the tiniest bit. Air hissing through a valve. It feels like I am getting permission to follow my heart and ignore my brain. But I'm not ready to do it. Plus, he would need to do the same.

"That was a tricky situation to handle," she says. "I'm not saying he made the right choice, but was there a good way? Would you have stuck around if he was transparent? We all make mistakes, right? Even me."

"Yeah, but you're *you*."

"And he's him. And a looker to boot." She wiggles her eyebrows in jest.

"It's just . . . messy." I frown.

"I mean, yes," Celeste agrees. "But, then again, what isn't?"

Back at the apartment, I settle in front of my computer at the kitchen table and bask in the glory of a finished job. Derek and Stephanie love the footage and, aside from a couple tiny tweaks, we are good to

go. It will be a few weeks before the story goes live, but, in the meantime, they'll use clips from the video content as teasers.

I am about to forage in the fridge for a reward when a separate
email from Stephanie lands in my inbox:

Sash! Thought you might appreciate this excerpt from the
feature. For your eyes only. Still needs an edit. But a couple
of grafs are copied below. Call me when you read!
xx S.

When it finally opens its doors after a soft launch, Citrine
Cay will no doubt wow guests. This is not an average hotel.
Rather, there's a sense of quid pro quo between nature
and what's been erected here, a wildness that infuses the
experience with intoxicating possibility and abandon. This
place is not sterile. There are no golf courses or manicured
tennis courts. Unlike more corporate or conventional
top-end resorts, here, dust blows up from unpaved roads,
framed by deceptively rugged terrain. The land is owned
more by a thriving population of protected iguanas than
by the human beings playing house.

And, yet, the issue of ownership is paramount here: this
new destination is the vision of onetime actor-cum-mogul
Martin Bernard. And his presence on property is sure to
attract the glitterati—at least members of that set who still
find him fit for fraternity. While Bernard has most certainly
discovered a paradise—a deeply special as yet unspoiled
place, ideal for a hyperexclusive escape of this kind—all
the beauty cannot compensate for the ugliness he himself
projects. Though his handlers have managed to spin the tale
of his retirement in a way that sounds voluntary, speculation
has circulated that perhaps he was one of many men forced
to reckon with his repeated poor treatment of women,
minorities and others working under him for years.

I am stunned. Breath gone. This is major.

I call Stephanie right away. And, when she picks up, I am still catching up.

"Oh my God!" I say.

"Right?" she says. "We debated whether I should write it, but, ultimately, Ethan felt like it was irresponsible not to speak up about Martin's behavior. He offered to write this part as an addendum, as part of his editor's letter, and take the heat, but you know me—I'm here for it! I don't mind a little extra attention."

"I'm so impressed!" I really am. By her. By Ethan. Especially considering his job hangs in the balance. "I didn't know if you'd be up for something like this—?"

"What? Why not? You know I have no fear!"

"Well"—how do I say this delicately?—"I thought you guys boned." Why be delicate with Stephanie? The beauty of knowing her is not having to be.

"What?! Ew! Me and Martin? Sasha! That man is thirty years older than me!"

I shrug at myself in the wall mirror. "Well, you were kind of tolerant of him on that first night."

"You can't be intolerant of someone you want to get to dish for a story!"

"And then the next night, you were . . . gone! All night."

"Oh my God!" Stephanie is cracking up. "Derek! Derek! Come here."

I hear Derek's irritated "What?" faintly in the background.

"I'm talking to Sasha. She thought I slept with Martin on the trip!"

I cover my eyes though they can't see me.

"No way!" I hear him laugh. "Well, to be fair, one never knows with you."

"Sasha," she says, her voice quieter. "You know I was just trying to give you space. That's why I stayed out. Which it does not seem like you took advantage of, BTW!"

At least Ethan and I escaped without the others realizing what happened between us. "Right. I know. I appreciate the effort."

Larry the cat wanders over to me, stops and then stares up at me like he knows I'm a liar.

"So, you were just sharing Jackie's room that whole time?" I ask.

"Jackie! No. I was with Charlie!"

Charlie. It all starts to click into place. Derek's discomfort at the lunch table. Charlie's hefty appetite the next day. The subtle innuendo. Which I, of course, missed because I was too busy panicking about my own.

"Charlie. Right. Well, that makes much more sense."

"Um, yeah."

I'm late to the game, but I'm happy they found each other. "Ahhhh. Steph! He's *so* cute."

"Yeah, no kidding! And recently single. And not a handsy, racist, misogynist, old dude. We're grabbing a drink tonight! The saga continues."

I don't know why this stops me in my tracks. "Oh, you're still seeing Charlie now? Like back here?"

"Sure! Why not?!"

I think about Charlie and Stephanie, out somewhere in New York together. The vibe so different from those chill evenings by the beach. Could they carry what they found at Citrine into their real lives? Grab drinks and dinners at dim restaurants, wander museums, binge watch shows on their couches? What is it that's making my words catch in my throat? Is it guilt? Recognition? Jealousy?

I realize Stephanie is kind of my hero. She truly is fearless.

"Hang on," Stephanie says. "Derek wants to talk to you. *Privately.* Very intriguing. I'm going to transfer you to his office. Bye!"

"Martin. Ha!" I hear her murmur before putting me on hold.

I stand up and start pacing. Suddenly, I am flooded with nervous energy.

I wait, anxiously, for Derek to pick up. And, when he does, I am still startled by the way his voice breaks in. *What is wrong with me? Why am I so on edge?*

"Sasha, hi. Great work on the video."

I picture him at a large glass desk in one of a row of offices, a segment of the skyline visible out the window. No doubt his desk is spotless.

"You really did a fantastic job," he says. "The footage came out so well. We're all thrilled. I shared it with Ethan earlier, and he's also really pleased."

"I'm so glad!" I chirp. Because I am. But also because—is he? Something ricochets through me at the mention of his name.

"So, I wanted to talk to you about the full-time position. If you're interested, we'd like to connect you with HR and begin serious conversations about it."

The job! My heart sings. And then hits a sharp note and nosedives. *How do I even say this delicately? This isn't Stephanie. I trust Derek to be discreet, but I also don't want him to judge me.*

"Derek," I say, staring at myself in Nettie's full-length mirror as I speak. *Would I take me seriously?* I am wearing a "Maryland is for crabs!" T-shirt. "Um. I'm not sure I can work for Ethan. Or that it would even be ethical for him to consider hiring me." I bite my lip, cringe at myself.

There is a weighty pause. "Right, well, he has already officially recused himself from the hiring process because he knows you personally, outside of work. As *parents*. At the school."

He says these last words with emphasis. Because that's how Ethan and I know each other. Not from the outdoor shower. Only, I get the sense that Derek knows more than he's letting on. As usual.

"But what about working for him? Won't that also be a conflict? Because of . . . the school connection?"

"HR will designate someone else as your supervisor, likely me, so that you can be assured of objective treatment."

"Wait, really?" *Is this happening?* It dawns on me that all my worry over having tanked this opportunity was for nothing. So much wasted energy. The position can still be mine! The money! The 401(k)! The Christmas parties (where Professional Sasha will *not* get drunk and make out with the boss)! Well. Probably not.

Relief drops through me.

"Really," says Derek. "So? Interested?"

I am blown away. I have not blown it all. The job is still a possibility. And Ethan has paved the way for me without ever being asked.

"I am interested. Beyond interested. It's my dream job, and I would love to be considered."

"Good." I can hear the smile in Derek's voice. "For what it's worth, I'm hopeful that, even without this official HR process in place, you and Ethan would not have let . . . school . . . get in the way."

"Really?" I am feeling more bold. "But you seemed dubious from the start."

"Only because I thought you were married. And I could see what was happening."

"What was happening?"

"*School* was happening." *School* has clearly become a synonym for *sex*, which is deeply awkward, but still less awkward than saying *shower sex*.

"What made you think it would happen?"

"Because I've been working with that man for long enough," says Derek, in a rare moment of candor. "I could tell how much he liked you from the second I saw you together. When he passed your name on initially, I had no idea he actually knew or had any opinion about you. He didn't let on. And, when I realized . . . man, it stressed me out."

"You think he really liked me? From the beginning?" A fresh kaleidoscope of nerves flutters through me. But, in the mirror, I can't keep the smile off my face. It's embarrassing even to me. What am I doing? Ethan lied to me. Can he even be trusted? Can I? Can we show our faces at school? Is he even still interested? Probably not. He's certainly given me a lot of space.

"I think he likes you, currently. I think he's an amazing catch. And as your potential supervisor, I think I should not be having this conversation with you."

"Right," I say. "Conversation over. Almost. I don't know, Derek. The situation is already so complicated. It all seems less than ideal."

"Maybe," says Derek. "But love is never convenient."

Love.

When we get off the phone, I sit down on Nettie's bed. In her sweet room. With its white walls and pastel bedding, stray friendship bracelets and owl paraphernalia lining the shelves.

And I recognize in this moment, I have at least given my children this. Stability. Cheer. Love. With this job, maybe I can give them more.

But what have I not given myself? What are my barriers to happiness? To partnership? To love? What have they been all along?

Cliff. Money. Time. Stress. Parenting. The mental load. These demands have cock-blocked my peace for years. At least, that's what I would have told myself before.

Now I wonder: Was it me all along?

As I look at my reflection in the mirror—which looks okay "for my age"—I realize that one enormous barrier is the way that I see myself. As a worker bee or a vessel before a woman. I have stopped viewing myself as autonomous.

That's the most surprising thing about the changes of the last few weeks to me—the mental leap about my own identity.

I have always liked to remain a step removed. Kaitlin wasn't wrong about that. Not for the sake of a set of values but for my own protection, I realize now. I like people to see me with that sheen that Kaitlin remembered—easier to maintain with some distance. I like to look clean and crisp and not try too, too hard. I like them to think that they're lucky to be my friends.

Only it's been a long time since I really felt that way. It's been a long time since my skin glowed and my hair looked perfect and my stomach was flat and I got my liquid cat-eye liner just right and I didn't have giant dark circles under my eyes and a small smudge of kid food somewhere on my sweater. It's been a long time since I caught a glimpse of myself in a mirror midday and looked as together as I thought I had when I left the house. It's been a long time since I looked in the mirror and wasn't surprised by the older face that gazed back at me.

I am a different person now. That's the truth. I am no longer the prettiest girl in school—or at least the one who did the most with what she had. Who knew how to coolly attract the right attention and just a bit of fear. I am not untouchable or sparkling. I am not wild or even really fun. I pee when I jump. I pee at night when I try to sleep. I pretty much pee all the time. And I've lived enough to know that a correct Kegel is only an urban legend.

I am an old lady. Or I might as well be. I like herbal tea and lavender hand cream and walks in the fall down dirt roads. I like hot toddies and bingeing TV shows and wearing sweaters. I like my mom's edibles. And that is nothing spectacular or revelatory, since it has happened to millions of women before me, except in so far as it shocks me every single fucking day.

And maybe, just maybe, it doesn't mean that I can't be something else too.

I guess it never occurred to me that someone else could see me differently than that. Could see me sparkle. Could see me as more than utilitarian. After kids and Cliff and years of single-minded survival. That someone could see me as a whole human instead of a figment of my former self. That I could *be* a whole person again.

47 | Vow of Celibacy

FATHER ETHAN

TO-DO
- Call with corporate.
- Dr. Feldberg: 144 W. 86th Street, 1A—9:00 a.m.
- ~~Move on.~~
- Move on.

I see Sasha at drop-off, but I disappear before she can spot me.

I have stuff to do. Kaitlin to help (whether she likes it or not). Adjustments to make. Come-to-Jesus moments to accept. I'm watching Ruby like a hawk to make sure she's fairing okay. Corporate is poised to make a decision about our jobs.

But I still have to actively try not to think about Sasha. She's told me where she stands, and I can't blame her. Now, I just need to accept defeat.

48 | Uptown Girl

KAITLIN

When our divorce was finalized, Ethan and I stopped seeing our couples counselor. For obvious reasons.

You can't fix something you've already returned to sender.

After the Harvest Festival debacle, when he and Ruby arrived home to his apartment (even though it wasn't his night), he called me and insisted we go back for a therapy session.

"But we aren't a couple!" I protested. But I knew I had no leg to stand on.

"Kaitlin, we're in this together," he whispered, so Ruby wouldn't hear. "Whether we like it or not."

The man loves a lecture. It's so annoying when he's right.

Of course I know I went off the deep end. Of course I know I took it too far. I know I am not *fine*. I knew that before I blew it all up. In retrospect, that's probably why I did it.

So I didn't have to pretend anymore.

On the downside, I no longer have access to the school's office copier. Lisa has been handed those responsibilities, and she is already drunk with power. I can't wait for her to organize a PS421 field trip to Target to shop for jumpsuits.

Those administrators will miss me when she gets to talking. And never stops.

Today, I am back on the Upper West Side for our therapy session. Back in my childhood hood.

Once in the psychologist's office, with its requisite Matisse print and World Market cushions, I actually don't mind being there. At least I'm not holding my breath anymore—despite the doctor's over-powering floral perfume. I have hit rock bottom. The truth is out.

And, more than anything, it's a relief.

I sit on one side of the couch, counterbalanced by Ethan, as she faces us, hand poised above her notepad. We are farther apart than ever.

Ethan begins by explaining what happened at the festival, in his words. What he describes is an admittedly ugly scene, involving aired dirty laundry near hay bales. And I sit ready to spew venom back. About how he chose the very worst possible person to date. About disrespect! But I discover, when it's my turn, I am no longer fired up to prove my point.

Years before, the same doctor—with the same short curly salt-and-pepper hair and tortoiseshell glasses—once asked us, with re-gard to our arguments, "Would you rather be right or loved?"

I guess now that we're not in love, being right seems significantly less important too. I am too tired to fight. Especially when part of me knows he's mostly in the right. And it is when I admit that fact out loud that I start to cry. It is a surprise even to me.

Ethan is kind about it. He is kind, full stop, I allow myself to admit. The therapist is too. They eye me with concern, emphasize all the change I've experienced lately, suggest I take "some time" to visit with my sister in the Bay Area. Take a time-out from mom-dom. From ex-wife-dom. From PTA-dom. From work. Pluck ripe fruit from her orange groves. Reset. A California infusion.

I don't say no.

I don't miss Ethan, I realize. Not in the way my reaction to his being with Sasha suggested. I don't think I even felt betrayed by his choice, though he knew I disliked her. I think I was more jealous that Sasha liked *him*—saw value in him and not me—than the other way around.

That's a lot to admit. I don't like it one bit.

It took a total implosion for me to realize that Sasha isn't even Sasha at all for me. She's just an idea of something that feels stolen from me—a symptom of what the therapist calls my "scarcity mentality." The idea that one person's success is another's failure. Sasha is a stand-in for the harsh lens through which I see myself. Something tantamount to fluorescent lights in an airport bathroom. And who likes that?

For all my "compulsion," as the doctor gently labels it, I rarely check Hugo's social media anymore. In fact, since the scene at school, I have erased the apps off my phone. I never text him either. That relationship petered out in the worst way, anyway. Not with a dramatic big to-do, as a torrid affair might suggest. First came the end of my marriage. (Even in that, Ethan was maddeningly tepid.) And, eventually, the affair ended with a bleary dulling of edges. It, too, proved insufficient. He, too, proved boring. A figment of another time. A ghost of homeboys past. Not the missing piece that would make me whole.

Why was I never enough?

"Why do you think Sasha became the arbiter of value in your mind?" the doctor asks.

But I am unsure. Maybe the answer lies in the streets just outside the entrance to this doorman building. Down just a few manicured blocks to Eighty-Sixth and Broadway, where all my first joys and fears were awakened. Where both doubt and possibility began.

It's time to start again.

Before we leave the couch, Ethan turns to me unprompted. "Kait," he says, carefully. "I want to say something while I have the chance."

We've decided I will be returning to this office for weekly visits, but he will not be joining me. I did not resist this plan. Now that I have blown things sky high so publicly, I no longer need to worry that people will judge me for needing help. There are so many better things to judge me for.

"I just want to say that I should have been there more," Ethan says, his familiar eyes earnest and searching mine. "When things were off between us, I shouldn't have responded by avoiding our life. I should have been there for the difficult day-in and day-out of parenting. I should have supported you more. And I know I'm complicit in how you've been feeling . . . and struggling. I'm going to do better."

I both appreciate his words and know they're eons too late. Not for saving our relationship—that was never possible. But for saving me.

After our appointment ends, Ethan and I ready to part ways awkwardly outside, under a green awning with gold lettering. I'm sure he is headed back to his office. The proximity to Midtown was why we started seeing a doctor way up here in the first place. So he could squeeze us in at lunch.

I can already see he will not be that kind of dad anymore. And, with a twinge, I realize he won't be that kind of husband either, when he gets the chance for a redo.

It stings.

But maybe I could be better for someone else too.

I watch Ethan as he checks his phone. Finds nothing. Sighs. He is still handsome. He always will be. But he looks tired—and sad.

"Go get her, tiger," I say lamely. I am trying to give him the go-ahead.

He might as well move on. Maybe it will help me to do the same. Move on from everything.

I remind myself of the new philosophy I am trying to adopt: It can only be good for Ruby to have more people in her life to love her. It can only be good for our daughter to have more family.

I feel a little sick imagining a part of her life that doesn't involve me, but I have decided I am committed to keeping the peace for her sake. From now on.

At least I'll try.

Ethan furrows his brow in confusion, but then smiles and cocks his head as he registers what I mean by, "Go get her."

"Really?"

"Really," I say. "You're obviously miserable. It makes it harder to hate you."

"Well, thanks—sort of." He frowns. "But I think that door may be closed now."

I shake my head. *Men!* "Don't be an idiot," I say. "The door is not closed. I saw how Sasha looked at you."

He looks up at that. "You really think so?"

He must be feeling desperate if he's open to insight from me, on this, after everything. I do know him though. And, for better or worse, I know her.

"Just don't be passive," I say. "Don't just let life happen to you. Fight for it."

He nods slowly, like he's considering this.

"My two cents," I say. An old woman strolls by us with a fluffy white dog. I turn to walk the same way.

"Is that something you think I do?" he asks. "Let life happen to me?"

I turn back to face him. "I don't think it, Ethan. I know it," I say. "It's how you wound up with me."

He bites his lip, like he had not considered this.

"Make choices," I say. "Don't just sit in it. Don't wait for someone to choose *you*. Take it from me. It doesn't get you anywhere good."

"Thanks, Kait," he says, nodding. "That's good advice."

"It is." I bring a hand to my hip. "Maybe I'll become a life coach."

He narrows his eyes. "Mm. Maybe not."

We both smile. For a second, I remember that there were good times.

"Anyway, go!" I say. "Seize the day!"

He waves goodbye. Turns. I watch him as he heads down Columbus Avenue, first strolling, then speed-walking, then eventually running for the train. *Go get her, tiger.*

I walk down the street to my train too, wishing I wasn't underdressed. Maybe I do need some California sun.

I am not better yet. But maybe I can be.

In the shade, the warm day turns brisk. But there is a comfort in being here again. I peer up at the glowing windows of the prewar buildings I know from my childhood, down at the sidewalk etched with names. And, though I know it isn't here, I search for my own.

49 | The Long Run

SASHA

I am on the loop. But, instead of running three miles, I am running as long as it takes to exorcise this agitated warble in my chest. And I am moving in the "wrong" direction.

I still take umbrage with that label. *Wrong.* Let's say *unconventional.* Let's say *renegade.* I am running in the direction of free thought.

Prospect Park is crowded today. People jog, walk, chase their dogs. Dogs jog, walk, chase their pigeons. It's not surprising. The weather is getting colder—you can feel winter warning—and today may very well be our last gasp of relative warmth.

It is fifty-six degrees and sunny. The sky is glass. And I know there's no way he resisted. I am here later in the day, but it's like I can feel Ethan's presence here in the morning, hours before, blowing past me with his hands up. This loop will never be the same.

I am listening to Olivia Rodrigo. If anyone asks, it's the Clash. The music is carrying me for now. I told myself I'd run as long as it takes, but, after about a mile, I am already tired.

That's when I sense someone run up beside me. See? I'm not the only person who prefers the road less traveled!

"Hi," my new running partner says. Only he doesn't say it, he pants it.

I turn to face him. And I am confronted with Demon Dad. Only he does not look quite like himself. First of all, instead of running gear, he's wearing jeans, a PT, a perfect hoodie and a streamlined army-green backpack. Second, all are drenched in sweat. He looks like me after two miles. Which is like him after ten.

But he's still annoyingly sexy as hell.

For a moment, I am thrilled to see him . . . until I remember that maybe I'm not. "What is actually happening?" I say with wide eyes, not breaking stride.

"I came," he huffs, "to find you."

"To find me?"

He nods vigorously, unable to catch his breath.

"How did you know where I'd be?"

He shakes his head. "I didn't. That's why I went to your apartment. The supermarket. The café. Now . . . here. Around the loop. Multiple times."

He points to the road below our feet. In case I don't know what "here" means.

I have to admit this makes happiness swell inside me, despite my reservations. But why is he here?

"Is everything okay?"

"Yes. No. It depends who you ask. Can we talk?"

"Mm. I'm kind of in the middle of something," I say. "This isn't the best time for a talk." We both know I'd love any excuse to abandon my run. But I'm not stopping everything for anyone who can't be bothered to do the same.

Not today, sir. Not today.

Not that I reached out either, but where has he been? He has been absent since the festival. He gave up so easily. Didn't even offer an explanation.

At least, that's what I tell myself. It's not fear; it's wisdom that keeps me running.

Although in his defense, it does seem as if maybe he has derailed his day to find me. And possibly ruined his tee. Will that neckline ever be the same? Still. I will not be so easily swayed.

"Fine," he breathes. "We don't have to stop or talk. I'll just keep running with you until you're done. Until you're ready."

If I'm honest, I am *ready*. My Lululemon sports bra is being tested. But I am committed to showing him who's boss.

Me. That's who.

I drop my arms intentionally low, my hands dangling down by my thighs. I raise my eyebrows, baiting him. He purses his lips shut. Nope. He will not lecture me. He will not give me an excuse to flee.

"Don't you want to tell me to hold my hands higher?"

"Not really," he grunts.

"What about my gait? How's my gait?" I say, throwing my legs around in the world's most erratic way.

I watch him suppress a smirk. "It's perfect."

That's when I get my earbuds tangled up on my wrist and, while looking down trying to sort it, trip over—maybe nothing? "Shit!"

I am about to hit the ground, surrendering to a scraped knee and shattered ego, when I am caught around the rib cage by two strong hands. Poking out from a perfect hoodie.

"Whoa!" he says, helping me to standing and ushering me to the side of the loop and onto the grass. "What is wrong with you?"

"Why do you always ask me that when I fall? Whatever happened to 'Are you okay?' When did that become not enough?"

"Be honest," he says. "When you said 'all tied up,' you meant with your earbuds."

I shoot him a look, smooth my pony.

"Do you want to keep going?"

I don't. I really don't. I am sick of running. From him. From this. On the loop. But I don't want to admit it. Admitting it means confronting all the things.

If I hear him out and we can't make sense of things, I have to give up all hope. If I hear him out and we both want to try, I'll be vulnerable.

How do I know he's different? That he won't turn into a Cliff?

Do I want to keep going? "Do *you*?"

His hands are planted on both hips as he leans over. He is breathing like an elderly bulldog. But he calls my bluff: "I'm in until you're done. I'm on *your* clock."

"What if I go ten more miles?"

He doesn't even point out the absurdity—no, sheer impossibility—of that notion. Or the fact that he's wearing jeans and has been running all over the city. He is a man who is willing to wait on me.

"I can go all day," he says, looking at his watch. "Well. Until pick-up."

That gets my attention. I snap to it. My eyes on his. I feel myself sucked in by the gravity of his pupils, dwarfing the flecked brown. "Pick-up?" I repeat. "But you don't *do* pick-up."

He stands up a little taller, holds my gaze. Like he's a kid announcing he's become a man. "I do now."

I consider him, this person who has quite literally run all over town to find me. Who has risked his job to hire me. Risked his career to call out a figure like Martin, the misogynist shit face. A man who is trying his best.

The rest of the mad goes out of me.

"Okay, fine," I say. "I'll talk." If I ever catch my breath.

"Okay, great. I'm going to start, if that's okay?" He looks genuinely relieved, but also focused. "Look, I'm sorry. I need to say that first and foremost. I'm sorry I didn't tell you about the job before putting you up for it. I'm sorry I didn't make sure you understood who my ex-wife was and how much she . . ."

"Detests me?"

"Yes. That. I won't even sugarcoat it. For what it's worth, she has never been a great judge of character. Present company included."

"Fair enough," I sigh, hugging myself. A hand on each of my own shoulders. "But why did you do it? Why omit all those details?"

"Sasha," he says, his eyes boring into mine in a way that hits me in all the places. "I like you. Like *really* like you. Maybe even . . . anyway. There are reasons, for sure. Qualities that draw me to you. But, more than that, it's that feeling. Like I've known you forever and always will. But you have been poised to run since the first moment I met you—for the second time." He breaks eye contact, kicks a pebble with his shoe. Boots. He's been running in his *boots*. "I think I was afraid to scare you off."

I know there is truth in his words. I cannot deny my instinct to flee—at a moderate to slow clip. "Fair enough," I say, crossing my arms over my chest. "But how do I know it won't happen again?"

"You don't," he says.

We sit with that for a moment.

"You don't. You want honesty and there it is. I'm coming off a relationship where we shared minimal information that mattered. Where I avoided interacting—even showing up—in order to keep the peace. Even if I tell you now that I will always be forthcoming about every detail of every single element of our lives together, that I will try as hard as I can, which I will, you can't know. No one ever can in a relationship. And that's one of the risks with this."

Our lives together. Those words hover in the air between us, strange and magnetic. A whole life. And, actually, to my surprise, the words don't scare me. I like how they look, how they sound. I want to try them on my tongue.

I realize with a jolt: I am in.

"I can't make this decision for you," he is saying, running a hand up and down his stubble. "I wish I could. But I can't decide what you want or what you can handle. You have to get there on your own. That was my hesitation after our argument in Turks and Caicos too. You have to want this as badly as I do or it isn't going to work. I'm willing to wait as long as it takes. But I can't have the pendulum swing back and forth—because one minute you're inviting me into the shower; the next you're swearing we're doomed."

"I feel like there was some stuff in between those two things."

He gazes toward the path for a beat, then back up at my face. There is an intensity in his eyes, a furrow in his brow that unravels me. Now that I realize I want this, I know I also want to take away his pain. He takes a step toward me. I drop my hands. "I ran here to find you to ask you not to choose fear," he says. "Choose nights on the couch. Days in the park. Crispix shopping in tandem. Choose annoying events and ridiculous photo shoots. Choose the awkward blending of our families and run-ins with my ex. Choose getting screwed. With *me.*"

And there is no way I can say no. To any of it. I want it all. Messiness be damned.

I take a step closer to Ethan. I pretend it's because I want to give us some privacy. But really I just want to be as near to him as possible.

"It's true that you come with some baggage," I say. "And you could have told me your ex-wife hated me with the fire of a thousand suns. That might have been helpful forewarning. I'm not sure our kids like each other, and also you are very condescending when it comes to making cotton candy. And running." I sigh, stick my chin in the air. "But you're a really good kisser and that's not something I want to live the rest of my life without experiencing again."

This last part catches him by surprise. He works to suppress a smile. Manages, sort of. "So, what does that mean?"

"It means," I say, forcing myself to hold his gaze no matter how naked I feel, "that I will stop with the push and pull. No one will be drawn and quartered today. That I'd like to date you. I choose *us*."

To my surprise, what I feel, more than anything, in accepting his proposition, in giving in to my base desires despite the obvious complications, is relief. Not panic. Not worry. I trust him. I trust us. I don't want to fight myself anymore.

"You want to date me?" he says.

"Yes."

"And kiss me?"

"That seems like an implicit part of the package, but yes. Sure. If I need to lay it all out: I'd like to date you and make out with you. Regularly. Because, the thing is, I really, *really* like you. And that doesn't happen to me—ever."

"You do?" He shoots me a small smile.

"Yes. Because you're smart and funny and kind and good—and you look really great in T-shirts."

"Hm. Even if I wear Tevas? You'll still like me then?"

I toggle my head. "Yes. Even then . . . probably."

He eyes me sideways, his lips pressed together as he assesses. *Is this real?* "It's not always going to be simple."

"I know. I can handle it."

As if on cue, Green Vest jogs by in a green workout set. She spots us and raises a hand in greeting. "Hi, guys!"

We wave back.

"Has Kaitlin assigned each of her friends a color to wear?"

"It's possible." Ethan sighs. "But that's a perfect example: that woman will likely report on us. People will be in our business. And you may not always like what they say or do." His voice grows quiet. "Your kids may hear things and not always like that too."

I nod. This has occurred to me. Multiple times as I lay awake in my bed, staring at my ceiling and wondering how my kids managed to stick a unicorn puffy sticker all the way up there. And, to be honest, my desire to block for my children is one of the biggest obstacles to overcome. But this is the work.

"Ethan. Are you talking me into this or out of this?"

"I don't want to talk you in any direction at all." He shakes his head. "I want you to know. On your own. I want you to be ready. And know that I'm here when and if you are."

How can I explain? Encapsulate everything that has gotten me to this place?

"I've spent a lot of time worrying about what I can't give my kids," I say. Now, it's my turn to kick a pebble, smash some leaves with my toe. "But I've realized I need to accept the reality of inevitably failing them sometimes, no matter the pain. It's not possible to protect them entirely. Not without robbing all of us of something. They need to learn resilience. So, perfection is no longer the goal." It was never attainable anyway. "Ethan, I think the reason I didn't remember you after we first met and had what I'm sure was a significant conversation is that I wasn't open to seeing the truth yet. And I think that's been a big barrier for me all along, in many ways. I haven't been truly open to what I want."

Ethan runs a hand through his hair. Nods. I want to do the same.

Run my fingers over his head and down his neck, lodge myself in the crook of his arm. Inhale his mowed-lawn cologne. But I realize we're not there yet.

I can't believe I was ever willing to let him go.

"I understand that it's not the same for us," he is saying. "I know that being a mother is different from being a father. But, for the sake of my relationship with my ex-wife too, I'm taking more on. Not only the logistical stuff, but also the sense of compromise. The load."

"They should come up with a better word for that."

"Agreed."

He runs a hand along his jaw again, a stress tell—and I can see how worried he's been. "Ethan," I say, "I'm sorry things have been so hard—with Ruby, with Kaitlin. It's all going to be okay."

He exhales sharply. "Thank you."

"What's the latest with Kaitlin?" I ask.

"She's going to stay with her sister for a few weeks in Northern California."

"That sounds nice."

"That sounds necessary. She definitely needs to regroup. *We* need to regroup."

"Of course."

"But we talked this morning," he says. "I think she's really going to try to accept this—us."

I am not Kaitlin's biggest fan. And I do not look forward to future interactions with her. But, I have to admit, I do understand some of what motivated her. What do you do when you've misplaced your identity? Become a jumble of errands and dinners? A snack dispenser? A nag? How do you construct a new sense of self? If the present doesn't look how you'd hoped, maybe you look to the past. To the moment when things went awry or when you last remember feeling whole. Or when you last recall feeling a thrill. Or hopeful. Or full of promise. Or maybe, if you're me, you hunker down and become an immutable object, fixed to the spot where you've landed, whether it serves you or not.

In the not too distant future, I will catch Kaitlin's eye from down the street outside of school, as families weave in and around us like space dyed yarn. And we will not look away.

"I didn't steal her boyfriend," I say again. "At least not on purpose." I don't know why it matters at this point. But it bothers me that Ethan might think that about me.

"She always had a little hang-up about you," he says. "I guess it turned into a full-blown projection."

"And now her worst nightmare confirmed," I say, gesturing between the two of us.

"Well, ironically, all her sabotage kind of forced us to get to know each other. Maybe unconsciously she was pushing us together to prove herself right."

"Right?" I crinkle my nose.

He twists his mouth to one side. "She saw me looking at you at some event a few months ago, long after we separated," he admits. "She thought I had a crush on you." He looks shyly down at the ground. "Maybe I did."

I try not to grin, but I can't help it. "You liked me even before you stole the sweatshirt!"

"Well, I don't know about liked. I thought you were hot. And we had one good conversation on the playground—that you promptly forgot. The sweatshirt debacle made your personality seem questionable at best."

"I knew it!"

"You *knew* it?"

"Well, no. Not at all. But I like it!"

"I bet you do." He tilts his head. "How's your sting, by the way? All healed?"

"I've filed for worker's comp," I deadpan. "That jellyfish will be hearing from my lawyer. No, seriously. I'm just glad my fall got cut from the video before anyone saw it."

His expression glitches in a deeply suspicious way.

"Excuse me," I say, pointing at him. "What was that on your face?"

"Nothing!"

"Ethan?"

"I may have watched that clip—on repeat this last week."

"Oh my God!" I punch him in the arm. He rubs the spot where I made contact in mock pain.

"I couldn't help it! It's hilarious!" He smiles. And it's dreamy. Asymmetrical dimple and all. I could get lost in that smile. Who needs a map?

"But you liked it?" I say. "Derek said you liked how it turned out?" I'm surprisingly anxious to hear his thoughts.

He nods. "Not just me."

"Corporate? The publisher?!"

He smiles. "Our jobs are all safe, for now."

"Ethan! That's amazing!" I grab his hands. They're warm and strong.

"Sasha," he says, hanging on.

"You know it kills me when you say my name."

"Sasha. Sasha. Sasha."

"Are you trying to destroy me?" I pretend to faint into his arms.

"I could ask you the same thing," he says, looking down at me as I turn to face him, pressing my body up against his. He smells like him. And I missed it.

"You sure about this?" he asks.

I nod, my lips now inches from his mouth. I am hypnotized. "I was afraid and all over the place," I say quietly. "And you were an idiot. But now I'd like to get on top of things. On top of *you*."

His eyes crinkle and spark. He narrows his gaze. "That can be arranged."

Then, he leans in and kisses me, in the middle of that park for all the moms and dads and their vests to see. And I am all about it. It starts shallow and goes deep, his arms encircling me, his hands pressed into the small of my back. It hits me at my core and I melt into him on every level. This is the kind of daily workout routine I can get behind.

This, I dare say, could be love.

When we finally pull apart, reluctantly as hell, he says, "We should get going. Before this gets obscene." His lids are heavy.

"Or after," I suggest, and wiggle my eyebrows. "Give the people a show!"

"Did you finish your three miles?"

"I actually don't know! But I am definitely done running for today."

"Wow," he says. "You broke your rule! You didn't run *exactly* three miles."

"I'm rewriting lots of rules these days." I give him one of my signature winks. It is terrible.

He shakes his head, laughs. "You should never do that. Not in public."

I realize I love his laugh. And his T-shirts and his generosity and even his stupid-ass lectures. Well, sort of. I think back to our time on the island. How hard I tried to fight it.

"You look tired," I say now, sweeping my fingers over his jaw. "We should go to bed."

"Ah, I wish," he says, his hand drifting lower on my back. "You have no idea how much. But I have somewhere to be. And so do you."

"What? Where?" I look at my phone. "Oh, damn! It's time for pick-up."

"Want to go together?"

"Ethan. Are you asking me out to pick-up? Our first date!"

"So, this is a date, but dinner on the moonlit beach wasn't? You're a very strange woman," he says. Then he stops short. "Oh, wait! I almost forgot!"

I feel the absence of his hands, when he swings his backpack off one shoulder and unzips it from the top. He digs inside and pulls out a super-squished plastic-wrapped pink cotton candy.

"For you," he says, presenting the pastel lump to me like a bouquet.

I am touched. Like for real. "For me? It's like an edible corsage!"

"That's the best kind. They were selling it at the stand up by the park entrance. It seemed like an ideal peace offering. Sorry it's mushed."

"It's not mushed," I say, cradling it to my chest. "It's artistic!"

"If you say so."

I remove the plastic and toss it in the garbage, rip off a fluffy chunk and let it disintegrate on my tongue. "Mmm."

"Good?"

"Best thing to happen to me all day."

He shoots me a *Really?* look.

"Okay. Second best."

"You don't want to wait to eat it?"

"What? And have to share it with the kids?"

I pull off a chunk and pop it in his mouth. He lets it melt. Nods like it's pretty good. I kiss him one more time for good measure. It's sticky and sweet. I want seconds.

But I will have to wait.

He weaves his fingers through mine, and we start walking around the loop toward school, runners rushing past us in various states of hyperventilation. I hear a rustle in the trees above us. Some birds are having a rap battle. Maybe in our honor.

As we near the park's exit, we pass the playground on our right. I glance over at some toddlers squealing as they take turns throwing themselves down the mini slide, and I don't know if I'm inventing it or if it's real, but, all at once, I am flooded with a memory of pushing Nettie in a swing. Beside me is a dad, pushing his own daughter as we chat. He's adorable and funny and, I think, maybe in another lifetime. . . .

Could it be?

Now, Ethan leans into me. Nudges me with his elbow. Then throws his arm around my shoulders. Sends a shiver of electricity coursing through every part of me. I reach up and nuzzle into his neck.

I am happy. Sexually frustrated. But happy.

"Rain check for tomorrow?" I say. "For the going-to-bed thing?"

"Hmm." He narrows his eyes, like he's considering it. "No. I don't think so."

"What! Why?"

"The thing is, now that you have this edible corsage and everything, I think maybe we shouldn't waste it. I think I need to take you out. Tonight."

I stop short and look up at him. I want to go so badly, but there is no way.

"Ethan! I don't have a babysitter."

"Actually, you do."

"I do? How?"

He nods, placing a hand on each of my shoulders. "Celeste is taking your kids for the night."

"What? How?" I am in shock.

He tucks my hair behind my ear. "I may have reached out. And, before you ask, no, she doesn't mind. She seemed pretty supportive, actually."

I lean my cheek against his palm. "Ethan."

"Sasha."

"That's so nice. And so cocky. What if I hadn't forgiven you?"

He shrugs, sheepish. "I rolled the dice. I hoped. Optimism."

I am touched. And excited. A puddle. A ball of bliss.

I step forward and meld to his chest, my eyes welling. I feel so lucky to have landed here in this hopeful place.

"So, is this a yes?" he asks, looking down at me with eyes that dance.

"Hmm. I don't know if I'm free." I shrug. "You know me. I'm all tied up."

"I can work with that," he says. And he leans down and kisses me again.

Epilogue

SASHA (+DEMON DAD 4-EVA)

"The universe is vast and ever-expanding," booms a deep voice that seems to emanate from all sides at once. "As different as we may feel, the 8.1 billion humans on Earth today all exist within the same cosmos."

"The stars—they're just like us!" I stage-whisper through pitch-blackness in Ethan's general direction.

"Four and half billion years ago, our solar system formed from a combination of interstellar gas and dust . . ."

I lean over and, this time, I whisper in his ear, "There's some dust collecting under my fridge. Should we try to make our own galaxy later?"

"We're not going home tonight," he says.

"I know. I just meant *later* in our lives."

It's too dark to see him, but I can feel his grin.

I am immediately thrown back to the night we stargazed on the beach, the night we first kissed for real—but *not* our true first date, in my opinion. I had to sense Ethan beside me then too. Imagine his reactions. The subtle nuances of his face.

Even then, I felt like I knew him like he was mine.

Of course, this memory jog is precisely what Ethan had in mind.

He and I are on our non-first-date date—*finally*. We are at the planetarium. Which somehow he has managed to secure for us alone.

I could not have loved anything more. This man gifted me the night sky.

"But *how?*" I asked when we first arrived at the empty theater, after museum hours. My mouth agape.

"I play basketball with the assistant director." He shrugged.

This basketball game is a gold mine. Maybe I need to work on my jump shot?

And yet I knew Ethan was downplaying the favor he called in. There is, no doubt, an expectation of some major quid pro quo.

"There are eighty-eight official constellations in the sky," says the all-knowing voice now, "from Canis Minor to Boötes to Triangulum Australe, or Southern Triangle."

Maybe now is a good time to finally tell Ethan my theory about constellations being named like sexual positions.

"Hey, Ethan," I whisper.

"Sasha," he says. "Are you bored?" Like I am a child who cannot sit still. Like he might offer me his phone to play on.

I get it. He is not wrong. I am oddly chatty. But I have never been less bored.

On the contrary, I am giddy. Awake. Abuzz. I'm just so blissed out—by Ethan's proximity, his fingers woven through mine, the freedom of this night, the fact that I can kiss (or even bone!) him whenever I want—that I'm having trouble settling in.

It is still so new. And yet I feel like I've known him forever.

"I'm not bored at all!" I say. "This is incredible."

"Good."

"Can I just tell you one last thing?"

"Of course. But why are you whispering? We're the only people here!"

"I know. But I don't want to be disrespectful."

"To the recording?"

"Yes. And to the little green men."

"Oh boy." I can feel him roll his eyes, but smile too.

"One last question, and then I promise to pay attention," I say. "Yes?"

"Where are you taking me after this?"

"Sasha!" he groans. "We've been over this. What part of *surprise* don't you understand?"

"The part that involves me being insanely hungry and you taking me to some super-chic hipster bar where the only snack is dried shiso leaves."

"Do you really think I would miss the chance to watch you demolish the best burger in New York?"

"Aw," I say, all warm inside. "You really *know* me."

He squeezes my hand, and fireworks ignite inside me. Blinding light. Crackling waterfalls of shimmer. Circular explosions of red, blue, purple and green that pop up as if out of nowhere, to gasps and sighs.

I tingle from head to toe.

"Hey, Ethan?"

"Yes?" he says, all patience. And I give him big props for not telling me to shut up.

"If no one else is here, why do I have to sit in my own seat?"

He laughs, softly. "Now, *that* is a good question." He pulls me onto his lap, where I curl up and burrow into him. My head in the crook of his grass-scented neck.

He wraps his arms around me and pulls me close.

I rise and fall with his breath.

I will stay here for infinity and a day, if they let me. No matter how much I want that burger.

"The moon is four hundred times smaller than the sun, but four hundred times closer to Earth," the voice explains. "It appears bright, but is actually dark on the surface."

It's all about perspective.

"Sasha," Ethan whispers.

I still melt when he says my name.

"Yes?"

"The thing is . . . I might love you. I mean, I do. Love you."

I can feel his breath hitch in his chest. We both know it's soon. But when you know, you know.

"Hey, Ethan?"

"Yeah?"

"I might love you too. A lot."

He squeezes me tight. I am aglow. All tied up—with him.

From this vantage point, with Ethan as my armchair, I look up and finally focus on the show.

With wonder, I take in the stars—the ones projected on the ceiling and the ones twinkling inside of me.

Acknowledgments

I first came up with the idea for this book while standing on the sidewalk in a large circle, chatting with a group of parents outside of my kids' school after drop-off. Thank you to that crew—and our extended school circle—for brightening my mornings and afternoons (and often evenings too). You started as fellow parents and became true friends.

I am forever grateful to my agent, Faye Bender of the Book Group, who is always open to my harebrained schemes and has been in lockstep with me since the moment I told her I wanted to write romance. Your impeccable taste and easy energy elevates the whole experience. What would I do without you? An enormous thank-you to my editor Carrie Feron at Gallery Books, who saw potential in *Pick-Up* and put her boundless expertise to work in order to make it shine. I feel beyond fortunate to be in your orbit. We couldn't have done any of this without the delightful Ali Chesnick. Thank you for championing this book from the get-go. I am so appreciative of the enthusiastic support of Jen Bergstrom and the whole wonderful Gallery Books team at Simon & Schuster, particularly Erica Ferguson, Michelle Lecumberry, Mackenzie Hickey, Lucy Nalen, Sally Marvin, Lisa Litwack, Esther Paradelo, Sarah Wright, Jen Long, Eliza Hanson, the entire sales team, and so many more. And I have gifted illustrator Sandra Chiu to thank for this cool and vibrant cover.

Thank you is not enough for Sarah MacLean, my dear friend for now almost a decade. You have been my biggest cheerleader and the most invaluable guide a person could imagine throughout this process. I literally wouldn't be here without you and your limitless generosity. Someday, at our meetups, I promise I'll let you work.

To Nicola Wheir, Hanna Neier and Katie Schorr, I am so grateful to you for reading the manuscript and giving insightful and honest notes. And, to Emily Barth Isler, your unchecked encouragement means so much. Thank you to Peter Harris for sharing publishing-world wisdom and for always insisting I sparkle. You guys are my community. I am so thankful for you.

Melissa Haggerty, your insight on producing video shoots for editorial was clutch. A huge thanks to you—and, of course, to my anonymous friends who shared openly and generously with me about their personal experiences with divorce.

To the Tabers and Weiners, thank you for being excited about my wins and forgiving of my losses—and for always, always showing up.

To Meg and Rach, who are my lifelines: I am so beyond lucky to have you both in my life and feel grateful for you every single day. Thank you for tolerating my endless vegan pastry runs and late mornings. And thank you to Tova, who reminds me to always keep trying.

To my big sister, Claudia, whose opinion I trust implicitly and who is always willing to read my drafts, even when they're messy as hell: you helped me build an entire rom-com reference library in my head and fully curated my high-low cultural touchstones, from Joan Didion to *Clueless* (and, of course, *Revenge of the Nerds*). A giant thank-you to Annie, for always trekking to Brooklyn for our cherished *Bachelor* nights, and to Katia for running "Katia Class," two rituals—and friendships—that have kept me sane in light and dark times. A big shout-out to my "hell no" squad, who keeps me laughing when things get messy, and to my high school girls, who knew me when.

An infinite thank-you to my mother, Lynn, who first read me *Pride and Prejudice*, paving the way for everything I know and love about strong female characters and writing. And to my father, Paul, who taught me dry humor and truly believes his daughters could run the world.

To my children, who give the best hugs in the entire universe: you amaze me every day with your imagination, perceptiveness, humor and love. And no—you cannot have more dessert.

To my husband, Andrew, with whom I share my own enemies-to-lovers story: I may complain when you snack audibly while I write, but the truth is you're the greatest sounding board. Thank you for always believing I'm capable of great things—and for being an Ethan, never a Cliff.

I am so thrilled to put *Pick-Up* out into the world. Thank you to anyone and everyone for reading!

About the Author

Nora Dahlia is a lifestyle writer whose work has appeared in the *New York Times*, *Elle*, the *Wall Street Journal* and *Vanity Fair*, among others. Nora is also a branded content expert, book doctor/collaborator, ghostwriter and writing coach. She lives in Brooklyn with her husband, two kids and enormous cat, Waldo. *Pick-Up* is her first romance novel.